I'm
我識出版社
17buy.com.tw

I'm

我識出版社
17buy.com.tw

I'm

我識出版社
17buy.com.tw

想要和你
用英文聊聊天

CHAT!!

1

全圖解漫畫式問答句，讓自己彷彿身歷其境。

❶ 在每單元的最開始都可以看到 6 個問句，以及搭配該問句的 4-5 句回答。打破傳統的 AB 對話模式，不管是想先用問句與老外破冰展開話題，或是被老外搭話時，都能立刻且正確地應答。

❷ 每組問答隨時補充台灣人最容易說錯的回答句，還有對話時可以多多參考的小技巧，以及豐富的單字及好用句式解說，讓你／妳避免掉文化差異可能產生的尷尬，和老外聊天更加如魚得水。

Word Power!
· ready for phr 對…有準備 → 後面接名詞或動名詞
· go back to bed phr 去睡回籠覺
· get out phr (使)出去

詞性符號說明

n 名詞	phr 片語
v 動詞	abbr 縮寫
a 形容詞	conj 連接詞
ad 副詞	

2

虛擬實境練口說，任何情境都有聊不完的話題！

最豐富實用的情境例句攏底加！除了按照使用場所區分篇章之外，陳子李老師還設想了每個地方最容易出現的四種情境，搭配 2 到 3 句會話，再提供 3 個單字替換，1,000 多句會話讓你／妳隨便聊，成為英語聊天大師不是夢！

★本書附贈 CD 片內容音檔為 MP3 格式★
★音檔即頁碼編號★

∩ 018

3

超擬真網路聊天室，
再遠的距離都能聊！

❶ 想和外國網友們在聊天室哈啦嗎？那你／妳一定得學會這些超夯用語！老外用網路都在聊、即時訊息都在瘋傳，沒學到就遜掉啦！

❷ 跟不上老外打字的速度時，先用生動可愛的貼圖擋一下準沒錯。

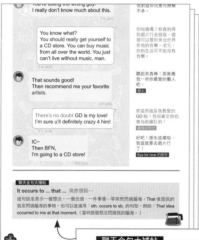

4

搶救英文口說大作戰，
與老外面對面也不怕！

神來一筆的好用句子、美國人每天都在説的慣用句型，通通幫你／妳補充到位。不會讓你／妳愈唸愈想睡，史上最簡單的英文會話書就在手中！

> **聊天金句大補帖**
>
> **It occurs to ... that ...** 突然想到…
>
> 這句話是表示一個想法、一個念頭、一件事情…等突然閃過腦海。That 後面說的就是閃過腦海的事物，也可以直接用：sth. occurs to sb. 的句型，例如：That idea occurred to me at that moment.（當時那個想法閃過我的腦海。）

　　各位讀者朋友們好，很高興能這麼快就再次與大家見面。自去年和 Dennis 老師一同出版了《用英文打開話匣子》後，收到了不少熱烈的迴響。一方面，很感謝各位的支持，另一方面，也決定不辜負讀者朋友們的熱望，因此和出版社共同努力，終於順利的讓新書《想要和你用英文聊聊天》在 5 月和各位見面。

　　這本書的概念，以採用問句的方式與外國人開啟對話為出發點，不僅更貼近模擬真實的情境，也可幫助讀者，若面對外國人突然拋出的一個問題，該如何應對得更漂亮、更精準。這之中也補充了許多英語母語使用者的愛用詞彙、以及那些較不正式，甚至說出來會顯得無禮的 NG 用法，避免因文化的不同，和外國朋友起了衝突，那可就適得其反了。除了以問句開啟話題之外，為了幫助讀者應對生活中的各種情境，因此當然也有符合各種情境的會話例句，而同一句話，更換一個字就能是一句全新的話的概念，相信若您是前作的讀者，必定對於這種學習模式不會陌生。

　　另外，隨著科技進步，用英文聊天早已不被侷限在現實生活中。面對面的聊天比起書信來說更簡單，那用簡訊或即時通訊聊呢？本書為此，特地規劃了虛擬實境網路聊天的單元，不僅收錄擬真即時通訊內容、更富含符合時下潮流的網路用語。無論你是想透過網路和外國人交朋友，或是在國外認識朋友後交換臉書、skype 以保持聯絡，都千萬別錯過這個單元，這樣才不會 out of fashion 喔！

　　最後，再次感謝讀者朋友們對於我的肯定，衷心期許我的英語教學經驗，能帶給各位些許的幫助。英文是很有趣的語言，它其實學起來一點也不難，重點是，學到了就要會用，若是僅僅只會紙上談兵，語言就會失去了它的功用，因此希望各位，學了就要用，用的意思就是要開口說！不要害怕自己的文法、發音會不會出錯、會不會被嘲笑，只要敞開心胸與外國人交流，相信他們都會很樂於回應你的！

陳子秀

2016.04

Contents
目錄

使用說明 ……………………………………… 002
作者序 ………………………………………… 004

Chapter 1　008
一切就從家開始

Unit1 早起的鳥兒有蟲吃
Unit2 哈囉！今天天氣晴
Unit3 人要衣裝佛要金裝
Unit4 準備出門走跳去
Unit5 當顆沙發馬鈴薯
Unit6 祝你有個好夢

Chapter 2　046
地鐵站大冒險

Unit1 向左走向右走
Unit2 短程旅行必搭
Unit3 長途旅行必搭
Unit4 趕時間必搭
Unit5 東奔西跑的每一天
Unit6 道聲珍重再見

Chapter 3　084
環遊世界免煩惱

Unit1 訂票快狠準
Unit2 連接世界的橋樑
Unit3 出境入境必經
Unit4 做好起飛準備
Unit5 休息是為了玩更久
Unit6 下次再接再厲

Contents
目錄

Chapter 4　122
校園密室逃脫

- Unit1 充滿回憶的所在
- Unit2 結伴讀書去
- Unit3 朋友是一輩子的
- Unit4 來場三對三
- Unit5 揮灑青春汗水
- Unit6 保持好品格

Chapter 5　160
工蜂嗡嗡嗡

- Unit1 請多多指教
- Unit2 小資族的第二個家
- Unit3 您好請問哪裡找
- Unit4 恭喜恭喜恭喜你呀
- Unit5 神仙打鼓有時錯
- Unit6 春神來了怎知道

Chapter 6　198
令人食指大動

- Unit1 卡好位才有得吃
- Unit2 燈光美氣氛佳
- Unit3 吃飯也有潛規則
- Unit4 趕時間也要吃
- Unit5 台灣最美的風景
- Unit6 最方便的好鄰居

Contents
目錄

Chapter 7 236
找點樂子吧

- **Unit1** 購物狂的天堂
- **Unit2** 唱出閃亮的歌聲
- **Unit3** 週五電影夜
- **Unit4** 來點動次動次
- **Unit5** 瘋狂派對夜
- **Unit6** 少不了的是祝福

Chapter 8 274
出發社區巡禮

- **Unit1** 信件集散地
- **Unit2** 錢財通通交到這
- **Unit3** 沒事別進出的地方
- **Unit4** 店員什麼都會
- **Unit5** 記得守規矩
- **Unit6** 個人情報保衛戰

Chapter 9 312
聊得更深入

CHAT!!

- **Unit1** 有話就是要直說
- **Unit2** 十萬個為什麼
- **Unit3** 請告訴我
- **Unit4** 信不信由你
- **Unit5** 真相只有一個
- **Unit6** 給認真的自己比個讚

Chapter

1

一切就從家開始

Unit 1 早起的鳥兒有蟲吃

Unit 2 哈囉！今天天氣晴

Unit 3 人要衣裝佛要金裝

Unit 4 準備出門走跳去

Unit 5 當顆沙發馬鈴薯

Unit 6 祝你有個好夢

Unit 1

早起的鳥兒有蟲吃

90% 的老外都是用這些句子開始聊天。

Is it time to get up?
現在該起床了嗎？

- No, I don't want to. 不，我還不想起。
- Yes, it is already 8:00. 是的，現在已經八點了。
- Yes, I must go to school later.
  是的，我等一下就要去上學。
- No, I don't need to work today.
  不，今天不用上班。

不能不會的小技巧

不只是小朋友或青少年，就連許多大人也常常會在鬧鐘響的時候賴床，硬是不起床吧。要記得，提醒他人起床時，態度一定要堅定，尤其是對於賴床慣犯，口吻一定要強硬一點。

Word Power!
- get up phr 起床
- already [ɔl`rɛdɪ] ad 已經
- later [`letə] ad 較晚地
  → late 的比較級

Are you ready for breakfast?
你準備用早餐了嗎？

- Yes. What are we going to eat this morning?
  是的，我們今天要吃什麼？
- No. I don't usually have breakfast.
  我通常不吃早餐。
- No. I'm going back to bed.
  不，我要去睡回籠覺。

Word Power!
- ready for phr 對…有準備 → 後面接名詞或動名詞
- go back to bed phr 去睡回籠覺
- get out phr （使）出去

這樣說不禮貌

Get out of my room. I'm still sleeping.
滾出我的房間。我還在睡耶。

Did you have breakfast yet?
你已經吃過早飯了嗎？

- Not yet. Feel like joining me for breakfast?
  還沒。想和我一起早餐嗎？
- Yes, about an hour ago.
  是的，大約半個小時前就吃過了。
- No, I'm going to have breakfast.
  沒有，我正準備去吃早飯。

Word Power!
- breakfast [`brɛkfəst] n 早餐
- feel like phr 想要 → 多用於疑問句和否定句，以人作主詞，後面接名詞或動名詞。
- treat [trit] n 請客

Sentence Power!
- Not yet. 到目前為止尚未。

這樣說不禮貌

No. How about giving me a treat?
沒。還是你要請客？

What do you like to eat for breakfast?
你早餐喜歡吃什麼？

- Scrambled eggs and mashed potatoes. 炒蛋和薯泥。
- I like to keep it simple. A glass of milk and toasts. 我喜歡簡單的早餐。一杯牛奶加吐司。
- Black coffee, pancakes with fresh strawberries, and hash browns are my favorite. 黑咖啡、草莓鬆餅和薯餅是我的最愛。
- I always have porridge for breakfast. 我早餐總是吃稀飯。

Did you brush your teeth yet?
你已經刷過牙了嗎？

- Yes, I did it one minute ago. 是的，我一分鐘前刷過了。
- No, I got up just now. 沒有，我剛剛起來。
- No, I will brush my teeth later. 不 我會晚點再刷牙。

這樣說不禮貌

Don't talk to me. I am brushing my teeth now.
別跟我說話，我現在正在刷牙。

Coffee or tea for breakfast?
早餐想喝咖啡還是茶？

- Coffee, please. 咖啡，謝謝。
- Can I have caramel macchiato instead? 我可以改喝焦糖瑪奇朵嗎？
- I usually have a glass of soybean milk. 我通常都喝一杯豆漿。
- Neither, thanks. 都不要，謝謝。

2 虛擬實境口說練習 on your iMessenger 　從最簡短到最豐富，讓你實際和老外練習口說和聽力

| 當你一早起床，想問候家人和室友們時 |

❶ Morning! Are you going to wash your face?
早安！你要去洗把臉嗎？

have some breakfast 吃早餐
exercise 運動
change your clothes 換衣服

❷ Good morning! Today is a beautiful day.
早安！今天是美好的一天。

sunny 晴朗的
nice 不錯的
happy 快樂的

❸ Did you sleep tight last night?
昨晚睡得好嗎？

well 好
comfortably 舒服
early 早

| 當你要叫你的家人或室友們起床時 |

❶ Wake up! The breakfast is ready.
起床！早餐已經準備好了。

the school bus 校車
your sister 你的姊姊 / 妹妹

❷ It's almost noon! Wake up right now.
快中午了！趕快起來。

9 o'clock 9 點
lunch time 午餐時間

│當有人問你早餐想吃什麼時│

❶ **I would like to have a smoothie.**
我想喝些果昔。

a steamed bun 包子
some millet porridge 小米粥
a hamburger 漢堡

❷ **I want a cup of black coffee.**
我要一杯黑咖啡。

a glass of fresh juice 新鮮果汁
a glass of wine 紅酒
a cup of breakfast tea 早餐茶

❸ **I don't know what I should eat for breakfast.**
我不知道我早餐要吃什麼。

could 可以
may 應該

│當有人問你準備好出門了沒時│

❶ **Yes, I've already dressed up.**
是的,我已經打扮好了。

changed my clothes 換好衣服
put on my shoes 穿好鞋子
put on my make-up 化好妝

❷ **Of course. Let's go!**
當然。走吧!

Sure 當然
No problem 沒問題
Wait a moment, OK 等我一下,好了

3 虛擬實境網路聊天
on your iMessenger

在手機或電腦上，利用打字就可以聊出千言萬語

Tom B.

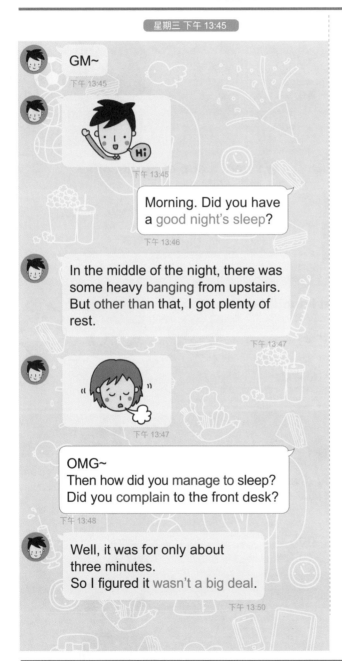

星期三 下午 13:45

GM~
下午 13:45

Hi
下午 13:45

早安〜
Good Morning 的簡寫

Morning. Did you have a good night's sleep?
下午 13:46

早安。昨天晚上睡得好嗎？
安穩的睡眠

In the middle of the night, there was some heavy banging from upstairs. But other than that, I got plenty of rest.
下午 13:47

半夜時樓上傳來很大的碰撞聲，除此以外，我休息得挺充分的。
砰砰的聲音
除了

下午 13:47

OMG~
Then how did you manage to sleep?
Did you complain to the front desk?
下午 13:48

那你怎麼睡得著？有去跟櫃台抱怨嗎？
Oh, my god. 的簡寫
設法
訴苦、抱怨

Well, it was for only about three minutes.
So I figured it wasn't a big deal.
下午 13:50

喔，那聲音大概只延續了三分鐘左右，所以我想沒什麼大不了的。
沒什麼要緊的

Tom B.

星期三 下午 13:45

IC.
And have you had breakfast yet?

下午 13:51

這樣啊。那你吃過早餐了

I see. 的簡寫

Yes, I have.
It was a very nice spread at the breakfast table.

下午 13:51

吃過了,早餐準備得非常豐盛。

盛宴

That's good.
Because it might be a while until lunch.

下午 13:55

太好了。因為我們可能得過一些時間才會吃午餐。

That is no problem! I'm ready for a busy schedule.

下午 13:56

沒問題,我已經準備好迎接滿滿的行程了。

Great! I'll pick you up in front of your hotel.

下午 13:57

太好了!那我到時就在旅館前接你。

接送

No problem. See you then!

下午 13:58

沒問題,到時見!

聊天金句大補帖

What's on your agenda for...? 你有什麼計畫?

當我們想詢問他人某段時間有沒有什麼計畫時,有很多說法。比如說:

• Do you have any plans...?

• Got any special plans...?

而「What's on your agenda for...?」其實是比較正式的用語,但卻常被用在日常對談中以幽默的口吻呈現。

Unit 2

哈囉！今天天氣晴

How's it going?
近況如何？

不能不會的小技巧
通常當對方問這個問題時，比較禮貌地回答是客套表示自己過得還不錯，然後再問對方近況如何。

Word Power!
- mid-term **a** 學期中的
- burn the midnight oil **phr** 熬夜

- Everything is going well. What about you?
  一切順利，你呢？

- Next week is ours mid-term exam, so I'm working hard now. 下周就是期中考了，我正在努力用功。

- A little tired. I've been burning the midnight oil for three nights. 有點兒累。我已經連續熬夜三天了。

How are you doing?
最近好嗎？

不能不會的小技巧
回答自己很好時可以使用：fine, well, good, ok 等，同時也可以加上感謝對方的話，接著也可以詢問對方的情況。

Sentence Power!
- All is well. 一切順心；萬事順利。
- Of course. 當然。

- Oh, I'm well. 喔，我很好。

- All is well. What about you? 一切都好。你呢？

- Of course. I'm well. And you? 當然，我很好。你呢？

這樣說不禮貌
I'm doing nothing. 我沒在幹嘛。

How is the weather?
天氣如何？

Word Power!
- weather [ˈwɛðɚ] **n** 天氣
- rain cats and dogs **phr** 傾盆大雨

Sentence Power!
- It's raining cats and dogs! 傾盆大雨！
  = What a downpour!

- It's sunny today. 今天天氣晴朗。

- It looks like rain today. 看樣子今天會下雨。

- The sky is getting very cloudy. 天空中的雲越來越多了。

- It's raining cats and dogs! 雨下的真大啊！

這樣說不禮貌
How should I know?
我怎麼會知道？

It looks like it's going to be sunny. What will you do?
今天好像會是晴天。你要做什麼呢？

Chapter 1 一切就從家開始

- I will go camping with friends. 我要跟朋友去露營。
- I'll visit one of my friends; I have been waiting for a long time. 我要去找一個朋友；我已經等很久了。
- Someone is waiting for me to travel! 有人正等我去旅遊呢！
- Maybe I will enjoy a rest at home! I'm so tired. 也許我想在家休息！我太累了。

不能不會的小技巧
一般來説，當有人問你這類型的問題時，目的是想約你一起出去打發時間。所以若要拒絕對方，使用委婉的口氣會比較禮貌。

Word Power!
- go camping **phr** 露營
- visit [ˋvɪzɪt] **v** 拜訪
- rest [rɛst] **n** 休息

How do you do?
你好嗎？

- How do you do? 我很好，你好嗎？
- I'm fine. Thank you. How about you? 我很好，謝謝你。你最近怎麼樣呢？
- Not well. Recently I met a little trouble. 不。我最近遇到了一些麻煩。
- Not so good. I got cold yesterday. 不太好。我昨天感冒了。

不能不會的小技巧
How do you do? 問的不是「你在做什麼？」，而是見面時人們相互之間的問候語。

Word Power!
- recently [ˋrisn̩tlɪ] **ad** 最近
- trouble [ˋtrʌbl̩] **n** 麻煩；紛爭
- get cold **phr** 感冒

It seems to be clearing up. What do you think?
天氣好像要轉晴了。你認為呢？

- I wish it would stay this way for the weekend. 希望這種好天氣能維持到週末。
- I really don't think the good weather will last. 我覺得好天氣不會維持太久。
- Yes, it's not what the weather report predicted at all. 是啊，和氣象報告預報的不一樣。

Word Power!
- clear up **phr** 放晴
- last [læst] **v** 持續
- predict [prɪˋdɪkt] **v** 預料

更多⋯
晴時多雲偶陣雨
- windy 風大的
- hurricane 颶風
- typhoon 颱風
- thunderstorm 大雷雨
- snowstorm 暴風雪

2 虛擬實境口說練習
on your iMessenger

從最簡短到最豐富，讓你實際和老外練習口說和聽力

┃當你要向你的朋友打招呼時┃

❶ Hey man, what's up?
嘿兄弟，最近怎麼樣？

> what's happening 發生什麼事
> what's going on 過得如何
> what's new 有什麼新鮮事

❷ How have you been doing lately?
你最近過得如何？

> these days 這幾天
> recently 最近
> since I last saw you 距離我上次看到你

❸ Hello! Thanks for seeing me.
哈囉！謝謝你來看我。

> Thanks for coming 你過來
> Thanks for meeting up 你來會面
> Thanks for spending some time
> with me 你花時間陪我

┃當你被問到近況如何時┃

❶ I've been just scraping by.
我現在有努力地過日子。

> eking out 過得還可以
> barely getting 勉強地過活
> scrounging 掙扎地過日子

❷ I'm looking forward to getting a new promotion!
我正期待著要升遷到新職位呢！

> moving in to a new apartment 搬到新公寓
> getting a new espresso machine 收到新咖啡機
> making a new boyfriend 交新男友

|當有人問你今天天氣如何時|

❶ The weatherman said to expect rain.
天氣播報員說好像會下雨。

> thunderstorms 大雷雨
> showers 陣雨
> a light drizzle 毛毛雨

❷ It warmed up nicely in the afternoon.
下午變得比較溫暖了。

> heated up 氣溫升高
> cooled down 氣溫降低
> cooled off 變涼爽

❸ If I had known, I would have worn my overcoat.
如果我早知道的話,我應該就會穿著我的大衣了。

> raincoat 雨衣
> mittens 連指手套
> thermal underwear 發熱衣

|當有人告訴你今天天氣不是很好時|

❶ It's been raining cats and dogs.
一直都下著大雨。

> raining buckets down 下著傾盆大雨
> raining unendingly 不停地
> snowing heavily 下著大雪

❷ It's going to be a long winter.
這將會是個很長的冬天。

> cold 冷的
> frigid 嚴寒的
> wet and cold 濕冷的

3 虛擬實境網路聊天
on your iMessenger

在手機或電腦上，利用打字就可以聊出千言萬語

Roy(Corp.)

星期三 下午 13:45

 If plans go smoothly between your company and mine, I might have to make frequent trips there.

下午 13:45

要是我們兩家公司的計畫談得很順利的話，我就得常飛到那裡了。
時常的

UR right.
I believe the same applies to me too.

下午 13:46

沒錯，我想我也是。
You are 的簡寫
適用於

 But you don't have to worry too much.
The climate over there is fairly temperate.
It may change day to day,
But I don't think it gets extreme like the weather here.

下午 13:47

但你不用太擔心，那邊的氣候相當宜人，天氣可能每天都不一樣，但是不會像這裡一樣有極端的變化。
相當地
溫和的、溫暖的

下午 13:47

We have some typhoons in summer,
droughts down south in the winter
But it's not that bad.

下午 13:48

我們這兒夏天有颱風，冬天時南部會有乾旱，但是情況不像你想得那麼壞。
乾旱

 Ez for you to say.

下午 13:50

你說得倒輕鬆。
Easy 的簡寫

Roy(Corp.)

星期三 下午 13:45

I wish the typhoon would be strong so that I don't have to come to work.

下午 13:51

我希望颱風能夠變得
很強烈，這樣我就不
用來上班了。
颱風
如此一來

下午 13:52

 I'm going to try to come during summer then.
Maybe there'll be a typhoon and I can get to miss work too.

下午 13:55

我打算夏天時回來這
兒，說不定也能遇上
一個颱風，放個假不
用上班。
錯過

Hope our wishes come true~

下午 13:58

希望我們的夢想成真
囉～

下午 13:59

聊天金句大補帖

Come again? 我沒聽錯吧？

當我們希望對方解釋他對於某事物的看法時，我們便可以說這句，但是此時表示你
對於你們談論的話題或情況感到訝異，因此你希望他好好解釋為什那樣說。除此之
外，此句也適用於我們沒聽清楚對方的話，希望他再說一次時

Unit 3 人要衣裝佛要金裝

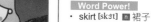

90% 的老外都是用這些句子開始聊天。

It seems sunny today. What should I wear?

今天天氣似乎很好。我該穿什麼呢？

Word Power!
- skirt [skɜt] n 裙子
- suit [sut] n 西裝
- fit [fɪt] v 適合於

更多…
- trousers 長褲
- jeans 牛仔褲
- hoodie 連帽 T 恤
- pullover 套頭毛衣

- You can wear your new skirt. It's so beautiful!
  你可以穿你的新裙子。它好漂亮！

- Your new suit fits you! You have an important meeting today! 穿新西裝吧！你今天有一個重要的會議要參加！

- Be careful! The weather will change this afternoon.
  小心！今天下午會變天。

這樣說不禮貌

Whatever. 隨便。

Are you going to get dressed for work?

你穿好衣服準備要上班了嗎？

Word Power!
- get dressed phr 穿衣服
- make-up [`mek.ʌp] n 化妝品

Sentence Power!
- Just a moment. 等一下
  = Wait a minute.
  = Hold on.

- No, not yet. 還沒有。

- Yes, everything is ready. 一切準備就緒。

- No, I'm putting on make-up. 還沒有，我正在化妝。

- Just a moment. I'm brushing my teeth. 等一下，我正在刷牙。

- Yes, I'm waiting for you. 是的，我在等你。

It looks like raining. What should I wear?

看起來要下雨。我該穿什麼呢？

Word Power!
- jacket [`dʒækɪt] n 外套
- raincoat [`ren.kot] n 雨衣
- rain boots n 雨鞋

更多…
- coat 大衣
- boots 靴子
- leather jacket 皮衣
- trench coat 風衣

- You should wear that jacket, it must be cold.
  你可以穿那件夾克，天氣肯定很冷。

- You can wear your raincoat or you'll be wet.
  你可以穿雨衣，否則會被淋濕。

- You may wear your rain boots.
  你可以穿上你的雨鞋。

這樣說不禮貌

Who knows? It's ok that you dress like this.

誰知道？你現在穿的就可以了。

How will you dress on you date?

你約會時穿什麼呢？

Chapter

1

一切就從家開始

Word Power!
· dress [drɛs] **v** 打扮；
  穿著
· sort of
  phr 到某種程度的
· a pair of
  phr 一雙；一對
· date [det]
  n 約會對象；約會

Sentence Power!
· It's no use to... 做……
  沒有用。後接原形 V.
  = It's no use + Ving

- I want to wear my long white dress. 我想穿我的白色長洋裝。

- It's no use to dress up, I will wear what I usually wear. 沒有必要刻意去打扮，我就穿平時的衣服去。

- I will wear my suit, it's a sort of respect to others. 我將穿西裝去，那也是對別人的一種尊重。

- I bought a pair of new shoes just for tonight. My date will love the shoes. 我為了今晚（的約會）買了一雙新鞋。我的約會對象會愛死這雙鞋。

Which dress is more beautiful?

哪件洋裝比較好看呢？

Word Power!
· chic [ʃik] **a** 時髦的
· polka dots **phr**（衣料的）圓點花紋
· elegant [ˋɛləgənt]
  a 優美的；雅緻的
· old-fashioned
  [ˋoldˋfæʃənd]
  a 老派的；過時的

- The red one. It fits you. 這件紅的，它適合你。

- If you ask me, you look very chic in the black cocktail dress. 如果你問我的話，我覺得你穿這件黑色的雞尾酒洋裝看起來會非常時髦。

- The white dress with polka dots. It is simple and elegant. 這件白色有圓點的洋裝，它簡單又優雅。

| 這樣說不禮貌 |

Neither. You look old-fashioned in all of them.

都不好看。你穿每件都看起來很老氣。

Why not choose the red one? It fits you better.

為什麼不選紅色的那件？那個更適合你。

Word Power!
· so [so] **n** 像這樣
· agree with sb. **phr**（尤用於否定句或疑問句）適合
· sense [sɛns]
  n 意識；見識

Sentence Power!
· Don't you think... 你不覺得 / 認為……？

- Do you really think so? 你真是這麼認為嗎？

- I can't agree with you more. 我非常同意你的意見。

- Don't you think the yellow one is better? 你不認為黃色的更好嗎？

| 這樣說不禮貌 |

No. The red one is ugly. You really don't have any sense of fashion.

不。紅色那件很醜。你真是一點品味也沒有。

2 虛擬實境口說練習
on your iMessenger

從最簡短到最豐富，讓你實際和老外練習口說和聽力

| 當你想請朋友提供穿搭建議時 |

❶ Do these pants go with this top?
這件長褲適合搭配我的上衣嗎？

match 和…相配
complement 與…相配
highlight 使…亮眼

❷ Would you be seen wearing something like this?
你可以讓人看到你穿這樣嗎？

dressed in 穿
robed in 穿
garbed in 穿

❸ What's the appropriate attire for a hike?
你覺得適合的健行服裝是什麼？

suitable 適合的
recommended 推薦的
traditional 傳統的

| 當你要幫助朋友選擇外出服時 |

❶ Let's see what you've got in your closet.
我們先來看看你的衣櫃有什麼。

drawer 抽屜
wardrobe 衣櫥
shopping bags 購物袋

❷ I'd never pull this off, but you look good in it.
我絕對無法成功駕馭這件衣服的，但你穿起來還不錯耶。

get complimented on this 因為這件衣服而得到讚賞
look right 把這件穿得很好看的
turn heads in this 靠這件衣服吸引眾人目光

│當你被朋友問到他該怎麼穿時│

❶ **Don't worry, just put on something casual.**
別擔心那麼多,隨便穿件休閒服裝就好。

> get 穿
> dress 穿
> wear 穿

> clean 乾淨的
> smart 整齊的
> dark 暗色的

❷ **First off, you should throw away that shirt.**
首先,你應該把這件襯衫丟了。

> iron 熨燙
> press 燙平
> cut the sleeves off 修剪…的袖子

❸ **Dress for the occasion.**
看場合穿。

> appropriately 適當地
> to impress 讓人印象深刻地
> down 隨便輕鬆地

│當你無法決定該穿哪一件│

❶ **I'm confused about what to wear.**
我現在非常煩惱要穿什麼。

> clueless as to 沒有想法
> indecisive about 無法決定

❷ **I'll wear whatever you tell me to.**
我會穿任何你叫我穿的。

> you think is best 你所想的,那樣就最好
> you pick out 你選擇的

3 虛擬實境網路聊天
on your iMessenger

在手機或電腦上，利用打字就可以聊出千言萬語

Vicky Chen

星期三 下午 13:45

Dear,
I've wanted to tell you something for a while.

下午 13:45

親愛的，我一直想要告訴妳一件事。
一會兒

What is it?

下午 13:46

什麼事啊？

I'm telling you this for your own good.
You may have a good understanding of music,
but…
We have to do something about your clothes.

下午 13:47

我這麼說是為了你好。也許你對音樂的了解很足夠，但對於你的穿著，我們得做些改變了。
為你好

What's wrong with my clothes?

下午 13:48

我的穿著有什麼問題？

Nothing, if you are a hippy from the 70's.

下午 13:49

如果你是七十年代嬉皮的話，當然沒什麼問題。
嬉皮

下午 13:50

Listen,
We have got to get you out of those rags and into some real clothes.

下午 13:50

聽著，我們得去買些真正的衣服，取代你身上那些破布。
破布

Vicky Chen

星期三 下午 13:45

下午 13:55

Are the shops here up to date with the latest fashion?

下午 13:55

這裡的衣服跟得上時下的流行風潮嗎？

**Asia is the kingdom of clothing manufacturing!
Like music,
This place is influenced by other countries such as Korea and Japan.
A lot of the pricier boutiques carry up-to-the-minute fashion designs from Europe.**

下午 13:57

亞洲可是服飾製造王國呢！就像音樂一樣，這兒的服飾也受到鄰近國家的影響，比方說韓國、日本等。很多高級的精品店也都有來自歐洲最新的時尚款式。

製造業
精品店
現代的

I'm not so sure about this.

下午 13:58

我不確定。

Don't worry, you're in good hands.

下午 13:59

別擔心，你不會有問題的。

 聊天金句大補帖

I've been considering... 我一直考慮…

當我們心中一直在盤算、思考著某事，同時希望提出來與他人討論時，常常用這個句型作為對話的開頭。這麼說的用意通常是在一開始就想讓對方明白，這個想法或念頭已經在腦海裡認真地思考過了，現在提出來很可能是希望與對方分享或者獲得意見。

Unit 4 準備出門走跳去

1 一定要會的問答句

90% 的老外都是用這些句子開始聊天。

When will you start your summer vacation?
你們什麼時候開始放暑假？

- Maybe it will begin from the 15th of July.
  大概從七月十五號開始吧。

- I don't know , but I think it's coming.
  我不知道，但我想快了。

這樣說不禮貌

I'm too busy to care.
我忙得沒有時間在乎。

- Soon I guess. I can't wait.
  我想快了吧。等不及啦。

Do I have time to get a cup of coffee?
我有時間喝杯咖啡嗎？

- Yes, we will enjoy it! 有的，喝杯咖啡不錯！

- Sure. I'd like to have some hot coffee too.
  當然，我也想喝點熱咖啡。

這樣說不禮貌

You can help yourself!
你可自便。

- No, we do not have enough time.
  不，我們沒有時間了。

What do you do in your spare time?
你沒事的時候都做些什麼？

- I like to play football with my schoolmates. 我喜歡和學校的朋友去踢足球。

- Most of the time, I tutor! 大部分時間我在做家教！

這樣說不禮貌

- I enjoy going shopping with my friends and family.
  我喜歡跟家人或朋友去逛街。

I am not interested in anything except for reading.
除了閱讀以外我對任何事情都不感興趣。

Don't you think it would be better to go out for a walk?
你不覺得出去走走會比較好嗎？

- Yes, maybe I should.
  是呀，也許應該出去走一走。

- That sounds reasonable.
  這主意聽起來很合理。

這樣說不禮貌

Are you crazy? It's raining cats and dogs outside!
你瘋了嗎？現在外頭下著大雨！

I don't like taking a walk. It's pretty boring.
我不喜歡散步。那蠻無聊的。

Shall we go out tomorrow?
我們明天出去走走好嗎？

- Why not? What do you suggest?
  有何不可？你建議去哪裡？

- If I were you, I would stay home and rest. It's been a long week. 如果我是你，我會待在家中。這個星期很忙碌。

- Come on, stay in with me. I just want to be a couch potato. 拜託嘛，陪我窩在家。
  我只想當沙發上的馬鈴薯。

這樣說不禮貌

I'm going to stay home. But you can do whatever you like.
我要待在家。但你想做什麼都可以啊。

When will you have the date?
你什麼時候去約會？

- Well, my date is on Wednesday. 我的約會在星期三。

- After my supper. About half past nine.
  晚飯之後去，大概九點半。

- We will cut on this Saturday. There is a lantern carnival at Central Park.
  我們約這禮拜六。那天在中央公園有一個燈籠慶典。

這樣說不禮貌

Actually, I'm almost late. Can you give me a ride.
其實我快遲到了，你可以載我嗎？

2 虛擬實境口說練習
on your iMessenger

從最簡短到最豐富，讓你實際和老外練習口說和聽力

| 當你的朋友想約你出門時 |

❶ Oh sure, I am free.
當然好啊，我有空。

> am not busy 沒那麼忙
> have time to kill 有時間
> would love to 很樂意

❷ Let me check my schedule.
我先查看看我的行程表。

> ask my wife 問看看我老婆
> check and get back to you 查看看再回覆你
> make a check if I can make it
> 確認如果我騰得出時間的話

❸ Where do you have in mind?
你想要去哪裡？

> think we should go 覺得我們該
> suggest 建議
> like to visit 想去參觀

| 當有人告訴你應該出門走走時 |

❶ That would probably make me feel refreshed.
那可能可以讓你打起精神。

> rejuvenated 恢復精神
> better 好一點
> reenergized 重新振作

❷ Come with me, we can have a chat together.
跟我來嘛，我們可以一起聊個天。

> cigarette 抽根菸
> break 休息一下

| 當有人問你何時有空時 |

❶ **I'm generally free** on the weekends.
我通常假日都有空。

> every night 每天晚上
> whenever I want to be 想要有空時
> for lunch 午餐時間

❷ **I'm** starting a new job, **so I'm not sure yet.**
我即將要開始新工作，所以現在還無法確定。

> writing a novel 寫一部小說
> moving house 搬家
> working crazy hours 瘋狂加班

❸ **I keep busy, but I can always** change my plans.
我一直都很忙，不過還是都可以更改計畫的。

> alter my schedule 調整行程
> be spontaneous 保持彈性的
> follow my mood 隨心所欲

| 當有人問你要去哪裡約會時 |

❶ **You can't go wrong** going to the beach.
去海灘就絕不會出錯。

> It couldn't hurt 就不會有問題
> A good choice would be 會是最好的選擇
> Everyone loves 大家都愛

❷ **Asking her where she wants to go is the best** choice.
直接問她想去哪是最好的選擇。

> option 選擇
> policy 手段
> strategy 策略

3 虛擬實境網路聊天
on your iMessenger

在手機或電腦上，利用打字就可以聊出千言萬語

Matsumoto

星期三 下午 13:45

Yo!
What do people here do when they want to get out of town for a bit?

下午 13:45

嘿！假如這邊的民眾想到城外走走的話，他們都怎麼辦？

和 Hi 意思相近的問候

一點點

Oh, there's a world of options.

下午 13:46

噢，有幾千幾百種方法，

選擇

Hmmm...

下午 13:47

Where should I begin?

下午 13:47

我該從哪一點開始說起呢？

Well,
Just tell me about the things you do then.

下午 13:48

只要告訴我你是怎麼做的就行了。

Well, on weekends, I go fishing with my friends sometimes.

下午 13:49

這個嘛，有時候週末時，我會和我的朋友去釣魚。

釣魚

Just sit there and wait for fish to come?

下午 13:50

光是坐在那裡等魚兒自己上鉤？

. . . . ."

下午 13:51

Isn't it kind of boring?

下午 13:51

那樣不是很無聊嗎？

有一點

Matsumoto

星期三 下午 13:45

Haha
There's more to it than just fishing though. The chatting and catching up with friends goes along with it.

下午 13:55

 Still sounds too quiet for me.

下午 13:56

下午 13:57

 I prefer something more active.

下午 13:57

You should come with us next time. You never know, you might find that you actually enjoy yourself.

下午 13:58

 OK. I might have a try next time.

下午 13:59

哈哈，不光只有釣魚而已啦，我們還會和投緣的朋友聊天、敘舊。

趕上某人
一起

聽起來對我而言還是太靜態了。

我比較喜歡活潑一點的。

活躍的

你下次應該跟我們一起去。誰也說不準，說不定你會發現自己很陶醉其中呢。

好吧。我下次可能會試試看的。

試試看

聊天金句大補帖

Let me see. 讓我想想。

這句是很常用的口語，當別人詢問你任何問題，特別是跟日程表、個人計畫、每日活動有關的問題，而你無法馬上給予確定的回應，需要緩衝的時間時，就可以說這句。同時也告訴對方，你需要一點兒時間想想，才能針對他的問題給予回應。

Unit 5

當顆沙發馬鈴薯

Did you watch the volleyball game last night?
昨天晚上你看排球比賽了嗎？

> **Word Power!**
> · exciting [ɪk`saɪtɪŋ]
>   🅰 令人興奮的
> · result [rɪ`zʌlt] 🇳 結果
>
> **Sentence Power!**
> · forget about... 忘記…
> · What a pity! 真可惜！

- Yes. It was very exciting. 是的，非常精彩。

- No, I forgot about it. 沒有，我忘了。

- What a pity! I was too busy.
  真可惜！我昨晚太忙了。

- No. How about the results?
  沒有，結果怎麼樣呢？

> 這樣說不禮貌
> Who cares?
> 誰在乎什麼比賽？

What's program is on tonight?
今晚有什麼節目？

> **Word Power!**
> · final [`faɪnl] 🇳 決賽
>   v.s. 🄰🄱🄱🅁 versus 的縮寫。
>   對決，對抗
> · TV guide
>   🄿🄷🅁 電視節目表
>
> **Sentence Power!**
> · ...is on 正在播…

- Tonight is football night. 今晚是足球之夜。

- Your favorite show is on. 你最喜歡的節目。

> 這樣說不禮貌
> Why don't you check the TV guide?
> 你為什麼不查查節目表？

- There's an NBA Finals game, Knicks vs Lakers. 有場 NBA 冠軍賽，尼克對湖人。

What is your favorite program?
你最愛看什麼節目？

> **Word Power!**
> · favorite [`fevərɪt]
>   🅰 特別喜愛的
> · program [`progræm]
>   🇳 節目
> · waste [west] 🇳 浪費
>
> 更多…
> · talk show 脫口秀，談
>   話性節目
> · reality show 真人實境
>   節目
> · TV series 連續劇

- My favorite program is Oprah's talk show. 我最喜歡的節目是歐普拉的脫口秀。

- I love TV series such as *Revenge*, *The Walking Dead*, and *House of Cards*. 我喜歡看影集，像是《復仇》、《陰屍路》還有《紙牌屋》。

- I only watch CNN and BBC on TV.
  電視我只看 CNN 和 BBC。

> 這樣說不禮貌
> Watching TV is a waste of time.
> 看電視是浪費時間

What do you think about this advertisement?
你認為這個廣告怎麼樣？

Word Power!
· advertisement
[ˌædvɚˋtaɪzmənt]
n 廣告
· creative [krɪˋetɪv]
a 有創造力的
· pay attention to
phr 注意；關心
· appealing [əˋpilɪŋ]
a 有魅力的
· make sense
phr 具有意義

- Not so much. It's not creative or funny at all.
  不太好。既沒創意又不好笑。

- I don't usually pay attention to commercials.
  我通常不太注意廣告。

- It is not very appealing. 並不怎麼吸引人。

- The commercial doesn't seem to make sense to me.
  這個廣告對我來說不太合理。

When does the sports program begin?
體育節目幾點開始？

Word Power!
· sports [sports]
a 運動的
· miss [mɪs]
v 錯過；想念
· have no idea
phr 不知道
· promptly [ˋprɑmptlɪ]
ad 準時地

- In fifteen minutes. Trust me, you don't want to miss the game. 再十五分鐘，相信我，你不會想錯過這場比賽的。

- It's starting soon. 馬上就開始了。

- I have no idea. 我不知道。

- It will start at 6:30 p.m. promptly. 晚上六點半準時開播。

Would you mind if I open the window?
你介意我打開窗戶嗎？

Word Power!
· mind 這個字當動詞使
用時，後面接的動詞
要加 ing。
→ Do you mind
turning off the light
你介意關燈嗎？
· catch a cold phr 感冒

- No, of course not. 不，當然不介意。

- Yes, I'm feeling kind of cold.
  介意，我覺得有點冷。

- Oh, that's what I want to do.
  噢，那正是我想做的。

這樣說不禮貌

I would. I don't want to catch a cold.
我介意，我可不想感冒。

2 虛擬實境口說練習
on your iMessenger
從最簡短到最豐富，讓你實際和老外練習口說和聽力

┃當有人問你愛看什麼電視節目時┃

❶ **I don't even own a TV.**
我根本沒有電視。

> turn on the 沒打開過
> bother with the 不會花時間在
> like 不愛看

❷ **I watch crime shows any chance I get.**
我只要有空都會看犯罪劇。

> reality TV 實境秀
> sitcoms 情境喜劇
> soap operas 肥皂劇

❸ **I tend to binge watch older programs.**
我喜歡馬拉松式地追老一點的劇看。

> whole series 整個系列劇
> a season at a time 一次一整季
> established shows 已完結的劇

┃當有人想請你推薦好看的節目時┃

❶ **You should catch up on X-Files.**
你應該去追 X 檔案。

> definitely watch 一定要去看
> get into 應該追
> check out 應該去看看

❷ **Have you ever seen _Twin Peaks_?**
你有看過《雙峰》嗎？

> Do you know about 你知道
> Would you consider 你有考慮看
> When did you last see
> 你最後一次看⋯是什麼時候

| 當有人問你昨晚是否有看球賽時 |

❶ I couldn't believe that touchdown in the closing seconds.
我真不敢相信最後那秒的觸地得分。

alley-oop 灌籃
penalty kick 罰球
foul 界外球

❷ The league needs to do something about the refs.
聯盟應該要好好的處理裁判們。

instant replay 即時重播回放
the pace of the game 比賽的節奏
all the injuries 所有的受傷事件

❸ I missed it; who won?
我錯過了，結果誰贏？

didn't catch 沒看到
forgot about 忘了
skipped 跳過沒看

| 當節目進行到一半進廣告時 |

❶ I'm going to go to bed when this is over.
這段結束之後我要去睡覺了。

get some popcorn 去拿些爆米花
stretch my legs 伸展一下我的腿
see what else is on
轉台看還有哪些節目

❷ I've got time to go number one.
我終於有空去上個廁所。

hit the head 上廁所
take a pee break 上廁所休息
relieve myself 解放一下

3 虛擬實境網路聊天
on your iMessenger

在手機或電腦上，利用打字就可以聊出千言萬語

Sam

星期三 下午 13:45

 Are those headphones you have on?
What are you listening to?

下午 13:45

The Asia Music Billboard
top one hundred.

下午 13:47

你頭上戴的是耳機
嗎？
你在聽什麼？
頭戴式耳機

我在聽亞洲音樂排行
榜前一百名歌曲。
音樂排行榜

 You're what?

下午 13:48

你在聽什麼？

下午 13:49

 OMGoodness!
You're becoming a local!
Not saying there's
anything wrong with that,
just that you are fitting in
better than I thought.

下午 13:49

我的老天，你都快要
變成當地人了！並不
是說這樣有什麼不好，
只是，你適應的情況
比我想像得要好。
當地人
適應環境

I'm noticing something in this
music.
Although there's rock, pop,
slow songs, and R&B, there's a
certain similarity to all of them.
I think a lot of it is influenced by
western music.

下午 13:51

這些音樂讓我注意到
一件事。雖然裡頭有
搖滾、流行、慢歌及
饒舌等不同類型的歌
曲，但是都有一種類
似的感覺。我想他們
受到西方不少的影響。
注意
相似點
影響

Sam

星期三 下午 13:45

You're telling the wrong guy!
I really don't know much about this.

下午 13:52

You know what?
You should really get yourself to a CD store. You can buy music from all over the world. You just can't live without music, man.

下午 13:53

That sounds good!
Then recommend me your favorite artists.

下午 13:54

There's no doubt GD is my love!
I'm sure u'll definitely crazy 4 him!

下午 13:53

IC~
Then BFN,
I'm going to a CD store!

下午 13:54

你這可找錯對象了，我對這些玩意兒瞭解不多。

你知道嗎？你真的得到唱片行去逛逛，裡頭可以買到來自世界各地的音樂。老兄，你的生活可不能沒有音樂。

聽起來真棒！那推薦我一些你最愛的藝人吧。
藝人

那當然就是我最愛的 GD 啦！我很確定你也會為他瘋狂的！
毫無疑問地

好吧！那先這樣啦，我這就要去唱片行了！
Bye for now 的簡寫

聊天金句大補帖

It occurs to ... that ... 突然想到…

這句話是表示一個想法、一個念頭、一件事情…等突然閃過腦海。That 後面說的就是閃過腦海的事物，也可以直接用：sth. occurs to sb. 的句型，例如：That idea occurred to me at that moment.（當時那個想法閃過我的腦海。）

Unit 6 祝你有個好夢

一定要會的問答句

90% 的老外都是用這些句子開始聊天。

What do you usually do before you sleep?

睡覺前你通常幹什麼？

- Brush my teeth and have a bath. 刷牙、洗澡。

- I like to do yoga to stay fit.
我喜歡練一會兒瑜伽以保持身材。

- Read books. I'm recently getting hooked on Harry Potter.
看一些書，我最近迷上看哈利波特。

Word Power!
- yoga [ˋjogə] n 瑜珈

Sentence Power!
- stay fit 保持身材
- get hooked on sth. 迷上（某事物）；完全陷於（某事物）之中
- keep it a secret 保密

這樣說不禮貌

I'd rather keep it a secret.
我寧願不告訴你。

What's the time now? I'm sleepy.

現在幾點了？我想睡了。

- It's just seven o'clock. It's so early to go to sleep.
才七點，睡覺太早了。

- It's time to go to bed, hurry up! 到睡覺的時候了，快點上床吧。

- You look very tired, go to bed please. 你看起來很累，去睡吧。

Word Power!
- sleepy [ˋslipɪ] a 想睡的
- tired [taɪrd] a 疲倦的

Sentence Power!
- Hurry up! 快一點！

Can I eat something before I go to bed?

上床之前我可以吃東西嗎？

- Yes, you can. Just a little.
可以，但只能吃一點點。

- You'd better not, if you want to stay in shape.
如果你想保持良好的身材，最好別那樣做。

Word Power!
- a little phr 少量的
- had better not phr （勸告，建議）最好不要

Sentence Power!
- stay in shape 保持身材
- It's up to you. 隨便你；你自己決定。

這樣說不禮貌

It's up to you. 你自己看著辦。
No, Look how fat you are.
不行，你太胖了。

Why are you going to bed so early today?
為什麼今天睡覺這麼早？

- I have a fever and a headache. 我發燒了，頭痛。
- Many works are waiting for me tomorrow, so I need a good rest. 明天有好多工作要做，因此我要好好休息下。
- I find my skin is very bad because of lack of sleep. 我發現因為沒有足夠的睡眠導致我皮膚很差。

這樣說不禮貌

'Cause you're very annoying.
因為你很煩。

Would you like to go shopping with me tomorrow?
明天我們一起去逛街好嗎？

- That sounds very nice. 那聽起來很好。
- Sure! Let's go to that newly opened shopping mall. 好哇！我們去那間新開的購物中心。
- Sorry, I would love to, but I have to meet a friend. 抱歉，我很想去，但明天我要見一個朋友。

這樣說不禮貌

I don't feel like going shopping.
我不想逛街。

Would you be free to come to a book show on Saturday?
你星期六有空去看書展嗎？

- Sure. Thanks for asking. 當然，謝謝你邀請我。
- Sorry, but I have a meeting to attend on Saturday night. 對不起，但星期六晚上我有個會議要參加。
- What a splendid idea. Thank you. 真是個好主意，謝謝。
- I'm terribly sorry. I don't think I can. 真的很抱歉，我想我沒辦法去。

2 虛擬實境口說練習
on your iMessenger

從最簡短到最豐富，讓你實際和老外練習口說和聽力

| 當你和朋友差不多準備上床睡覺時可以說 |

❶ **Sleep tight!**
祝你睡個好覺！

> Nighty night 晚安
> Sweet dreams 祝你有個好夢

❷ **Time for some shut-eye.**
該睡覺了。

> to hit the hay 上床睡覺
> to call it a day 到此為止去睡覺
> for my beauty sleep 去睡美容覺

❸ **What a long day! I'm bushed.**
好長的一天啊！我累慘了。

> exhausted 累死
> beat 要倒地
> worn out 筋疲力盡

| 當你想先做點什麼再睡時 |

❶ **I know it's late, but there's got to be something to do.**
我知道已經很晚了，但一定還有些事情可以做。

> somewhere to go 有些地方可以去
> some bars open 有些酒吧開著
> some game we could play
> 有些遊戲我們可以玩

❷ **Hey Barry, get out of bed and come meet me.**
嘿巴瑞，快起床來找我玩吧。

> don't act so old 別像個老頭子一樣
> stop what you're doing 停下你正在做的事
> get dressed 快穿上衣服

| 當你想約朋友出去吃消夜時 |

❶ Come with me to see if the nightmarket is still open.
跟我來吧，去看看有沒有夜市還開著。

any food stand 小吃攤
the beef noodles shop 牛肉麵店
one of the tea houses 茶店

❷ Let me show you a great place for crepes that only opens late.
讓我帶你去一家賣超棒可麗餅的店，它都很晚才開。

fried wontons 炸餛飩
stinky tofu 臭豆腐
matcha tea 抹茶

❸ Don't worry, one snack now won't make you fat.
別擔心啦，吃一份消夜而已不會變胖。

kill you 殺了你
make you have bad dreams 害你做惡夢
ruin your diet 毀了你的節食計畫

| 當你想提早就寢，而室友們仍在閒聊時 |

❶ Guys, I've got a big test tomorrow morning. Could you keep it down?
各位，我明天早上有場大考試。你們可以小聲點嗎？

an interview 面試
a meeting 會議
a breakfast date 早餐約會

❷ Pipe down! It's too late to be so loud.
安靜點！已經很晚了不能太吵。

Put a lid on it 嘴巴閉起來
Knock it off 停下來不要鬧了

3 虛擬實境網路聊天
on your iMessenger

在手機或電腦上，利用打字就可以聊出千言萬語

A.F.

星期三 下午 13:45

 Hey,
Tell me what do you
do to release stress?

下午 13:45

嘿，告訴我你平常都
做什麼來消除壓力？
釋放

I usually take a hot bath.
Which just washes away
my stress.
And if I'm able to fall asleep
at nite, my appetite comes
back in the morning.

下午 13:46

我會泡一個熱水澡，
然後壓力就會消失得
無影無蹤。假如我晚
上睡得好的話，隔天
早上我就會恢復食慾
了。
沖走
night 的簡寫
食慾

 I'm not much of an eater
when I'm stressed out either,
But I don't think that my
sleep patterns are affected
as much as you.

下午 13:47

我很緊張的時候胃口
不會像你這麼大，此
外，我的睡眠習慣也
不像你一樣這麼容易
受影響。
型態
受影響的

下午 13:48

 However,
When I'm stressed out, I get
really grouchy, n trust me,
you don't want to be around
me when that happens.

下午 13:50

然而，當我很緊張時，
我會變得很愛抱怨，
而且相信我，你不會
想靠近我的。
愛抱怨的
and 的簡寫

A.F.

What I do to deal with my stress is exercise.
Play some ball, do some swimming, and sweat the stress away.

下午 13:52

我都是靠運動來消除緊張的感覺。打打球、游游泳之類的，就可以把壓力流掉了。
出汗

No wonder you're in such great shape.

下午 13:53

難怪你身體這麼健康。
難怪

Yeah
Cuz I'm stressed out all the time!

下午 13:54

對呀！因為我一天到晚都很緊張啊！
because 的簡寫
緊張的

HEE HEE

下午 13:54

It is late now. U must be really tired. Sleep tight, dude!

下午 13:55

已經很晚了。你應該很累了吧。晚安，老兄！
傢伙

聊天金句大補帖

Not quite. 還沒／尚未。

當別人詢問你的計劃、情況等，而你正處於一種將完未完的不確定狀態時，就可以用這句話來表達你的情形。這句話意味著：雖然你幾乎要達到最後的結果了，但為了某些因素還差臨門一腳，因此尚未到達最終的穩定狀態。另外，

• Not completely.

也可以表達這種意思，但是是較為正式的用法。「Not quite.」則較不常出現在正式的交談中。

Chapter 2

地鐵站大冒險

It's adventure time!

Unit 1 向左走向右走

Unit 2 短程旅行必搭

Unit 3 長途旅行必搭

Unit 4 趕時間必搭

Unit 5 東奔西跑的每一天

Unit 6 道聲珍重再見

Unit 1 向左走向右走

I think we are lost. What should we do?

我覺得我們迷路了，我們該怎麼辦？

Word Power!
- direction [dəˋrɛkʃən]
  n 方向；指示
- hire [haɪr] v 僱用
- guide [gaɪd] n 導遊
- fault [fɔlt] n 錯誤

Sentence Power!
- no need to... 不需要…

- We should ask for directions! 我們應該問路！

- Maybe we should have hired a guide.
  也許我們應該請一位導遊。

- There is no need to worry. Let's just take a taxi.
  沒什麼好緊張的。我們搭計程車就好了。

這樣說不禮貌

Oh my god! It was all your fault.
哦我的天啊！這全是你的錯。

Excuse me. Could you please tell me how to get to Taipei 101?

對不起，你能告訴我怎樣去臺北 101 嗎？

Word Power!
- go along phr 一直走；
  繼續下去
- crossing [ˋkrɔsɪŋ]
  n 十字路口

- You can go along this road and turn left at the first crossing, then you'll see it. 沿著這條路一直往前走，在第一個十字路口左轉，你就可以看到它了。

- I'm going that way, follow me, please!
  我正要去那，請跟我走吧！

這樣說不禮貌

Just look up, you can't miss it!
自己查查吧，你不會錯過的！

Could you show me the way to the central park?

你能告訴我去中央公園的路嗎？

Word Power!
- go down
  phr 沿著…下去
- avenue [ˋævəˌnju]
  n 大道；大街
- block [blɑk] n 街區

Sentence Power!
- a five-minute walk
  五分鐘的路程

- Yes, you go down Fifth Avenue. You won't miss it. 哦，沿著第五街往前走就到了。你不會錯過的。

- Yes, you can go down from here, it's only about a five-minute walk. 是的，從這一直往前走，大約五分鐘左右就到了。

- You have to walk two blocks to the bus stop.
  再過兩條馬路到公車站牌那裡就到了。

Does the bus go to The Peninsula?

這輛公車會到半島酒店嗎？

- No, it doesn't. No direct bus goes to The Peninsula.
  不到，去半島酒店沒有直達的公車。

- No, it doesn't. You should take Bus No.15. It's only two stops from here. 不會，你該搭乘的是 15 路公車。從這裡過去只有兩站，

- Yes, it does. But there is something wrong with the bus. Please wait for another one. 是的。但公車出了點問題。請再等下一班吧。

How far is it to Universal Studios?

到環球影城還有多遠？

- Take the second road on the left and go straight on.
  沿著左邊第二條馬路一直往前走。

- Cross the street and you will find it.
  過個馬路，你就會看到它。

- Let me take you there.
  我帶你去好了。

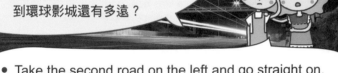

這樣說不禮貌

Almost there. Don't complain so much.
快到了。不要一直唸。

Excuse me. I'm trying to find my way to the flower market.

請問去花市的路怎麼走？

- Keep going until you come to an end. 這條路走到底。

- Turn left at the first corner, and it's the second building on your left. 在第一個街口左轉，左邊第二棟大樓就是。

- Take the No.6 or No.23 bus. 坐 6 路或 23 路公車。

- Sorry, I don't know. I am a stranger here. 對不起，我不知道，我第一次到這裡。

2 虛擬實境口說練習
on your iMessenger

從最簡短到最豐富，讓你實際和老外練習口說和聽力

| 當你在路上被問路時 |

❶ You're going the wrong way! You need to go back the way you came.
你走錯路了！你應該要先回到你來的那條路上。

> headed the wrong direction 走錯方向
> on the wrong path 走到錯的路
> wasting your steps 白走一段路

❷ I have never heard of that place. Let me ask somebody else.
我從來沒聽過那個地方。我問問看其他人。

> didn't know that place existed 根本不知道那個地方的存在
> didn't know that place was near here 不知道那裡離這邊近不近
> am not familiar with that place 對那裡不太熟

❸ You stay on this path, then hang a right after three blocks.
你繼續沿著這條小徑走，然後三個街區後右轉。

> turn left 左轉
> cross the street 過馬路
> hang a Louie (left) 左轉

| 當你要問別人路時 |

❶ Excuse me, Miss. Do you know the way to City Hall?
不好意思，小姐。妳知道市政府怎麼走嗎？

> Have you heard of 妳有聽過
> Could you direct me to 妳可以帶我去
> Where is 在哪裡

❷ Sir, can I bother you for a moment? I'm rather lost.
先生，可以打擾你一下嗎？我好像迷路了。

> get your attention 請你聽我說
> trouble you 麻煩你
> borrow you 借用你

| 當你想知道距離目的地還要走多遠時 |

❶ Is it far? I need to go to the bathroom.
那會很遠嗎？我需要先去上廁所。

> charge my cellphone 充我手機的電
> take a quick nap 小睡一下
> write a postcard 寫張明信片

❷ Do you know how long it will take?
你知道要多久才會到嗎？

> how many minutes it needs 需要幾分鐘
> if it'll be much longer 是否還要很久
> when we'll arrive 我們何時

❸ Could you give me an estimate of when I might arrive?
你可以估算一下我大概何時會抵達嗎？

> a clue 提示
> your best guess 猜
> a time frame 預設

| 當你想知道怎麼去一個地方比較近時 |

❶ Is there a shortcut?
這是一條捷徑嗎？

> faster way 比較快的路
> better way 好一點的路
> shorter route 比較短的路徑

❷ Tell me the most direct route.
請告訴我最直接可達的路徑。

> how to cut through 如何抄捷徑
> the quickest way 最快速的路線

3 虛擬實境網路聊天
on your iMessenger

在手機或電腦上，利用打字就可以聊出千言萬語

Dear KattyJ

星期三 下午 13:45

 Look at how many coffee shops there are!

下午 13:45

好多咖啡店呢！
咖啡店

下午 13:46

Rite~
Look at how many Starbucks there are just on that block.

下午 13:47

沒錯，光看那個街區有多少星巴克就知道了。
right 的簡寫

 Why are these cafés so popular?

下午 13:48

為什麼這些咖啡館這麼受歡迎呢？

I think people nowadays devote more time to leisure. They grab a cup of coffee in the afternoon while they browse the internet and sometimes do some work.

下午 13:49

我想是因為現代人更注重休閒生活了。他們在下午的時光喝杯咖啡，瀏覽網路，或者工作。
將……奉獻（給）
閒暇
瀏覽

 Oh,
I always thought that Asians were more connected with tea rather than coffee, what's the deal with that?

下午 13:50

我還以為跟咖啡比起來，亞洲文化跟茶的關係比較深，為什麼現在是這樣呢？
與……聯繫
怎麼回事

Dear KattyJ

星期三 下午 13:45

I would hav to say, It's people's fondness for western civilization.

下午 13:52

下午 13:53

Also an image we see many times in movies.
For example,
When was the last time the hero and the heroine of a movie met in a teashop rather than a coffee shop?

下午 13:54

 You have a point there.

下午 13:55

可以說是因為人們對西方文化的喜好吧。
`have 的簡寫`
`喜愛`
`文明`

同時也受到我們從電影當中接收到的意象影響。比方說你上次看到電影裡面的男女主角相約在茶館見面而不是在咖啡館是什麼時候的事了？
`例如`

你講得有道理。
`你說得有道理`

`聊天金句大補帖`

Can I trouble you to...? 能不能麻煩你？

當我們很需要別人幫我們一個忙，而又覺得有點兒不好意思時，可以直接用這個句子詢問對方能否伸出援手。類似的說法還有：

• Could I bother you to...? 能不能麻煩你⋯？

• I was wondering if you could / might...? 不知道你能不能幫我⋯？

Unit 2 短程旅行必搭

Where should I get a ticket for the MRT?
我要到哪裡才能買捷運的票？

Word Power!
- automatic [ˌɔtəˋmætɪk]
  a 自動的
- ticket machine
  n （自動）售票機
- next to **phr** 在…旁邊
- attendant [əˋtɛndənt]
  n 服務人員
- booking office
  n 售票處

- You can use the automatic ticket machine over there.
  你可以使用那裡的自動售票機。

- You can buy an Easy card next to the ATMs.
  你可以到提款機旁邊買悠遊卡。

- You can ask the attendant in the booking office.
  你可以問問售票處的服務人員。

這樣說不禮貌
How should I know?
我怎麼會知道？

What's wrong with the MRT?
捷運發生什麼問題？

Word Power!
- accident [ˋæksədənt]
  n 意外

Sentence Power!
- What's wrong with...?
  …有什麼問題？

- The MRT is late. There may have been an accident.
  捷運誤點了。可能有什麼意外吧。

- Sorry I don't know. Maybe we should take the taxi to catch the meeting on time.
  抱歉，我不清楚。或許我們該搭計程車才趕得上開會了。

這樣說不禮貌
I'm already late! Make the MRT leave right now!
我已經遲到了！叫捷運現在趕快開！

When does the MRT stop running?
捷運什麼時候停駛？

Word Power!
- sometime
  [ˋsʌmˌtaɪm] **ad** 在（將來或過去）某一時候

更多…
捷運的英文在不同國家有不同的表示方法，例如：在台灣為 MRT、在香港為 MTR、在美國為 Subway / Underground、在英國則為 Tube。

- It closes at 12:00 midnight. 午夜十二點。

- I'm not sure. I think sometime around midnight.
  我不確定。我想大概是半夜吧。

- I'm pretty sure it closes at one in the morning.
  我十分確定停運時間是凌晨一點。

- The trains run 24 hours a day.
  捷運二十四小時營運。

這樣說不禮貌
How could I possibly know?
我怎麼可能知道？

How long **does it take to the destination by** MRT?

搭捷運到達目的地我們需要多久？

Word Power!
· destination
　[ˌdɛstəˋneʃən] **n** 目的地
· service counter
　n 服務台
· look up **phr** 查詢

Sentence Power!
· How long...? 要多久？
· It depends. 看情況。

- About 30 minutes. 大概三十分鐘。
- You can Google it. 你可以 Google 一下。
- You can ask the service counter. 你可以到服務台問一下。
- It depends. 視情況而定。
- Let's look up the timetable. 我們來查查看時刻表。

Does the MRT supply a food service?

捷運供應食物嗎？

Word Power!
· supply [səˋplaɪ]
　v 供應，提供
· food service
　n 提供食物的服務

Sentence Power!
· You must be kidding me. 你一定是在開我玩笑。

- No. I'm sure it doesn't. 不，我很確定不提供。
- No, I don't think so.
  不，我不這麼認為。

這樣說不禮貌

- I'm not sure, maybe it does.
  我不確定，也許提供吧。

You must be kidding me. You even can't eat or drink on the MRT!
你在開玩笑吧，捷運上甚至不能吃或喝東西！

Can I drink my soda on the MRT?

可以在捷運上喝汽水嗎？

Word Power!
· definitely [ˋdɛfənɪtlɪ]
　ad 明確地；明顯地
· fine [faɪn]
　v 處⋯以罰款
· go ahead
　phr 進行；發生
· get a ticket **phr** 開罰單

- No. You definitely can't. 不，你絕對不行。
- No. If you do that, you'll be fined.
  不行，如果你喝了，會被罰錢的。

這樣說不禮貌

- You better not. Look, there is nobody drinking or eating on the MRT.
  最好不要。你看，捷運上沒有人在吃或喝東西。

Go ahead if you want to get a ticket.
如果你想被罰款的話就喝吧。

2 虛擬實境口說練習
on your iMessenger

從最簡短到最豐富：讓你實際和老外練習口說和聽力

│當你想問站務員如何搭捷運時│

❶ How do I connect to the red line from here?
我該怎麼從這裡搭去紅線呢？

> blue line 藍線
> airport 機場
> line that goes to the zoo 會到動物園的路線

❷ Where can I get a yoyo card?
我要去哪裡才能買到悠遊卡呢？

> day pass 一日券
> ticket 票
> token 代幣

❸ What time will the MRT stop running?
捷運何時會停駛呢？

> start running 開放
> come 來
> arrive at Tamsui 抵達淡水

│當你在教外國人如何搭捷運時│

❶ You can top up your card at the machine.
你可以用這台機器儲值卡片

> add value 加值
> add money 加錢

❷ If you get on here, this train will intersect with the green line.
如果你搭這班車的話，就會搭到綠線。

> run into 前往
> cross 經過

| 當你想問站務員有關票價的問題時 |

❶ Can I get a discount if I use a yoyo card?
我用悠遊卡的話可以得到折扣嗎？

> pay for a whole month 預付一個月
> make a transfer 轉車
> give a senior my seat 讓座給老年人

❷ Is the fee calculated by distance?
費用是依照距離計算的嗎？

> time of day 一天的時間
> the number of stations I pass 經過的站數
> my weight 我的載重

❸ What if I want to get reimbursed the money on my card?
如果我想從卡片拿錢出來呢？

> I lose 弄丟
> I don't know how much money is on
> 不知道⋯有多少錢在裡面
> the gate doesn't open when I swipe
> 刷⋯過閘門，門卻沒開

| 當你被問到有關搭捷運的規則時 |

❶ A bottle of water is okay, but otherwise drinks are not permitted.
一瓶水還可以，但是其他飲料就不行。

> not allowed 不被允許
> not to be opened 不能打開
> against the rules 會違反規定

❷ You have to eat it before you cross the MRT gate.
你要吃的話請在跨入捷運站前吃。

> after you get off 出捷運站後
> either before or after 在進去前或後
> anywhere but on the train
> 在哪都可，就是不能在車上

3 虛擬實境網路聊天
on your iMessenger

在手機或電腦上，利用打字就可以聊出千言萬語

J. S.

星期三 下午 13:45

So,
Were you able to find everything
you were looking for?

下午 13:45

那，你順利找到你要
買的東西了嗎？
尋找

Yup,
The directions U gave
me were very helpful.

下午 13:46

是的，你提供的指引
相當精確。

 Glad to hear it.

下午 13:47

很高興聽到你這麼說。
高興的

下午 13:47

I did notice one thing.
Though it's still packed,
The traffic has gotten a lot better
since the last time I was here.

下午 13:48

不過我注意到一件事，
雖然路上還是很多車，
但是交通狀況跟我之
前來的那一次比起來
改善很多。
擁擠的
交通

I think we have the MRT to
thank for that.
Since it was built, more and
more people have been taking it
for their daily commute,
As well as for traveling to nearby
attractions during weekends.

下午 13:49

我想這多虧了我們的
捷運系統。捷運路線
建成後，人們每日利
用它通勤上班，假日
也透過捷運到鄰近的
景點去遊玩。
通勤
而且
附近的

J. S.

星期三 下午 13:45

Rite.

下午 13:50

對呀。

With the increasing amount of people going out,
other public transportation systems have benefited as well.

下午 13:51

隨著搭乘人數的增加，其他的大眾運輸也跟著受益。

數量
大眾運輸系統
有益於

When I was taking the bus I realized that.
I mean it wasn't rush hour but the bus was packed full of people.

下午 13:52

我搭公車的時候就明白到這點了。雖然不是尖峰時間，但車上仍舊坐滿了人。

領悟
尖峰時段

下午 13:52

聊天金句大補帖

That's quite true! 一點兒也沒錯！

這句話是用以表示贊同對方的意見、想法、作法，或者對方所提出的某項事實等。
也有「我再同意不過了」的意思。另外，

• You can say that again.

也可以表達同樣的意思，而且語氣顯得更強烈。

Unit 3

長途旅行必搭

一定要會的問答句

90% 的老外都是用這些句子開始聊天。

Which train do I take to Barcelona?

去巴塞隆納要坐哪趟火車？

> **Word Power!**
> · platform [ˈplætˌfɔrm]
>   **n** 月臺
> · cancel [ˈkænsl]
>   **v** 取消，中止
> · snowstorm [ˈsnoˌstɔrm]
>   **n** 暴風雪

- Platform 4 at 9:30. 坐第四月臺九點半的那一趟。
- I think it should be K181. 我想應該是 K181 次列車。
- The train to Barcelona has been cancelled because of a heavy snowstorm. 開往巴塞隆納的火車因為暴風雪而被取消了。

這樣說不禮貌

Why Barcelona? That is a boring place.
為什麼要去巴塞隆納？那裡很無聊。

When will we get to our destination?

我們什麼時候到達目的地？

> **Word Power!**
> · arrive [əˈraɪv] **v** 抵達
> · earthquake [ˈ3θˌkwek]
>   **n** 地震
> · high-speed rail
>   **n** 高鐵
> · shut down **phr** 停止
> · have no clue
>   **phr** 不知道

- We will arrive by noon. 中午前就會到了。
- I heard that there was an earthquake last night, the high-speed rail has been shut down all day. So we can't leave here until tomorrow morning.
  我聽説昨晚那場地震讓高鐵今天停駛一整天。所以我們最快也要明天才能出發。
- Sorry, I have no clue. 抱歉，我不大清楚。

這樣說不禮貌

We will get there when when we get here.
該到的時候就會到。

What's round-trip fare?

來回票多少錢？

> **Word Power!**
> · round-trip [ˈraundˌtrɪp]
>   **a** 來回的；雙程的
> · fare [fɛr] **n** 費用
> · total [ˈtotl] **n** 總數
> · correct [kəˈrɛkt]
>   **a** 正確的
> · discount [ˈdɪskaunt]
>   **n** 折扣
>
> **更多…**
> · one-way ticket 單程票
> · monthly pass 定期票
> · ticket books 回數票

- 628 dollars. 六百二十八美元。
- The total is ￡90. 總共是 90 英鎊。
- I don't know its correct number. 我不知道確切的數字。
- 600 dollars, after discount. 折價後是六百元。

Do I have to change trains?

需要換車嗎？

Word Power!
- local train **n** （中途停多站的）慢車
- direct train **n** 直達車
- figure out **phr** 【口】想出；理解

更多…
- express 快車
- night express 夜間快車
- berth 臥鋪火車
- doodlebug 短程往返火車

- Yes, you will have to. 是的，你必須要換車。
- No. It's a local train. 不用，這班是慢車。／這班車每站都停。
- You don't need to change trains. It's a direct train. 不必換車，這一班是直達車。
- Sorry. I'm still trying to figure that out, too. 對不起，我也還在試著要搞清楚。

Who is traveling with you?

誰和你一塊旅遊？

Word Power!
- seem [sim] **v** 看來好像，似乎
- manager [ˋmænɪdʒɚ] **n** 經理
- business trip **phr** 出差

- I'm traveling with my wife. 我與妻子一同旅遊。
- I always travel by myself. 我總是獨自旅遊。
- My friends. But I can't seem to find them now. 和我朋友，可是我現在似乎找不到他們。
- My manager. We are on a business trip this time. 和公司經理。我們這趟是出差之旅。

Should I reserve seats on the train?

我應該預訂火車車票嗎？

Word Power!
- reserve [rɪˋzɝv] **v** 預約
- full [ful] **a** 滿的
- peak season **n** 旺季
- off season **n** 淡季

- Yes, this train is always full, and it is peak season. 是的，這趟車總是人很多，而且現在是旅遊旺季。
- No, you don't have to. It is off season now. But you can book it to make sure you have seats then. 沒有必要，現在是旅遊淡季。不過你還是可以先訂票以確定到時有位置。
- There is no need to reserve seats on that train. It's never full. 那班車不必訂位，總會有空位。

2 虛擬實境口說練習
on your iMessenger

從最簡短到最豐富，讓你實際和老外練習口說和聽力

| 當你想向火車站務員買票時 |

❶ I'd like two tickets to Taitung, please.
我想要買兩張到台東的票，謝謝。

to Pingtung 到屏東
North 北上
on the next train 下一班

❷ Do you have any business class tickets?
你們有任何經濟車廂的票嗎？

first class 頭等艙
sleeper train 臥鋪
cheaper 便宜一點

❸ Where is the platform?
月台在哪裡？

time table 時間表
information on my ticket 票上的資訊
best seat 最好的位置

| 當你的票弄丟，在火車上要補票時 |

❶ (toward your friend) Check your pockets; I can't find my ticket.
（對你的朋友說）檢查看看你的口袋，我找不到我的票。

the floor 地板
your purse 你的皮包
your seat 你的座位

❷ I can't find my ticket, so I guess I'll have to buy another one.
我找不到我的票，所以我猜我可能要再買一張。

pay again 再付一次錢
purchase a new one 買一張新的
get off the train here 在這邊下車

| 當你要告訴外國朋友如何搭火車時 |

❶ Just listen to the announcements, and you'll know when you arrive.
聽車上的廣播，你就可以知道什麼時候會抵達。

check the sign outside the window 確認窗外的標誌
see digital display above the door 看門上的跑馬燈
watch your position on Google maps
看著你在 Google 地圖上的位置

❷ Let me show you on your ticket where it tells you your seat number.
讓我指給你看你票上的座位號碼。

car number 車次
departure time 出發時間
train type 車種

❸ You can just fall asleep and they'll wake you up when you arrive.
你可以先睡一下，他們到了時會叫你起來。

you'll be there before you know it 在你醒來前就會抵達了
because it'll take a little while 因為會要一陣子才到

| 當你想詢問路人如何看時刻表時 |

❶ What do those codes mean?
這些代碼代表什麼意思？

symbols 符號
abbreviations 縮寫

❷ I don't see my train; are they listed alphabetically by city?
我看不到我的火車，它們是按照城市的開頭字母順序排列的嗎？

by departure time 出發時間
according to their direction 根據目的地

3 虛擬實境網路聊天
on your iMessenger

在手機或電腦上，利用打字就可以聊出千言萬語

Jessica Lee

星期三 下午 13:45

 U know what?
I went to the history museum the other day.

下午 13:45

你知道嗎？我前幾天去了歷史博物館。
You 的簡寫

I'm not much into history, but I definitely appreciate a good piece of historical art when I see one.

下午 13:56

我對歷史不是那麼有興趣，但是當我看到一件歷史悠久的優質藝術品時，我會相當欣賞。
賞識

 You like historical art?

下午 13:47

你喜歡歷史悠久的藝術？
有關歷史的

Yup, and contemporary art too. Not just paintings and sculptures, but also dance and musicals.

下午 13:48

也喜歡當代藝術。而且不只是繪畫、雕刻，我也喜歡舞蹈、音樂劇等。
當代的
不只…還有

 U should take me to an art museum then!
And why haven't U take me to a musical theater yet?

下午 13:49

那麼帶我去看看美術館吧！還有，你為什麼都還沒帶我去音樂劇院呢？
美術館
音樂劇院

下午 13:49

 You never take me out anymore.

下午 13:50

你很久沒帶我出去玩了。

Jessica Lee

星期三 下午 13:45

Plzplzplz…………
下午 13:52

拜託拜託啦…。
Please 的簡寫

Fine...
下午 13:53

好吧…。

……"
下午 13:53

I'll give you the names of some art museums. But!
You'll have to check the opening hours of the museums and the schedule for the dances yourself.
下午 13:54

我給妳一些美術館的名字，不過妳得自己查詢博物館的開放時間以及舞蹈表演清單。
營業時間

Thx!!! Luv U!
下午 13:55

感謝啦！愛你！
Love 的簡寫

聊天金句大補帖

Why wouldn't I? 為什麼不呢？

這句話表達的是一種個人主觀的感受，意味著說話者覺得某人的某個行為、作法、決定等沒有什麼不對、沒有什麼不可行之處，有理所當然的感覺包含其中。

Unit 4 趕時間必搭

Taxi, Can you take me to the British Museum?
計程車，可以載我去大英博物館嗎？

- Yes. I can take you to there in passing. Hop in please.
  可以，我可以把你順道載過去。請上車。
- Sorry, there is a traffic jam, you'll wait for a longer time. 對不起，那邊塞車了，你還得再等等。
- Sorry, it's not my turn. You can take that one in front of me. 對不起，還沒輪到你，你可以坐我前面的那輛。

> **不能不會的小技巧**
> 到了國外，有時也難免發生想去一個景點，但大眾交通工具無法抵達的窘境。通常在這種時候，叫一台計程車確實是最方便又快速的辦法。
>
> **Word Power!**
> - museum [mjuˋzɪəm]
>   n 博物館
> - in passing = by the way phr 順便
> - hop in = step in phr 上車
> - traffic jam phr 交通阻塞

How exactly do you figure out the fare?
你是怎樣計算車費的？

- According to the kilometer. 根據公里數來計算的。
- The first 5 kilometers are 5 dollars, and every kilometer extra costs you 50 cent. 前五公里是五美元，之後每五公里五十分。
- Don't worry. I don't take advantage of people.
  別擔心，我不會騙你的。

> **Word Power!**
> - exactly [ɪgˋzæktlɪ]
>   ad 確切地
> - kilometer [ˋkɪləˌmitɚ]
>   n 公里
> - take advantage of
>   phr 利用；佔便宜

How long will it take to get there?
去那裡要多久？

- Maybe half an hour. 也許半小時。
- Don't worry. I'll try to take some short cuts to suit your time. 別擔心，我會儘量抄近路來配合你的時間。
- Maybe it is about ten minutes if the traffic isn't too heavy. 路上要是不太擠的話就十分鐘。
- It's hard to say. It's rush-hour now. 很難說，現在是尖峰時段。

> **Word Power!**
> - short cut
>   phr 捷徑、近路
> - suit [sut]
>   v 配合；適合
> - heavy [ˋhɛvɪ]
>   a 大量的
>
> **Sentence Power!**
> - It's hard to say. 很難說，不好說。
>   = It's difficult to say.

Did you call a taxi?
你叫計程車嗎？

Chapter 2 地鐵站大冒險

- Yes. Please take me to this address. 請載我去這個地方。
- Yes, where is the taxi stand? 是的，計程車招呼站在哪裡？
- Drive me to the National Museum of Natural Science, please. 請載我到科博館。
- Yes. Please hurry up! I'm late. Please take me to the train station. 是的，快點，我遲到了。請載我去火車站。

不能不會的小技巧

叫計程車，除了最簡單的在大馬路上招手之外，也可以到飯店、車站、百貨公司外的計程車招呼站，那裡總是會有排隊等待載客的計程車們。而現在，你也可以用手機下載 APP，讓系統自動幫你定位叫車，省去老是招不到計程車，還要受外頭日曬風吹的麻煩哦！

Word Power!
- address [ə`drɛs]
  n 住址
- taxi stand
  n 計程車招呼站

How much should I pay?
我該付你多少錢？

- That's 20 dollars. 總共二十美元。
- The meter reads 30 dollars. 儀表顯示三十美元。
- It costs 100 dollars. 一百美元。
- Let me see. It's 25 dollars in total.
  讓我看一下。總共是二十五美元。

這樣說不禮貌

Just watch the Meter.
自己看看儀表吧。

Sentence Power!
- How much 多少（錢）
  →這句也可以用來詢問不可數名詞的數量，例如：
  How much coffee did you drink today? 今天你喝了多少咖啡？

Can you stop right over there for a moment?
你可以在前面停一下車嗎？

- Look, there is a "No Parking" sign over there.
  瞧，那邊有「禁止停車」的標誌。
- I'm afraid it's a restricted area.
  這裡是管制區，不能停車。
- Sorry, I can't stop here.
  對不起，我不能停在這。

這樣說不禮貌

Suit yourself.
隨你了。

Word Power!
- over there phr 在那裡
- sign [saɪn] n 標誌
- restricted area
  n 禁止通行地區

更多…
- parking lot 停車場（可數）
- parking space 停車位
- parking ticket 違規停車罰單。

Sentence Power!
- Suit oneself. 隨某人自己的意願行事。

2 虛擬實境口說練習
on your iMessenger
從最簡短到最豐富，讓你實際和老外練習口說和聽力

| 當你要告知計程車司機你要去哪裡時 |

❶ I'd like to go to the train station.
我想要去火車站。

> airport 機場
> city hall 市政府
> art museum 美術館

❷ Do you know the way to Tin Pan Alley?
你知道去叮盤巷（台南的美式餐廳）的路嗎？

> best route 最好路線
> quickest way 最快方法
> shortcut 捷徑

❸ Go past the intersection and turn right down the alley.
過交叉路口後右轉進巷子。

> around the block 繞過街區
> 5 more blocks 過五個街區
> one more mile 一英哩過

| 當你被司機問到該如何走時 |

❶ If you can go around the heavy traffic, that'd be great.
如果你可以繞過那個車陣的話會很好。

> take the scenic route 走風景優美的小徑
> not let us wait in traffic 讓我們不用塞車

❷ Use any road besides Jianping Rd, and turn down Wennan Rd when we get there.
不要開建平路其他都可以，我們快到時轉進文南路。

> go past 過
> turn left on 左轉

| 當你要打電話叫車時 |

❶ I don't know how to operate the machine; could you call a taxi for me?
我不知道該怎麼操控這台機器，你可以幫我打電話叫計程車嗎？

> the phone number 電話號碼
> where I am 我在哪
> how to go 怎麼去

❷ Pick me up at the corner.
在**轉角**讓我上車。

> I'll walk to 我會走過去
> Meet me at 在…讓我碰面
> I will stand on 我會站在

❸ I'd like to schedule a pickup at 6 in the morning.
我想要預先叫早上 6 點的車

> at noon 中午
> at my house 到我家
> every evening this week 這個禮拜每天晚上

| 當你詢問計程車司機收費標準時 |

❶ Do I pay per mile?
我是按表付費嗎？

> kilometer 公里數
> city block 城市街區
> the distance 距離

❷ How do you calculate the rate?
你是怎麼計算費率的？

> cost 價錢
> fare 價錢
> final price 最後價格

3 虛擬實境網路聊天
on your iMessenger

在手機或電腦上，利用打字就可以聊出千言萬語

Haku-sun

星期三 下午 13:45

 How do taxis survive with all the advancements in public transportation?

下午 13:45

既然大眾運輸這麼發達了，計程車怎麼生存呢？
存活

下午 13:45

It is great but there are limitations to it as well.

下午 13:46

大眾運輸是很棒，但是也有其侷限。
限制

 Really? Like what?
I mean,
With so much public transportation available, there is hardly any need for taxis.

下午 13:47

真的嗎？像什麼呢？我是說有這麼多大眾運輸工具，誰還需要計程車呢？
可用的
幾乎不

But don't you ever find yourself in a hurry to get somewhere?

下午 13:48

但，難道你不曾碰過趕時間到某處的狀況嗎？
趕著要…
某處

  Hmmm...

下午 13:49

Or, after a night out on the town, you find that there are no public transportation services operating?

下午 13:50

或者晚上很晚回家發現大眾交通工具都停駛了？
運送

星期三 下午 13:45

Or that you're just too lazy to walk beyond your front door?

下午 13:51

下午 13:52

或是你懶到不想用走的出門？

越過

Taxis definitely do their part in providing transportation services to the public.

下午 13:53

計程車必定也為了運輸服務業盡了一份心力。

盡自己的職責

No wonder I find myself riding taxis a lot.

下午 13:54

難怪我常常搭計程車。

難怪

You take the taxi because you get lost. And taxis get you to the front door! Haha~

下午 13:55

你搭計程車是因為你迷路了。而計程車會把你送到家門口！哈哈～

聊天金句大補帖

Have any advice? 你有什麼建議？

當我們希望從對方那邊得到對於任何事情的忠告、意見時，這句話經常會被用到。

完整版其實就是：

• Do you have any advice?

但是在口語中我們經常以這樣簡略的形式說話。

Unit 5
東奔西跑的每一天

How do you go to the office?
你怎麼去上班？

Word Power!
- office [`ɔfɪs] n 辦公室
- driver [`draɪvɚ] n 駕駛
- sport car n 跑車
- commuter [kə`mjutɚ]
  n 通勤者

- By bus. 搭公車
- I usually go to the office by bicycle.
  我通常騎車去。
- My driver often drives me to the
  office. 我司機開車送我去。
- I go to the office on foot. 我步行去

這樣說不禮貌
Of course drive my fancy sports car! I'm
not going to be a poor commuter.
當然開我的跑車呀！我才不要當可憐的通勤者。

Do you own a car?
你有汽車嗎？

不能不會的小技巧
在台灣，許多通勤族都會
選擇騎機車上班，但其
實，在歐美大部分國家，
騎機車通勤是很少見的。
下次若碰到國外的同事
們，不妨問問他們是如何
去辦公室的吧。

Word Power!
- own [on] v 擁有
- expensive [ɪk`spɛnsɪv]
  a 貴的

- Yes, I have an old car. 有，我有一輛舊車。
- No, I don't. It's too expensive for me.
  沒有，對我來說太貴了。
- Yeah, I just bought a sports car. 我剛買了一輛跑車。
- No, I always take the MRT. 沒有，我總是搭捷運。

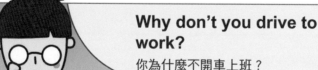

Why don't you drive to work?
你為什麼不開車上班？

Word Power!
- break down phr 故障
- lend [lɛnd] v 借出
- price [praɪs] n 價格
- afford [ə`fɔrd] v 負擔

- My car broke down. 我的車壞了。
- I lent it to my uncle today. 我今天把它借給我舅舅了。
- The gas price is so expensive,
  I can't afford.
  油價太貴，我負擔不起。

這樣說不禮貌
Because I don't drive and I don't
have a driver.
因為我不會開車而且我也沒有司機。

Which kind of transportation do you like?

你喜歡哪一種交通工具？

Word Power!
· transportation
[ˌtrænspɚˋteʃən]
n 運輸
· convenient
[kənˋvinjənt] **a** 方便的
· save time **phr** 省時間
· environmentally
friendly **phr** 環保

Sentence Power!
· Which kind of...?
哪一種…？

- I like cars, they're very convenient. 我喜歡汽車，很方便。
- I like planes, they can save much time.
  我喜歡飛機，可以節省好多時間。
- I like bicycles, they're very environmentally friendly.
  我喜歡自行車，很環保。
- I like the bus, it's cheap. 我喜歡公車，很便宜。

What do you think about this city's traffic system?

你覺得這個城市的交通系統怎麼樣？

Word Power!
· system [ˋsɪstɪ]
n 交通系統
· disordered [dɪsˋɔrdɚd]
a 混亂的
· stand [stænd] **v** 忍受

- It is too disordered. 太亂了。
- You can always see so many traffic jams. 你總是能看到交通阻塞。
- It's too crowded! I just can't stand it. 實在太擁擠了！我真的快忍無可忍了。
- I think the bus system is convenient. 我認為公車系統非常的方便。

What do you think about driving a car in the city?

你認為在市區開汽車怎麼樣？

Word Power!
· city [ˋsɪtɪ] **n** 城市
· economic [ˌikəˋnɑmɪk]
a 經濟的

Sentence Power!
· It's difficult to... 難以做到
· more...than 更…（多用於比較級）

- It's difficult to find a parking space. 很難找到車位。
- The gas price can't be afforded. 油價難以負擔。
- It's not environmentally friendly. 不環保。
- It is not more economic than a bus. 沒有公車省錢。

2 虛擬實境口說練習
on your iMessenger
從最簡短到最豐富，讓你實際和老外練習口說和聽力

| 當有人問你都乘坐什麼交通工具上班／課時 |

❶ I live close by, so I walk.
我住得很近，所以我用走的。

> ride a bike 騎腳踏車
> only take a bus when it rains 只有下雨時會搭公車
> take my Segway 騎賽格威

❷ It takes me forever, so I take a nap on the train.
要搭很久，所以我都在車上睡覺。

> I get stuck in rush hour 尖峰時間我都被卡在車陣中
> I put so many miles on my car
> 我的車累積了很多哩程
> the bus is slow 巴士很慢

❸ Sometimes I car pool to work.
有時候我和別人共乘去上班。

> give my coworker a ride 載我的同事
> have my wife drive me 請我老婆載我
> ride my scooter 騎機車

| 當你想和朋友討論用車情形時 |

❶ There's too much traffic on the 101; I always take back roads instead.
101 號公路前面總是太塞了，我都走後面的小路。

> an alternate route 替代路線
> I-75 75 號州際公路
> Alhambra Road 阿罕布拉路

❷ It's so lucky that the price of gas has gone down.
油價降了真是太幸運了。

> there's no snow on the roads 路上都沒有雪
> we can park for free 可以免費停車
> we have a company car 有公司用車

| 當你想知道其他人都怎麼去上班時 |

❶ What's the best way to the office from your house?
從公司去你們家最好的路線是什麼？

> the factory 工廠
> the customer's office 客戶公司
> the supply shop 供應店

❷ Doesn't it take you forever to get there? How early do you have to leave?
你到公司不會超久的嗎？你都多早就出發？

> head out 前往
> take off 離家
> be on the road 在路上

❸ What's your commute like?
你的通勤生活如何？

> the morning traffic 早上的交通
> the roads 路況
> the highway in the morning 早上的高速公路

| 當朋友問你要不要一起開車出去兜個風時 |

❶ I've got nothing to do tomorrow; we can drive all night.
我明天沒事做，可以去兜風一整晚。

> as far as you like 不管多遠隨你喜歡
> all the way up the coast 一直到海濱

❷ We have to take lots of breaks; my butt gets sore easily.
那我們要休息很多次，我屁股很容易痠。

> I get sleepy 我…想睡
> my bladder gets full 我…想跑廁所

3 虛擬實境網路聊天
on your iMessenger

在手機或電腦上，利用打字就可以聊出千言萬語

Tiffany

星期三 下午 13:45

Watching movies is one of my favorite pastimes.
下午 13:45

看電影是我最喜歡的消遣之一了。
休閒、消遣

Me 2!
下午 13:46

我也喜歡！剛好幾天前才看了一部。
too, to 的簡寫

下午 13:46

I just saw one the other day. Why haven't U gotten yourself to a theater?
下午 13:47

那你怎麼不進電影院看呢？
電影院

Well, It's not like I'm going to understand what they are talking about.
下午 13:48

我又聽不懂他們說的語言。
又不是…

I don't understand what you are talking about.
下午 13:49

我不了解你在說什麼。

Most of the movies are from America and are in English, Or they have English subtitles. You do understand English, rite?
下午 13:51

大部分的電影都是美國電影，而且都講英文，要不然就是有英文字幕。你聽得懂英文嘛，不是嗎？
字幕

Tiffany

星期三 下午 13:45

Haha, very funny.
So you mean to say I've been miss-ing out on good movies all this time?

下午 13:52

哈哈，真有趣。所以你是説我一直錯過好電影嗎？

錯過

總是

Hmmm...

下午 13:53

Well~
It's never too late to start.

下午 13:53

這個嘛，開始永遠不嫌晚。

太…以致於無法

IC. I've got nothing to do tonite, do you fancy going to the cinema with me?

下午 13:54

我懂了，我今晚剛好沒事，你想和我去趟電影院嗎？

tonight 的簡寫

想要

電影院

Haha. That would be my pleasure!

下午 13:55

哈哈，我很樂意！

I don't want to miss good movie again. C u then!

下午 13:56

我不想再錯過好電影了。到時見！

See you. 的簡寫

聊天金句大補帖

Hurry up and...! 快點……！

當我們想要催促比較熟的人趕緊做一件事情時，這個句型會相當好用。這麼説可以讓對方知道你希望他動作快點，或暗示他你接下來還有別的事情，必須趕緊處理眼前的情況。

Unit 6 道聲珍重再見

I must go now, see you!
我必須走了，再見。

- See you. Take care of yourself! 再見。多保重！
- Ok. I hope see you again. 希望可以再見到你。
- In that case, I won't keep you any longer. Drop in any time. 如果是那樣的話，我不再挽留你了。（歡迎）隨時到我這裏來。
- Right now? But the night is still young. 現在就要走嗎？可是時間還早呢。

Word Power!
- drop in phr 來訪
- right now phr 現在，馬上

Sentence Power!
- See you. 下次見。
- Take care. 多保重。
- In that case 既然那樣

這樣說不禮貌
Oh, Sure. 噢，好。你可以走了。

See you.
再見。

- See you next week. 下週見。
- See you then. 再見。
- OK, bye until we meet again. 好，下次再見。
- Don't be sad. I'm sure we'll see each other soon. 別難過，我相信我們很快就會再見面的。

不能不會的小技巧
要跟自己的朋友或是家人道別時，可以提醒對方要繼續保持聯絡。可能的話，也可以先約好下次會面的時間哦。

Word Power!
- until prep 直到…時
- each other phr 彼此

I come here to say goodbye to you.
我是來跟你道別的。

- I can't believe how time flies. Take care of yourself! 我真不敢相信時間過的這麼快。保重！
- Why not stay a little longer? 為什麼不多留一會呢？
- I am sorry to hear that. Nice to meet you, I hope to see you again. 真可惜。見到你很高興，我希望再次見到你。

Sentence Power!
- Time flies. 時光飛逝。
- Why not...? 為什麼不…？
- I am sorry to hear that. 真遺憾。

這樣說不禮貌
Ok. Bye! I'm glad never see you again.
好吧，再見。很高興不用再見到你。

It's very nice of you to see me off. But I have to say goodbye to you.
你能來送我真好，但我不得不說再見了。

- You're welcome! Have a good time!. 不用客氣，祝你玩得開心！
- Take care and give my best wishes to your parents. 保重，代我向你父母問好。
- Bye. Please call me if you arrive. 再見，到了記得給我打電話。
- It's my pleasure .Wish you a wonderful journey 沒什麼，祝你旅途愉快。

I had a great time with you. See you later.
和你在一起真高興。回頭見。

- Me too! See you tonight. 我也是！晚上見。
- I wish I could meet you again soon. 但願能很快再次見到你。
- See you soon! I will miss you until then. 待會見！我會想你的。
- When can we meet again? 我們何時才能再見面。

這樣說不禮貌
Why should we meet later?
我們等下為何要見面？

Thank you for inviting. But I must say goodbye.
謝謝你的邀請，但我得說再見了。

- When will you leave? 你什麼時候離開呢？
- When are you off? 你什麼時候走呢？
- Please give my regards to your families and have a good journey. 代我向你家人問好，路途愉快。
- What a pity! I wish to see you again soon. 太遺憾了！但願能很快再見到你。

2 虛擬實境口說練習
on your iMessenger

從最簡短到最豐富，讓你實際和老外練習口說和聽力

| 當你要和朋友道別，且有一陣子不會再見時 |

❶ Take care of yourself, and don't forget to send me some postcards.
照顧好你自己，別忘記寄明信片給我。

call once in a while 偶爾打給我
check in from time to time 偶爾回來看看
share lots of pictures 多分享一些照片

❷ I can't believe you're really going, I never thought this day would come.
我不敢相信你真的要走了，我從未想過這天的到來。

you'd really go through with it 你真的要去面對
we'd be apart for so long 我們要分離這麼久
you had so much courage 你有這麼大的勇氣

❸ Hope I see you in another country sometime.
希望有天能在另一個國家見到你。

in another life 能在另一段人生
before my hair turns white 能在我頭髮白之前
and you have lots of stories to tell
能…而且你有很多故事能告訴我

| 當你和同學、老師或家人說再見時 |

❶ Don't cry; we'll always be friends.
別哭，我們會一直都是朋友的。

keep in touch 保持聯絡
have each other 擁有彼此
have our memories 擁有回憶

❷ I love you; now it's time for me to step out on my own.
我愛你，但已經是時候該踏出屬於我自己的路了。

show the world what I'm made of 讓世界看到我
prove myself 證明我自己
find myself 找尋我自己

| 當和國外的朋友玩了一天，準備先回家時 |

❶ I can drive everybody out, but I need to leave the party early.
我可以載大家出去，但我要先提早離開派對。

head home by midnight 要在午夜前回到家
excuse myself before it's too late 不能太晚，請原諒我要先離開
can't give you a ride back 不能載你們回來

❷ I've got something on in the morning, so I'm about to take off.
我白天還有事，所以我差不多要離開了。

I need to call my mom 我要打個電話給我媽
My girlfriend is waiting for me 我女朋友還在等我
I'm pooped 我累了

❸ Guys, something came up. You'll have to have fun without me.
各位，有狀況。你們就撇下我好好玩吧。

do 做
keep the partying going 讓派對進行
move on 繼續

| 當你想提早離開朋友的聚會時 |

❶ Party hard! And be safe.
玩得開心點！然後也要小心安全。

don't do anything I wouldn't do
別做任何我不會做的事
have a drink for me 替我喝點飲料

❷ Let me know what I missed.
記得讓我知道我錯過了什麼。

how everything turned out 最後發展如何
when you get home 你到家後

3 虛擬實境網路聊天

on your iMessenger

在手機或電腦上，利用打字就可以聊出千言萬語

Bowyer

星期三 下午 13:45

 Hey, bro
Have you ever thought about
What UR going to do when you retire?

下午 13:45

嘿，老兄
你有想過你退休要做什麼嗎？

you are 的簡寫
退休

I'll definitely travel for a while.
C the lifestyle of different cultures and visit the wonders of the world.
How about you?

下午 13:47

我鐵定會先去旅行一陣子，去體驗一下不同文化的生活，然後還要去參觀世界奇景，你呢？

絕對
一陣子
See 的簡寫
奇景

 Well, as you know,
I'm a big fan of food. So I might travel the world as well,
But for different reasons.

下午 13:48

嗯，你知道的，我是個大老饕。我一樣也會到世界各地旅行，不過，是為了不一樣的理由。

下午 13:48

I want to share all the wonderful things that I encountered with the world.

下午 13:50

我希望我能把這一路上所遇到的美妙事情和這個世界分享。

遭遇

U aren't going to be doing that at 65, RU?

下午 13:51

你不會要等到你六十五歲的時候才去做吧？

are you 的縮寫

Bowyer

星期三 下午 13:45

No~
I'm thinking of retiring earlier.
I think ultimately after I've
tasted all the foods of the world,
I'll want to open a restaurant.

下午 13:52

下午 13:51

 It sounds like you're going to retire early!
Alright, I still have some work to do,
Need to go right now. Bye!

下午 13:53

CYA!

下午 13:54

我想早一點退休。我想，等到最後我嚐盡了世界上的各種食物以後，我會想開一間餐廳。

最後

聽起來好像你要很早退休似的！好啦，我還有些工作要做，該走了，掰！

聽起來

掰啦！

See ya 的簡寫

聊天金句大補帖

That's a shame. 真可惜／真遺憾。

這句話用以表達我們的情感，通常是你對於一件事甚有感觸時說的，有時是懷念，有時是遺憾的感覺，有時則是同情等。也可以說：

• What a shame.

更可以加強語氣強調哦。

Chapter

3

環遊世界免煩惱

English spoken all over the world.

Unit 1 訂票快狠準

Unit 2 連接世界的橋樑

Unit 3 出境入境必經

Unit 4 做好起飛準備

Unit 5 休息是為了玩更久

Unit 6 下次再接再厲

Unit 1 訂票快狠準

South Air. How may I help you?

南方航空公司。有什麼能幫你的？

- I would like to make a reservation to Seattle, please. 我想訂往西雅圖的機票。
- I would like to fly in economy. 我想訂一張經濟艙票。
- I prefer a morning flight. How much is a return ticket? 我要一早起飛的班機，來回票多少錢？
- What's the baggage allowance? 行要限重是多少？

Word Power!
- reservation [ˌrɛzəˈveʃən] n 預約
- economy [ɪˈkɑnəmɪ] n （飛機的）經濟艙
- return ticket n 【英】來回票
- baggage [ˈbæɡɪdʒ] n 行李
- allowance [əˈlauəns] n 允許額；限額

更多…
- first class 頭等艙
- business class 商務艙

One-way or round-trip ticket?

單程票還是來回票？

- One-way is OK! 單程票就行！
- Round-trip ticket, please. 請給我來回票，謝謝。
- Wait a moment, please. I should ask my mother for some ideas. 等一下，我得問一下我媽媽。

Word Power!
- ask sb. for,,, phr 問（某人）…
- actually [ˈæktʃuəlɪ] ad 事實上

Sentence Power!
- Wait a moment. 等一下。

這樣說不禮貌
Uh, I don't know which one is better actually.
呃，我其實也不知道哪個比較好。

Do you prefer a direct flight?

你比較偏好直飛班機嗎？

- Definitely. 沒錯。
- Whatever is cheaper is fine with me. 只要便宜一點就都可以。
- No, I'd rather turn around on route. 不，我寧願中途轉機。
- That's even better. 那樣更好。

Word Power!
- prefer [prɪˈfɜ] v 寧願；更喜歡
- would rather phr 寧可；倒不如
- on route phr 中途轉機
- even [ˈivən] ad 甚至；更

Sentence Power!
- Do you prefer...? 你偏好哪種…？

Are there any discount tickets available?

還有任何有折扣的票嗎？

不能不會的小技巧
訂票前，最好先確認每家公司或網站提供的不同折扣，且也應確認清楚時間和日期等資訊。越早訂票，通常優惠也會更多，因此旅行前記得要早做準備哦！

- Yes. How many tickets do you want to order? 有，你想訂幾張呢？
- Let me check it. 讓我查看看。
- Sorry, tickets are already all fully booked. 抱歉，票已經全部訂完了。
- There is still a ticket available. 還有一張票。

Word Power!
- discount [ˈdɪskaʊnt]
  n 折扣
- available [əˈveləbl]
  a 可利用的
- order [ˈɔrdə] v 訂購
- fully [ˈfʊlɪ] ad 完全地

Have you ordered your tickets?

你訂到票了嗎？

Word Power!
- done with
  phr 完成了的
- recently [ˈrisṇtlɪ]
  ad 最近

- Yes, I'm done with that. 是的，我已經處理好了。
- No, it is very difficult to order recently.
  沒有，最近很難訂到票。
- Yes, a friend helped me to do it.
  訂好了，一個朋友幫我訂的。

這樣說不禮貌

I'm leaving tomorrow morning. Of course I've ordered the tickets.
我明天早上就要飛了，當然已經訂到票了。

What's the fare to Los Angeles, first class?

往洛杉磯的頭等艙票價是多少？

不能不會的小技巧
對於大部分想省錢的乘客，搭乘飛機時通常會選擇經濟艙，但有時候若你提早抵達機場報到，航空公司有可能會幫你免費升等喔。

Word Power!
- system [ˈsɪstəm]
  n 系統
- website [ˈwebˌsaɪt]
  n 網站

- It's $600. 600 美元。
- You can check it online. 你可以上網查一下。
- There is something wrong with system, you can call back later. 系統有點出錯了，請等一下再打過來吧。

這樣說不禮貌

Go check it on the website. 直接去查網站啦。

2 虛擬實境口說練習
on your iMessenger
從最簡短到最豐富，讓你實際和老外練習口說和聽力

| 當你要以電話訂機票時 |

❶ **I'm calling to make a reservation from Philadelphia to Los Angeles.**
我想要訂一張機票從費城到洛杉磯的。

> out of Miami 從邁阿密出發的
> to Hong Kong 到香港的
> from KHH to CDG
> 從高雄小港機場到巴黎戴高樂機場的

❷ **Can you tell me what flights are available on the 31st?**
請告訴我 31 號還有哪些班次有座位呢？

> the schedule is like 航程推薦
> time the flights take off 起飛時間
> is the availability 可訂機位

❸ **I fly out of LAX or Bob Hope Airport.**
我要從洛杉磯國際機場或鮑勃霍普機場起飛。

> LaGuardia only 只…拉瓜地亞機場
> either Seattle or Portland 西雅圖或波特蘭
> anything in the surrounding area
> 附近任何區域的機場

| 當你詢問朋友該如何訂機票時 |

❶ **How do you search for plane tickets?**
你在哪裡搜尋機票資訊？

> Where do you look 你都在哪裡找
> What website do you use 你都在哪個網站看
> Do you know an app
> 你知道哪個 APP 可以得知

❷ **Have you ever tried booking through an agent?**
你有透過旅行社訂過機票嗎？

> with Skyscanner
> 透過 Skyscanner（訂票網站）
> a mobile app 用手機 APP
> at the airport 在機場

| 當你想請旅行社幫你代訂機票時 | -

❶ I would like you to book me a flight to Tokyo for any week in May.
我想請你們幫我訂一張到東京，五月任何一周都可的機票。

> leaving on the 2nd 2 號出發
> that returns on a Sunday 且週日回程
> round-trip 來回

❷ What cities do you have the best deals to?
你們的機票到**哪個城市**最划算？

> can you get me a good rate
> 你們可以幫我訂到…最好的價格
> do you offer a sale 你們訂機票到…有特價
> get your best rates 你們飛…有最好的價格

❸ Here are my dates and my budget; make it happen.
這是我的日期跟預算，請幫我訂票。

> get me the best rate 請幫我訂最優惠的價錢
> let me know when it's booked
> 請再告知我訂到何時的票
> get me a decent hotel 再幫我訂一間像樣的旅館

| 當你想詢問服務人員如何訂票較划算時 | - - - - - - - - - - - - - - - - - -

❶ Can I get a discount if I fly on a different day?
如果我搭不同日的航班話會有折扣嗎？

> on a later flight 較晚
> at a different time 不同時間

❷ If I'm flexible with my schedule, what deals are available?
如果我的行程可以彈性調整的話，還有哪些優惠可以訂？

> discounts might I find 我可以找到的折扣
> days have lower priced flights 有便宜航班的日期可訂

3 虛擬實境網路聊天
on your iMessenger

在手機或電腦上，利用打字就可以聊出千言萬語

Lilian

星期三 下午 13:45

Ann,
Ive a couple of days off.
And I want to go somewhere far away.
Do U hav any suggestions?

下午 13:45

下午 13:45

安安，我有幾天假期，而且我想要去遠一點的地方。妳有什麼建議嗎？
I have 的簡寫
休息
建議

How nice~

下午 13:46

下午 13:46

真棒～。

Well, I think cruises are great.
U get to meet all sorts of
different people while relaxing
on the ocean.

下午 13:47

我認為遊輪旅行不錯。在海上放輕鬆的同時，又可以認識各種不同的人。
遊輪
當…的時候

I dun think taking a cruise is an option.
Cuz I'll get seasick.

下午 13:48

遊輪之旅可能不會在我的選擇範圍內，因為我會暈船。
don't 的簡寫
暈船

Then…
How about fly to UR destination?
U want to travel alone or with a
tour?

下午 13:49

那…搭飛機去目的地怎麼樣？你想要自助旅行還是跟團？

Lilian

星期三 下午 13:45

 I don't really care.
Just let me go somewhere I can leave my worries behind.

下午 13:50

我沒有很在乎。只要讓我去一個能完全把煩惱拋下的地方就好。

把煩惱拋諸腦後

  HEE HEE

下午 13:50

In that case,
I'd suggest going to one of the islands around south east Asia.
And find URself a villa and take it from there!

下午 13:51

如果是這樣的話，我建議你去東南亞的一個小島，找間別墅然後自己享受吧！

小島

別墅

 Then I should go to book the ticket right now.
Thx anyway.

下午 13:52

那我現在就趕快去訂機票吧，不管怎樣謝啦。

 GL~

下午 13:53

祝你好運囉～

Good luck. 的簡

聊天金句大補帖

Would / Could you mind...? 你可以…？

在談話當中，要拜託對方事情時，可試著用這個句型加上動名詞來造句，這樣的語氣聽起來較禮貌、客氣。通常說話時若語氣是尊重的，對方便會較為樂意接受。

Unit 2 連接世界的橋樑

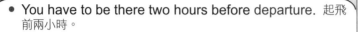

What time should I check-in?
什麼時候辦理登機手續？

- You have to be there two hours before departure. 起飛前兩小時。

- Just now. You can follow the red lines if you have anything to declare. 才剛開始。如果有東西需要申報，請走紅色通道。

- Your flight has been cancelled due to heavy fog. 你的航班因大霧被取消了。

Word Power!
- check-in [ˈtʃɛkˌɪn]
  n (旅客登機前)驗票並領取登機卡
- departure [dɪˈpartʃɚ]
  n 出發
- declare [dɪˈklɛr] v 申報
- flight [flaɪt] n 航班
- fog [fɑg] n 濃霧

Sentence Power!
- Just now. 剛才。

Do you prefer a window seat or an aisle seat?
你偏好靠窗座位還是靠走道的座位？

- A window seat is better. 我比較喜歡靠窗的座位。

- Maybe an aisle seat is more convenient. 也許靠走道座位比較方便。

- Perhaps, a window seat is more comfortable. 或許靠窗座位更舒服。

Word Power!
- window seat
  n 靠窗的座位
- aisle seat
  n 靠走道的座位
- perhaps [pɚˈhæps]
  ad 或許

Sentence Power!
- It doesn't matter. 沒關係；不要緊。

這樣說不禮貌

It doesn't really matter.
這真的不重要。

Is the flight going to take off on time?
航班能準時起飛嗎？

- No problem. 沒問題。

- It should be. 應該可以的。

- Maybe, if the weather gets a little better. 如果天氣轉好的話就有可能。

- Don't worry, it must be. 別擔心，肯定會的。

不能不會的小技巧
搭乘飛機時，最好能跟航空公司確認起飛時間，若要轉機，也要確認轉機時保留足夠的時間，以免造成更多麻煩。記得，就算飛機已經延誤，詢問起降時間時還是要盡量保持有禮的態度。

Word Power!
- take off
  phr （飛機）起飛

Sentence Power!
- No problem. 沒問題。

When can we board the plane?
我們什麼時候登機？

不能不會的小技巧
搭乘飛機旅遊時，一定要注意飛機起飛的時間以及登機的時間。一般來說，登機時間會是飛機起飛前的半個小時到一個小時。若你不小心遲到，航空公司有權拒絕讓你登機。所以務必要注意。

Word Power!
- board [bord] **v** 上（船，車，飛機等）
- look at **phr** 檢查

- Check-in time is 6:30. 登機時間是 6:30.
- It's half past seven. 7:30 時可以。
- I'm afraid our flight is delayed. 我們的班機可能誤點了。

這樣說不禮貌
You can look at your ticket.
你可以看看你的機票。

Do you have any luggage to check in?
你還有其他行李要登記嗎？

Word Power!
- luggage [ˈlʌgɪdʒ] **n** 行李
- another [əˈnʌðə] **a** 另一個的

- Does this little bag need to be checked-in?
  這個小包也要登記嗎？
- Yes, there are another two boxes. 是的，還有兩個大箱子。
- Yes, this is the last one. 這是最後一個。
- All of them have been checked-in. 所有的都登記完了。

May I help you?
有什麼可以幫你的？

Word Power!
- confirm [kənˈfɝm] **v** 確認
- often [ˈɔfən] **ad** 常常

Sentence Power!
- How often…? 有多常…？
  → 多用於詢問比例、頻率相關的問題。

- I want to know where I can board. 我想知道我從哪登機。
- I want to confirm my flight. 我想確認我的班機。
- What time should I check-in?
  什麼時候該辦理登機手續？
- How often is there a flight to New York? 去紐約的班機多久一班？

這樣說不禮貌
What's the problem with your plane? I've been waiting for 2 hours!
你們的飛機到底有什麼毛病？我已經等 2 小時了！

2 虛擬實境口說練習
on your iMessenger

從最簡短到最豐富，讓你實際和老外練習口說和聽力

| 當你詢問機場服務人員部分設施的位置時 |

❶ Is there a VIP lounge nearby?
請問附近有 VIP 室嗎？

a place to take a shower 沖澡的地方
a yoga room 瑜珈室
somewhere with some privacy
提供私人空間的地方

❷ Where can I get a shoeshine?
請問哪裡可以取得鞋油？

a magazine 雜誌
a neck pillow 頸枕
some gum 一些口香糖

❸ I'd like to shop at the duty free shop.
我想要在免稅店購物。

find the bathroom 找廁所
find the restaurants 找些餐廳
get a view of planes taking off
去看飛機起降

| 當你想詢問機場的何處可以過夜時 |

❶ Excuse me, may I stay overnight at the airport?
不好意思，請問我可以在機場過夜嗎？

live in a capsule hotel 住膠囊旅館
find someplace to take a rest
找個地方休息

❷ Is there a lounge for passengers to rest?
請問有給旅客休息的休息室嗎？

a bathroom 浴室
an area 區域

take a shower 淋浴
spend all night 過夜

| 當你被問到機場的轉乘站在哪時 |

❶ There will be a big sign for rental cars if you walk the past baggage claim.
你走過行李提領區時，會看到一個出租車輛的大招牌。

> the buses 巴士站
> taxis 計程車招呼站
> ground transportation 地面交通站

❷ People here don't stand in lines for the buses; it's chaotic.
人們在等公車時都不排隊，真是一團混亂。

> for the taxis 計程車
> to buy train tickets 買火車票
> for anything 任何事物

❸ The signs are confusing; look for people lined up and ask how to go.
標誌很容易讓人搞混，直接找有人在排隊的地方然後問怎麼去吧。

> talk to another passenger at baggage claim
> 和行李提領區的其他乘客搭話
> grab somebody in uniform 找穿著制服的人
> check the information desk 去服務台

| 當你想問機場人員有關航班的問題時 |

❶ How much longer will the flight be delayed?
請問航班還會遲飛多久？

> be grounded 要⋯才會降落
> be unable to take off 要⋯才會起飛
> take to arrive 要⋯才會抵達

❷ Is the issue due to mechanical failure?
請問是因為機器故障而導致的問題嗎？

> the engine 引擎
> a leak of some kind 有什麼漏洞
> anything suspicious 任何疑慮

3 虛擬實境網路聊天
on your iMessenger
在手機或電腦上，利用打字就可以聊出千言萬語

Jimmy Chou

星期三 下午 13:45

Hey Pete
It's been a while since I've been to the hot springs.
You wanna go with me?

下午 13:45

嘿，彼特，我已經有好一陣子沒去泡溫泉了，你想跟我去嗎？

want to 的簡寫

Sure!
The weather has been a little chilly and I've heard lots about them.
Is it true they have healing powers?

下午 13:46

當然好啊！
天氣一直有點冷，我也聽說過好多關於溫泉的事。它們真的有治病的能量嗎？

治療功效

下午 13:49

Define healing powers.

下午 13:50

你先替治病的能量下個定義。

為…下定義

Like if you have an illness of some kind, and you take a dip, then you're cured?

下午 13:51

比方說你生病了，去泡個溫泉，病就好了。

生病

浸泡

治癒

Dude, it's not holy water!
I think you're been watching too many infomercials.

下午 13:52

老兄，那不是聖水好嗎？我想你看太多購物節目了。

購物節目

Jimmy Chou

星期三 下午 13:45

> Then,
> are hot springs good for
> anything other than relaxation?

下午 13:53

> Hot springs in different areas contain
> different minerals.
> And those minerals can have different
> effects on the body.
> I go cause it helps my skin look nice~

下午 13:54

> I didn't know you were
> so ladylike haha.

下午 13:55

下午 13:55

那麼，除了放鬆身心以外，溫泉還有什麼功效呢？
放鬆

不同的溫泉區含有不同的礦物質，這些礦物質對身體有不同的功效。我泡溫泉是因為它能讓我的皮膚看起來很好～
包含
礦物

我不知道你這麼淑女耶哈。
如貴婦的

聊天金句大補帖

Cheer up！加油！

這句是常用來鼓勵人的話，就是要別人高興一點，不要難過。當別人灰心喪志時，說這句話再適合不過了。另外，

• cheer sb. up

則是指「使某人高興起來」。

097

Unit 3 出境入境必經

What do you have in your bag?
你的袋子裝了些什麼？

Word Power!
- cosmetic [kɑz`mɛtɪk]
  n 化妝品
- husband [`hʌzbənd]
  n 丈夫
- packing [`pækɪŋ]
  n 打包
- allow [ə`lau] v 允許

- They are some toys of my son. 一些我兒子的玩具。
- Just my cosmetics and shoes.
  只是我的化妝品和鞋子。

這樣說不禮貌

Just a bottle of milk. What? Is it not allowed?
一瓶牛奶。怎麼了？這有不合法嗎？

- I don't know, my husband did the packing. 我不知道，我老公打包的。

What's the purpose of your visit to here?
你來此地的目的為何？

不能不會的小技巧
通常在過海關時，海關官員會檢視你的護照，並詢問你來訪的目的，此時只要態度堅定，據實回答就可以。顯得過於緊張只會讓海關官員覺得可疑。因此只要記得回答問題時的態度誠懇有禮就行。

Word Power!
- purpose [`pɝpəs]
  n 目的
- attend [ə`tɛnd] v 出席
- offer [`ɔfɚ] n 提供

- I am going to attend a meeting. 我去開會。
- I'm here to visit my parents. 我去看望我的父母。
- I got a job offer. 我得到一份工作。
- Just to travel. 就是旅遊而已。

Do you have anything to declare?
你有什麼要申報的嗎？

Word Power!
- personal [`pɝsn̩l]
  a 私人的
- effects [ɪ`fɛkts]
  n （作複數）財物
- excess [ɪk`sɛs]
  n 超額量
- duty-free [`djutɪ`fri]
  a 免稅的

- No, I have only personal effects. 沒有，我只有一些私人用品。
- Oh, I've got 2 bottles of whisky. 哦，我還帶了兩瓶威士忌。
- Well. Are two bottles of Merlot wine in excess of the duty-free allowance?
  這個嘛，兩瓶梅洛紅酒有沒有超過免稅限額？

這樣說不禮貌

No. Look, just a small bag.
沒。你自己看，我只有一個小包包而已。

Do you have any relatives in America?
你在美國有沒有親戚？

· Yes, my uncle lives in Miami. 有的，我舅舅住在邁阿密。

· No, My relatives all live in Asia. 沒有，我的親戚都住亞洲。

· I'm not sure. Hold on, let me think about it.
  我不確定。讓我想一下。

· As far as I now, nobody.
  就我所知沒有人住美國。

這樣說不禮貌

Uh… Say it again? I was checking something else on my phone.
呃可以再說一次嗎？我剛在看我手機的東西。

Hello, this is the duty-free shop, what can I do for you?
你好，這是免稅商店，有什麼可以幫你的嗎？

· I want to buy some liquor. 我想買點酒。

· Thank you, I'll just look around. 謝謝，我只是看看。

· Can you tell me where the chocolate-covered toffees are? 你能告訴我巧克力太妃糖在哪嗎？

· This pink Birkin bag is gorgeous. Can I take a look? 這款粉紅柏金包太美了。我可以看一下嗎？

What do you think about the duty free shop?
你覺得免稅商店怎麼樣？

· Well, it helps kill time at the airport. 嗯，它可以讓我在機場打發時間。

· It's pretty convenient, and the goods are cheap and the quality is better. 很方便，而且他的商品物美價廉。

· I don't like it. It is all cheap goods.
  我不喜歡，所有的東西都是便宜貨。

2 虛擬實境口說練習
on your iMessenger

從最簡短到最豐富，讓你實際和老外練習口說和聽力

| 當你被海關問到是否有攜帶違禁品時 | -

❶ **I brought several guns, but I have a permit.**
我帶了一些槍，但我有獲得許可。

> my collection of 18th century katanas
> 我的收藏品，18 世紀的武士刀
> toxic chemicals 有毒的化學物
> a nonnative species 非本地種的生物

❷ **No, I have nothing.**
不，我沒攜帶任何違禁品。

> nothing of that sort 沒有任何那類的東西
> that'd be silly 那樣也太蠢了吧
> of course not 當然沒有

❸ **I already threw it in the trash.**
我已經丟到垃圾桶裡了。

> disposed of it 把它們丟棄
> had it confiscated 把它們充公
> got rid of it 丟掉它們

| 當海關詢問你是否有需要申報物品時 | -

❶ **No, nothing to declare.**
不，沒有任何要申報的東西。

> nothing 沒有
> not a thing 沒有任何東西

❷ **Do I need to declare my fruits?**
我需要申報我的水果嗎？

> my pet turtle 我的寵物烏龜
> this antique 這件古董

| 當你有物品要向海關申報時 |

❶ I think I need to declare these items from the duty free shop.
我想我需要申報這些我從免稅店買的東西。

> all the money I have 我身上所有的錢
> the thing I inherited after my grandfather's funeral
> 這個我從我爺爺葬禮後繼承的東西
> the gift for my mom 我從我媽那得到的禮物

❷ Who should I tell about these items? I'm desperate to declare them.
我應該向誰告知關於這些物品呢?我急需申報它們。

> my goods 我的物品
> these products for my business
> 這些我生意上要用的商品
> my traveler's checks 我的旅行支票

❸ Do I need to fill out a form?
我會需要填個表格嗎?

> to tell you their value 告知你它們的價值
> to leave it with you 把它們留下來給你
> to provide with documentation 提供文件

| 當海關詢問你入境目的時 |

❶ I was visiting my family, and had business with clients.
我來探望我家人,以及和客戶談生意

> friends 朋友
> father's grave 父親的墓
> son 兒子

> in Orlando 到奧蘭多
> at a conference 開會
> to attend to 去

❷ I took a vacation to New York and Little Rock.
我去紐約跟小岩城度假。

> on the East coast 去東岸
> with my friends 和我朋友們去
> to climb Denali 要去爬迪納利山

3 虛擬實境網路聊天
on your iMessenger

在手機或電腦上，利用打字就可以聊出千言萬語

Lala

星期三 下午 13:45

下午 13:45

Sry for the delay~
There was a hold up during customs.

下午 13:46

抱歉遲到了～在海關那邊弄了好久。
Sorry 的簡寫
阻礙

下午 13:47

Don't worry about it!
How was UR flight?

下午 13:48

不要緊的！旅途怎麼樣呢？

The flight was smooth and the service was great.

下午 13:49

很順利，機上的服務品質很好。
平穩的

Good to hear that.
Well, what would you like to do first?

下午 13:50

那真是太好了。你現在想先做什麼呢？

What R my choices?

下午 13:51

我有哪些選擇？
are 的縮寫

We can check you in at the hotel,
Or we can have dinner if you are hungry now.

下午 13:52

我們可以先去旅館辦理入住，或者要是你餓了，我們可以先吃晚餐。
飢餓

Lala

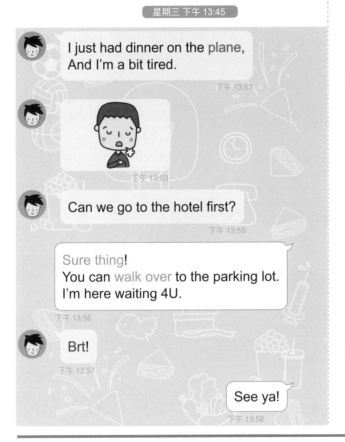

星期三 下午 13:45

I just had dinner on the plane,
And I'm a bit tired.

下午 13:53

下午 13:53

Can we go to the hotel first?

下午 13:55

Sure thing!
You can walk over to the parking lot.
I'm here waiting 4U.

下午 13:56

Brt!

下午 13:57

See ya!

下午 13:58

我剛在飛機上吃過晚餐了了，而且我有點累。

飛機

可以先去旅館嗎？

當然，你先走來停車場吧。我在這兒等你。

必然之事

穿過

馬上過去！

Be right there. 的簡寫

掰掰！

聊天金句大補帖

I'm not sure. 我不確定。

這句話是當你對於一件事情、一個情況，在他人詢問你的時候，尚未有確定答案時經常回應的話。有時也許可能有答案，但為了避免對方完全採用你的話，你可以先說這句，讓對方明白你並不能保證實際的結果是什麼。

Unit 4 做好起飛準備

1

Do you mind switching seats?

介意換一下位子嗎？

Word Power!
- switch [swɪtʃ] **v** 位子
- as a matter of fact **phr** 事實上

Sentence Power!
- Never mind. 沒關係

- Never mind. 不要緊的。

- As a matter of fact, I do.
  事實上，我介意。

- Sorry, but I want to sit with my friend.
  對不起，但我想和我的朋友坐在一起。

這樣說不禮貌

No, I can't, I don't want to move.
不行，我不想動。

Of course I mind. I paid for my seat.
當然介意，我付了錢耶。

Could I have a blanket, please?

能給我一條毯子嗎？

Word Power!
- blanket [ˈblæŋkɪt] **n** 毯子

Sentence Power!
- Here you are. 給你。

- Yes, just a moment. 好的，請稍等。

- Yes, here you are. 好的，給你。

- One minute. It's coming. 等我一分鐘，馬上就來。

- Will one or two be enough? 你要一條還是兩條？

這樣說不禮貌

Please wait. I'm pretty busy now. 請等一下，我現在很忙。

What kind of meals will be served on the plane?

飛機提供什麼食物？

不能不會的小技巧
對於有特殊餐點需求的乘客，例如不吃牛肉、回教餐及素食餐…等。請在訂票時就跟航空公司確認。航空公司通常都會貼心地為這些乘客另外準備適合的餐點。

Word Power!
- meal [mil] **n** 餐點
- dish [dɪʃ] **n** 菜餚

- All kinds of meals. 各種各樣的。

- Hot dishes, cold dishes, and drinks. 有熱食、冷食和飲料。

- You can choose what you like. 你可以選你喜歡的。

- Chicken, beef, seafood, and vegetarian. 雞肉、牛肉、海鮮以及素食。

Could I use the toilet now?

現在我可以使用洗手間嗎？

不能不會的小技巧
飛機起降時通常會要求乘客待在座位上，待座位上方的指示燈熄滅後才可以站起來走動哦。

Word Power!
- toilet ['tɔɪlɪt] n 廁所
- aisle [aɪl] n （戲院、列車等座位間的）走道
- stable ['stebl̩] a 平穩的
- occupied ['ɑkjupaɪd] a 被占用的

- Just a moment. The plane is taking off. 請稍等，飛機正在升空。

- Yes, it's at the end of aisle. 可以。廁所在走道盡頭處。

- Please wait until the plane become stable. 等飛機平穩就可以。

- The toilet is occupied. 洗手間正有人用。

What can I do to kill time on the airplane?

在飛機上，我能做些什麼來消磨時間呢？

Word Power!
- option ['ɑpʃən] n 選擇
- video game n 電動遊戲
- next to phr 緊鄰著

- How about watching movies? We have lots of options on the plane. 看部電影怎麼樣？機上有許多電影可供選擇。

- If I were you, I would play video games. 假如我是你的話，我會玩電動遊戲。

- You can talk to the person next to you. 你可以跟旁邊的人聊天。

The kids are making loud noises. Is there anything you can do about it?

小孩子太吵，有辦法解決嗎？

Word Power!
- noise [nɔɪz] n 噪音
- trouble ['trʌbl̩] v 擾亂
- solve [sɑlv] v 解決
- take care of phr 處理

Sentence Power!
- As soon as possible. 盡快。

- Sorry to trouble you. I'll solve this as soon as possible. 對不起，打擾你了，我會盡快處理的。

- I'm sorry. Kids, keep quiet, please. You're bothering people. 抱歉。小朋友們，請保持安靜，你們打擾別人了。

- Let me take care of it. 我來處理。

這樣說不禮貌

They are kids. What do you expect? 他們是小孩子嘛。你想怎樣？

2 虛擬實境口說練習
on your iMessenger

從最簡短到最豐富，讓你實際和老外練習口說和聽力

| 當你要請空服員幫你準備餐點時 |

❶ I need a vegetarian meal. Can you take away this tray of meat?

我需要一個素食餐點。可以幫我把這盤肉的拿走嗎？

> get me a salad 拿一份沙拉
> serve me veggies only 只提供我素食
> get me something appropriate 拿適切的餐點來

❷ Sorry, I had a special request for turkey. I already paid for it.

抱歉，我有特別要求要火雞肉，也已經付款了。

> an early order plate 預先點餐
> a combo order with my plane ticket
> 加購餐點在我的機票
> requested a special meal 要求特別餐點

❸ Do you have any other options besides fish?

你們有除了魚肉以外的選項嗎？

> beef 牛肉
> rice 米飯
> veal 小牛肉

| 當你想向空服員要求服務時 |

❶ Stewardess, could I have a hot towel?

空服員，可以給我一條熱毛巾嗎？

> some headphones 一些頭戴式耳機
> a glass of chardonnay 一杯白酒
> a blanket 一條毯子

❷ Miss, my son would like to see the cockpit.

小姐，我的兒子想看看駕駛艙。

> eat more peanuts 再來一點花生
> request a pillow 跟妳要一個枕頭
> be escorted to the bathroom 找人陪他到廁所

| 當你想問空服員航程時間及狀況時 | - - - - - - - - - - - - - - - -

❶ **Do you know how I connect after we land?**
妳知道我們降落後要怎麼接通電話嗎？

touchdown 落地
disembark 著陸

❷ **Is my connecting flight on time?**
請問我的轉機航班會準時抵達嗎？

in the same gate 在同一個登機門
serving the same meal 供應同樣的餐點
expecting any delay 有可能會延遲

❸ **Do you think I'll land before 4pm?**
你認為我們下午四點前能夠降落嗎？

make it out of the airport 離開機場
get through customs 通過海關
have my luggage in hand 拿到我的行李

| 當你想請鄰座的人降低音量時 | - - - - - - - - - - - - - - - - -

❶ **Could you turn that down? I can hear it while I read.**
請你把音量轉小好嗎？我在閱讀時都聽得到。

as sit here and meditate
坐在這且在沉思時
over my own audio
透過我的耳機還是
from over here 即使在這裡

❷ **Ma'am, don't you realize that you're annoying everybody around you?**
女士，妳難道沒發現妳打擾了所有坐妳周圍的人嗎？

the volume is too high 妳的音量過高
there are other people on this plane, too
這輛飛機上還有別人

3 虛擬實境網路聊天 在手機或電腦上，利用打字就可以聊出千言萬語
on your iMessenger

Bob White

星期三 下午 13:45

 So,
did anything interesting
happen on the plane?

下午 13:45

耶，在飛機上有沒有
什麼有趣的事情呢？
有趣的

Nothing exciting really,
but it was a pleasant flight.

下午 13:46

沒什麼有意思的事，
不過是一趟很愉快的
航程。
愉快的

 Tell me about it.

下午 13:48

説來聽聽吧。

For starters, the food was
better than expected.
I mean I didn't even know that
they had steak on the plane.

下午 13:49

首先呢，餐點比預期
得要好，我還真不知
道飛機上有提供牛排
呢。
首先

下午 13:49

 Well, you did fly first class.

下午 13:50

那當然，你坐的可是
頭等艙。

I suppose so.
As for the service, the
air stewardesses were
attentive to my needs.
They even tucked me in!

下午 13:52

我想是的，至於服務
呢，空姐們相當照顧
我，甚至幫我蓋好被
子呢。
至於
空姐
體貼的
幫某人蓋好被子

Bob White

星期三 下午 13:45

Wow, I wish I had a stewardess to tuck me in.

下午 13:53

下午 13:54

Then next time you come visit our company, we'll fly you in with a first class ticket and a stewardess to tuck you in as well.

下午 13:56

I'll be looking forward to that!

下午 13:55

嗯，我希望也能有個空姐幫我蓋好被子。

那麼下次你來訪問敝公司時，我們會為你買頭等艙的機票，同時請一個空姐幫你蓋好被子。

也

我相當期待。

期待

聊天金句大補帖

That explains it. 這就說得通了。

當別人對你解釋一件事情、一個情況等，而你對於他的說明若有所悟時，你就可以說這句，代表你先前所不了解的謎團得到了解答。除此之外，也可以使用

• That make sense.

來表達相同的意思。

Unit 5 休息是為了玩更久

I would like to book a double bedroom, please.
我想訂一間有雙人床的房間。

Word Power!
- double bedroom
  n 雙人房（一張雙人床）
- vacancy [ˋvekənsɪ]
  n 空房
- twin room n 雙人房（兩張單人床）
- single room n 單人房
- left [lɛft] v 剩下

- Yes, wait for a minute, please. 好的，請稍等！
- Sorry, there is no vacancy. 對不起，沒有空房間了。
- Sorry, there is no double bedroom, but there is a twin room.
  對不起，沒有雙人床的房間了，但有一間雙人房。

這樣說不禮貌
No double-bed room, there is only a single room left.
沒有雙人床的房間了，只剩一間單人房。

Do you have any special requests?
你還有其他特殊的要求嗎？

Word Power!
- special [ˋspɛʃəl]
  a 特別的
- request [rɪˋkwɛst]
  n 要求
- Internet access
  n （連線）上網

- No, I don't. 沒有了。
- I need to have Internet access in my room. 我的房間必須可以上網。
- Can I watch CNN on TV? 房間電視能看 CNN 嗎？
- Well, I want to know the price of a double room. 我想知道雙人床的價錢。

How long will you stay here?
你將在這停留多久？

Word Power!
- a couple of phr 兩個
- overnight [ˋovṇˋnaɪt]
  a 一整夜的

Sentence Power!
- It's up to... 這由…決定

- About a couple of days. 可能是兩天。
- I'm only staying here overnight. 我只住一晚。
- It's up to my meeting plan.
  這取決於我的會議安排。
- I will go back tomorrow. 我明天就回去。

這樣說不禮貌
I don't know. My plans are always changing.
我也不知道，我的計畫總是變動的。

What facilities are free for hotel guests?
飯店旅客可以免費使用哪些設施呢？

zWord Power!
- guest [gɛst] **n** 客人
- gym [dʒɪm] **abbr** 運動場（gymnasium 的縮寫）
- range [rendʒ] **n** 靶場
- carriage [ˈkærɪdʒ] **n** 四輪馬車
- for free **phr** 免費

- You can use our swimming pool and sauna. 你可以使用我們的游泳池和三溫暖。

- The gym and bowling alley. 運動場及保齡球館。

- The shooting range. 射擊場。

- You can enjoy a horse-driven carriage for free. 你可以免費乘坐馬車。

這樣說不禮貌

You should pay for all facilities if you want to use them.
你使用任何設施都要付錢。

Is there anything I can do for you?
我能為你做些什麼嗎？

Word Power!
- restroom **n** 洗手間
- lounge [laundʒ] **n** （飯店、旅館等的）會客廳

Sentence Power!
- Excuse me. 不好意思

- Can you tell where the restroom is? 可以告訴我洗手間在哪嗎？

- I cannot find the way to my room. 我找不到我的房間。

- What time does breakfast start at Lounge café? 大廳咖啡廳的早餐何時開始？

- Excuse me, I want to change my room. 我想換房間。

What's the check-in and check-out policy?
登記住房和退房的規定是什麼？

Word Power!
- policy [ˈpɑləsɪ] **n** 政策
- at least **phr** 至少
- regret [rɪˈgrɛt] **v** 為…抱歉
- accommodate [əˈkɑmədet] **v** 提供…住宿
- prior [ˈpraɪə] **a** 在前的
- arrangement [əˈrendʒmənt] **n** 安排
- guaranteed [ˈgærənˈtid] **a** 必定的

Sentence Power!
- In general 一般來說

- In general, check-in time is 3 o'clock in the afternoon. 一般來說，登記住房時間是下午三點。

- We regret that we cannot accommodate pets. 本飯店不提供寵物入住。

- Early Check-in or late check-out is by prior arrangement only and not guaranteed. 提前入住以及延遲退房請提前告知以便安排，但不保證有空房。

2 虛擬實境口說練習
on your iMessenger

從最簡短到最豐富，讓你實際和老外練習口說和聽力

| 當你要打電話確認你的訂房資料時 |

❶ **I just want to make sure my wife made the correct arrangements.**
我只是想確認一下我太太的安排正確。

spelled our names correctly 拼對我的名字
got us a non-smoking room 訂到禁菸的房間
got the dates right 訂的時間正確

❷ **Can I have my reservation next week extended one night?**
我可以把我下周的訂房延長一個晚上嗎？

canceled 取消
moved to the following weekend 改成再下一周
upgraded 升級

❸ **Do you mind that I'll be checking in very late tonight?**
你們會介意我今晚很晚去登記入住嗎？

after 10pm 晚上 10 點過後
after I have dinner 晚餐後
after hours 一小時候

| 當飯店人員在櫃檯向你核對 check-in 的資料時 |

❶ **Hi, I have a room tonight under the name Coughlin.**
你好，我今晚有用 Coughlin 的名字登記一間房。

a reservation 預約
booked two rooms 兩間房

❷ **I can carry my bags by myself.**
我可以自己提我的行李。

find the room 找到房間
explore the facilities 四處看看設施

│ 當你想叫客房服務時 │

❶ Hi, room service? Could send up a Hawaiian chicken platter?
你好，可以幫我送一個夏威夷雞肉拼盤來房間嗎？

a salad and a bottle of red wine
一份沙拉及一瓶紅酒
your biggest steak 你們最大的牛排
a baguette 一條法式長棍麵包

❷ I'm having trouble turning the lights on in the bathroom; could you come up?
我房間浴室的燈有問題，可以請你們上來一下嗎？

getting hot water 房間的熱水
opening my bottle of wine 開紅酒時
with the air-conditioner 房間的空調

❸ Do you offer any special services, such as leaving in massage?
你們有提供任何特殊服務嗎？例如留言？

turndown service 夜床服務
a wake-up call 晨喚服務

│ 當你向飯店人員詢問附近的景點及交通時 │

❶ Is it true the only way to the hot spring is over an old wooden bridge?
去溫泉唯一的路只能經過一條老舊的木橋是真的嗎？

on foot 用走的
to hike up the mountain
爬過一座山
to pay a taxi driver to take me
付錢請計程車載

❷ Will there be a bus stop near the historic battlegrounds?
那座歷史性的戰場會有巴士站嗎？

taxis waiting 計程車等候
signs pointing the way 路標指路
tuk-tuk drivers 嘟嘟車司機

3 虛擬實境網路聊天
on your iMessenger
在手機或電腦上，利用打字就可以聊出千言萬語

Momo

星期三 下午 13:45

Knock, knock~
下午 13:45

有人在嗎？

**Hi!
Wassup?**
下午 13:46

哈囉！怎麼啦？
What's up 的簡寫

I noticed that there's an awful lot of red on the streets and at the office. What's going on?
下午 13:47

我看到街上和辦公室裡有一大堆紅色的東西，是怎麼回事啊？
非常的

It's the Chinese New Year coming, haha!
下午 13:48

是中國新年快到了啦，哈哈！
中國的

下午 13:49

**New Year?!
Wasn't January 1st a long time ago?**
下午 13:50

新年？一月一號不是已經過去很久了嗎？

**The Chinese New Year runs on a different calendar~
It is celebrated with a bang here.**
下午 13:51

中國新年的時間是用另一種曆制～在這兒我們會盛大地慶祝。
曆制
轟動

**So...
Which day is the Chinese New Year exactly, according to say...
The American Calendar?**
下午 13:52

那麼，中國新年是哪一天呢…根據美國曆制的話？
根據

Momo

星期三 下午 13:45

It is based on solar and lunar movements.

下午 13:53

中國人的曆制是依據太陽及月球的運行而定。

太陽的
月亮的

Hmmm...

下午 13:53

Every year, the CN New Years falls on a different date according to the American Calendar.

下午 13:54

每年我們的春節都落在陽曆的不同時間上，美國曆制就是陽曆。

Chinese 或 China 的簡寫
遇上

 IC.
So, is it going to be fun?

下午 13:55

這樣子喔。那你告訴我，春節好玩嗎？

Why don't you see for yourself?

下午 13:56

你自己體驗看看吧！

 Sure!
Happy Chinese new year!

下午 13:57

祝你中國新年快樂！

聊天金句大補帖

Give me a break. 饒了我吧！

這句話有兩種意思，一種是說「饒了我吧」，另一種則是「別説笑了」。第一種説法通常用在很忙又很累的時候，渴望休息，希望別人不要再壓榨你；而第二種説法則是別人講了一件很誇張的事，有點嗤之以鼻的味道。

Unit 6

下次再接再厲

Why did you cancel the ticket for the train？
你為什麼要取消火車票的預訂？

Word Power!
- impromtu [ɪmˈprɑmptju] a 事先無準備的
- agenda [əˈdʒɛndə] n 行程
- crowded [ˈkraʊdɪd] a 擁擠的

- Because I have an impromptu meeting to attend.
  因為我臨時要參加一個會議。

- My travel agenda has been changed.
  我的行程改變了。

- Because the train is so crowded recently.
  因為最近火車太多人搭。

這樣說不禮貌

I would rather take an airplane.
我寧可搭飛機。

When did Mr.Wang cancel the reservation at the Four Seasons Hotel?
王先生什麼時候取消他在四季酒店的訂位？

Word Power!
- terribly [ˈtɛrəblɪ] ad 很，非常

- He cancelled it yesterday. 他昨天取消的。

- I'm sure he called to cancel the reservation last week. 我確定他是上星期打電話取消的。

- I don't remember. I'm terribly sorry.
  我不記得了，非常抱歉。

這樣說不禮貌

I don't know. You should ask the manager.
我不知道，你該問經理才對。

Sir, I need to cancel my reservation for tonight.
先生，我必須取消今晚的訂位。

Word Power!
- advance [ədˈvæns] a 事先的
- notice [ˈnotɪs] n 通知
- require [rɪˈkwaɪr] v 需要
- adhere to phr 遵守
- strict [strɪkt] a 嚴格的
- refund [rɪˈfʌnd] n 退款
- deposit [dɪˈpɑzɪt] n 訂金

- 72-hour advanced notice is required for cancellations. 若要取消訂位，請於七十二小時前（三天前）通知。

- We adhere to a strict cancellation policy. So if you cancel the reservation tonight, you won't get a refund of the deposit. 我們訂有較嚴格的取消訂位政策。所以若您要取消今晚的訂位，訂金將不會退還。

Hello, can I cancel my reservation of my ticket?
你好，我能取消我的機票預訂嗎？

Word Power!
· up to phr 多達
· charge [tʃɑrdʒ] n 費用
· issue [ˋɪʃju] v 核發

- Yes, when did you make your reservation? 可以，你是什麼時候預訂的？

- If a confirmed ticket is cancelled up to 3 days before the event, cancellation charges shall be 25% of the fare. 若三天前取消訂票，取消手續費為票價的百分之二十五。

- Yes. But no refund will be issued for cancellations within 24 hours. 可以。但是二十四小時之內取消訂票將無法退款。

How did you cancel the reservation in the hotel?
你是怎樣取消酒店預訂的？

Word Power!
· phone call n 電話
· secretary [ˋsɛkrə͵tɛrɪ] n 祕書
· myself [maɪˋsɛlf] pron （反身代名詞）我自己

- It's easy. I made a phone call. 簡單，我打了通電話。

- I had my secretary do it for me. 我請我祕書取消的。

- I sent on e-mail to cancel it. 我寄電子郵件取消的。

- I went to the hotel to cancel it by myself. 我親自到酒店取消的。

這樣說不禮貌
Why don't you ask the hotel directly? 你幹嘛不直接問酒店？

Why did you cancel the booking for the air ticket?
你為什麼取消機票？

Word Power!
· booking [ˋbukɪŋ] n 預訂
· car accident n 車禍
· personal [ˋpɝsn̩l] a 個人的

Sentence Power!
· ...in the end 最後

- I cancelled the reservation because my best friend had a car accident. 我取消機票因為我的好朋友出車禍了。

- I decided to go home by train in the end. 我最後決定搭火車回家。

- Because I need more time to deal with personal matters. 因為我需要多一點時間處理個人事務。

這樣說不禮貌
Mind your own business.
干你什麼事。

2 虛擬實境口說練習
on your iMessenger

從最簡短到最豐富，讓你實際和老外練習口說和聽力

┃當你想要取消預訂的機票時┃

❶ **Are my tickets refundable?**
請問我的票是可以退款的嗎？

transferable 可轉讓的
able to be refunded 可以退款的
unchangeable 不可轉讓的

❷ **What's the fee for me to cancel these tickets?**
取消這些票的話費用多少呢？

How much 要多少錢
What percentage does it cost 會扣百分之幾呢
What's the damage 賠償金多少

❸ **My boss won't let me take the vacation; I need to cancel.**
我的老闆不願讓我放假，所以只好取消。

My mom is sick 我媽媽生病了
Something came up 有狀況發生
I figured out that I can't afford it
我發現我負擔不起

┃當你被朋友問到取消行程的理由時┃

❶ **I just wasn't really in the mood to go.**
就只是沒有心情去了。

don't actually like my travel partner
不太喜歡我的旅伴
have so much work to catch up on
有太多工作無法趕上

❷ **I haven't had much motivation lately.**
我最近變得很沒有動力。

inspiration 活力
interest 興趣

| 當你要取消飯店的訂房時 |

❶ Sorry, it looks like we won't be making it.
抱歉，因為我們好像沒辦法過去。

able to arrive 抵達
taking the trip 去旅行
checking in 登記入住

❷ We read some reviews, and we don't think this is the hotel we want to stay in.
我們讀了一些評價，然後我們想這家飯店應該不是我們想住的。

saw the news 看到新聞
looked at your website 看到你們的網站
googled some pictures 搜尋到一些圖片

❸ Unfortunately something came up, and we will not be going to that city.
不幸地，有些狀況發生，所以我們不會去那座城市了。

we ran out of time 我們的時間來不及
our plans changed 我們的計畫改變
we're stuck 我們被塞在車陣

| 當飯店回應你取消訂房會索取手續費時 |

❶ What? That's outrageous!
什麼？這太令人吃驚了！

out of the question 不可能
unacceptable 我無法接受
ridiculous 太可笑了

❷ I don't think that's fair, because I am giving you 7-days notice.
我覺得這不公平，因為我有提前 7 天告知。

ample notice 在足夠的時間內告知
early notification 提前告知
plenty of time to rent to someone else
提供很多時間讓你們去讓別人入住

3 虛擬實境網路聊天
on your iMessenger

在手機或電腦上，利用打字就可以聊出千言萬語

Samuel Porter

星期三 下午 13:45

Bro, U no what?
I just got word from a friend.
He has been laid off because
his company is losing money.

下午 13:45

我剛聽說我的一個朋友由於公司一直虧本而遭受解僱。

know 的簡寫
話語
解僱
公司

下午 13:46

Well,
At least he wasn't fired.
I have a friend, whose
company fired him because
business was slow.

下午 13:46

但至少他不是被開除。我有個朋友被公司開除了，原因是公司營運不佳。

開除
不景氣的

 @@...
The story with your
friend is just unfair.

下午 13:47

你朋友所遭遇的的情況太不公平了。

情況
不公平的

下午 13:47

I told my friend,
It's good that he no longer needs
to work at a company like that.

下午 13:48

我告訴我朋友，不再為那種公司工作也未嘗不是好事。

不再

Samuel Porter

星期三 下午 13:45

That's one thing our company never does, lay off people.
I mean,
There are other ways such as taking a cut in pay.

下午 13:49

我們公司絕不會開除員工。總是有其他方式能夠解決問題，比方說減薪。

刪減
薪水

It just depends if the management is willing to work up a salary cut plan.

下午 13:50

這得看管理階層是不是願意實施減薪計畫囉。

願意
薪水

It's moments like these that remind me to be grateful.
I still get promotions and raises.

下午 13:51

說到這些事就提醒我自己要心懷感激了，我還能升職及調薪呢。

感激
升遷
加薪

UR such a lucky dog!

下午 13:52

你真幸運哪！

幸運兒

Good

下午 13:53

聊天金句大補帖

I can't make head nor tail of... 我搞不清楚…。

當我們想不透某件事情、或不清楚別人講話的意思，除了直接問「What do you mean?」之外，也可以用這句話來表達。硬幣的正反面在英文中就是「heads and tails」，因此分不清楚正反面就用來比喻搞不清楚事情的的來龍去脈。

Chapter 4

校園密室脫逃

Unit 1 充滿回憶的所在

Unit 2 結伴讀書去

Unit 3 朋友是一輩子的

Unit 4 來場三對三

Unit 5 揮灑青春汗水

Unit 6 保持好品格

Unit 1

充滿回憶的所在

What's your favorite subject? Why?
你最喜歡哪一學科？為什麼？

- Geography. It makes me understand the magic of nature. 地理，它讓我瞭解大自然的神奇。

- English. It helps me communicate with my foreign friends. 英語，我可以與外國友人交流。

- Woodshop. We can enjoy the process of creating.
木工課，我們可以享受製作的過程。

Word Power!
- subject [ˈsʌbdʒɪkt]
  n 科目
- geography [ˈdʒɪˈɑgrəfɪ]
  n 地理學
- nature [ˈnetʃɚ] n 自然
- communicate
  [kəˈmjunəˌket] v 交流
- process [ˈprɑsɛs]
  n 過程

Sentence Power!
- What's your favorite...?
  你最喜歡的…是什麼？

Have you finished your homework?
你的作業寫完了嗎？

- I finished it yesterday. 我昨天就寫完了。

- I'll do it right away! 我現在馬上寫！

- Not yet. I'll do it after the game.
還沒。等下玩完遊戲我再寫。

Word Power!
- right away phr 馬上
- rush [rʌʃ] v 催促

這樣說不禮貌

I'll do it later. Don't rush me!
我等下會寫。不要催啦！

Do you reside at school?
你住在學校嗎？

- Yes, I live in a dorm with my roommates.
我和同學們住在宿舍。

- No, I live at home. 不，我住在家裡。

- I rent a house to live. 我租房子住。

- I live in a dorm most of the time, but sometimes I stay at home. 大部分時間我住在宿舍，有時在家。

不能不會的小技巧
在美國，通常大學離自己家中距離遙遠，所以大部分的學生選擇住在學校宿舍。下次，不妨問問你的室友來自哪個城市，又為何選擇住校，相信這會是增進你和室友感情的好方法。

Word Power!
- reside [rɪˈzaɪd] v 居住
- dorm [dɔrm] n 宿舍
  （dormitory 的簡稱）
- rent [rɛnt] v 租用

Who is the naughtiest boy in our class?
誰是我們班上最調皮的男孩呢？

Word Power!
- naughty [ˋnɔtɪ]
  a 調皮的
- play jokes on phr 戲弄
- in trouble phr 陷入麻煩
- lively [ˋlaɪvlɪ] a 活潑的
- fight [faɪt] v 打架

- I think it's Tom. He always plays jokes on me. 我認為是湯姆，他經常捉弄我。

- It's Jim. He always gets himself in trouble. 是吉姆，他經常惹麻煩。

- Most of them are lively, but it's not naughty. 大部分男生都很活躍，但不調皮。

- I think it is Sam. He always starts fights with others. 我認為是山姆，他經常和人打架。

Do you like your teacher?
你喜歡你的老師嗎？

Word Power!
- teaching [ˋtitʃɪŋ]
  n 教學
- kind [kaɪnd] a 和藹的
- sleepy [ˋslipɪ]
  a 想睡的

- I like her very much. 我非常喜歡她。

- I like her way of teaching. It's relaxing. 我喜歡她的授課方式，很輕鬆。

- She is kind, I love her. 她非常和藹，我喜歡她。

這樣說不禮貌

Her boring class makes me sleepy.
她的課很無聊，讓我想睡覺。

Why didn't you do well on final exam?
你為什麼期末考沒考好？

Word Power!
- final exam n 期末考
- go over phr 復習
- carelessness
  [ˋkɛrlɪsnɪs] n 粗心
- make mistakes
  phr 犯錯誤
- stay up phr 熬夜

- I didn't go over the material well. 我沒有復習好。

- It is because of carelessness, I made so many mistakes. 由於粗心，我犯了很多錯誤。

- I had a fever last night so I lost the chance to review one last time. 昨晚我發燒了害我沒時間復習最後一次。

- I stayed up late to watch TV last night. 昨晚我熬夜看電視了。

這樣說不禮貌

What is done is done.
過去的事就過去了。

2 虛擬實境口說練習 on your iMessenger

從最簡短到最豐富，讓你實際和老外練習口說和聽力

| 當同學問你喜歡上哪個老師的課時 |

❶ Who is your favorite teacher at school?
你在學校最喜歡的老師是哪一位？

the best 最好的
the most popular 最受歡迎的
the most outstanding 最出色的

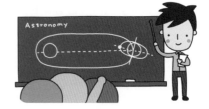

❷ Which teacher do you like the most?
你最喜歡的老師是哪一位？

of them all 在他們之中
at this school 在學校
the best 最

❸ Tell me who the teacher you like the best is.
告訴我你最喜歡哪一個老師。

Let me know 告訴我
Inform me of 告訴我
Whisper to me 偷偷告訴我

| 當你要跟同學分享你上某一堂課的心得時 |

❶ Let me tell you what I think about this class.
讓我告訴你關於這堂課我的想法吧。

how I feel 我的感覺
what my opinion is 我的建議
all 的一切

❷ There are some things about this class I should tell you.
關於這堂課有些事我一定得告訴你。

warn you of / against 提醒你
fill you in on 告訴你
let you know about 讓你知道

| 當你問同學剛剛考試考得如何時 | ------------------------------

❶ Did you pass the last exam?
你上次的考試通過了嗎？

ace 考得好
not fail 沒被當
do well on 考得好

❷ How did you do on the last exam?
你上次的考試考得如何？

the previous 前一次的
yesterday's 昨天的
the most recent 最近一次的

❸ How are you feeling about that last exam?
你覺得上次的大考如何？

test 小考
pop quiz 隨堂測驗
homework assignment 功課

| 當你想抱怨學校課業太難時 | ------------------------------

❶ This homework is no joke!
這份作業真的不是開玩笑的！

really difficult 非常難
not easy 很不簡單
super tough 非常困難

❷ Does anyone else feel like this homework is impossible?
有人也覺得這份功課不可能達成的嗎？

too hard 太難了
crazy 根本瘋了
a piece of cake 很輕鬆

3 虛擬實境網路聊天
on your iMessenger

在手機或電腦上，利用打字就可以聊出千言萬語

Franky J.

星期三 下午 13:45

Hey Peter man,
RU into theater?

下午 13:45

嗨彼得，你熱衷舞台
表演嗎？
熱衷於
戲院

Hmmm...

下午 13:46

I've got some free tickets to the
"Hunchback of Notre Dame".
Maybe you can take your girl
to see it.

下午 13:47

我有一些鐘樓怪人的
免費入場券，或許你
可以帶你的女友一起
去欣賞。
駝背

下午 13:48

Sure, but why aren't U going?

下午 13:49

當然好啊，但是你為
何不去呢？

To be honest, I'm not a big fan of
musicals.
But there's no point in letting some
perfectly good tickets go to waste,
Rite?

下午 13:50

老實說，我並沒有很
迷音樂劇。不過，總
不能白白浪費了這麼
好的門票。
音樂劇
沒有意圖的
浪費

IC.
So then, how did you
get these tickets?

下午 13:51

我想也是。那這些票
你哪兒弄來的？

Franky J.

星期三 下午 13:45

 Well, I have a friend who's in the performing arts industry n he sends me tickets all the time.

下午 13:52

這個嘛，因為我有一個朋友在表演藝術這行工作，他都會把票寄給我。

產業

and 的簡寫

下午 13:53

 But the only things I really care to watch are dance performances.

下午 13:54

不過，我想看的只有舞蹈類的表演而已。

想要

I really had no idea you were into dance!
What type of dance are you into?

下午 13:55

我完全想不到你會喜歡舞蹈耶！那你喜歡的是哪一類的呢？

不知道

 Exotic.

下午 13:56

異國風的。

異國情調的

That's pretty cool~

下午 13:57

蠻酷的耶～

聊天金句大補帖

You haven't been yourself... 你不太對勁…

這句話指的是一個人的行為舉止或表現跟平時的他不太一樣，似乎有什麼不尋常的事情發生，導致他不太對勁。當我們察覺一個人有這樣的傾向時，我們就可以用這個句型來表達。比如：

• John hasn't been himself recently. 約翰最近不太對勁。

Unit 2

結伴讀書去

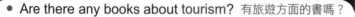

How may I help you?
我能幫你嗎？

Word Power!
- tourism [ˋturɪzəm]
  n 旅遊
- stack [stæk] n 大書架
- cyber [ˋsaɪbə] n 與電腦相關的事物
- magnetically [mægˋnɛtɪklɪ] ad 帶磁性的
- code [kod] v 為⋯編碼

- Are there any books about tourism? 有旅遊方面的書嗎？

- I can't find this book in the stacks. 我在書架上找不到這本書。

- I want to get these books on cyber culture and check them out for overnight use. 我想借這些關於網路文化的書，借一個晚上。

- Are the books in the library magnetically coded? 圖書館的書都有磁性編碼嗎？

Do you always go to the library?
你經常去圖書館嗎？

Word Power!
- library [ˋlaɪˏbrɛrɪ] n 圖書館
- environment [ɪnˋvaɪrənmənt] n 環境
- nerd [nɜd] n 書呆子

- Yes, I like the quiet environment. 是的，我喜歡安靜的環境。

- No, I like staying in the dorm. 不，我喜歡待在宿舍。

- Yes, there are so many books to read. 是的，這裡有很多書可以讀。

這樣說不禮貌

No, do I look like a nerd? 不，我看起來像書呆子嗎？

Can you recommend a top selling book?
你可以推薦一本最暢銷的書嗎？

Word Power!
- recommend [ˏrɛkəˋmɛnd] v 推薦
- top selling book n 暢銷書
- shelf [ʃɛlf] n 架子
- latest [ˋletɪst] n 最新的事物

Sentence Power!
- How about...? ⋯怎麼樣？

- How about this one on the second shelf? 第二層這本怎麼樣？

- Of course, firstly, can you tell me which kind of book do you like? 可以，你可以先告訴我你喜歡那類書？

- The latest top selling books will arrive tomorrow. 近期最暢銷的書明天送到。

I'm looking for thrillers, can you help me?
我在找驚悚類的書籍，你能幫我嗎？

Word Power!
- thriller [ˈθrɪlə]
  n 恐怖小說（或電影）
- librarian [laɪˈbrɛrɪən]
  n 圖書館員

更多…
- essay 散文
- poetry 詩歌
- fable 寓言

Sentence Power!
- be familiar with...
  phr 對…熟悉

- I'm sorry, I'm not familiar with the library. 抱歉，我對圖書館不熟。

- Maybe you can ask the librarian.
  也許你可以問圖書館員。

- I also want to borrow those books.
  Let's go together.
  我也正要借那類的書，我們一起找吧。

這樣說不禮貌

Do I look like a librarian?
我看起來像圖書館員嗎？

Why are your books overdue?
你的書為什麼逾期未還？

Word Power!
- overdue [ˈovəˈdju]
  a 過期的
- library card n 借書證

- I lost my library card. 我把借書證弄丟了。

- I haven't been at school until today. 我今天才回學校。

- I can't find the book that I borrowed.
  我找不到我借的書。

- How much should I pay as a fine?
  我得交多少罰金？

這樣說不禮貌
I just forgot. Any problem?
我就忘了，有什麼問題嗎？

How long am I allowed to keep the books for?
書可以借多久呢？

Word Power!
- renew [rɪˈnju] v 更新
- otherwise
  [ˈʌðəˌwaɪz] ad 否則
- magazine [ˌmæɡəˈzin]
  n 雜誌
- take out phr 帶…出去

- You must renew the books if you wish to keep them longer than a month. 一個月後如果要續借，必須辦理續借手續。

- Two months. Otherwise, you should pay a fine. 兩個月，否則要收罰金。

- A month. But magazines can't be taken out. 一個月，但雜誌不外借。

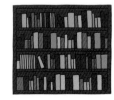

2 虛擬實境口說練習
on your iMessenger

從最簡短到最豐富，讓你實際和老外練習口說和聽力

┃當你要請圖書館員幫你找一本書時┃

❶ **Can you help me locate this book?**
可以請你幫我確認這本書的位置嗎？

> find 找
> look for 尋找
> search for 尋找

❷ **I need your help because I am having trouble finding this book.**
我需要你的幫忙，因為我找這本書時遇到困難。

> aid 援手
> expertise 專門知識
> knowledge 知識

❸ **Can you tell me which section of the library this book is in?**
可以請你告訴我這本書在圖書館的哪一區嗎？

> what part 哪一塊
> which area 哪一區
> what floor 哪一樓

┃當館員告知你圖書館的注意事項時┃

❶ **Talking on your phone is strictly forbidden in the library.**
圖書館是嚴禁講電話的。

> Eating food 吃東西
> Sleeping 睡覺
> Yelling 喧鬧

❷ **The library's computers are for research purposes only.**
圖書館的電腦只能用來搜尋資料。

> database 資料庫
> periodicals 期刊
> academic journals 學術期刊

┃當你詢問館員借書的規定時┃

❶ How long can I borrow these books for?
我可以借這本書借多久？

> How many days 幾天
> What period of time 多長時間
> How much time 多久

❷ What is the policy of this library regarding returning books late?
圖書館對於遲還書籍的政策是什麼？

> about 關於
> as far as 對於
> in terms of 在…方面

❸ How many books can I borrow at one time?
我一次可以借幾本書呢？

> today 今天
> at once 一次
> now 現在

┃當館員阻止你做某件事時┃

❶ Stop that right now!
馬上停下來！

> instantly 立刻
> immediately 馬上
> right away 立刻

❷ Give me that gum you have.
給我你的口香糖。

> Hand over 交出
> Relinquish 交出
> Spit out 吐掉

3 虛擬實境網路聊天
on your iMessenger

在手機或電腦上，利用打字就可以聊出千言萬語

Randy

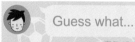

星期三 下午 13:45

 Guess what...
下午 13:45

下午 13:46

你知道嗎？
猜猜怎麼了

...I saw on TV last night with lots of cussing and fighting!
下午 13:47

我昨晚在電視上看到一堆打鬥咒罵的場面！
詛咒

I don't know some late night kung-fu movie.
下午 13:48

我不知道這麼晚了還有功夫電影。
功夫

No, they were trying to pass a bill. And there was a lot of arguing, Suddenly, a microphone flew over and hit someone on the head!
下午 13:50

不是，他們正嘗試要通過一項新法案。爭吵越演越烈，接著一支麥克風飛了出來擊中其中一人的頭部！
法案
爭吵
麥克風

下午 13:51

Oh man, it was better than "Kill Bill."
下午 13:52

喔，那比「追殺比爾」還精彩。

134

Randy

星期三 下午 13:45

If you like that, then you'll love voting season.
下午 13:53

 What's in store for me during voting season?
下午 13:54

Oh, you'll get to see drama beyond your wildest imaginations.
下午 13:55

下午 13:56

From sabotage to espionage, blackmail to betrayal,
And if you're lucky enough, you might even catch an episode of assassination!
下午 13:57

假如你喜歡那種場面的話，那你一定會更愛選舉季！
選舉

選舉季到底為我準備了什麼？
…在未來等待著某人

噢，你將會看到你連作夢都想像不到的戲劇情節。
寬宏的
想像力

從破壞行動到間諜活動、黑函到背叛都有，而且，假如運氣夠好的話，你說不定會目睹一場暗殺的戲碼喔！
破壞
諜報
連續劇
暗殺

聊天金句大補帖

I'll tell you what. 讓我來告訴你吧。

當你有非常確切、果決的意見或想法想要傳達給對方時，就可以說這句。這也是 "I'll tell you what I will do." 或 "I'll tell you what might be a good idea." 的省略形式，在口語上自然更常使用。

Unit 3 朋友是一輩子的

How do you get along with your new friend?
你和你的新朋友相處的怎樣？

Word Power!
- get along with
  phr 與…和睦相處
- friendly [ˋfrɛndlɪ]
  a 友好的
- together [təˋgɛðɚ]
  ad 一起
- creepy [ˋkripɪ]
  a 毛骨悚然的

- I think we will be good friends in the future.
  我想我們將來一定是好朋友。

- He's very friendly. I like him.
  他很友好，我喜歡他。

這樣說不禮貌

- I don't know, we didn't spent much time together. 我不知道，我們相處時間不多。

Not well. He's a creepy guy.
不是很好。他是個令人毛骨悚然的傢伙。

Here's something for you!
這裡有東西要給你！

不能不會的小技巧
接受他人的禮物時，表達謝意是很必要的禮節之一。要記得：對方送禮是一種貼心並表示心意的行為，因此，禮貌地收下禮物並表示自己對禮物的喜好才是最符合禮儀的行為喔！

Word Power!
- exactly [ɪgˋzæktlɪ]
  ad 確切地

- It's very nice of you. 你真好。

- It's lovely! Thank you. 真可愛！謝謝。

- You're so sweet. That's exactly what I want. 你真好。
  這正是我想要的東西。

- What a beautiful painting! Thank you.
  這幅畫真漂亮！謝謝你。

I thought I'd drop in to see how you're doing. How is it going?
我順道過來看看你的近況如何，你最近怎麼樣？

Word Power!
- catch a cold phr 感冒

Sentence Power!
- Have a seat. 請坐。
- Funny you should ask.
  你問得真好。

- That's very nice of you. Have a seat. 你真好，請坐。

- All right. Just caught a cold. 沒事，只是一個小感冒而已。

這樣說不禮貌

- Funny you should ask. I am actually in trouble now. 既然你都提了，
  其實我碰到了一點麻煩。

I'm pretty busy recently. Please leave after the cup of tea.
我最近比較忙。喝完這杯茶你就走吧。

I have a headache now. Oh, God, who can help me?

我的頭現在好痛。天呀，誰可以幫幫我？

Word Power!
- feel well `phr` 覺得舒服
- aspirin [ˈæspərɪn] `n` 阿斯匹靈
- plenty [ˈplɛntɪ] `a` 大量的

Sentence Power!
- Take it easy. 放輕鬆

- I'm sorry to hear you're not feeling well. 聽到你不舒服我感到很難過。

- Take it easy and get lots of sleep tonight. 放輕鬆。今晚好好休息。

- Just take an aspirin. 吃顆阿斯匹靈吧。

- Do get plenty of rest and drink lots of water. 好好休息並多喝水。

這樣說不禮貌

Why don't you go to see a doctor?
你幹嘛不去看醫生。

Who is your best friend in your class?

誰是你在班上最好的朋友？

Word Power!
- friendship [ˈfrɛndʃɪp] `n` 友誼
- loner [ˈlonə] `n` 獨行俠

- The friendship is very good between my classmates and I. 我和同班同學的友誼都很好。

- Anyone who loves playing football is my best friend. 凡是喜歡足球的都是我的好朋友。

- I like all of them. 每個人我都喜歡。

- I don't have best friends. I'm a loner. 我沒有好朋友。我是獨行俠。

There's something wrong with my original plan. What should I do?

我原本的計畫出了點問題，我該怎麼辦呢？

Word Power!
- solution [səˈluʃən] `n` 解決辦法
- back-up [ˈbæk‚ʌp] `a` 備用的

Sentence Power!
- There's something wrong with... …出了狀況
- Calm down. 冷靜下來。

- Don't worry about that. Calm down. 不要擔心。冷靜一點。

- Cheer up! You will find the solution. 打起精神來！你會找到解決辦法的。

- I'm terribly sorry to hear that. Is it too late to change your plan? 我很遺憾聽到這個。現在改變計畫會太晚嗎？

- Do you have a back-up plan? 你有備用計畫嗎？

2

虛擬實境口說練習
on your iMessenger

| 當你跟你的朋友分享你現在的心情時 |

❶ I've been feeling really down lately.
我最近覺得心情真的很不好。

> very 非常
> totally 超級
> extremely 極度地

❷ I'm sad, and I don't know what to do.
我很難過，而且我不知道該怎麼做。

> torn 不安
> lonely 寂寞
> confused 困惑

❸ I want you to know why I've been so happy recently!
我要你知道為什麼最近我總是那麼開心！

> this week 這週
> these past few days 這幾天
> when I am with you 跟我一起時

| 當你想約好久不見的朋友出來見面時 |

❶ It's been ages! Want to grab a coffee?
好幾年沒見了！想去喝杯咖啡嗎？

> so long 久
> too long 長時間
> forever 像一輩子

❷ I haven't seen you in forever. Let's meet and catch up this week.
我好像一輩子沒見過你了。我們這禮拜見個面聯絡感情一下吧。

> soon 盡快
> when you're free 等你有空時
> when you're in town 等你進城時

| 當你的朋友很難過，而你想安慰他時 |

❶ I'm here for you if you want to talk.
如果你想找人聊聊的話我都在這兒。

say anything 說任何事
cry 哭
complain 抱怨

❷ What can I do to make you feel better?
我該做些什麼讓你覺得好一些呢？

cheer up 高興起來
come around 恢復精神
perk up 振作起來

❸ I know what will cheer you up: a hug!
我想到什麼可以鼓勵你了：一個擁抱！

an ice cream 來點冰淇淋
some wine 一些紅酒
a bike ride 去騎腳踏車

| 當朋友問你關於某件事的建議時 |

❶ I'll do my best to help you out.
我會盡我最大努力幫助你的。

what I can 我所能
whatever is in my power 我所有的權力
anything I am able to 我任何所能做的

❷ I'll give you the best advice I can.
我會給你我所能給的最好建議

know 知道
am able to 可以給
heard before 之前聽過

3 虛擬實境網路聊天
on your iMessenger

在手機或電腦上，利用打字就可以聊出千言萬語

H. K.

星期三 下午 13:45

Hey, Larry!
I was just in the bathroom
and there was a weird guy.

下午 13:45

下午 13:45

喂，賴瑞，我剛剛在廁所的時候，有一個很奇怪的男子。

奇怪的

He kept looking over at my
urinal when I was peeing.
What was his problem?!!!

下午 13:46

一直盯著我的小便斗耶，他到底有啥問題啊！

看過來 / 去
小便斗
小便

下午 13:47

I see you've met Dick.
His name really is Dick! And he
can be a real dick sometimes!

下午 13:48

喔，看來你已經見過狄克了。而且，他的名字真的就叫狄克！有時候真的還滿像渾球的！

渾球

Is that a tongue twister or something?

下午 13:49

這是一個繞口令還是什麼東西啊？

繞口令

Larry

星期三 下午 13:45

No~
Just that some of the people here
can get on your nerves sometimes.

下午 13:50

不是～只是有些這裡
的人真的是會讓你精
神煩躁。

刺激或煩擾某人

 Like whom for example?

下午 13:51

例如像誰啊？

Do you know Katherine? The pretty
girl in our class.
It's great to be sociable at parties
but…
In the class on a Monday morning...

下午 13:52

你知道凱瑟琳嗎？就
我們班那個正妹。聚
會上善於交際很不錯，
但是，一到星期一上
課的時候…

善交際的

派對

下午 13:53

It just annoys the heck
out of people here.

下午 13:54

就會讓所有人都很受
不了。

見鬼

 Look on the bright side, at least
she's pretty.

下午 13:55

想想好的一面啊，至
少她很漂亮。

往好處想

聊天金句大補帖

I owe you one. 我欠你一次。

當你覺得談話的對方讓你心生感激時，為了表達你的謝意，我們可以說這句話。在
適當的情境下，這句話會比說 "Thank you." 更為生動、輕鬆，但卻能使對方明白
他所做的事情或所說的話對你有實質上的注意。通常這麼說還帶有幽默的意涵在裡
頭。

Unit 4 來場三對三

Who is that on the basketball court?

在籃球場上的哪個人是誰？

Word Power!
- court [kort] n 場地
- famous [ˈfeməs] a 有名的
- be interested in phr 對…有興趣
- captain [ˈkæptɪn] n 隊長
- referee [ˌrɛfəˈri] n 裁判

- He is the most famous player on our school basketball team. 他是我們學校籃球隊最有名的隊員啊。

- He is my best friend ,and he is interested in basketball. 他是我最好的朋友，他很喜歡籃球。

- He is the captain of the basketball team. 他是籃球隊隊長啊。

這樣說不禮貌

He is the referee. Idiot.
那是裁判啦。呆子。

Do you want to play basketball with me?

你想和我一起打籃球嗎？

Word Power!
- bell [bɛl] n 鈴

Sentence Power!
- Sounds... 聽起來…

- Sure, I want to play basketball as well. 好的，我正好也想打籃球。

- No, the bell is ringing. I must go back to my class. 不了，上課鈴響了，我得回去上課了。

- Sorry, I'm busy now. After thirty minutes, I'm free. 對不起，我現在有點忙。過半個小時後我有空。

- Sounds great. Let's go. 這想法聽起來不錯，走吧。

Why don't you play basketball with us?

你為什麼不和我們一起打籃球？

Word Power!
- injure [ˈɪndʒɚ] v 受傷
- suck [sʌk] v 爛

Sentence Power!
- The reason is that... 原因是…
- To be honest... 老實說…

- Because I was injured last week. 因為我上星期受傷了。

- **The reason is that** my skill is so bad.
因為我的球技太爛了。

- I am too tired. Maybe next week. 因為我太累了，也許下星期吧。

這樣說不禮貌

To be honest, it's because you suck at it.
老實說，因為你們打太爛了。

How many players are on the basketball court?

籃球場上有多少名球員？

- I guess there are six. Except those on the bench. 我猜有六個。除了那些坐板凳的球員。

- It has to be ten. You know the rules. 肯定十人，你知道這是規定。

- There are so many people now, I can't check them clearly. 有很多人，我數不清楚啊。

這樣說不禮貌

You can count by yourself. 你可以自己數一下。

Don't talk to me when I'm focused on the game! 我在專心看比賽時別跟我說話！

When will we have a basketball game?

我們什麼時候有籃球比賽？

不能不會的小技巧
比賽賽程對於球員來說十分重要。萬一弄錯時間，通常就不會再有重賽的機會了。

- On Tuesday. God bless us. 星期二。祝我們好運。
- The day after Labor Day. 勞動節後的那天。
- Tomorrow morning. 明天上午。
- I should ask our teacher first. 我得先問一下我們老師。

What is the score of this game?

這場比賽比分是多少？

不能不會的小技巧
到球場打球或是踢球都是交到新朋友的好方法，但在球場比賽時，心情難免心浮氣躁，因此還是要時時注意說話禮儀，以免造成口角或演變成肢體衝突喔。

- It is 79 to 60 now. But the game is still not over. 現在是 79 比 60，但比賽還沒結束。

- The scores are even. Who will be the winner finally? 比分相同，但最後誰會贏呢？

- I don't know. But this is the second round; A team was the winner in the first round. 我不知道，但這已經是第二場比賽；第一場是 A 隊贏了。

2 虛擬實境口說練習
on your iMessenger

從最簡短到最豐富，讓你實際和老外練習口說和聽力

| 當你想約朋友和你一起看球賽時 |

❶ Come over to my place later, and we'll watch the basketball game.
等下來我那邊吧，然後我們可以一起看籃球。

> house 家
> crib 小屋
> apartment 公寓

❷ Are you busy later? Do you want to watch the basketball game together?
你最近會很忙嗎？想要一起看個籃球比賽嗎？

> Do you have plans 有任何計劃嗎
> Are you free 有空嗎
> What are you up to 怎麼樣

❸ I need some company to watch the basketball game with.
我需要找些夥伴一起看球賽。

> someone 某個人
> some friends 些朋友
> some other fans 些球迷

| 當你想約朋友出去打球時 |

❶ You want to go shoot some hoops?
你想去投幾個球嗎？

> play ball 打球
> shoot around 練投籃
> to the courts 籃球場

❷ Do you have time to play basketball today?
你今天有時間一起打籃球嗎？

> Are you free 有空
> Do you want 想要
> How's about we go 要跟我

| 當你和朋友在討論昨晚的球賽時 |

❶ Did you see that dunk last night?!
你昨晚有看到那個灌籃嗎？

> block 防守
> rebound 籃板球
> buzzer beater 壓哨球

❷ I can't believe what happened at the end of the game.
我真不敢相信昨晚比賽快結束時發生的事。

> I'm speechless about 對於…我整個無言
> I'm flabbergasted at 讓我大吃一驚
> I can't accept 我無法接受

❸ The referees in last night's game were terrible, don't you think?
昨晚比賽時的裁判真是爛透了，你不覺得嗎？

> wouldn't you agree 你不同意嗎
> didn't you see 你有看到嗎
> right 對吧

| 當朋友找你去幫忙加油時 |

❶ You have to support my favorite team!
你一定得支持我最愛的隊伍！

> cheer for 幫…加油
> back 支持
> side with 站在…這邊

❷ My team needs our support.
我的隊伍需要我們的支持。

> requires 需要
> has to have 一定得
> must have 一定需要

3 虛擬實境網路聊天
on your iMessenger

在手機或電腦上，利用打字就可以聊出千言萬語

Juli, Jane(2)

星期三 下午 13:45

U look very fit!
Have U always been like this?

下午 13:45

你看起來蠻健康的
耶！你一直都這樣
嗎？
健康的

Believe it or not, I once
weighed over 200 pounds.

下午 13:46

信不信由你，我曾一
度重達 200 磅。
秤…的重量

I can't believe it!!!!
How is it possible?

下午 13:47

我不相信！怎麼可
能？
可能的

It's true. I've seen a picture
of her back in those days.

下午 13:48

那是真的。我親眼看
過他那時候的照片。
照片

I told you so~

下午 13:49

就説吧～
早跟你說過

下午 13:50

Well, back in my senior high years,
I did nothing but sit around and
study. I ate whenever I studied.
And before I knew it, I barely fit
through the door.

下午 13:51

我高中的時候，除了
坐著唸書之外啥都不
做，只要我在唸書，
我的嘴就沒停過。在
我有警覺心之前，我
差點肥到過不了門了。
高中
幾乎不

Juli, Jane(2)

星期三 下午 13:45

下午 13:52

Then... How did you lose all that weight?

下午 13:53

那…你後來怎麼擺脫那些肥肉的？

減重

I tried everything like diet pills, diet supplements, eating nothing... But in the end the only thing that worked was exercising and fitness.

下午 13:55

我試過各種方法，像是減肥藥、補給品、斷食，不過，到最後唯一有用的是運動和健身。

減肥藥

補給品

UR telling me you lost all that weight just by exercising?

下午 13:56

你的意思是你能瘦下來全是靠運動的關係？

Yeah! But believe me, it wasn't easy at all.

下午 13:57

對呀！不過，相信我，這一點都不容易。

一點也不

聊天金句大補帖

Keep your chin up. 保持正面的態度。

照字面的意義看，就是把下巴抬高，用以勉勵別人不要垂頭喪氣，不管遇到什麼事都要用最正面的態度去面對！

Unit 5 揮灑青春汗水

90% 的老外都是用這些句子開始聊天。

Do you think working out is important to students?
你認為健身對學生來說重要嗎？

- Yes, it can prevent disease. 是的，這有助於預防疾病。
- Yes, I totally agree. Students in Taiwan spend too much time in their classrooms. 對，我完全同意。台灣學生待在教室的時間太多了。
- Maybe, but every student has his or her own opinion. 也許吧，但每個學生都有自己的觀點。

> 不能不會的小技巧
> 均衡發展也是教育很重要的一環。下次遇到外國朋友，也可和他們談談對學校教育的想法哦。
>
> **Word Power!**
> - work out phr 健身
> - prevent [prɪˋvɛnt] v 預防
> - disease [dɪˋziz] n 疾病
> - totally [ˋtotl̩ɪ] ad 完全地
> - opinion [əˋpɪnjən] n 意見

Do you like sports?
你喜歡體育運動嗎？

- I love sports, such as basketball and baseball. 我很愛體育運動，例如籃球和棒球。
- Well, tennis is probably my favorite. 呃，網球可能是我最喜歡的吧。
- A little. I like ball games, such as table tennis.
  一點點，我喜歡輕鬆的運動，如打乒乓球。

> **Word Power!**
> - ball games n 球類運動
> - table tennis n 桌球（也稱 ping-pong）
>
> 更多…
> - softball 壘球
> - soccer 【美】足球
> - football 【美】橄欖球

> 這樣說不禮貌
> I hate all the sports.
> 我討厭所有的體育運動。

Do you think Federer will win the match?
你認為費德勒會贏得比賽嗎？

- Of course, he is an amazing player. 當然，他可是一個傳奇球員。
- No matter if he wins or loses, I will always support Federer. 無論輸贏，我都會支持費德勒。
- As long as the game is exciting, I don't really care about who will win. 只要比賽精采，我沒有真的很在乎誰會贏。

> **Word Power!**
> - match [mætʃ] n 比賽
> - amazing [əˋmezɪŋ] a 令人驚奇的
> - support [səˋport] v 支持
> - as long as phr 只要
>
> **Sentence Power!**
> - No matter... 無論…

Do you usually go to the stadium?
你是否經常到體育館？

● I go there almost every weekend.
幾乎每個週末我會去那。

● I used to go there every day. But I haven't been there since I sprained my ankle last year. 我以前每天去，但自從去年我扭傷腳後就沒再去過。

● I usually go to the stadium to watch the sports games.
我經常去體育館看比賽。

這樣說不禮貌

Sports are boring so I never go there.
我不喜歡體育運動，所以我從來不去那裡。

Why are you so slender?
你為什麼這麼苗條了？

● I usually eat more vegetables and less meat. 我都多吃蔬菜少吃肉。

● I work out every single day. 我每天健身

● I didn't eat junk food. 我不吃垃圾食物。

● That's because summer is coming, so I want to lose weight. 因為夏天快到了，所以我想減肥。

Do you think every match must have winner and loser?
你認為比賽一定要有輸贏嗎？

● Yes, the winner receives great honor and a big trophy. 是的，贏的人會得到很高的榮譽及大獎盃。

● Yes, it can help every team find a higher pursuit. 可以，因為這幫助每個人去追求更多。

● Sportsmanship is much more important than the result. 運動家精神比輸贏重要多了。

這樣說不禮貌

It's nothing to me.
對我來說無所謂。

2 虛擬實境口說練習
on your iMessenger

從最簡短到最豐富，讓你實際和老外練習口說和聽力

| 當你問你的朋友有在做哪些運動時 |

❶ Are you playing any sports in your free time?
你平時空閒玩任何運動嗎？

> recently 最近
> when you are free 平常有空
> that you like 喜歡

❷ What sports are you into?
你熱衷於哪些運動？

> do you play 有在玩
> do you participate in 有參與
> are your favorite 最喜歡

❸ How have you stayed so fit?
Are you playing sports?
你是怎麼保持好身材的？你有在運動嗎？

> in shape 身材
> healthy 健康
> svelte 苗條

| 當你和朋友在討論該如何維持身材時 |

❶ You should be exercising every day for at least thirty minutes.
你應該每天至少運動三十分鐘

> around 大概
> about 約
> up to 以上

❷ Diet and exercise are both important to staying fit.
節食和運動都對保持身材很重要。

> parts of 是⋯的一部分
> necessary to 對⋯很必要
> ingredients in 是⋯的要素

| 當你的朋友約你周末一起去運動時 |

❶ **If I have free time, I'll definitely join your Saturday runs.**
如果有空的話，我一定會跟你一起周六去跑步。

> totally 絕對
> absolutely 絕對
> without a doubt 毫無疑問會

❷ **Of course I'd love to exercise with you on the weekends!**
我周末當然願意和你一起去運動！

> get back in shape 健身
> play badminton 打羽毛球
> go hiking 健行

❸ **I can't exercise with you every weekend, but when I have free time, sure!**
我不能每個禮拜都和你去運動，但如果是我有空時當然可以！

> am free 方便
> am able to 可以
> don't have other plans 沒有其他事

| 當你跟你的朋友說你想減肥時 |

❶ **How can I lose some weight?**
我該怎麼減掉體重呢？

> drop 降低
> get rid of 甩掉
> take off 削減

❷ **You have to tell me the secret to losing weight.**
你一定得告訴我你減肥的祕密。

> getting thin 變瘦
> getting a better figure 身材變好
> proper dieting 正確飲食

3 虛擬實境網路聊天
on your iMessenger

在手機或電腦上，利用打字就可以聊出千言萬語

Tarzan

星期三 下午 13:45

下午 13:45

What's with the hype about being fit these days?

下午 13:46

It's the trend these days! Which explains why there are so many exclusive exercising clubs opening up.

下午 13:47

Got it.
But it seems as if everything now is about membership.

下午 13:48

Yup~

下午 13:49

The more you pay for membership, the better it must be. A lot of people see it as a symbol of their status.
But some don't even go that often!

下午 13:50

下午 13:51

最近關於健康觀念的大肆宣傳到底是怎麼回事呀？
天花亂墜的大肆宣傳

這是最近的潮流趨勢，這就解釋了為什麼有這麼多高級的健身俱樂部成立。
潮流
高級的
開展

嗯，我知道了。不過現在好像任何東西都脫離不了會員制。
會員制

是啊～

你支付的費用越高，也就表示你的會員階級越高。也有很多人把這個當作身份地位的象徵，但有些人還不常去呢！
象徵
地位

Tarzan

星期三 下午 13:45

> Well~ Not everybody is like that. Some people make full use of the facilities, like me.
>
> 下午 13:52

不過，不是每個人都這樣啦，像我就會充分使用每一項器材

利用

充分地

器材

下午 13:52

> There's nothing like a good workout after work
>
> 下午 13:54

工作一天後上健身房好好運動流汗一下，那種感覺是什麼都沒得比的！

健身

 Definitely!
> So I love a good game of badminton after work.
>
> 下午 13:55

一點都沒錯！所以我都喜歡在工作結束後，好好打一場羽球。

羽毛球

下午 13:55

聊天金句大補帖

Give it your best shot. 全力以赴。

當我們發現身旁的人因某事而對自己沒信心、裹足不前的時候，就可以用這句話來鼓勵他，告訴他凡事盡力就好。

Unit 6 保持好品格

Here you are. This is a gift for your birthday. Do you like it?
哪，這是給你的生日禮物，喜歡嗎？

不能不會的小技巧
接受他人的禮物時，表達謝意是很必要的禮節之一。

Word Power!
· obliged [ə`blaɪdʒd]
  a 感激的
· appreciate [ə`priʃɪet]
  v 感激；欣賞

- Thanks! I really enjoy it. 謝謝！我很喜歡。
- Much obliged. 非常感謝！
- Thanks! I appreciate it. 謝謝！我很感激。
- Thank you very much again, I like it.
  再次謝謝您，我非常喜歡。

這樣說不禮貌
Not bad, I like it.
不錯啊，我喜歡。

Oh, no! You sprained your ankle. Can I do anything to help?
哦，真糟糕，你扭傷了你的腳踝。我能幫你什麼嗎？

Word Power!
· ankle **n** 腳踝
· thankful [`θæŋkfəl]
  a 感謝的

Sentence Power!
· thankful to sb. for 為…感激

- Thanks. You are very kind. 謝謝，你真是好心。
- I'm thankful to you for all this help.
  我要感激你所幫的忙。
- Thank you very much indeed.
  真是謝謝你。

這樣說不禮貌
Leave me alone! You can't do anything about it.
走開！ 你什麼忙也幫不了。

How come you look prettier and prettier every day?
你怎麼愈來愈漂亮？

Word Power!
· compliment
  [`kɑmpləmənt] **n** 讚美
· sweet [swit] **a** 溫柔的
· make sb.'s day **phr**
  讓某人一整天都開心
· flatter [`flætɚ] **v** 奉承

Sentence Power!
· How come...? 怎麼會…？

- Thanks for your compliment. 謝謝你的讚美。
- Really? Thank you very much. 真的嗎？太感謝你了。
- Thanks. It's very sweet of you. 謝謝，你真是貼心。
- Thank you. You made my day.
  謝謝。你會讓我一整天都開心不已。

這樣說不禮貌
Don't flatter me.
別奉承我。

Do you mind if I help you wash your car?
你介意我幫你洗車嗎？

Word Power!
- grateful [ˈɡretfəl]
  a 感謝的
- stay away from...
  phr 與⋯保持距離

Sentence Power!
- Do you mind if I...? 你介意我做⋯？
  →此句型為要做某事前的婉轉說法。

- Of course not. Thanks a lot! 當然不會。太感謝了！

- Not at all! I appreciate it. 一點也不！我很感激。

- No. I'm very grateful to you.
  不介意，真是感激不盡。

- Are you sure? Thank you anyway.
  你確定嗎？總之謝啦。

這樣說不禮貌

I do! Stay away from my car please.
非常介意！請遠離我的車。

Thanks for helping my sister find her way home. Would you have supper with me?
謝謝你幫我妹妹找到回家的路，我能邀你共進晚餐嗎？

Word Power!
- supper [ˈsʌpɚ] **n** 晚餐
- pleasure [ˈplɛʒɚ]
  n 喜悅
- unfortunately
  [ʌnˈfɔrtʃənɪtlɪ]
  ad 不幸地

Sentence Power!
- It's my pleasure. 這是我的榮幸。

- I would love to have dinner with you. 我非常願意。

- It is very kind of you. But no, thanks.
  你人真好，但不用了。

- It's my pleasure. 榮幸之至。

這樣說不禮貌

Thanks. But unfortunately I have no time.
謝謝，但我實在沒時間。

Thank you for carrying my bag for me. Is it heavy?
謝謝你幫我提購物袋。袋子重嗎？

Word Power!
- carry [ˈkærɪ] **v** 提；帶
- heavy [ˈhɛvɪ] **a** 重的
- lady [ˈledɪ] **n** 淑女
- gentleman [ˈdʒɛntlmən]
  n 紳士
- light [laɪt] **a** 輕的
- strong [strɔŋ] **a** 強壯的
- a piece of cake
  phr 小事一樁。

- Helping ladies is what a gentleman should do. 幫助女士是紳士該有的行為。

- No ,It's light to me. 不累，對我來說很輕。

- Don't worry, I'm strong. 別擔心，我很強壯的。

- It's a piece of cake for me. 這對我來說是小事。

2 虛擬實境口說練習
on your iMessenger
從最簡短到最豐富，讓你實際和老外練習口說和聽力

| 當某人因為某事向你表示感謝時 |

❶ You're very welcome!
你太客氣了！

> more than 太過
> extremely 過度
> totally 真是太

❷ Don't mention it.
不用提了。

> worry about 擔心
> think about 想多
> consider 細想

❸ It's not a problem.
這不是什麼大問題。

> nothing 沒什麼
> no big deal 不是什麼大事
> not an issue 不是問題

| 當你為了某事要向某人表示感謝時 |

❶ Thanks so much!
真的非常感謝！

> a million 十萬分的
> very much 真的很
> a lot 非常

❷ You're the best!
你是最棒的！

> my hero 我的英雄
> my savior 我的救星
> such a big help 我的一大助力

| 當你建議某人應該向對方表示感謝時 |

❶ You had better thank him/her.
你最好謝謝他／她。

> ought to 應該要
> probably should 或許應該
> would be wise to 聰明的話就要

❷ A little thank you will go a long way.
小小的謝謝就很受用了。

> is all he/she needs to hear
> 是他／她唯一需要聽到的
> is enough 足夠
> will be plenty 很多

❸ People will think you are a bad person if you don't thank them.
如果你不謝謝他們，人們會覺得你是個壞人。

> have no manners 沒有禮貌
> are uncouth 沒有教養
> are selfish 很自私

| 當你詢問其他人是否該向某人表示感謝時 |

❶ Should I thank him/her for the gift?
我應該謝謝他的禮物嗎？

> compliment 讚美
> good news 好消息
> help 幫助

❷ Do I need to thank him/her for such a small thing?
我應該為了一點小事謝謝他／她嗎？

> Must I 我一定要
> Would it be the right thing 是正確的事
> Is it necessary to 我需要

3 虛擬實境網路聊天
on your iMessenger

在手機或電腦上，利用打字就可以聊出千言萬語

Bonnie

星期三 下午 13:45

Dear,
You know, I'm really grateful to be working among some of the most talented people in this industry.

下午 13:45

I wish I could say the same about the people in my company.

下午 13:46

Whassup?

下午 13:48

My boss is one of the nicest guys out there.
But the problem is,
When it comes to selecting employees, he's clueless.

下午 13:49

下午 13:50

A lot of people in my company are slackers!
They procrastinate because they are very irresponsible.

下午 13:51

親愛的，你知道，我很高興能夠跟業界最有才能的其中一些人一起工作。

在…之中
有才華的
產業

但願我公司裡的同事也能帶給我同樣的感覺。

公司

怎麼了？
What's up 的簡寫

我們老闆是一個最好心的人，但問題是，當我們談到挑選工作伙伴時，他完全一無所知。

當提到…
一無所知的

我們公司裡有許多人都很沒有責任感，愛混水摸魚，又老愛拖延時間。

偷懶的人
拖延
不負責任的

Bonnie

星期三 下午 13:45

Oh, that's terrible.
下午 13:53

下午 13:53

I'm sorry to hear that.
But I'm sure there are some
coworkers who are dedicated to
their work like you!
下午 13:55

Thank you~
I just hope one day the boss
realizes that he's losing
money by employing these
people, and fires them!
下午 13:56

這真是太糟了。

我很遺憾聽到這樣的
事。但是我相信一定
還是有一些同事跟你
一樣對工作盡心盡
力！
同事
對⋯有貢獻

謝謝你～我只是希望
老闆有一天能了解到
這些人一直讓他虧錢，
然後把他們給開除！
明白

聊天金句大補帖

Is that so? 真的嗎？

這句的用法跟意思與

• Really?

是大同小異的。對於別人提出的任何話題我們都可以用這句話
來回應，除了可以繼續發展話題外，也可以表示你對於對方所
說的事情感興趣。

Chapter
5

Unit 1 請多多指教

Unit 2 小資族的第二個家

Unit 3 您好請問哪裡找

Unit 4 恭喜恭喜恭喜你呀

Unit 5 神仙打鼓有時錯

Unit 6 愛神來了怎知道

Unit 1 請多多指教

What do you do for a living?
你是做什麼工作的？

- I'm a teacher in a junior high school. 我在一所中學當老師。
- I have been an accountant for almost 12 years. 我當了快十二年的會計師。
- In fact, I don't have a stable job. 事實上，我並沒有穩定的工作。
- I am an engineer. 我是一名工程師。

Word Power!
- living [ˈlɪvɪŋ] n 生計
- junior high school phr 國中
- accountant [əˈkauntənt] n 會計師
- engineer [ˌɛndʒəˈnɪr] n 工程師

更多…
職業萬花筒
- astronaut 太空人
- chef 廚師
- lawyer 律師
- nurse 護士

Do you get along with your colleagues?
你和你的同事處的還好嗎？

- Yes, my colleagues are friendly. 是的，我的同事都很好。
- No, it's hard for me to get along with my colleagues. 對於我來說，跟同事友好相處很難。
- I try to keep a distance between my job and personal life. 我試著在工作和私人生活間劃清界線。

Word Power!
- colleague [ˈkɑlig] n 同事

Sentence Power!
- It's hard for sb. to... 對某人來說很難…
- keep a distance between...and... 與…保持一段距離

這樣說不禮貌
Some of them are difficult to work with.
有些人真的很難共事。

How many people are there in your family?
你家有多少人？

- There are three people in my family. My parents and I. 我家有三個人，父母和我。
- I live with my parents and my wife. My parents retired last year. 我和父母親還有老婆住一起，我父母親去年已經退休。
- I live with my mother. I'm the only child. 我跟媽媽住一起，我是獨生子（女）。

Word Power!
- parent [ˈpɛrənt] n 雙親
- retire [rɪˈtaɪr] v 退休
- only child n 獨生子（女）

更多…
都是一家人
- twin 雙胞胎（之一）
- sibling 兄弟姊妹
- cousin 表兄弟姊妹
- great-grandparents 曾祖父母

What kind of jobs do you like ?

你喜歡什麼樣的工作？

- I prefer to work indoors. 我喜歡室內的工作。
- I am an outgoing person. so I like to work outside. 我是一個外向的人，因此我喜歡室外工作。
- I like venturesome jobs. 我喜歡具冒險性的工作。
- I want to be a police officer so that I can help people. 我想成為一名警察，這樣我才可以幫助人民。

這樣說不禮貌
I don't want to do any jobs.
我什麼工作也不想做。

Which city do you want to work in?

你想在哪個城市工作？

- The big apple. I've always wanted to work in a big city. 大蘋果（紐約）。我一直想在大城市工作。
- I want to work in a small town. 我想在一個小鎮工作。
- I dont like working in a metropolis. 我不想在大都會區工作。
- I want to work in the foreign country. 我想在國外工作。

Can you fix me up with a full-time job?

你可以幫我安排一份全職工作嗎？

- Have you had any experience? 你有工作經驗嗎？
- Does a gardener's job appeal to you? 園藝工作你感興趣嗎？
- Is it a permanent job you're after? 你要找固定工作嗎？
- Sorry, there is no full-time job available. 對不起，沒有全職工作了。

2 虛擬實境口說練習 on your iMessenger　從最簡短到最豐富，讓你實際和老外練習口說和聽力

▎當你的朋友告訴你他將來想從事的工作是什麼時 ▎-------------------------

❶ **Whichever field you work in, I know you will be successful!**
不論你在哪個領域工作，我知道你一定會成功的！

area 地區
department 部門
country 城市

❷ **That sounds like a great career choice.**
那聽起來是個不錯的職業選擇。

job opportunity 工作機會
career prospect 職涯前景
work environment 工作環境

❸ **Do you really see a future for yourself in that career?**
你真的在這個職業中可以看到自己的未來嗎？

yourself succeeding 自己的成功
long-term potential 長期的潛力
yourself making enough money 讓自己溫飽

▎當你的朋友請你介紹工作給他時 ▎-------------------------

❶ **I'll see if there are any openings at my company.**
我會看看我們公司是否有任何職缺開放。

available jobs 工作可做
potential spots 可能的職務
employees planning to leave 員工要離職

❷ **Have you checked for jobs online?**
你有在網路上先看過工作了嗎？

in the classifieds 分類廣告上
in other cities 其他城市
at a job center 就職中心

| 當你告訴某人你現在從事的行業時 |

❶ **I'm working part-time until I finish university.**
我打零工直到我大學畢業為止。

while I am in university 在我讀大學時
for the time being 作為暫時的工作
in order to have more free time
是為了要有更多空間的時間

❷ **I'm an assistant sales manager at a clothing company.**
我在服飾公司擔任助理銷售經理。

steel 鋼鐵
toy manufacturing 玩具製造
cosmetics 化妝品

❸ **I work in the accounting department of a multinational company.**
我在一家跨國公司的會計部門工作。

human resources 人力資源
legal 法務
marketing 行銷

| 當你被問到關於工作上的情況時 |

❶ **My work is quite monotonous.**
我的工作相當單調無聊。

interesting 有趣
a handful 麻煩
important 重要

❷ **Work has been so hectic recently!**
我的工作最近變得非常忙亂！

since the merger 自從公司合併後
the past month or so 這幾個月來
ever since I received a promotion 自從我升職後

3 虛擬實境網路聊天
on your iMessenger

在手機或電腦上，利用打字就可以聊出千言萬語

CEO group(6)

星期三 下午 13:45

Jenny joins the group.

Jenny, this is our CEO group. Miss Kate and others, let me introduce you Jenny, the representative from the company abroad.

下午 13:45

珍妮，這是我們公司的執行長小組。凱特小姐及各位，這位是珍妮，客戶公司從海外派來的代表。

代表
海外的

Nice to meet you all.
Hello, dear Miss Kate.
Your company has done many great things for this industry.

下午 13:46

很高興認識你們。你好，親愛的凱特小姐。貴公司對這個產業有許多貢獻。

很高興認識你

下午 13:48

Call me Kitty plz.
I'm glad you took the time to come all the way here to visit us.

下午 13:48

請叫我凱蒂，同時很感謝你大老遠到這兒來進行參訪。

Please 的簡寫
老遠地來

下午 13:49

I'm really honored to be here.

下午 13:51

能夠到這兒來，我真的倍感榮幸。

榮幸的

Don't be so humble!

下午 13:52

別這麼客氣！

謙虛的

CEO group(6)

星期三 下午 13:45

下午 13:53

 I've heard about how you closed the Johnson's deal back in March.

下午 13:54

Thank you very much, but I couldn't have done it without the support of my team.

下午 13:55

I like a woman who's humble and doesn't hog all the credit. Let's welcome Jenny again!

下午 13:56

下午 13:57

我已經聽説三月份的時候你是怎麼解決強森那項交易了。
聽說

謝謝，要是沒有我的團隊的幫忙，我不可能成功。
支持

我欣賞謙虛且不獨佔功勳的人。我們再次歡迎珍妮！
霸佔
功勞

聊天金句大補帖

Let me help you with... 讓我幫你…
當我們看到他人有需要幫助的地方，而我們又有能力及時提供幫助時，這句話可以簡潔明瞭地讓對方知道自己願意且能夠幫助他。"with"的後面通常只能加名詞。

Unit 2 小資族的第二個家

Why are you late to the office?
為什麼你上班遲到呢？

- The traffic was too crowded this morning. 今早路上大塞車。
- I helped my neighbor to the hospital. 我送鄰居去醫院看病。
- My car broke down on the way to office. 來上班的路上，我的車壞了。
- My clock stopped. 我的鬧鐘停了。

不能不會的小技巧
在職場上，若是毫無理由並經常性的遲到，不僅會讓上司感到不滿，更有可能使你的形象大打折扣。

Word Power!
- late to phr 遲到
- neighbor [`nebɚ] n 鄰居
- hospital [`hɑspɪtl] n 醫院
- on the way to... phr 要去⋯的路上

Can you check the form for me please?
你可以幫我檢查一下這張表格嗎？

- Sure I can. 當然可以。
- Absolutely. What is wrong with the form? 當然。表格有什麼問題嗎？
- I'm awfully sorry. But I'm in a hurry right now. 真的很抱歉，可是我正在趕時間。

Word Power!
- form [fɔrm] n 表格
- absolutely [`æbsəˌlutlɪ] ad 絕對地
- awfully [`ɔfulɪ] ad 非常地
- complicated [`kɑmpləˌketɪd] a 複雜的

這樣說不禮貌
That looks complicated. Maybe you should ask someone else.
看起來有點複雜。也許你該問問別人。

Is there something on your mind?
你在想什麼？

- I'm thinking how to figure this problem out. 我在想該怎樣搞懂這個問題。
- No, I'm just tired. 沒有，我只是累了。
- I'm considering our staff travel plan. 我在思考我們的員工旅遊計畫。
- I miss my cat. She passed away last night. 我好想我的貓，她昨晚過世了。

Word Power!
- on sb.'s mind phr 某人想著或煩惱著某事
- consider [kən`sɪdɚ] v 考慮
- staff [stæf] n （全體）員工
- pass away phr 過世

這樣說不禮貌
There's none of your business.
不關你的事。

Why did the manager yell at you?

為什麼經理對你大吼？

- I made a mistake on an important document. 我在一份重要的檔案上犯了錯誤。

- We lost the customer due to my fault. 由於我的失誤，我們失去客戶。

- I forgot to attend the meeting. 我忘記參加會議。

這樣說不禮貌

Who knows? The manager is too emotional.
誰知道？經理太情緒化了。

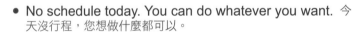

What is today's schedule?

今天的行程是什麼？

不能不會的小技巧
提醒自己的主管行程時，時間一定要正確確實，行程的內容及重點也要一併告知。告知他人行程時，語氣一定要堅決並果斷，切勿表現疑惑或不確定以致於誤導。

- No schedule today. You can do whatever you want. 今天沒行程，您想做什麼都可以。

- You have a meeting with the financial department at 3pm. 您今天下午三點要和財務部開會。

- You have a flight to Shanghai to attend the summit conference. 您要飛一趟上海參加高峰會。

How is the meeting going?

會議進行怎麼樣？

- We're discussing the scheme with others. 我們正與同事討論這個方案。

- The chairman is making a conclusion at the end of meeting. 主席在會議結束時總結發言。

- It will be ended in five minutes. 五分鐘後結束。

這樣說不禮貌

Hush! The president is giving a speech.
小聲點！總裁正在發言。

2 虛擬實境口說練習

on your iMessenger

從最簡短到最豐富，讓你實際和老外練習口說和聽力

┃ 當你詢問同事公司會議的日期時 ┃ --------------------------------

❶ Remind me when our next sales meeting is.
下次銷售會議時提醒我。

company-wide 全公司
interdepartmental 各部門
mandatory 例行

❷ Is our meeting with the Japanese clients tomorrow or next week?
我們和日本客戶的會議是明天還是下週呢？

the following day 接下的幾天中
this afternoon 今天下午
Thursday 星期四

❸ When did you schedule the interdepartmental meeting for?
各部門的共同會議你是排何時呢？

What day 哪一天
What time 什麼時間
How long 多久

┃ 當你詢問上司是否能請假時 ┃ --------------------------------

❶ Would it be possible for me to take a day off next month?
請問我下個月有沒有可能請一天假呢？

some leave 幾天假
some time off 幾個時間的假
a vacation 一段假期

❷ I need tomorrow off so I can go to the doctor.
我明天必須請假才能去看醫生。

visit my sick father 探望我生病的父親
file my taxes 申報稅務
register my son at his new school
帶我兒子到新學校報到

| 當當你要向新同事介紹環境時 |

❶ The break room is over there.
茶水間在那邊。

> bathroom 浴室
> communal kitchen 公用廚房
> copier 影印機

❷ You will be sharing an office with two other employees.
你會和另外兩名員工共享一間辦公室。

> a workspace 一個工作空間
> a desk 一張桌子
> your work 你的工作

❸ This is where you will be working.
這裡就是你之後工作的地方。

> sitting 坐
> answering the phone 接電話
> set up 安頓

| 當老闆問你工作做完了沒時 |

❶ Have those reports finished tomorrow.
明天請完成這些報告。

> case files 案件檔案
> sales documents 行銷文件
> order forms 訂購表格

❷ I see you've been swamped and haven't been able to finish.
我看你忙得不可開交而且還沒完成。

> super busy 超級忙碌
> running around 跑來跑去
> out of the office 離開辦公室

3 虛擬實境網路聊天
on your iMessenger

在手機或電腦上，利用打字就可以聊出千言萬語

Evelyn Wang

星期三 下午 13:45

 What's with all those empty cubicles?

下午 13:45

這些空隔間是做什麼用的？
小隔間

下午 13:45

That is the PR, or Public Relations department. Maybe everyone's either off to an early lunch, or out relating with other companies.

下午 13:46

那裡是 PR 部門，也就是公關部門，所有人不是提早去吃午飯，就是和其他公司接洽去了。
關係
使用聯繫

 IC. What about over there? Near the entry.

下午 13:47

我懂了，那邊呢？靠近入口那。

That's HR, Human Resources department. Where all the hiring and firing happens. Let's meet some of the staff here at this company later.

下午 13:48

那是 HR 部門，所謂的人事部門，決定員工的錄用或解雇。我們等下來見見公司其他人員吧。
資源

 Who are we going to meet?

下午 13:49

我們要見誰呢？

There's the Board of Directors

下午 13.50

董事會的成員們。
董事會

Evelyn Wang

星期三 下午 13:45

They're responsible for going over all the major decisions made by the CEO.
And the vice president, who's in charge when the CEO's on vacation
Lastly,

下午 13:51

他們要負責審查執行長所做的決策。還有副總裁，凱蒂休假期間都是由他代理職務。最後，

副的
負責
度假

More?
That's a lot of people to meet before lunch.

下午 13:52

還有？我看吃午飯前得拜會很多人哩。

The managers of the different departments along with their assistant managers.

下午 13:53

還有各部門的經理及其副理。

部門
輔佐的
經理

下午 13:54

Don't worry so much~ It'll be fine.

下午 13:55

別擔心啦～會很順利的。

聊天金句大補帖

Don't worry about it. 別擔心

這句通常出現在別人要向你道謝或覺得麻煩到你的時候，你希望別人不要放在心上或不用為你擔心，就會告訴別人這句話。此外，

• No problem.

也很常用在類似的情境中。

Unit 3

您好請問哪裡找

一定要會的問答句

90% 的老外都是用這些句子開始聊天。

Can I speak to Lucy?
請問露西在嗎？

- Yes, this is Lucy speaking. 我就是露西。
- Who's this please? 請問你是哪位？
- Hold on, please. Lucy is in the restroom. 等一下，露西去洗手間。
- She left just now. Please call back later. 她剛出去，請等下再撥。

Word Power!
- speak [spik] **v** 説
- just now **phr** 剛才

Sentence Power!
- Can I speak to...? 我找…
- This is...speaking. 這裡是…；我就是…
- Hold on. 等一下

Can I leave a message?
我能留個言嗎？

- Sure. Please hold on. 當然可以。請等一下。
- Please hold the line. Let me find a pen. 請別掛斷。讓我找支筆。
- Yes, I'm listening. 好的，請説。

Word Power!
- leave [liv] **v** 留下
- message [`mɛsɪdʒ] **n** 訊息
- hold the line **phr** 別掛斷

這樣說不禮貌

Please call back in an hour. I have no time right now.
請一個小時後再回電。我現在沒時間。

I'm afraid you have the wrong number.
恐怕你打錯電話了吧。

- Oh, isn't this Mike? I am so sorry. 喔，你不是麥克嗎？真對不起。
- I don't think so. The number I dialed is 5555-0000. 不會吧，我剛是撥 5555-0000。
- Come again, please? 可以再説一次嗎？

不能不會的小技巧

一旦確認打錯電話的一方是自己，則跟對方道歉，不需要感到難為情或過度抱歉，但態度要溫和，並對佔用對方時間表示歉意。

Word Power!
- have the wrong number **phr** 打錯電話
- dial [`daɪəl] **v** 撥

這樣說不禮貌

What did you say? 你説什麼？

The manager is not available at the moment.
經理現在沒空。

- Oh, sorry. I'll call back later. 喔，對不起，我等一下再打。
- Can I contact him this afternoon? 今天下午和他聯繫可以嗎？
- What time could I reach him? 什麼時候可以和他聯絡上呢？
- Could you take a message for me? 那你可以幫我留個話嗎？

不能不會的小技巧
代接電話的人態度一定要有耐心，除了告知對方要找的人暫時無法接電話以外，也可以問問對方是否需要留言，若有必要，可以留下對方的聯絡方式及公司行號，待對方要找的人回座位時，可以立刻回電。

Word Power!
- at the moment
  phr 暫時
- contact ['kɑntækt]
  v 聯繫
- reach [ritʃ]
  v 與…取得聯繫

Hello, is this Jamie?
你好，是傑米嗎？

- Speaking. 我就是。
- This is Jamie speaking. 我就是傑米。
- No, this is Claire speaking. 不是，我是克萊兒。

Sentence Power!
- What's up 怎了？
  →這個用法屬於比較隨性的說法，若在一般正式場合中最好少用。

這樣說不禮貌

Yes, what's up?
是的，有什麼事嗎？

What do you want?
你要幹嘛？

Did I have any phone calls?
有沒有我的電話？

- I don't know. I was absent then.
  我那時不在。所以我不知道。
- Miss Chao called and asked you to call her back. 趙小姐來電並請你回電。

Word Power!
- phone call n 電話
- absent ['æbsn̩t]
  a 缺席的
- call sb. back
  phr 回電給某人

這樣說不禮貌

How should I know?
我怎麼知道？

I'm not sure. Maybe.
我不確定。也許吧。

2 虛擬實境口說練習

on your iMessenger

從最簡短到最豐富，讓你實際和老外練習口說和聽力

|當你接到一通要找同事的電話時|

❶ You're looking for my co-worker, not me.
你應該是要找我的同事，不是我。

> colleague 同事
> assistant 助理
> manager 經理

❷ Wait a moment, and I'll transfer you to my coworker.
稍等一下，我會幫你轉接到我同事那邊。

> Hold on 等等
> One second 等我一下
> Hang on a minute 稍等一分鐘不要掛斷

❸ I'm sorry, but you have dialed the wrong extension.
我很抱歉，但你打錯分機了。

> Apologies 抱歉
> Terribly sorry 非常抱歉
> I hate to tell you 我很不想這麼說

|當你的同事告訴你剛剛有人來電找你時|

❶ Someone called for you while you were out.
有人在你出去時打給你。

> on the other line 接別的電話
> at lunch 用午餐
> using the restroom 去廁所

│當你現在不方便講電話時│

❶ I'm a bit busy. Can I call you back?
我現在有點忙，可以再回撥給你嗎？

> ring you later 等下打給你
> phone you another time 找時間再打給你
> return your call another time 找時間回撥給你

❷ Now is not really a good time to talk.
現在不是一個恰當的時間談話。

> to chat with you 和你聊天
> for me to be on the phone 講電話
> for me to take your call 接你的電話

❸ I don't have time to talk with you right now.
我現在沒時間和你講話。

> am unable 無法
> can't use my phone 不能用我的手機
> don't have enough time 時間不夠

│當你打電話給對方，對方卻不在時│

❶ Can I leave a message for him/her?
我可以留言給他／她嗎？

> give you a message 請你幫我留言
> leave a voicemail 留聲音訊息
> ask you to write a message down 請你寫個訊息

❷ Oh, do you know when he/she will be back?
哦，那你知道他／她何時會回來嗎？

> return 回來
> arrive 抵達
> be available 有空

3 虛擬實境網路聊天
on your iMessenger

在手機或電腦上，利用打字就可以聊出千言萬語

Nerdy

星期三 下午 13:45

Guess what!
下午 13:45

你猜發生什麼事！

下午 13:46

**I was in the break room
And I noticed the girls gathered together chatting with one another
Just as I walked in on them, they started giggling.
I think one of them likes me!**
下午 13:47

我在茶水間的時候，注意到一群女孩正聚在一塊兒聊天。當我走進去時，她們就開始咯咯地笑不停。我覺得一定是她們其中有人喜歡我！

茶水間
聚集
聊天
咯咯地笑

Trust me, it's not what you think. They're probably giggling about something else.
下午 13:49

相信我，才不是你想得那樣。她們一定是為了其他的事在竊笑。

下午 13:48

Why do you have to rain on my parade?
下午 13:50

你為什麼一定要掃我的興？
潑…冷水

Nerdy

星期三 下午 13:45

Take it EZ~ Man!
All I'm saying is: don't get
your hopes up.
They maybe were just carrying
on a regular conversation.

下午 13:52

放輕鬆點～老兄！我只是說：不要抱太大的希望，她們可能是在聊一些稀鬆平常的事。

`easy 的簡寫`
`進行`
`正常的`

 Or they could be talking about me.

下午 13:53

或者，她們也有可能正聊到我啊。

Not today, anyway.

下午 13:54

反正不會是今天啦。
`反正`

 And just exactly why not?

下午 13:55

那到底為什麼不會？
`確切地`

Cuz you have a trail of toilet
paper coming out of your pants!

下午 13:56

那是因為你的褲子後面拖著一條衛生紙啊！
`拖、曳`
`廁所衛生紙`

下午 13:57

聊天金句大補帖

Rome wasn't built in a day. 羅馬不是一天造成的

這句話在中文就常常聽到，其實就是從英文直翻過來的。人如果要有所成就總是需要時間經驗的累積，只要努力，假以時日一定可以成功。不過這句話也常被用來開玩笑，記得注意場合使用哦！

Unit 4

恭喜恭喜恭喜你呀

Congratulations on getting a job.
恭喜你找到工作。

Word Power!
- congratulation [kənˌgrætʃəˈleʃən] n 祝賀
- owe to phr 歸功於
- find out phr 得知

- Thanks a lot. 非常謝謝。

- Thanks. But I owe it to your help. 謝謝，不過這都多虧了你的幫忙。

- Thanks. It's what I have looked forward to for a long time.
謝謝，這是我期望已久的事了。

這樣說不禮貌
Uh, how did you find out that I got a new job?
呃，你怎麼知道我找到新工作的？

Best wishes. Happy birthday.
祝你生日快樂。

- Thank you. It's very kind of you. 謝謝，你對我真好。

- Thank you. I like your present very much. 謝謝我很喜歡你的禮物。

- Thanks. Can I invite you to join the party? 謝謝，我能邀請你參加我的生日宴會嗎？

- The same to you. I remember your birthday is also today. 你也是。我記得今天也是你的生日。

不能不會的小技巧
各個國家的人過生日時都有不同的習俗。在英國，小孩子生日時會在學校被抓住手腳舉起來，代表希望快快長高；在美國，也有從墨西哥傳入的打破皮納塔的習俗。皮納塔是一種色彩鮮艷的玩偶，通常是馬或牛的形狀，裡面則塞滿糖果。

Word Power!
- present [ˈprɛznt] n 禮物
- same [sem] a 同樣的

I have good news. I just got promoted.
告訴你一個好消息，我剛剛升職了。

Word Power!
- promote [prəˈmot] v 升遷
- fabulous [ˈfæbjələs] a 極好的

- Really? Congratulations! 真的嗎？恭喜呀！

- Fabulous! Let's make a party for you.
太好了！我們來開慶祝會吧。

- Good for you. 那太好了。

這樣說不禮貌
It should have been me.
我才應該被升職。

Could you attend my wedding?
你能參加我的婚禮嗎？

Word Power!
- wedding [ˈwɛdɪŋ]
  n 婚禮
- get married phr 結婚
- marriage [ˈmærɪdʒ]
  n 婚姻
- for the world phr 無論
  如何；怎樣也…

- Oh, my god. You are getting married. Congratulations! 喔，天啊。你要結婚啦，恭喜你。
- Best wishes to your wedding. But, sorry, I can't. I have something important to do. 祝賀你新婚快樂。但抱歉我無法參加。我有重要的事要辦。
- Many, many congratulations on your marriage. 恭賀你們喜結良緣。
- I won't miss it for the world. 我絕不會錯過的。

Have you heard about the football game? We won!
你聽到足球比賽的結果了嗎？我們贏了！

不能不會的小技巧
當你聽到對方球隊贏球時，最有禮貌的作法就是微笑表達喜悅。當然，若你支持的是不同球隊，也要秉持運動家精神，千萬不要做出挑釁的言論或動作。

Word Power!
- hear about phr 得知
- deserve [dɪˈzɝv]
  v 應得

- Yeah! We deserve to win! 好耶！勝利是我們應得的！
- What an exciting game! 比賽真是太刺激了！
- I must congratulate you. 我一定恭喜你！
- It's about time for us to win. 也該是我們贏球的時候了。

I got the first place in the sales competition finally!
這次銷售競賽我終於得了第一名！

Word Power!
- first place phr 第一名
- competition
  [ˌkɑmpəˈtɪʃən] n 競賽
- congratulate
  [kənˈgrætʃəˌlet] v 恭喜
- success [səkˈsɛs]
  n 成功
- pay off phr 回報
- fantastic [fænˈtæstɪk]
  a 極好的
- excellent [ˈɛksḷənt]
  a 傑出的

- Let me congratulate on your success. 恭喜你榮獲第一名。
- Your hard work has finally paid off. 認真工作終於有收穫了。
- Fantastic! I'm so proud of you. 太棒了！我真以你為榮。
- I'd like to be the first to congratulate you on your excellent performance. 我要為你的出色表現表示祝賀。

181

2 虛擬實境口說練習
on your iMessenger
從最簡短到最豐富，讓你實際和老外練習口說和聽力

| 當你祝賀朋友的人生大事時 |

❶ Congratulations on finally getting that promotion!
恭喜你終於升遷了！

> that new job 得到那份新工作
> that house you wanted 得到那間你想要的房子
> married 結婚

❷ You did it! You started a family!
你做到了！你組成一個家庭了！

> finished school 完成學業
> moved to Canada 搬到加拿大
> became a manager 成為經理

❸ I'm so happy you graduated that I could cry!
我太替你的畢業感到高興以致於我要哭了！

> kiss you 想親吻你
> dance for joy 都要跳起來了
> die 要死了

| 當你祝賀朋友找到工作時 |

❶ I knew you would find a good job.
我就知道你會找到一份好工作。

> was confident 對…有信心
> had no doubts 毫不懷疑
> was worried when 之前有擔心

❷ Congratulations on landing a new job!
恭喜新工作就職！

> getting 找到
> finding 找到
> being hired for 錄取

| 當你祝賀朋友獲獎時 |

❶ Great job on getting third place in the singing competition.
唱歌比賽拿到第三名做的太好了。

> runner up 第二名
> grand prize 大獎
> a participation award 參加獎

❷ Congrats on winning the tennis tournament.
恭喜你贏得網球錦標賽。

> speech contest 演講比賽
> lottery 樂透
> science fair 科展

❸ You really deserved that bonus.
你真的值得得到那份獎金。

> earned 賺到…了
> worked hard for 為了…很努力
> waited a long time for 為…等了許久

| 當你祝賀朋友出院時 |

❶ I'm just so relieved to hear that you're feeling better.
聽到你好一點後我就放心了。

> excited 高興
> overwhelmed 被沖昏頭
> overjoyed 狂喜

❷ It's fantastic to hear that you are out of the hospital!
聽到你出院真是太棒了！

> recovering at home 要在家裡復健
> feeling better 覺得好一點
> getting over your sickness 克服你的病

3 虛擬實境網路聊天
on your iMessenger

在手機或電腦上，利用打字就可以聊出千言萬語

Gin

星期三 下午 13:45

Hi
下午 13:45

Hey Gin!
下午 13:46

嗨！金。

U know the newlyweds over in the customer service department? They got a divorce!
下午 13:47

你知道客服部那對新婚夫妻嗎？他們離婚了！
新婚夫妻
離婚

Again?
What was it this time?
Did u know this was the third divorce they're had this month?
And they've only been married for two years.
下午 13:48

又來一次？這次又是什麼事啊？你知道這是他們這個月第三次離婚嗎？而且他們才結婚兩年而已。
第三

I heard them arguing over the coffee machine or something like that.
下午 13:49

我聽說他們好像是在爭吵咖啡機之類的事情。
為⋯爭吵
咖啡機

HEE HEE
下午 13:50

Not again!
You know why they got a divorce last time?
下午 13:51

又來了！你知道他們上一次為什麼離婚嗎？

Gin

星期三 下午 13:45

 Nope.
下午 13:52

The guy used the coffee machine to brew tea and didn't clean it out. And the wife caught him in the act! Just like that, they got a divorce.
下午 13:53

下午 13:54

I can't understand all these people getting divorces nowadays. R they trying to start a trend or something?
下午 13:55

They are not trying to start a trend, I think they're trying to keep up with it~
下午 13:56

不知耶。

先生用咖啡機泡完茶而沒有清乾淨。剛好被老婆捉個正著，就因為這樣，他們倆就離婚了。

煮
清乾淨
逮個正著

我真搞不懂現在這些鬧離婚的人。他們想要引領風潮嗎，還是什麼？

現今
潮流

他們不是想帶動潮流，我覺得他們是想跟上潮流～

跟上

聊天金句大補帖

I can't thank you enough. 真是太謝謝你了

當我們要對別人表達感謝之情，但覺得只說 "Thank you." 並無法讓對方感受到我們的滿懷感激時，可以用這個句子來表示。

185

Unit 5 神仙打鼓有時錯

Sorry that I didn't yield my seat to you earlier.
對不起，這麼晚才讓座給你。

Word Power!
- yield [jild] v 讓於
- about to phr 即將
- completely [kəm`plitlɪ] ad 完全地
- manner [`mænə] n 禮儀

Sentence Power!
- Never mind 沒關係的。
  = Not a bit of it

- That's okay. I'm about to get off the bus. 沒關係。我馬上就要下車了。
- Never mind it. 沒關係。
- I understand completely. 我完全瞭解。

這樣說不禮貌
You young people have no manners at all.
你們年輕人一點禮貌也沒有。

Excuse me. May I interrupt you for a second?
對不起，我能打斷你一下嗎？

Word Power!
- interrupt [ˌɪntə`rʌpt] v 打斷
- limited [`lɪmɪtɪd] a 有限的

- Sure, How may I help you? 當然。有什麼我能幫得上忙的嗎？
- Yes. What's up? 可以，怎麼了呢？
- Yes. Can I help you? 是的，我可以幫你嗎？

這樣說不禮貌
Go on. I'm listening. 你說吧。我在聽了。
Oh, sorry, you can't. My time is very limited. 喔，抱歉，你不能，我沒時間了。

Could you forgive me for being late last time?
你能原諒我上次遲到嗎？

不能不會的小技巧
當自己犯錯，需要請求他人原諒時，態度一定要真誠，堅定，謙遜地請求原諒才是最好的方法。

Word Power!
- forgive [fə`gɪv] v 原諒
- apologize [ə`pɑlə͵dʒaɪz] v 道歉
- all the time phr （在該段時間內）一直

- That's all right. 沒關係的！
- You don't have anything to apologize for. 其實並沒有什麼好道歉的。
- Please don't feel bad about it. 請不要因此而難過。

這樣說不禮貌
Why should I forgive you for being late all the time? 我為什麼要原諒你經常性的遲到。

Don't you find your words a little rude?

你難道不覺得你的話有點粗魯嗎？

Word Power!
- word [wɝd] n 言辭
- rude [rud] a 粗魯的
- offend [əˋfɛnd] v 冒犯
- overlook [ˏovɚˋluk] v 忽略
- rudeness [ˋrudnɪs] n 粗魯
- beg [bɛg] v 乞求
- pardon [ˋpɑrdn] n 原諒
- intention [ɪnˋtɛnʃən] n 意圖
- blame [blem] v 責怪

- Sorry, I didn't mean to offend you. 對不起，我不是有意冒犯你的。
- Please overlook my rudeness. 請原諒我的粗魯。
- I do beg your pardon, but my intentions are good. 請你原諒，我本來也是一番好意的。

這樣說不禮貌
How careless of me! You won't blame me for that, would you?
我真是粗心啊！你該不會為了這個責怪我吧？

Did you lose the magazine I lent you last week?

你是不是把我上星期借你的雜誌給弄丟了？

Word Power!
- lose [luz] v 丟失
- mean [min] v 意圖
- carelessness [ˋkɛrlɪsnɪs] n 粗心大意

- I'm sorry, I really didn't mean it. 對不起，我真的不是故意的。
- Please forgive me. It's entirely my fault. 都是我的錯，請原諒我。
- I hope you will pardon me for my carelessness. 希望你能原諒我的粗心大意。

I've come to apologize. I forgot to call you back last night.

我是來道歉的，我昨晚忘了回你電話。

Word Power!
- urgent [ˋɝdʒənt] a 緊急的
- best [bɛst] n 主要的
- worth [wɝθ] a 有…的價值
  →可接名詞、Ving、to be p.p.
- mention [ˋmɛnʃən] v 提起

- That really doesn't matter. It was not urgent. 沒關係，並不是什麼急事。
- That can happen to the best of us. 誰都會碰到這種事。
- It's nobody's fault. 這不是任何人的錯。

這樣說不禮貌
It isn't worth mentioning, actually. 這其實不值得一提的。

Just don't let it happen again. 下次別再犯了。

2 虛擬實境口說練習
on your iMessenger
從最簡短到最豐富，讓你實際和老外練習口說和聽力

┃ 當你發現忘記別人交代你的事，想要跟他道歉時 ┃

❶ **I totally forgot about that! My bad.**
我完全忘記那件事了！我的錯。

> one hundred percent forgot 完完全全忘記
> must have forgotten 一定是忘了
> seem to have forgotten 看樣子是忘了

❷ **I can't believe I forgot to do that! My apologies.**
我不敢相信我忘記做那件事了！我道歉。

> call you 打給你
> e-mail that document 寄文件給你
> order more tea 點更多茶

❸ **I'm so sorry I spaced out about our plans yesterday.**
我很抱歉我昨天搞不清楚我們的計劃。

> neglected 無視了
> misremembered 記錯
> forgot about 忘記

┃ 當你講話不小心冒犯了別人，想趕快跟他道歉時 ┃

❶ **I don't know what I did to upset you, but I'm sorry.**
我不知道我這樣做會使你生氣，但我很抱歉。

> make you angry 使你生氣
> frustrate you 使你沮喪
> raise your ire 挑起你的怒氣

❷ **Whatever I did, I apologize.**
不管我做了什麼，我道歉。

> I'm sorry 我很抱歉
> I take it back 我收回它們
> I wish I hadn't done it 我希望我沒做過那些

| 當你在工作上犯了錯，要向客戶道歉時 |

❶ I take full responsibility for the problem and would just like to apologize.
我會負起這個問題的全責並且願意道歉。

> error 錯誤
> typo 印刷錯誤
> misinformation 錯誤消息

❷ The delay in shipping your goods is my fault, and I am very sorry.
造成你們的貨物運送延遲是我的錯，然後我感到非常抱歉。

> mistake 錯誤
> bad 錯（不好）
> error 錯誤

❸ I'd like to ask for your forgiveness in the mistake on your order.
我想要要求你的原諒，為了我在你的訂單上犯的錯誤。

> beg 乞求
> pray 祈求

> purchase 所購之物
> confidential document 機密文件

| 當你的朋友因為放你鴿子而向你道歉時 |

❶ You had other plans, huh?
你有別的計劃。是嗎？

> a meeting 一個會要開
> an emergency 緊急狀況
> too much work 太多工作

❷ Are you sorry for ditching me yesterday?
你為了昨天爽約我而感到抱歉嗎？

> forgetting about 忘記
> leaving 離開
> not showing on 沒有出現在…面前

3 虛擬實境網路聊天
on your iMessenger

在手機或電腦上，利用打字就可以聊出千言萬語

Jennifer

星期三 下午 13:45

Hey, let me tell you something suprising.

下午 13:45

嘿，告訴妳一件驚人的事。

下午 13:46

As hard as it is to believe, I was headhunted by a rival company just the other day.

下午 13:47

雖然這很令人難以置信，但是幾天前我們公司的競爭對手想把我挖角過去。

挖角
競爭對手

You're too humble.
Any company would be happy to have you on their staff!

下午 13:48

你太謙虛了，任何公司都會想要你成為他們的一份子的。

lol..thx!

下午 13:49

哈哈哈哈謝啦！

laugh out loudly. 的簡寫

So what happened?

下午 13:50

跟我説發生什麼事。

發生什麼事

Well,
I received an email about an offer for a job from them a few days ago.
I ignored the e-mail, but then I received a phone call from them
They asked me to go to an interview.
I didn't want to go! But I didn't want her to keep bothering me, so
I ended up going.

下午 13:51

幾天前我收到一封電子郵件，提供一個工作機會給我。我沒理會那封信，但後來有個人打電話給我，要我去面試。我並不想去！但又不希望她繼續打擾我，所以還是去了。

無視
面試
打擾
最後以⋯

190

Jennifer

星期三 下午 13:45

I hope you guys met in a public place.

下午 13:52

我希望你們是在公共場合碰面的。
公開的

We met in a café and she introduced herself as a headhunter for the other company.

下午 13:53

我們在一家咖啡館見面，她說她為另一家公司做獵人頭的工作。
獵人頭者

下午 13:54

To make a long story short.
I turned her down and asked her not to look up my information again.

下午 13:55

我就長話短說吧，我拒絕了她，要求她別再搜尋我的個人資料了。
長話短說
拒絕
搜尋

下午 13:56

GJ for U!

下午 13:57

做得好！
good job. 的簡寫

聊天金句大補帖

I hope I didn't offend you. 希望我沒冒犯到你

當我們發現我們的行為或言語似乎可能對他人造成負面的作用或觀感時，我們馬上以這句話來作為彌補，一方面探知是否惹別人不高興，一方面讓對方明白我們並非有意觸犯他人。

Unit 6
愛神來了怎知道

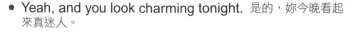

There are so many girls tonight, aren't there?
今晚這兒有很多女孩子，不是嗎？

Word Power!
- charming [ˈtʃɑrmɪŋ] a 迷人的
- attractive [əˈtræktɪv] a 有吸引力的
- loyal [ˈlɔɪəl] a 忠誠的

- Yeah, and you look charming tonight. 是的，妳今晚看起來真迷人。
- Yes, most of them look attractive. 是呀，她們看起來都很迷人。
- Right. But I will stay loyal to my wife. 恩，但我會對我老婆保持忠貞不二。

When was your first love?
你的初戀是什麼時候？

Word Power!
- fall for sb. phr 對…傾心
- secret [ˈsikrɪt] n 秘密
- close [klos] a 親密的

- The first time I fell for someone was in senior high school. 我的初戀是高中的時候。
- Sorry, it is a secret. 對不起，那是個秘密。
- I am not sure if I ever fell in love. 我不確定是否曾經陷入愛河過。

這樣說不禮貌

I don't think we're that close.
我不覺得我們有這麼熟。

What do you think about your date?
你覺得你的約會對象如何？

Word Power!
- company [ˈkʌmpənɪ] n 陪伴
- settle down phr 安頓下來
- some day phr 總有一天
- childish [ˈtʃaɪldɪʃ] a 幼稚的

- He's great. I enjoy his company. 他人很好。我很喜歡有他的陪伴。
- He's my kind of guy. 他是我喜歡的那種人。
- I just might settle down and get married some day. 我可能會跟他定下來，然後結婚。

這樣說不禮貌

I don't think I'll go out with him again. He is too childish!
我想我不會再跟他出去了。他根本是小屁孩！

How do you maintain a romantic relationship as a married couple?
你們夫妻之間的感情如何？

Chapter 5 工蜂嗡嗡嗡

- We treat each other with respect and we never yell at each other. 我們尊重彼此，而且從不對對方大吼大叫。
- My husband always takes me to romantic places. 我老公總是帶我到浪漫的地方。
- We always travel together once a year no matter how busy we are. 不管多忙，我們總是每年會一起旅遊一次。
- My wife always looks at me passionately. 我老婆總是深情地看著我。

Word Power!
- maintain [menˋten] v 維持
- romantic [rəˋmæntɪk] a 浪漫的
- couple [ˋkʌpl̩] n 伴侶
- treat [trit] v 對待
- respect [rɪˋspɛkt] v 尊重
- once [wʌns] n 一次
- passionately [ˋpæʃənɪtlɪ] ad 深情地

What type of love do you think is the most important?
你認為哪種感情最重要？

Word Power!
- type [taɪp] n 型式

Sentence Power!
- What is your idea? 你的想法是什麼？

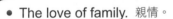

- The love of family. 親情。
- It is a difficult question to answer. 這是一個很難回答的問題。
- Different people have different ideas. 不同的人有不同的觀點。
- What is your idea of love? 你認為呢？

How long have you and your wife been married?
你和你老婆結婚多久了？

Word Power!
- forever [fɚˋɛvɚ] n 永遠
- silver [ˋsɪlvɚ] a 銀色的
- jubilee [ˋdʒublɪ] n （尤指二十五週年、五十週年等的）紀念

- Over ten years now, and our marriage will go on forever. 超過十年了，而我們將會一如既往的走下去。
- It's our silver jubilee now. 我們現在是銀婚。
- Our relationship is still going well. 我們的婚姻依然美滿。

這樣說不禮貌

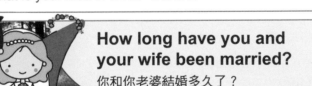

I can't believe I've been married to that crazy woman for three years. 我真不敢相信我和那瘋婆娘結婚三年了。

2 虛擬實境口說練習
on your iMessenger

從最簡短到最豐富，讓你實際和老外練習口說和聽力

| 當你詢問朋友的感情生活時 |

❶ How are things with you and your mister/missus?
你和你的男／女主人過得如何？

> husband/wife 丈夫／妻子
> boy/girlfriend 男／女朋友
> partner 伴侶

❷ Are you and your boy/girlfriend getting along alright?
你和你的男／女朋友相處得還好嗎？

> doing 過得
> feeling 感覺
> connecting 聯絡

❸ What's new with you and your boy/girlfriend?
你和你的男／女朋友有什麼新消息嗎？

> up 發生
> going on 發生
> the word 承諾

| 當你告訴朋友你想追一個女生時 |

❶ If I don't get a girlfriend soon, I'm going to go crazy!
我如果不趕快交個女朋友，我會發瘋的！

> lose my mind 瘋掉
> give up 放棄
> go mad 生氣

❷ All my life is missing right now is someone to share it with.
我的人生目前唯一的缺憾就是一個可以與我分享生活的人。

> a partner 一個伴侶
> a better half 一個好的另一半
> a boy/girlfriend 一個女／男朋友

| 當你和朋友說你和妻子的相處時 |

① Our marriage is quite rocky right now.
我們的婚姻目前相當的困難重重。

amazing 令人吃驚
difficult 困難
unfulfilling 令人不滿足

② My wife and I have been fighting constantly.
我和我的妻子最近很常吵架。

arguing 爭執
at each other's throats 互相攻擊
together 在一起

③ Don't let anyone tell you that marriage is easy!
別讓任何人告訴你說婚姻很簡單！

Don't believe for a second 一秒都別相信
Never think 別認為
You're naive if you think 你如果覺得⋯就太天真了

| 當你的朋友請你幫忙他求婚時 |

① I want you to hide and take pictures when I propose to my girlfriend.
當我和我女友求婚時，我要你躲起來並幫我拍照

surprise us 給我們驚喜
play music 放音樂
sing 唱歌

② The plan is for you to record the proposal.
這個計劃就是你幫我錄求婚影片

The idea is 想法就是
What I need is 我需要的就是
I would like 我會希望

3 虛擬實境網路聊天
on your iMessenger

在手機或電腦上，利用打字就可以聊出千言萬語

Robin W.

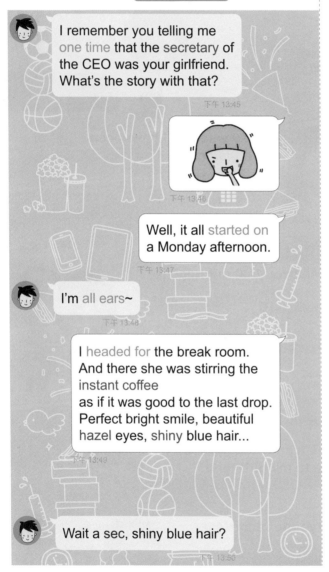

星期三 下午 13:45

I remember you telling me one time that the secretary of the CEO was your girlfriend. What's the story with that?

下午 13:45

下午 13:46

Well, it all started on a Monday afternoon.

下午 13:47

I'm all ears~

下午 13:48

I headed for the break room. And there she was stirring the instant coffee as if it was good to the last drop. Perfect bright smile, beautiful hazel eyes, shiny blue hair...

下午 13:49

Wait a sec, shiny blue hair?

下午 13:50

我記得有一次你告訴我執行長的祕書是你的女朋友。你們的故事是怎麼開始？

有一次

祕書

這個嘛，就要從某個星期一的下午開始說起。

開始於

我洗耳恭聽～

全神貫注地聽

我走到休息室去，她就站在那兒，攪拌著即溶咖啡，看起來好像那是一杯美味無瑕的咖啡。她有著完美的燦爛笑容、美麗的淡褐色眼睛以及光澤動人的藍色頭髮…

前往

即溶咖啡

榛果色的

閃亮的

等等，光澤動人的藍色頭髮？

second 的簡寫

Robin W.

Oh, it was Halloween and everyone was dressed up. Anyway, moving on,

下午 13:51

下午 13:52

I grabbed a bagel, knelt down in front of her, and asked her to marry me.
She wore the bagel on her ring finger and said to me,
"Where's the cream cheese?"
We broke into laughter then.

下午 13:54

OMG!!!

下午 13:55

It was smooth sailing from then on.

下午 13:56

喔，那天是萬聖節，大家都化妝打扮了。總而言之，往下說吧，

盛妝打扮
繼續

我拿起了一個貝果，跪在她面前，問她是否願意嫁給我。她把貝果戴在無名指上，對我說：「奶油乳酪醬在哪兒呢？」然後我們就發出很大的爆笑聲。

跪下
笑聲

我的天！

從此以後一切都順利進行至今。

從那時至今

聊天金句大補帖

Easier to say than done. 說得倒容易

在談話當中，倘若對方提出了一個天馬行空或不切實際的想法，而你認為不可行時，就可以用這句話來表達。不過這句話必須視當時情境來使用，以免冒犯了別人。

Chapter

6

令人食指大動

Unit 1 卡好位才有得吃

Unit 2 燈光美氣氛佳

Unit 3 吃飯也有潛規則

Unit 4 趕時間也要吃

Unit 5 台灣最美的風景

Unit 6 最方便的好鄰居

Unit 1

卡好位才有得吃

Do you prefer a smoking or a non-smoking area?

您較喜歡吸菸區還是禁菸區？

- A non-smoking area, please. 禁菸區，謝謝。
- A smoking area will be great, I'm a smoker. 吸菸區好了，我會抽菸。
- Both are fine. Thank you. 都可以。謝謝。
- I can't stand the smell of cigarettes. I prefer a non-smoking area. 我受不了菸的味道。我偏好禁菸區。

不能不會的小技巧
在預訂座位時，店員若是沒有主動告知是否要吸菸或禁菸區的話，也可以主動告訴他，你想要指定坐在怎樣的座位哦！

Word Power!
- non-smoking area
  n 禁煙區
- area [ˈɛrɪə] n 區域
- stand [stænd]
  v 忍受；站
- smell [smɛl] n 氣味
- cigarette [ˌsɪgəˈrɛt]
  n 香菸

How many seats do you need?

您需要幾個位置？

Word Power!
- adult [əˈdʌlt] n 成年人
- get back to sb.
  phr 之後再回覆

- Two adults, and two children under three-years old, please. 兩位大人，和兩位三歲以下小孩，謝謝。
- Just two, my wife and I. 只有兩個，我和我老婆。
- I need about five seats for my family. 我們家的話大概五位。
- Let me check and get back to you. 我查查看再告訴你。

All tables are booked.

所有的桌位都被預訂了。

Word Power!
- once [wʌns] conj 一旦
- look for phr 尋找
- arrange [əˈrendʒ]
  v 安排
- regular [ˈrɛgjələ]
  a 經常性的

- What a pity! 太可惜了！
- I can wait, please let me know once there's a table available. 我可以等，若有空位的話請儘快告知。
- Well, I guess I will look for another restaurant. 好吧，我想我只能去找另一家餐廳了。

這樣說不禮貌

Couldn't you arrange one more table? I'm a regular guest.
你不能再多安排一張桌子嗎？我是常客耶。

What is the dress code?
建議穿著什麼樣的服裝？

Word Power!
· dress code
　phr 服裝規定
· casual [`kæʒʊəl]
　n 便裝
· sandal [`sændl] n 涼鞋
· tuxedo [tʌk`sido] n【美】
　（男士無尾半正式）
　晚禮服
· cocktail dress
　phr 酒會禮服
· attire [ə`taɪr]
　n 服裝；衣著

- Casual. Please do not wear shorts or sandals. 便服即可。請勿穿著短褲或涼鞋。

- Formal, please. Men wear tuxedos, women wear cocktail or long dresses. 請著正式服裝。男士穿著晚禮服，女士穿著雞尾酒洋裝或是晚宴長洋裝。

- Cocktail attire. Men wear dark suits and women wear short, elegant dresses. 雞尾酒服。男士穿著深色西裝，女士穿著優雅的短洋裝。

這樣說不禮貌
Just don't act like a barbarian.
不要像個野蠻人就好。

Do you prefer a window table?
你想要一張靠窗的桌子嗎？

Word Power!
· window table n 靠窗
　的座位／桌子
· choice [tʃɔɪs] n 選擇
· sunburn [`sʌn,bɝn]
　n 曬傷

- It is the best choice. 那可是再好不過了。

- No, I'm afraid of getting sunburned. 不用，我怕曬。

- Of course, that's very romantic. 當然了，那樣很浪漫的。

- Sure. A window table will be better. 當然。靠窗的桌位比較好。

這樣說不禮貌
How about a table by the bathroom?
還是要坐廁所旁邊？

What kind of centerpiece do you prefer?
你喜歡哪種餐桌擺飾？

Word Power!
· centerpiece [`sɛntɚ,pis]
　n 放在餐桌中央的擺飾
· candle [`kændl]
　n 蠟燭
· gorgeous [`gɔrdʒəs]
　a 豪華的
· tacky [`tækɪ] a【美】
　俗不可耐的

- Some roses will be great. 一些玫瑰花就很棒。

- Anything gorgeous is great, please. I want everything to be perfect. 任何華麗的都可以，我要一切都很完美。

- I want some candles on the table. 我想要桌子上放些蠟燭。

- I will ask my girlfriend. 我問問我女朋友。

這樣說不禮貌
No centerpiece! It's so tacky.
不要餐桌擺飾！太俗氣了。

2 虛擬實境口說練習
on your iMessenger

從最簡短到最豐富，讓你實際和老外練習口說和聽力

| 當你要打電話向餐廳訂位時 |

❶ Yes, I'd like a table for two at eight o'clock tonight.
是的，我想訂兩人的座位，今晚八點。

> to reserve a table 訂位
> to know if there is a table 知道是否還有座位
> to book a private table 預訂私人座位

❷ Can I reserve a table for next Monday?
請問下周一我可以訂位嗎？

> book 訂
> make a reservation for 預約
> ask if there is 問是否還有

❸ Do you have any four-person tables available tonight?
請問你們今晚還有四人的座位嗎？

> Are there 請問還有
> Would you happen to have 請問你們…是否剛好有
> Can you tell me if there are 可以請你告知我…是否有

| 當餐廳打給你確認訂位資訊時 |

❶ I'm calling to double-check that you reserved a table at our restaurant tonight.
我打來是要再次確認您今晚有預約本餐廳的桌位。

> confirm that 確認
> make sure that 確定
> see if 看看…是否

❷ Did you book a table at our restaurant for tonight?
您今晚是否有預約我們餐廳的座位呢？

> for eight 八人
> by the kitchen 廚房區
> with an ocean view 海景

| 當你有特殊要求要先向餐廳提出時 |

❶ I'd like to book a table near the kitchen, please.
我想預訂靠近廚房的座位，麻煩你。

> if possible 如果可以的話
> if I can 如果可以的話
> thanks 謝謝

❷ We've got a little one, so could you prepare a booster seat for us?
我們有一位小朋友，所以可以麻煩你準備兒童椅給我們嗎？

> young child 小孩
> an infant 嬰兒
> a toddler 還不會走的小孩

❸ Because it's my husband's/wife's birthday, I'd like you to prepare a small cake.
因為當天是我丈夫／妻子的生日，我想請你們幫我準備一個小蛋糕。

> classmate's 同學的
> boss's 老闆的
> crush's 暗戀對象的

| 當餐廳問你是否有特殊需求時 |

❶ Are you vegetarian or vegan by any chance?
您有可能是吃蛋奶素或純素嗎？

> allergic to anything 對哪種食物過敏
> a picky eater 不吃哪種特定食物
> a new diner 第一次來用餐

❷ Do you have any food allergies we should know about?
請問您有對哪項食物過敏是我們必須知曉的？

> to tell us 需要告知我們
> that you know about 您已經知道的
> we need to consider 我們需要考慮到的

3 虛擬實境網路聊天
on your iMessenger

在手機或電腦上，利用打字就可以聊出千言萬語

Hannah

星期三 下午 13:45

 Tell me about what you feel in this country these days!

下午 13:45

跟我說說你在這城市的幾天裡覺得如何吧！

城市

這幾天

Sure!

下午 13:46

好啊！

下午 13:46

The one thing I love about this place so much is the assortment of foods from different cultures. What's more is that they are all close by and easily accessible! I don't have to drive half an hour to Chinatown to get Chinese food or another hour to get to little Saigon. And they are all delicious~

下午 13:48

這個地方有一點讓我很喜愛，那就是有許多異國美食。更棒的是這些地方都很近，很容易吃到！我不用開半個小時的車去中國城買中國菜，或者再多開一個小時到小西貢去。而且這些東西全都很美味～

可接近的

近

可取得的

 When it comes to eating, you just don't stop.

下午 13:49

一談到吃，你就停不下來。

當說到…

Why should I? There are so many foods to try yet so little time.

下午 13:50

我幹嘛得停下來呢？有這麼多好吃的東西，可是時間卻不夠。

但是

Hannah

星期三 下午 13:45

下午 13:51

Well, what have you had here so far?

下午 13:52

I've had Thai food.
You got to try the shrimp cakes, they were so good!
I've also tried Vietnamese food.
Oh, how delicious the soup noodles with grilled pork chops were!
And I shouldn't need to tell you about Chinese food.
It is so cheap as well!

下午 13:54

Alright, alright!
I'm fully understand how much you love it here!

下午 13:55

到目前為止，你吃過哪些東西呢？

到目前為止

我吃過泰國料理，你一定得吃蝦餅，太好吃了。還有越南食物，喔，那美味的又燒湯麵。至於中國食物我想就不需要跟你多說了，而且也很便宜。

蝦子

越南的

烤的

好了好了！我已經充分了解妳有多愛這個地方了！

聊天金句大補帖

I hate to say it, but... 我實在不想這麼說，但是…

當我們想要表達一個意見或者闡述一件事時，但這個意見或事實可能是趨向於負面的陳述時，為了緩和接下來所說的情境帶給對方尷尬、不適或負面的感覺，我們就可以說這句。

Unit 2 燈光美氣氛佳

Does the restaurant serve Korean food?
這裡的飯店有供應韓國菜嗎？

- For more than that, French and Italian cuisine are also served here. 不止這些菜，法國菜和義大利菜也很普遍。
- Yes, Korean food is very popular here. 是的，韓國菜在這非常流行。
- Not really, since it's a Chinese restaurant. 沒有，因為這是一家中國餐廳。

Word Power!
- serve [sɜv] v 供應
- cuisine [kwɪˈzin] n 菜餚
- since [sɪns] conj 因為

Sentence Power!
- more than that 不只這樣

更多…
各國料理大車拼
- taco 墨西哥捲餅
- tamale 墨西哥粽子
- nan 印度烤餅
- panna cotta 義式奶酪

Are you ready to order?
可以點餐了嗎？

- Yes, please. 好的，麻煩你。
- I have no idea. Could you give me some recommendations?
我也不知道，你能介紹一些嗎？
- Not yet. I'm still waiting for my friend.
還沒。我還在等我朋友。

Word Power!
- recommendation [ˌrɛkəmenˈdeʃən] n 推薦

這樣說不禮貌

Just wait for another minute.
再等一會吧。

Do you feel like starting with some appetizers?
你想從一些開胃菜開始嗎？

- Fine, what kind of appetizers do you have? 可以啊，你們這有哪些開胃菜？
- I want some drinks first, please. 我想先來一些飲料，麻煩你。
- I'd rather skip the appetizers. 我比較想跳過開胃菜。
- Thai style seafood salad sounds great. 泰式海鮮沙拉聽起來不錯。

不能不會的小技巧
在歐美，餐廳的習慣一般是先從開胃菜開始，然後是沙拉、熱湯和主菜，最後上餐後甜點及飲料。當然隨個人喜好，可以直接點主菜，沒有硬性規定要按照以上順序點菜。

Word Power!
- appetizer [ˈæpəˌtaɪzə] n 開胃菜
- skip [skɪp] v 跳過
- seafood [ˈsiˌfud] n 海鮮

Can you recommend some delicious dishes?
你能推薦一些好吃的菜嗎？

- Our steak is very juicy. 我們的牛排非常棒。
- Well, which kind of dish do you like? 那你喜歡什麼類型的菜？
- You have to try our Boston lobsters. 你一定要試試我們的波士頓龍蝦。
- We are famous for our strawberry cheese cake. 我們以草莓起司蛋糕而聞名。

這樣說不禮貌
You can look at the menu.
你可以看看菜單。

How would you like your steak to be cooked?
您的牛排要幾分熟？

更多…
牛排愛裝熟
- raw 生的
- rare 一分熟
- medium-rare 三分熟
- medium 五分熟
- medium-well 七分熟
- well-done 完全煮熟的

- Between medium-well and well-done. 八分熟好了。
- I want it medium-rare, please. 三分熟，謝謝。
- What's your advice? 你建議多熟？
- Well-done would be better. 全熟好了。

What's your favorite Chinese dishes?
你最喜歡哪道中式菜餚？

- All kinds of them. Like carp in sweet and sour sauce. 所有菜，比如像糖醋鯉魚。
- Fish-flavored pork shreds are the best. 最喜歡魚香肉絲。
- Spicy diced chicken with peanut is irresistible. 宮保雞丁令人難以抗拒。

這樣說不禮貌
Nothing. Such as twice cooked pork slices, is so terrible to me.
沒有，比如回鍋肉讓我覺得太難吃了。

2 虛擬實境口說練習
on your iMessenger

從最簡短到最豐富：讓你實際和老外練習口說和聽力

| 當服務生要向你推薦菜色時 |

❶ **You can't go wrong with our chef's special pasta.**
選擇我們的主廚特製義大利麵就不會錯。

won't do better than 是最棒的
ought to order 是一定要的
should try 你應該試試

❷ **Our special for this evening is a rack of lamb.**
我們今晚的特餐是羊排。

a poached bass 清蒸鱸魚
pasta with a cheese sauce 起司醬義大利麵
chicken cooked in red wine 紅酒煮雞肉

❸ **Our guests all seem to love our sushi.**
我們的客人似乎都很喜愛我們的壽司。

adore 極喜歡
go nuts for 為…而瘋狂
order 都會點

| 當你想向服務生提出特殊要求時 |

❶ **Could you bring us a pitcher of water for the table?**
可以請你幫我們拿一壺水到我們的桌子來嗎？

another menu 另一份菜單
some more napkins 更多餐巾紙
the check 帳單

❷ **Is it possible to turn down the music? It's quite loud.**
請問可否將音樂關掉呢？相當地大聲耶。

annoying 惱人
distracting 使人分心
terrible 可怕

當你要請服務生幫你點餐時

❶ **Which salad would you recommend?**
你推薦哪一種沙拉？

entrée 主餐
appetizer 開胃菜
side dish 配餐

❷ **I'm having trouble deciding what to order. What do you recommend?**
我在決定要點什麼時遇到困難。你推薦哪個？

choosing 選擇
finding 找
picking 選

❸ **I want to know what you would order.**
我想知道你會點什麼。

Tell me 告訴我
Let me know 讓我知道
You have got to tell me 你一定要告訴我

當你在結帳時

❶ **You accept credit cards here, right?**
你們可以用信用卡結帳，對吧？

don't you 不是嗎
correct 正確嗎
yeah 是吧

❷ **Was a service charge added to the bill?**
服務費有被加在帳單中了嗎？

put on 加進
included in 包含在
part of 當成…的一部分

3 虛擬實境網路聊天 on your iMessenger 　在手機或電腦上，利用打字就可以聊出千言萬語

Naomi

星期三 下午 13:45

Everywhere I see food stands that sell all kinds of intriguing foods.
But I don't dare sit down at any of them.
Because I'm not sure if they are sanitary><...

下午 13:45

我到處都看到那些賣著各種誘人美食的小吃攤，但我都不敢坐下來，因為我不確定他們是否衛生…

到處
引起興趣的
敢於
公共衛生的

下午 13:46

Food stands are definitely a part of Asian culture.
They have been around for the longest time, and even though the government tries to get rid of these vendors, their popularity just never dies.

下午 13:48

小吃攤自然是亞洲文化的一部分囉。他們的歷史悠久，即使政府試圖掃除這些攤販，他們依舊屹立不搖。

政府
擺脫
人氣

But…
How do you know if they're clean?

下午 13:50

但你怎麼知道他們乾不乾淨？

Well,
An important factor is to see if the business at the food stand is good.
Good business means their food is fresh and delicious.

下午 13:51

這個嘛，有一點很重要的是看看那個攤販的生意怎麼樣。好的生意通常意味著他們的食物新鮮而且味道可口。

因素
生意

Naomi

星期三 下午 13:45

 I notice sometimes that the price for the food at these food stands...
It is dirt-cheap! How good can it get?

下午 13:52

Well~
You'd have to taste for yourself.

下午 13:53

下午 13:54

 Alright! I've made up my mind to get stinky tofu, oyster omelet, bubble milk tea as well.

下午 13:56

Bon appetite!

下午 13:57

有時候我會注意到這些小吃攤的價格，便宜得嚇人！這麼便宜能有多好吃呢？

嗯，你得自己親身品嚐。
品嚐

好吧！我決定我要試試臭豆腐、蚵仔煎、還有珍珠奶茶。

祝你胃口大開！

聊天金句大補帖

Bring your appetite! 帶著你的食慾來吧！
當我們邀請他人前來做客或前往一個地方享用美食時，為了表示我們的殷勤，可以用這句話來讓對方感受到我們的誠心與熱情。

Unit 3 吃飯也有潛規則

一定要會的問答句

90% 的老外都是用這些句子開始聊天。

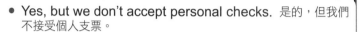

Do you accept credit cards?
你們接受信用卡付款嗎？

- Yes, but we don't accept personal checks. 是的，但我們不接受個人支票。

- Yes, but our system has been malfunctioning recently. 是的，但我們的系統最近有點毛病。

- Sorry, we accept cash only. 抱歉，我們只收現金。

不能不會的小技巧
現在大部分餐廳都接受信用卡付款，但最好還是事先詢問，以免造成身上現金不夠的窘境。

Word Power!
- accept [ək`sɛpt]
  v 接受
- credit card **n** 信用卡
- check [tʃɛk] **n** 【美】支票
- malfunction [mæl`fʌŋʃən] **v** 故障
- cash [kæʃ] **n** 現金

Did you give the gratuity to the waiter in the restaurant?
你有給餐廳服務生小費了嗎？

Word Power!
- gratuity [grə`tjuətɪ]
  n 小費
- tip [tɪp] **n** **v** 小費；給小費
- custom [`kʌstəm]
  n 習俗

- Oh, I forgot it. Thank you for reminding me. 哦，我忘了。謝謝你提醒我。

- In Taiwan, we don't give tips.
  在台灣，我們不給小費。

- Of course, 6 dollars.
  當然，我給了六美元。

這樣說不禮貌

I'm a foreigner, I don't know the custom.
我是外國人，不知道這個習慣。

Why do you give so much of a tip to the bartender?
你為什麼給酒保那麼多小費？

Word Power!
- bartender [`bɑr͵tɛndə]
  n 酒保
- bright [braɪt] **a** 明亮的
- Gin&Tonic **n** 琴湯尼（調酒名）
  →琴酒加通寧汽水及檸檬調製而成

更多…
微醺的夜晚
- martini 馬丁尼
  →琴酒加苦艾酒
- margarita 瑪格麗特
  →龍舌蘭酒加橙酒、檸檬汁、鹽巴

- Just because I am having a good time tonight. 原因是我今晚很愉快。

- Because he gave great service. 因為她服務很好。

- I like her smile, so bright. 我喜歡她的微笑，很燦爛。

- Well, he makes the best Gin & Tonic. 他調的琴湯尼超好喝。

Why didn't you receive a gratuity?
你為什麼沒收小費？

Word Power!
· worthy [ˈwɝðɪ]
  a 有價值的
· leave [liv] v 留給
· complain [kəmˈplen]
  v 抱怨
· spill [spɪl] v 使濺出
  →動詞三態為：spill-spilt-spilt
· laptop [ˈlæptɑp]
  n 筆電

Sentence Power!
· can't stop... 無法停止做某事
  → + Ving

● Because I made some mistakes, I am not worthy enough to get it. 因為我出了點錯，我不該拿。

● Because the customers didn't leave any gratuity. They couldn't stop complaining about the food. 因為客人沒留小費。他們不斷抱怨餐點。

● I didn't think I should because I spilt coffee on customer's laptop. 我覺得不該收小費，因為我把咖啡灑在客人的筆電。

How much gratuity did you get from that man?
那人給你多少小費？

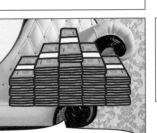

Word Power!
· abundant [əˈbʌndənt]
  a 豐收的
· stingy [ˈstɪndʒɪ]
  a 小氣的

● 20 dollars. What an abundant day!
二十美元。真是大豐收耶！

● 20 percent of his bill.
帳單金額的百分之二十

● Not much, really. 沒有很多，真的。

這樣說不禮貌

3 dollars. What a stingy customer.
三美元。真是小氣鬼。

How do you think about this phenomenon of gratuity?
你怎麼看待小費這種現象？

Word Power!
· phenomenon
  [fəˈnɑməˌnɑn] n 現象
· waitress [ˈwetrɪs]
  n 女服務生
· habit [ˈhæbɪt] n 習慣
· common [ˈkɑmən]
  a 平常的

Sentence Power!
· get used to... 漸漸習慣於…

● Waiters and waitresses should get it for their labor.
這是服務生提供服務應得的。

● Waiters shouldn't get it because they get paid by the restaurants. 服務員不該收小費，因為他們有工資呀。

● Different countries have different habits.
不同的國家有不同的習慣。

● It's very common. 很正常。

這樣說不禮貌

Taiwanese people could never get used to it. 台灣人永遠不會習慣這個的。

2 虛擬實境口說練習
on your iMessenger

從最簡短到最豐富，讓你實際和老外練習口說和聽力

┃當你問某人當地給小費的方式是什麼時┃

❶ **Who do you normally tip here?**
你們這裡一般來說會給哪些人小費？

often 經常
usually 通常
never 都不

❷ **What is the average tip for a meal at a restaurant?**
平均餐廳吃一頓飯的小費是多少？

the normal 一般
a good 一間好的
the necessary amount to 必須給

❸ **Should I add the tip to the bill or leave some cash on the table?**
我應該要把小費加進帳單，還是留現金在桌上？

total 總額
check 帳單
amount 總價

┃當你收到客人給的小費時┃

❶ **Thank you so much, sir/ma'am. You're too kind!**
非常謝謝您，先生／女士。您人真好！

You've made my day
您給了我美好的一天
You're the nicest 您真是最好的一位
Have a great day 祝您有個美好的一天

❷ **I greatly appreciate your tip.**
我非常地感謝您的小費。

truly 真心地
sincerely 誠心地
deeply 深深地

| 當你告訴朋友此地給小費的習慣是如何時 |

❶ It's normal to tip around 20% at restaurants in the US.
美國餐廳大都給差不多兩成的小費。

> about 大約
> up to 最多
> no less than 至少

❷ Pretty much everyone working in a service job here expects a tip.
幾乎每個在這邊做服務業的人都會期待有小費。

> should get 希望得到
> will ask for 會要求
> will demand 會要

❸ Don't ask if someone wants a tip. Just give it to them!
別去問對方是否需要小費。給他們就是了！

> hand it to 拿給
> pass it to 遞給
> leave it for 留下來給

| 當你和朋友聊到剛剛給小費的過程時 |

❶ The taxi driver who took me to the airport was over the moon when I tipped him.
我剛剛給載我去機場的計程車司機小費時，他欣喜若狂。

> so thrilled 興奮極了
> beside himself with joy 極度開心
> more than happy 超級高興

❷ I didn't know Americans tipped for everything!
我不知道美國人原來每件事都要給小費耶！

> all of the time 任何時候都
> incessantly 持續不停地
> so much 這麼多

3 虛擬實境網路聊天
on your iMessenger

在手機或電腦上，利用打字就可以聊出千言萬語

Eva Chen

星期三 下午 13:45

You know one thing I like about dining in this area?

下午 13:45

你知道我為什麼喜歡在這一帶用餐嗎？
用餐

下午 13:46

If you don't leave a tip, no one looks at you funny.

下午 13:47

要是你沒在桌上留下小費，沒有人會用訕笑的眼光看你。
好笑的

That may be true most of the time~
But if you go to a fancy restaurant, they do expect tips.

下午 13:48

大多數時候也許是這樣～不過要是到比較高級的餐廳，他們會要求收小費。
昂貴的

That reminds me of one thing.
I was in one of those theme restaurants.
When I got the check, I found out that the tip had already been added!

下午 13:49

這讓我想起一件事，有一次我去了一家主題餐廳。當我拿到帳單時，我發現他們已經把服務費算進去了。
提醒
主題餐廳

下午 13:50

Coming from a culture that usually doesn't expect tips, I felt cheated.

下午 13:51

在我們的文化裡面我們通常不會將小費算進帳單，因此我有被騙的感覺。
欺騙

Eva Chen

星期三 下午 13:45

For those restaurants which charge tips automatically, the waiters and waitresses must share their tips with the owner. And considering that their salary isn't exactly very high, the tips are an important part of their income.

下午 13:53

Look what you've done!
You've made me feel bad for them.

下午 13:54

Don't feel too bad, just leave a tip.

下午 13:56

下午 13:57

那些主動將服務費算進帳單的餐廳而言，大多數時候服務生的小費都得跟老闆分帳，而且他們的薪水也都不太高，所以小費對他們而言還蠻重要的。

收取
自動地
收入

看看你幹了什麼好事，現在你讓我為那些服務生感到難過了。

感到難過

別這麼難過，留下小費就是了。

留下

聊天金句大補帖

You'd be surprised. 你會很驚訝

當我們有絕對的把握説出來的事實會引起對方驚訝時，我們就可以説這句。意思是「等等要説的事情，説出來你會被嚇到，所以要有心理準備哦！」如果換成是你聽到這句話，也要小心哦！

Unit 4
趕時間也要吃

How may I help you?
有什麼可以為你效勞的嗎？

- I want to get some snacks. 我想來點點心。
- Are snacks served here? 這裡有供應點心嗎？
- I want to get a cup of root beer float. 我想要一杯漂浮沙士。
- A hot dog with everything. 一份熱狗，配料要全加。

Word Power!
- snack [snæk]
  n 快餐；小吃，點心
- root beer n 沙士
- float n 上面浮有冰淇淋的飲料

更多⋯
- popcorn 爆米花
- churros 吉拿棒
- fish and chips 炸魚薯條

Is it for here or to go?
在店內用餐還是外帶呢？

- Give me a second. I think I'll have it here. 等我一下。我想我在這吃好了。
- For here, please. 在這吃，謝謝。
- I want to have it here. 我想在這吃。
- It's better to go. 外帶好了。

Word Power!
- helmet [ˈhɛlmɪt]
  n 安全帽。

Sentence Power!
- For here or to go?
  內用或外帶？

這樣說不禮貌

Can't you see I'm wearing a helmet right now? To go, of course.
你沒看到我戴著安全帽嗎？當然是帶走。

Do you feel like upgrading your drinks and fries?
你想升級你的飲料和薯條嗎？

- Yes. please. 是的，請幫我加大。
- No, thank you. It will be too much.
  不，謝了。那樣會太多。
- That is a must. 那是一定要的。

Word Power!
- upgrade [ˈʌpˈgred]
  v 升級
- fries [fraɪz] n 薯條
  → French fries 的簡稱
- must [mʌst] n 必要的東西

這樣說不禮貌

No! Do I look like I'm be able to eat that much?
不！我看起來可以吃那麼多嗎？

Can I use my coupons?
我可以用我的優惠券嗎？

- Certainly. 當然可以。

- Let me check them, please. 讓我查查看。

- Sorry, they're out of date. 對不起，已經過期了。

- Yes, but there are no changes for your coupons.
  可以，但如果使用優惠券的話不找零。

這樣說不禮貌

They've been expired. Can't you read them?
這些已經過期了，沒看到上面有寫嗎？

Can I have extra cream cheese for the bagel?
我的貝果可以多加一份奶油起司嗎？

- Sure you can. 當然可以。

- Well, this is the last one.
  呃，但這是最後一個了。

- Sure. Ten dollars, please.
  可以，要再加十元。

這樣說不禮貌

No. One cream cheese per bagel. It's the rule.
不。一個貝果配一份奶油起司。這是規定。

Of these two drinks, which one do you like more?
這兩種飲料你喜歡哪一種？

- The red one. 紅色的。

- Neither of them. 兩種都不喜歡。

- I like the blue one. It looks so pretty.
  我喜歡藍色的。它好美。

- They're just not my cup of tea.
  這不是我喜歡的類型。

這樣說不禮貌

They both taste disgusting.
兩種喝起來都好噁心。

2 虛擬實境口說練習
on your iMessenger

從最簡短到最豐富，讓你實際和老外練習口說和聽力

| 當你在得來速點餐時 |

❶ **Yeah, I'd like two hamburger combos with fries and cokes.**
對，我要兩個漢堡，加薯條及可樂套餐。

chicken finger 雞柳
chicken sandwich 雞肉三明治
burrito 墨西哥捲

❷ **Can I get one hot dog, one cheeseburger, and a large chocolate milkshake?**
我可以點一個熱狗、一個起士漢堡、和一個大的巧克力奶昔嗎？

I'd like 我想要
Let me order 讓我點
Give me 給我

❸ **Give me three chicken sandwiches and three iced teas.**
給我三個雞肉三明治以及三杯冰茶。

large cokes 大可
sodas 汽水
popcorns 爆米花

| 當你要打電話叫外送時 |

❶ **I'd like to order two pizzas for delivery, please.**
我想要點兩個披薩，麻煩幫我外送。

to be delivered 要外送
to be sent to my house 送到我家
and for you to bring them to my house
請幫我送到家裡

❷ **About how long will it for take you to deliver to my address?**
送到我這個住址大概要多久？

Approximately how many minutes 大約需幾分鐘
Do you know how long 你知道要多久嗎
How much time 要多久

| 當店員跟你介紹點餐優惠時 |

❶ Would you like to add a drink for just $10 NTD more?
你想要加 10 元加購飲料嗎？

> dessert 甜點
> soup 湯品
> a salad 沙拉

❷ If you pay $50 NTD more, you can get another hamburger!
如果你多付 50 元的話，就可以得到另一個漢堡！

> extra 額外
> on top 再多
> additionally 另外

❸ This month we are doing a buy one get one free special on all desserts.
這個月我們所有的甜點都有買一送一的優惠。

> promotion 促銷活動
> offer 提供
> discount 折扣

| 當你的朋友約你去聊天順便吃東西時 |

❶ Do you want to get dinner and catch up sometime this week?
你這禮拜想抽空一起去吃晚餐和聯絡一下感情嗎？

> one day 找一天
> any day 哪一天
> within 在…內

❷ Are you free tomorrow to get lunch and chat for a bit?
你明天有空去吃午餐和聊個天嗎？

> Are you available 你…可以
> Do you have time 你…有時間
> Would you want to go 你…會想

3 虛擬實境網路聊天
on your iMessenger

在手機或電腦上，利用打字就可以聊出千言萬語

Kelvin King

星期三 下午 13:45

So Tom,
What would you like to eat?

下午 13:45

那麼，湯姆，你想吃什麼？

I don't know~
What's good around here?

下午 13:46

我不知道耶～這附近有什麼好吃的？

Would you like Eastern or Western food?

下午 13:47

你想要東方還是西式料理？

東方的

西方的

Eastern! Of course.

下午 13:48

當然要東方的！

We can have Chinese, Japanese, Korean, or Southeast Asian~

下午 13:49

我們可以吃中國菜、日本菜、韓國菜或者東南亞料理～

Then let's go with Chinese!

下午 13:50

那我們去吃中國菜吧！

You want to order a set meal or noodles and rice dishes?

下午 13:51

你想要吃套餐還是麵飯類？

套餐

下午 13:52

Wow~ So many choices!
Can't you just take me somewhere where they serve good food?

下午 13:52

哇～有這麼多選擇啊！能不能帶我到好吃的餐廳去就好了？

提供

Kelvin King

星期三 下午 13:45

Alright, how about soup noodles?

下午 13:53

下午 13:54

Yeah! I love noodles!
Where are we going to go?

下午 13:55

I know this place that has
the best beef soup noodles!

下午 13:56

I'm so hungry, I could eat a horse!

下午 13:57

Don't worry. It is a supersized meal.
Let's go!

下午 13:56

好的，你想吃湯麵嗎？
麵

當然，我愛麵食。我
們要去吃什麼呢？

我知道有個地方供應
最棒的牛肉湯麵！
地方

我好餓喔，我現在可
以吃下一匹馬。
非常的餓

別擔心，那是一道超
大份的餐點。我們走
吧！

聊天金句大補帖

What do you make of...? 你覺得⋯怎麼樣？

這句話是詢問他人對某事物的看法時比較口語的用語。類似但比較正式的用法有：

• What's your opinion on...?

• What are your thoughts on...?

Unit 5

台灣最美的風景

1 一定要會的問答句

90% 的老外都是用這些句子開始聊天。

What do you think about the night market?
你認為夜市怎麼樣？

- I think it's very good because the goods are very cheap. 我認為很好，因為商品很便宜。
- It is super convenient and the food is delicious. 夜市超方便而且食物很好吃。
- I don't like eating at the night market because public hygiene is my top concern. 我不喜歡在夜市吃東西，因為公共衛生是我最關心的事。

Word Power!
- night market phr 夜市
- hygiene [`haɪdʒin]
  n 衛生
- concern [kən`sɜn]
  n 關心

更多…
來認識台灣小吃
- pig blood cake 豬血糕
- oyster omelet 蚵仔煎
- tofu pudding 豆花
- ba wan 肉圓
- stinky tofu 臭豆腐
- bubble milk tea 珍珠奶茶

Do you usually go to the night market?
你經常去逛夜市嗎？

- Yes, there are so many choices. It's a shopping paradise. 是的，這有好多東西可選。根本是購物天堂。
- Sometimes, but I often go shopping at the department store. 有時候，但我比較喜歡在百貨公司購物。
- I often buy stuff at the night market.
  我經常在夜市買東西。

Word Power!
- paradise [`pærə,daɪs]
  n 天堂
- department store
  phr 百貨公司
- stuff [stʌf] n 東西
- messy [`mɛsɪ]
  a 混亂的

這樣說不禮貌

I never go to there. It's too messy and dirty.
我從來不去夜市。那裡太髒亂了。

Do you think the night market's goods are very expensive?
你認為夜市的商品很貴嗎？

- Yes, the prices are unreasonably high. 是啊，有點高的不合理。
- Not really. Most of the products and food are very cheap. 不。大部分的東西和食物都很便宜。
- I think the government should control the price. 我認為政府應該控制價格。

Word Power!
- unreasonably
  [ʌn`riznəblɪ] ad 不合理地
- product [`prɑdəkt]
  n 產品
- government
  [`gʌvənmənt] n 政府
- control [kən`trol]
  v 控制

Do you know the history of night markets?
你知道夜市的歷史嗎?

Word Power!
- history [ˈhɪstərɪ] n 歷史
- during [ˈdjurɪŋ] prep 在⋯的整個期間
- dynasty [ˈdaɪnəstɪ] n 朝代
- difficult [ˈdɪfəˌkəlt] a 困難的
- delicacy [ˈdɛləkəsɪ] n 美食

- Yes, they have a long history. It actually began during the Sung Dynasty.
  我知道,夜市有很長的歷史了,從宋朝開始。

- Sorry, it is too difficult to me.
  對不起,這對我來説太難了。

> 這樣說不禮貌

Why don't you just enjoy the delicious Taiwanese delicacies without thinking about the history?
你為什麼不好好享受美味的台灣美食就好,別想歷史這些有的沒的。

How much does the cap cost in the night market?
這頂帽子在夜市多少錢?

Word Power!
- cap [kæp] n 鴨舌帽
- appearance [əˈpɪrəns] n 外表
- quality [ˈkwɑlətɪ] n 品質
- imagine [ɪˈmædʒɪn] v 想像

- From its appearance, its quality is ok. Maybe $10?
  從表面來看,品質還行。10 塊嗎?

- I don't know, I am not good at beating down prices.
  我不知道,我不擅長殺價。

- It is very difficult to imagine the prices of the goods at the night market.
  夜市的東西很難估價。

> 這樣說不禮貌

It must be cheap, since it comes from the night market.
既然是夜市的東西,它一定很便宜。

Do you think that society should encourage people to go to the night market?
你認為我們的政府應該鼓勵大家到夜市消費嗎?

Word Power!
- encourage [ɪnˈkɝɪdʒ] v 鼓勵
- explore [ɪkˈsplor] v 開發
- disturb [dɪsˈtɝb] v 使⋯混亂
- opportunity [ˌɑpɚˈtjunətɪ] n 機會

- Sure. It allows foreigners to explore a different culture. 當然。對於外國人來説,夜市提供他們一個體驗不同文化的機會。

- Maybe, but I don't support it. It may disturb the regular market. 也許吧,但我不支持。這可能會導致正規的市場的混亂。

- Yes. It offers more job opportunities.
  是的。因為能提供就業機會。

> 這樣說不禮貌

I guess so. I don't really care about it. 我想是吧。我其實無所謂。

2 虛擬實境口說練習

on your iMessenger

從最簡短到最豐富，讓你實際和老外練習口說和聽力

| 當你向外國朋友介紹台灣夜市時 |

❶ **Night markets are great because they have so much different food.**
夜市因為有很多不同種類的食物所以很棒。

unique 特別的
special 獨特的
delicious 好吃的

❷ **The best place to try stinky tofu in Taiwan is at a night market!**
台灣品嚐臭豆腐最棒的地方就在夜市裡！

pig's blood cake 豬血糕
fried chicken 炸雞
squid 魷魚

❸ **Night markets are a very integral part of Taiwanese life.**
夜市是台灣人生活中不可或缺的一部分。

culture 文化
society 社會
identity 特色

| 當朋友想找你去逛夜市時 |

❶ **Come with me to the night market tonight!**
今晚跟我一起來夜市吧！

Let's go 一起去
Hurry 趕快前往
Take me 帶我去

❷ **I know you want to go to the night market with me.**
我知道你想跟我一起去逛夜市。

together 一起
soon 趕快
this week 這個禮拜

┃當你在夜市為了一件衣服和店家討價還價時┃

❶ **$300 NTD is way too much! I'll give you $200 NTD.**
300 塊太多了！我只會付你 200 塊。

> too expensive 太貴了
> outrageous 太可怕了
> highway robbery 根本搶劫

❷ **I'll pay you $500 NTD for the three shirts.**
這三件襯衫我出 500 塊。

> bag 個包包
> shoes 雙鞋子
> hat 頂帽子

❸ **If you don't reduce your price, I'll go somewhere else.**
如果你不降低價格的話，我就去別的地方買。

> lower your price 降價
> sell it to me cheaper 算我便宜一點
> want to haggle 再砍一點價格

┃當你和朋友聊起你逛夜市的心得時┃

❶ **Although I'm super excited to go to the night market later today, I'm not looking forward to the crowd that will be there.**
我雖然對於等下要去夜市感到很興奮，但也不想看到人山人海。

> dreading 有點擔心
> nervous about 對於…感到緊張
> going to try my best to avoid 會盡我所能避開

❷ **I don't want to go to the night market, but because they have the best barbeque there, I must!**
我不想去夜市，但是如果那兒有最棒的烤肉的話，我一定要去！

> think I will 想我會
> have no other choice 別無選擇只好
> have to 就會

3 虛擬實境網路聊天
on your iMessenger

在手機或電腦上，利用打字就可以聊出千言萬語

Jackson

星期三 下午 13:45

Hey~
Is there anywhere we can go for a late night snack?

下午 13:45

嘿～有沒有什麼地方我們可以去吃消夜的？

任何地方

消夜

I know just the place!
There's a night market nearby.

下午 13:46

我知道有個地方！旅館附近就有一個夜市。

附近的

Really?
What kind of things do they have there?
Is it like a flea market?

下午 13:47

真的嗎？那裡有什麼東西？是像跳蚤市場那樣的地方嗎？

跳蚤市場

下午 13:47

Sort of~
But not really.
Both a night market and a flea market may have things to eat and buy.
Unlike flea markets however,
A night market doesn't start its business until the sun goes down.

下午 13:49

大概是，但不完全一樣。跳蚤市場跟夜市都賣很多吃的跟用的。不過跟跳蚤市場不一樣的是，夜市是直到太陽下山以後才會開始營業。

有點算是

不完全是

不像

Jackson

星期三 下午 13:45

 So what kind of things are there to eat there?

下午 13:50

那那邊有什麼東西可以吃的呢？
種類

Well~
The night market is not a place for a three-course meal
But it's filled with snacks and local traditional foods as well as fusion foods from all over the world.
And there are lots of interesting things to buy.

下午 13:51

夜市裡沒有所謂的正餐，而是賣小吃、道地的傳統食物，也融合了世界各國的美食。還可以買許多有趣的東西。
正式用餐餐點
充滿
和
融合
全世界

下午 13:52

Well, let's get going then!

下午 13:53

那麼我們走吧！

聊天金句大補帖

In my opinion,... 在我看來，…

這句是用以表達自己的看法或想法時，直接了當的開啟話題的一種說法。在對話當中，如果我們想讓對方清楚地知道我們的想法，就可以先以這句作為開始，再接著講出自己的觀點即可。也可以用以下的句子代替：

• My view is that…
• I think that…

Unit 6 最方便的好鄰居

How do you like going shopping in the supermarket?
你覺得在超市購物怎麼樣？

Word Power!
- supermarket [ˈsupɚˌmarkɪt] n 超市
- low [lo] a 低的
- specialty [ˈspɛʃəltɪ] a 專賣店

Sentence Power!
- can't say no to... 無法拒絕…

- I like it. The price is lower than specialty stores.
  我喜歡，超市的價格比專賣店的價格低。

- I can't say no to discounts so I love it very much. 我非常喜歡。我無法拒絕折扣。

這樣說不禮貌
I prefer going shopping at a nicer place.
我比較喜歡去高級一點的地方。

Do you need plastic bags?
你要塑膠袋嗎？

Word Power!
- plastic [ˈplæstɪk] n 塑膠
- necessary [ˈnɛsəˌsɛrɪ] a 需要的

- Yes, please. 要，謝謝。

- Sure. Please give me the largest one. 好。請給我最大尺寸的。

- Can I have a paper bag? 你們有紙袋嗎？

- That's not necessary. Thank you.
  不需要，謝謝。

這樣說不禮貌
Put these in different bags for me.
把這些東西給我放到不同的袋子。

Where can I find the information desk?
在哪兒可以找到服務台？

Word Power!
- information desk n 服務台
- swing door n 旋轉門
- give you a hand phr 幫忙
- cashier [kæˈʃɪr] n 收銀員

- Just around that swing door. 在那個旋轉門附近。

- I'll come and give you a hand. 我可以跟你一起去，幫你的忙。

- Walk along the lockers, then turn right.
  沿著置物櫃一直走，然後向右轉。

這樣說不禮貌
Why don't you ask the cashier?
你為什麼不問收銀員？

What can I do for you?
我可以為你做點什麼嗎？

Word Power!
· dairy product
  n 乳製品

更多…
來去大採購
· frozen food 冷凍食品
· canned food 罐頭食品
· beverage 飲料
· baked goods 麵包蛋
  糕類

- Yes, I'd like to buy a pair of sneakers for my son. 是的，我想為我兒子買一件 T 恤。
- I am looking for the dairy products area. 我在找乳製品區。
- I'm just browsing. 我只是隨便看看。
- I'm here to return this broom. 我來是想退還這件掃帚。

I want to buy a jacket, can you give me some advice?
我想買一件夾克，你能給我一些意見嗎？

Word Power!
· pattern [ˈpætən]
  n 花樣
· youth [juθ] **n** 青年

更多…
穿出自己的 style
· polka dot 圓點花樣
· stripe 條紋花樣
· plaid 格子花紋
· leather 皮革
· denim 單寧（牛仔布）

- Sure. Please follow me. 好，請跟我來。
- Which style do you want? 你想要什麼樣式的？
- This pattern is very popular in youth culture. 這個花樣在少年們之間很流行。
- I think that one suits you. 我想那件夾克會很適合你。

What do you think about the new fabric?
你覺得這種新的布料怎麼樣？

Word Power!
· fabric [ˈfæbrɪk] **n** 布料
· on the whole
  phr 一般來說
· be superior to **phr** 優於
· nylon [ˈnaɪlɑn] **n** 尼龍
· match [mætʃ]
  v 和…相配
· stylish [ˈstaɪlɪʃ]
  a 有型的
· economical
  [ˌikəˈnɑmɪk!] **a** 經濟的

- On the whole, I consider it to be superior to nylon. 大體上來說，它比尼龍好。
- Well, no one can match it on quality. 這個嘛，在品質上它是無可匹敵的。
- It is less stylish. 但是，它看起來不是很好看。
- It is not economical enough. 的確，只是不夠經濟。

2 虛擬實境口說練習 on your iMessenger

從最簡短到最豐富，讓你實際和老外練習口說和聽力

| 當你在超市要找某樣東西時 |

❶ Where can I find laundry detergent?
我可以在哪裡找到洗衣粉？

frozen pizza 冷凍披薩
shrimp 蝦子
the produce 農產品

❷ Which aisle are the condiments in?
調味料放在哪條走道？

What area 哪一區
Which section 哪個區塊
What part of the store 店裡的哪個部分

❸ I'm having trouble finding where the cereal is.
我找不到麥片在哪。

I can't find 我找不到
I'm losing my patience because I don't know
我快因為不知道…而失去耐心
Ask someone 問別人

| 當你找不到超市的出口時 |

❶ Where's the exit to this labyrinth?!
這座迷宮的出口到底在哪？

maze 座迷宮
massive store 個大超市
place 個地方

❷ Can you point me in the direction of the exit, please?
你可以指給我看出口的指示嗎，麻煩你。

Could 可以
Will 會
Would 能

當你的朋友告訴你他要去超市買點東西時

❶ Can you buy some milk for me while you are at the supermarket?
你去超市時可以順便買些牛奶給我嗎？

bread 麵包
butter 奶油
salt and pepper 胡椒鹽

❷ Can I come with you to the supermarket?
我可以跟你一起去超市嗎？

May 能…嗎
Could 可不可以
Is it okay if 如果…好嗎

❸ Would you mind picking some things up for me while you are there?
你會介意去那裡時順便幫我買些東西嗎？

grabbing 帶
getting 拿
buying 買

當你跟家人或朋友說你今天逛超市的收獲時

❶ Ground beef was dirt cheap today, so I bought a whole lot!
牛絞肉今天超級無敵便宜，所以我就買了全部！

super inexpensive 超級便宜
on sale 在特價
discounted 有打折

❷ I stocked up on yogurt today because they were having a big sale.
我囤了一堆優格因為它們今天有大促銷。

bought a lot of 買了許多
got so much 買了太多
purchased a whole bunch of 買了一整堆

3 虛擬實境網路聊天
on your iMessenger

在手機或電腦上，利用打字就可以聊出千言萬語

Luna

星期三 下午 13:45

Explain something to me, Baby.
下午 13:45

有件事我搞不清楚，你跟我解釋一下吧，寶貝。
解釋

Sure thing, whazzup?
下午 13:46

沒問題啊，什麼事？
What's up 的簡寫

**I joined Rita, your manager, the other day for lunch.
And the most interesting thing happened,
She insisted very strongly on paying for the bill!**
下午 13:47

幾天前我跟你們的經理瑞塔一起吃午餐，有趣的事情發生了。她強烈地堅持一定要她買單。
加入
堅持
強烈地
付賬

下午 13:48

I mean, I could understand it if it was a business lunch, but it wasn't!
下午 13:48

如果是為了公事而共進午餐，我可以理解她為什麼這麼做，但那並不是。
商務的

I think that's just the way she shows her kindness to U~
下午 13:50

我想那是她展示好意的方式啦～
好意

下午 13:51

Luna

星期三 下午 13:45

In my opinion,
Although it was a very kind gesture,
It almost seemed as if she was
going to get mad at me if I didn't let
her pay.

下午 13:52

Ohhhhh~ Get used to it.
You're going to see a lot of that
around here.
This gesture goes beyond business.
If you walk into a restaurant, pay
attention to what happens near the
cashier, there's bound to be a fight
over the bill.

下午 13:53

Well, don't you worry.
I'll never fight with you over the bill.
You can pay every time! Haha~

下午 13:54

在我看來，她的舉動是出於好意，但好像要是我不讓她買單，她會非常生氣似的。

表示
好像
生氣的

喔～習慣就好，在這裡你會經常看到這種情況。這種舉動無關乎做生意。當你走進一家餐廳時，不妨注意一下收銀機附近。絕對有一場帳單之爭發生。

超過
注意
收銀機
一定會

別擔心，我永遠不會跟你搶著買單，可以每次都由你付！

爭執

聊天金句大補帖

It slipped my mind. 我都忘了這回事了。

當我們要表達本來應該知道或記住的事情但是卻一時忘了或一時沒想起來時，就可以用這句話來表示。類似的用法還有：

• Oh, I forgot.
• I didn't think of that right away.

Chapter
7

找點樂子吧

Unit 1 購物狂的天堂

Unit 2 唱出閃亮的歌聲

Unit 3 週五電影夜

Unit 4 來點動次動次

Unit 5 瘋狂派對夜

Unit 6 少不了的是祝福

Unit 1 購物狂的天堂

90% 的老外都是用這些句子開始聊天。

When does the department store close?
百貨公司什麼時候停止營業？

- In general, it closes at 11:00 P.M.　一般是晚上十一點停止營業。

- I'm not sure. I think sometime around midnight on weekdays.　我不確定，我想上班日的話大概是半夜吧。

- The department store trades 24 hours a day.　百貨公司二十四小時營業。

Word Power!
- close [kloz] v 關（商店）
- sometime [`sʌm͵taɪm] n 某一時候
- midnight [`mɪd͵naɪt] n 半夜
- weekdays n 上班日

Sentence Power!
- In general,... 一般來說

How are the department store's goods?
百貨公司的商品怎麼樣？

- The quality is very good.　商品品質很好。

- They look fine, but they're not my style.　商品看起來不錯，可是不是我的風格。

- The style is a little out of date.　款式有點落伍。

Word Power!
- out of date phr 退流行

Sentence Power!
- Between you and me. 只有我們兩個人知道

這樣說不禮貌

Between you and me. I never buy anything in this department store.
偷偷告訴你，我從來不在這家百貨公司買東西。

What are you doing in the department store?
你在百貨公司做什麼？

- I'm just shopping around with my friends.　我和我朋友在這裡逛街。

- I'm a marketing supervisor here.　我是這裡的行銷主管。

- I'm a security guard in the department store.　我是百貨公司的保安人員。

- I work here as an elevator girl.　我在這裡當電梯小姐。

Word Power!
- shop around phr 四處逛逛
- marketing [`markɪtɪŋ] n 行銷
- security [sɪ`kjurətɪ] n 安全
- guard [gɑrd] n 守衛
- elevator [`ɛlə͵vetə] n 電梯

How long is the warranty on the product?

這個產品的保固期有多久？

不能不會的小技巧
不論是購買何種產品，一定要向店家詢問保固期限，而且要要求加蓋店章，對自己才有保障。詢問這一類商品的資訊時，一定要得到確切的答案，千萬不要讓店員給予你敷衍或是含糊不清的答案。

- It's generally three years. 通常是三年。
- You can read the manual. 你可以看看說明書。
- I'm sure no more than three years. 我敢肯定不超過三年。
- Sorry, I can't confirm the dates from the manual. 對不起，我從說明書中找不到確切的日期。

Word Power!
- warranty [ˈwɔrəntɪ] n 保固期
- manual [ˈmænjuəl] n 說明書

When was the department store built?

百貨公司是什麼時候建的？

Word Power!
- build [bɪld] v 建造
- ancient [ˈenʃənt] a 古老的
- specific [spɪˈsɪfɪk] a 確切的

- About ten years ago. 大概十年前建的。
- It was built in 2000. 它從 2000 年開始建的。
- It was built when I was ten years old. 我 10 歲時蓋的。
- It's an ancient building, I don't know its specific date. 它是一座古老的建築，我不知道確切的時期。

Can I change the product if I don't like it?

如果我不喜歡，能否換貨？

Word Power!
- on sale phr 特價中
- remain [rɪˈmen] v 保持
- intact [ɪnˈtækt] a 未受損傷的
- within [wɪˈðɪn] prep 不超過

- You can't if you bought it on sale. 如果是打折時購買的就不行。
- Yes, if the product remains intact. 如果商品尚未開封就可以。
- You can change it within seven days. 七天之內可以換貨。

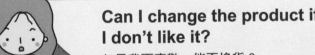

這樣說不禮貌
Changing and returning products are not allowed.
本櫃恕不接受退換貨。

2 虛擬實境口說練習
on your iMessenger

從最簡短到最豐富，讓你實際和老外練習口說和聽力

┃當你正在逛百貨公司，並詢問他人你要買的東西所在樓層時┃

❶ **Can you tell me where I can find the sportswear?**
請問可以告訴我哪裡可以買到運動服飾嗎？

> footwear 鞋（總稱）
> headwear 帽（總稱）
> underwear 內衣

❷ **Is the male clothing department on the fifth floor?**
男裝部在五樓嗎？

> female department 女裝部
> cosmetics department 化妝品部
> household appliances department 家電部

❸ **Can I get to the top floor by elevator?**
我可以搭電梯到頂樓嗎？

> escalator 手扶梯
> stairs 樓梯
> ladder 梯子

┃當你的朋友告訴你他昨天在特賣會大血拼時┃

❶ **What did you buy?**
你買了什麼？

> get 得到；買到
> purchase 購買

❷ **It must have been very packed!**
一定塞滿了人吧！

> crowded 很擁擠
> full 擠滿了人

┃當你想詢問櫃哥／姐關於商品的訊息時┃

❶ What size do you have for this shirt?
這件衣服有什麼尺寸？

> color 顏色
> discount 折扣
> style 款式

❷ How much is this necklace?
這條項鍊多少錢？

> bracelet 手鐲
> pair of earrings 一對耳環
> mascara 睫毛膏

❸ Can I get a discount?
可以給我折扣嗎？

> take a look 看一看
> take a glimpse 瞥一眼
> request a refund 要求退費

┃當你的朋友向你推薦好用的化妝品時┃

❶ Wow! It looks great on me!
哇！這用在我身上看起來超級棒！

> gorgeous 極其漂亮的
> fantastic 極好的

❷ Does it match my dress?
這跟我的服裝搭嗎？

> go (along) with 與… 一致
> complement 為…增色

3 虛擬實境網路聊天　在手機或電腦上，利用打字就可以聊出千言萬語
on your iMessenger

Mr. Thomas

星期三 下午 13:45

 I was thinking,
Could we do some shopping
before this trip ends?

下午 13:45

我在想，這趟參訪結束以前我們能不能去購物？

Sure thing!
Tell me the kind of things you
want to shop for and I'll point
you in the right direction.

下午 13:46

當然！你想要買些什麼，我再推薦你去好地方？
指出

下午 13:47

 I have a couple of requests
from the ladies back home to
buy some brand name purses.
And I would also like to shop
for some souvenirs.

下午 13:49

我家那群小姐們要求我回去時買一些名牌的包包。而我也想買一些紀念品。
要求
紀念物

Well, those two interests
don't usually come together.
We might have to go to
different places to find what
you are looking for.

下午 13:50

嗯，這兩種東西不會同時出現。我們得到不同的地方去找你要的。

感興趣的事物或人

下午 13:51

Mr. Thomas

星期三 下午 13:45

下午 13:52

Why? Don't you have just a big shopping center with everything?

下午 13:52

為什麼？你們沒有什麼都賣的大購物中心嗎？

Those places with everything in it are aimed at foreigners~ You don't want to go there or you'll get ripped off.

下午 13:54

裡面的東西全都是專門賣給外國人的～你不會想要去那兒被剝削。

針對

敲竹槓

下午 13:55

To get the most out of your dollar, it's best that we look around.

下午 13:56

為了花錢花得其所，我們最好四處看看。

得到最大效用

聊天金句大補帖

There is no doubt about it. 毫無疑問。

當我們要表達相當同意對方的說法或肯定一件事物時，常會用這句話來表示強調。對方聽到這個說法時，往往能更有信心地將對話持續下去。

Unit 2

唱出閃亮的歌聲

May I ask what you need to order?
請問你們需要點些什麼？

- We need five bottles of water. 我們需要五瓶水。
- A couple of menus, please. 兩份菜單，謝謝。
- Please give us two glasses of Coke. 請給我們兩杯可樂。
- We need a fried platter and a bottle of Diet Coke. 我們要一個炸物拼盤和一瓶健怡可樂。

Word Power!
- bottle [ˋbɑtl̩] n
  一瓶的容量
- a couple of
  phr 兩個；一對
- platter [ˋplætɚ]
  n 大淺盤
- Diet Coke
  n 健怡可樂（無糖）

更多…
量詞百百種
- a can of 一罐
- a barrel of 一桶
- a carton of 一盒
- a drop of 一滴

Could you give us a private room?
請問有包廂嗎？

- Sorry, we don't have spare room. 對不起，我們沒有空房間了。
- Sorry, We have not started operating. 對不起，我們還沒開始營業。
- Yes, we have already prepared one for you. 好的，我們已準備好了。

不能不會的小技巧
台灣的 KTV 通常都是私人包廂，比較具有隱密性。當然，若你有額外的要求，例如人數眾多等，則要記得事先提出，方便店家作安排。

Word Power!
- private room phr 包廂
- operate [ˋɑpəˌret]
  v 營業

Where is the restroom?
請問洗手間在哪裡？

- It's upstairs. 在樓上。
- Perhaps it's that room. 也許是那間。
- Along this road you will find it.
  沿著這條路走你就會看到了。

Word Power!
- upstairs [ˋʌpˋstɛrz]
  a 樓上的
- perhaps [pɚˋhæps]
  ad 也許

更多…
廁所的說法
- restroom
- toilet
- W.C.
- lavatory
- bathroom

這樣說不禮貌
Ask the waiter.
你可以問問服務員。

What are your favorite kinds of songs?
你最愛唱哪種類型的歌曲？

- I am the king of KTV, so I sing all kinds of songs. 我是 K 歌之王，所以所有的歌我都會唱。

- I love songs which make for an exciting atmosphere. 我喜歡可以炒熱氣氛的歌曲。

- Love songs. 愛情歌曲。

- Rock n' roll or heavy metal. 搖滾或重金屬的歌。

這樣說不禮貌
I'm not into any pop music. I only listen to classical music.
我對流行樂不感興趣。我只聽古典樂。

Will you be able to come to my birthday party at Holiday KTV on Sunday night?
星期天晚上你能來參加我在好樂迪辦的生日派對嗎？

- I'm afraid not. I'll be travelling back from Hawaii. But I will send you a little surprise. 可能不行，我那時正要從夏威夷旅行回來，不過我會寄個小驚喜給你。

這樣說不禮貌

- I will be there on time. 我一定會準時到達。

No, I won't. I'll be busy.
不，我沒辦法。我很忙。

Do you want to hang out some other time?
你想找時間出去玩嗎？

- I want to go to KTV with my friends. 我想和我的朋友一起去 KTV。

- Sure I do! I think we can go road cycling in the morning, and then get to the KTV for happy hour in the evening. 當然想！我想我們可以早上去騎公路單車，然後晚上再去 KTV 歡唱一下。

這樣說不禮貌
But I don't seem to have time lately.
但這段時間我沒空。

2 虛擬實境口說練習
on your iMessenger

從最簡短到最豐富，讓你實際和老外練習口說和聽力

| 當櫃台人員向你介紹 **KTV** 的消費方案時 |

❶ Is food included in this package?
這個方案有包含食物嗎？

> drink 飲料
> dessert 甜點
> appetizer 開胃菜

❷ Thanks for your explanation.
謝謝你的講解。

> I appreciate 我對…非常感謝
> I'm grateful 我很感激
> I'm happy to hear 我很高興聽到

❸ How long can we sing?
我們可以唱多久？

> How much time 多久
> How many hours 幾個小時
> Where 在哪裡

| 當你要使用包廂內的服務電話向服務生提出要求時 |

❶ Could you send in more ice?
你可以送更多冰塊進來嗎？

> napkins 餐巾紙
> water 水

❷ I'd like to extend our session by an hour.
我想要延長一小時。

> two hours 兩小時
> three hours 三小時

當朋友問你都愛唱什麼類型的歌曲時

1. I like pop songs.
我喜歡流行歌曲。

classical music 古典音樂
rock and roll 搖滾
blues 藍調

2. I'm not really into singing.
我不是很喜歡唱歌。

dancing 跳舞
clubbing 去夜店
shopping 逛街

3. I prefer female singers to male singers.
我喜歡女歌手勝過男歌手。

apples 蘋果
juice 果汁
lying 躺著

bananas 香蕉
milk 牛奶
standing 站著

當你告訴別人你對 KTV 的感覺時

❶ **It's the best place to release pressure.**
那是釋放壓力最好的地方。

relax yourself 放鬆自己
go on a date 約會
go on a picnic 野餐

❷ **People usually drink alcohol and smoke in KTVs.**
人們通常會在ＫＴＶ喝酒與抽菸。

night clubs 夜店
restaurants 餐廳
lounge bars 酒吧

3 虛擬實境網路聊天
on your iMessenger

在手機或電腦上，利用打字就可以聊出千言萬語

Will

星期三 下午 13:45

Yo, buddy!
It's Amy's b-day tomorrow, she's invites us to celebrate it with her at a KTV not so far from here.
Would u like to go?

下午 13:45

嘿老兄！明天是艾咪的生日，她邀請我們到附近的一家 KTV 去陪她慶祝一番，你想去嗎？

夥伴

birthday 的簡寫

下午 13:46

A KTV?
Isn't that the place where people sing karaoke, and there will be a bunch of people we don't know?

下午 13:47

KTV？那不是一般人去唱卡拉 OK，而且裡頭還有一堆不認識的人在的地方嗎？

一群

下午 13:48

You're thinking of the traditional karaoke with a stage and a large audience!

下午 13:49

你所想的是傳統的卡拉 OK，有舞台、觀眾席的那種。

舞台

Am I misunderstanding something?

下午 13:50

我誤會什麼了嗎？

誤會

Will

星期三 下午 13:45

 The KTVs here have private rooms with room service.
You can order snacks, drinks or a complete meal.
It's almost like a hotel room with the addition of being able to sing.

下午 13:51

OIC~

下午 13:52

 The price is cheap and you can party as hard as you want without having to clean up the next day.

下午 13:53

So that's why I see so many people lined up outside KTV on weekends.

下午 13:54

 Hmmm...

下午 13:55

現在的 KTV 是提供包廂服務的私人包廂。也可以點吃的、喝的或者全套餐點。幾乎就像是飯店的房間，只不過多了可以唱歌這一項。

哦我懂了～
`Oh, I see. 的簡寫`

價格便宜，而且可以盡情歡樂，又免去了隔天清理的麻煩。
`儘量`
`清理`

難怪週末的時候總是看到 KTV 外頭大排長龍。
`排隊`

`聊天金句大補帖`

What put that idea in your head? 你怎麼會這麼想？

當別人說出一件事情、想法、意見等，讓你覺得有點兒不以為然，或者很不解對方為何這樣想時，為了促進對方針對他的想法提出解釋，我們就可以說這句。

Unit 3 週五電影夜

What is the name of this film?
這部電影的名稱是什麼

Word Power!
- film [fɪlm] n 電影
- space [spes] n 太空
- sequel [ˋsikwəl] n 續集
- animation [͵ænəˋmeʃən] n 動畫片
- pirate [ˋpaɪrət] n 海盜

- It's called *Interstellar*. It's a movie about space adventure.
  這部片叫《星際效應》。是一部關於太空歷險的電影。

- *Avengers 3*. It's one of the sequels.
  《復仇者聯盟3》，這是續集之一

- It's an animation called *Zootopia*.
  這是一部動畫片，叫《動物方程式》。

這樣說不禮貌

Don't tell me that you've never heard of *Pirates of the Caribbean*. It's very popular.
別跟我說你沒聽過《神鬼奇航》。這很有名耶！

Why do you like going to the movie theater?
為什麼喜歡來電影院？

Word Power!
- theater [ˋθiətə] n 電影院
- surrounding [səˋraʊndɪŋ] n 環境

- I think it's a romantic place. 我覺得它是一個非常浪漫的地方。

- I can see the newest movies here. 我可以來這裡看到最新的電影。

這樣說不禮貌

- The theater I go has a very good surrounding. 我去的那間電影院環境很好。

Who doesn't like going to the movie theater?
誰不喜歡去電影院？

What do you think about today's film?
你感覺今天的電影怎麼樣？

Word Power!
- special effect n 特效
- lead [lid] a 最重要的
- actor [ˋæktə] n 演員
- vampire [ˋvæmpaɪr] n 吸血鬼
- werewolf [ˋwɪr͵wʊlf] n 狼人

- I loved the special effects in the movie. 我愛極了這部電影的特效。

- The lead actor is the only reason why I decided to see the movie. 男主角是我想看這部電影的主要原因。

- I'm tired of vampires and werewolves.
  我真是受夠吸血鬼和狼人了。

Do you often go to the cinema and watch film?

你經常去電影院看電影嗎

- Yes, I think it is very cool. 是的，我認為這樣很酷。
- No. I usually watch movies on my computer. 不，我通常用我的電腦看電影。
- Sometimes. After all, the tickets are very expensive. 有時會去，畢竟門票太貴了。
- Yes, I do. I love the smell of popcorn and nachos. 是的，經常去。我好愛爆米花和玉米片的味道。

不能不會的小技巧
每個人喜歡的影片類型都不盡相同。下次碰到老外，卻不知道要聊什麼的時候，不妨談論電影，這會是個很棒的聊天話題，而且也能更進一步了解對方。

Word Power!
- cinema [ˈsɪnəmə] n 電影院
- after all phr 畢竟
- smell [smɛl] n 氣味
- popcorn [ˈpɑpˌkɔrn] n 爆米花
- nachos [ˈnætʃoz] n 玉米片

How may I help you?

我可以為你服務嗎？

- Can I have a large popcorn and a medium Coca-Cola? 我想點一份大包爆米花和中杯可樂。
- Two tickets for Sherlock-The *Abominable Bride*. 兩張《福爾摩斯：地獄新娘》的票。
- Can you cancel my booking for me, please? 可以幫我取消訂票嗎？

Word Power!
- large [lɑrdʒ] a 大的
- medium [ˈmidɪəm] a 中的
- abominable [əˈbɑmənəbl] a 糟透的
- bride [braɪd] n 新娘

Which film do you want to see next time?

下次你想看什麼電影？

- A film about the Tudor Dynasty. 關於都鐸王朝的電影。
- A thriller, just like *Before I Go To Sleep*. 驚悚片，像是《別相信任何人》。
- I want to see some 3D films. 我想看些 3D 電影
- I love seeing horror movies in the movie theater. I definitely will go to see that again. 我好愛在電影院看恐怖片。我一定還要再去看一次。

Word Power!
- Tudor Dynasty n 都鐸王朝
  → 1485-1603 年間統治英格蘭地區的王朝
- thriller [ˈθrɪlɚ] n 驚悚片
- horror [ˈhɔrɚ] n 恐怖

更多…
電影類型百百種
- action movie 動作片
- documentary 紀錄片
- chick flick 文藝片
- romcom 愛情喜劇片

2 虛擬實境口說練習
on your iMessenger

從最簡短到最豐富，讓你實際和老外練習口說和聽力

| 當你在電影院的窗口買票時 |

❶ **Two tickets for Toy Story. Thank you.**
玩具總動員，兩張票。謝謝你。

> Star Wars 星際大戰
> Harry Potter 哈利波特
> Fast and Furious 玩命關頭

❷ **I'd like to pay by cash.**
我想付現。

> by credit card 刷卡
> by debit card 刷金融卡
> in advance 預先支付

❸ **I'd like to sit in the back row.**
我想坐在後排。

> front row 前排
> first row 第一排
> second row 第二排

| 當售票人員向你推薦搭餐優惠時 |

❶ **Thank you. But I just had dinner.**
謝謝，但我剛吃過晚餐。

> lunch 午餐
> breakfast 早餐
> snacks 零食

❷ **No, I'm good. Thanks!**
不用了，我很好。謝謝！

> I'm fine. 我很好
> I'm full. 我飽了
> I don't need anything.
> 我不需要任何東西

| 當你告訴朋友你看完電影的感想時 | - - - - - - - - - - - - - - -

❶ I really like the cast!
我真的很喜歡這部電影的演出陣容。

> plot 情節
> setting 背景
> audio effect 聽覺效果

❷ The leading actress nailed it!
女主角根本技壓全場！

> did a great job 做得很好
> won an Oscar 贏了一座奧斯卡
> married a famous actor 嫁給一個知名演員

❸ The setting of the movie is spectacular!
電影的場景實在是太豪華了！

> magnificent 壯麗的
> attractive 吸引人的
> tranquil 寧靜的

| 當你和朋友討論電影院的環境時 | - - - - - - - - - - - - - - -

❶ The guy sitting next to me was talking on his phone non-stop!
坐我隔壁的傢伙不停地講手機！

> beside me 在我旁邊
> in front of me 在我前面
> behind me 在我後面

❷ The couple in the front row blocked my view.
前排的那對情侶擋住我的視線了。

> raised their hands 舉起他們的手
> made a request 做出一個要求
> asked for help 請求幫助

3 虛擬實境網路聊天
on your iMessenger

在手機或電腦上，利用打字就可以聊出千言萬語

Cathy

星期三 下午 13:45

Going to the theaters is great, but sometimes you just want to watch some of those special moments over and over again. U know what I mean?

下午 13:45

去看電影很棒沒錯，但是有時候你只想一直重複看一些片段而已，你了解我的意思嗎？

一再

Yeah, I no.

下午 13:47

是的，我了解。

know 的簡寫

And u know what, I missed out on a couple of good films during my stay here. Because we've been so busy sightseeing.

下午 13:48

還有你知道嗎，我在這裡的這段期間錯過好多很不錯的電影，因為我都忙著觀光。

失去獲得樂趣的機會

遊覽

下午 13:48

Do u think they are released on rentals?

下午 13:49

你覺得它們在出租店發行了嗎？

出租業

I'm not sure, but we can go check.

下午 13:50

我不太確定，不過我們可以去看看。

Is it ez to get a membership?

下午 13:51

申辦會員容易嗎？

easy 的簡寫

Cathy

Sure. But there is a slight difference.

下午 13:52

Hmmm...

下午 13:53

當然容易。不過有一
些不同。
微少的

In other countries, you pay each time you rent.
But here, you have to deposit money into an account and money is deducted every time you rent something.

下午 13:54

在別的國家，每租一
次付一次錢。但是在
這兒，你必須先在你
的戶頭儲值，每次消
費的時候再從裡面扣
款。
扣除

Well, whatever works, let's go get some.

下午 13:55

怎樣都行啦，我們去
租些片子吧。

Fine~

下午 13:56

好啦～

聊天金句大補帖

Whatever you say. 隨便你怎麼說。

在談話當中，倘若對方一直說著讓你聽起來很沒建設性或根本不可能的事，或者對
方一直固執己見，你也沒耐心和他爭論了，就可以對他說這句話。或簡化為：

• Whatever.

Unit 4 來點動次動次

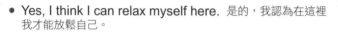

Do you often go to the night club?
你經常來夜店嗎？

Word Power!
- night club **phr** 夜店
- situation [ˌsɪtʃuˈeʃən] **n** 情況
- interesting [ˈɪntərɪstɪŋ] **a** 有趣的
- theme party **n** 主題派對
- rule [rul] **v** 控制
- strictly [ˈstrɪktlɪ] **ad** 嚴厲地

- Yes, I think I can relax myself here. 是的，我認為在這裡我才能放鬆自己。
- It depends on the situation. 這要看情況而定。
- Only if there's some interesting theme party. 有什麼有趣的主題派對我才會來。
- No. My girlfriend rules me strictly. 不。我女朋友管我很嚴。

Let's go get something to eat, OK?
我們去找點吃的，好嗎？

Word Power!
- buffet [ˈbʌfɪt] **n** 自助吧
- help yourself **phr** 自己來；請自便

- But I am not hungry now. 可是我現在不餓啊。
- Well, we can ask the waiter to take our order. 嗯，我們可以找服務生幫我們拿啊。
- Let me get some food for you. What do you want to eat? 我去幫妳拿吧，妳想吃什麼呢？

這樣說不禮貌

There's a buffet. You can help yourself.
那裡有自助吧。妳可以自己去拿。

What do you want to drink?
你想喝點什麼呢？

Word Power!
- Cosmopolitan **n** 柯夢波丹（調酒名）→伏特加、橙酒、蔓越莓汁、加上新鮮萊姆汁調製而成
- olive [ˈɑlɪv] **n** 橄欖
- soft drink **n** 軟性飲料（無酒精飲料）

- Six pack of Heineken will be great. 一手海尼根啤酒就可以了。
- No, thanks. I'm just waiting for a friend. 不，謝謝，我只是在等一個朋友。
- A Cosmopolitan with an olive. 一杯柯夢波丹加橄欖
- Soft drinks, please. 無酒精飲料，謝謝。

Do you know how long does this night club has been running?

你知道這家夜店經營了多長時間嗎？

Word Power!
- run [rʌn] **v** 經營
- detail [ˈditel] **n** 細節
- clearly [ˈklɪrlɪ]
  ad 明確地
- shot [ʃɑt]
  n （烈酒的）一小杯

- About three years, I think. 我想大概三年吧。

- I 'm not sure. I don't know any detail about it.
  我不確定，我不大了解它的情況。

- Yes, I remember it clearly. The night club has been running for over 6 years.
  是的，我記得很清楚。這家夜店已經營業超過六年了。

Who knows? Why so serious? Have another shot, bro!
誰知道？幹嘛那麼認真？再來拼一杯吧老兄！

Would you like to dance with me?

你願意和我跳支舞嗎？

Word Power!
- dance with
  phr 與…共舞
- take a rest **phr** 休息

- Sorry, I want to take a rest now. 不好意思，我現在想休息一下。

- I'm really sorry, I already have a date. 實在抱歉，我已經有一個舞伴了。

- I'd like to, however, I'm not a very good dancer. 我很樂意，但是我舞跳得不是很好。

Do you like the life of the night club?

你喜歡夜店的生活嗎？

Word Power!
- party animal **phr** 熱衷於社交聚會的人
- active [ˈæktɪv]
  a 活潑的
- complicated
  [ˈkɑmpləˌketɪd]
  a 複雜的
- junkie [ˈdʒʌŋkɪ]
  n 有毒癮者
- gangster [ˈɡæŋstə]
  n 流氓

- Yes, I love it. Because I'm a party animal. 嗯我喜歡。因為我是派對狂。

- Yes, there are so many youths, they are all active.
  是的，這裡有許多年輕人，他們都好有活力。

- No. It is a complicated place.
  不。這是一個龍蛇混雜的地方。

I don't like it. There're full of junkies and gangsters.
我不喜歡，那裡都是毒蟲跟流氓。

2 虛擬實境口說練習
on your iMessenger

從最簡短到最豐富，讓你實際和老外練習口說和聽力

| 當你在夜店要搭訕別人時 |

❶ Hey, can I buy you a drink?
我可以請你喝一杯嗎？

sent you some flowers 送妳一些花
treat you a meal 請妳吃頓飯
give you a present/gift 送妳一個禮物

❷ Can I take you out to dinner tomorrow?
明天我可以邀請你吃晚餐嗎？

hang out with you 和你出去逛逛
go on a date with you 跟你約會
ask you out 約你出去

❸ What's your name?
你的名字是什麼？

address 住址
gender 性別
opinion 意見

| 當你的朋友告訴你夜店有多好玩時 |

❶ You really had a blast last night!
你昨晚真的玩得很盡興！

had fun 玩得開心
had a good time 玩得很開心
had a ball 玩得很開心

❷ I would love to go with you next time!
下次我很樂意跟你一起去！

share with you 與你分享
work with you 與你一起工作
collaborate with you 與你合作

| 當你要向酒保點飲料來喝時 |

➊ A Cosmopolitan, please.
一杯柯夢波丹，謝謝！

Screwdriver（雞尾酒）螺絲起子
Whisky Coke 威士忌可樂
Long Island Iced Tea 長島冰茶

➋ Can you make it less strong?
你可以調淡一點嗎？

more strong 濃一點
less iced 少一點冰塊
straight up 不要冰塊
（指用調酒器調完並瀝除冰塊）

➌ Do you have any soft drinks?
這裡有任何軟性飲料嗎？

beer 啤酒
water 水
juice 果汁

| 當你回應朋友要帶你去夜店的邀約時 |

➊ Sorry! I've got work to do.
不好意思，我有事要忙。

had plans 有計畫了
got kids to take care of 有小孩要照顧
had no spare time 沒有空閒時間

➋ Please keep an eye on me. I get drunk easily.
請看好我，我很容易喝醉。

lost 迷路
confused 陷入困惑
rejected 被拒絕

3 虛擬實境網路聊天   在手機或電腦上，利用打字就可以聊出千言萬語
on your iMessenger

Leslie

星期三 下午 13:45

Hey
Wanna go out for some
late night exercise?

下午 13:45

嘿，妳想去做點夜間
運動嗎？

Well, there are 24-hour
gyms that we can go to,
but I have a better idea
Let's go clubbing.

下午 13:46

哦，的確是有 24 小時
的健身房，不過我有
更好的主意，我們去
夜店吧。

去夜店玩

That's a great idea!

下午 13:48

好主意！

下午 13:49

But I'm not too much of a dancer.
Those night clubs can get a little
wild with all the alcohol and dancing.

下午 13:50

不過我不太會跳舞，
那些充滿酒精及舞蹈
的夜店肯定有些狂野。

酒精

Well....
Or we could go to a lounge.
We can sit, relax, and chat.

下午 13:52

這樣哦…或我們就去
沙龍吧。可以坐下來
放鬆、聊天。

沙龍

Leslie

星期三 下午 13:45

 But we were supposed to **exercise.**
下午 13:53

可是我們打算要運動啊。

應該要

下午 13:54

Rite lol! I forgot.
How about a nightclub with a live band?
You can dance without worrying about hangovers because these clubs are more focused on music.

下午 13:55

對，哈哈！我都忘了。那我們到有現場樂團演奏的夜店怎麼樣？你可以在旁邊跳舞，不用擔心宿醉，因為在那類夜店的重點是音樂，不是酒。

宿醉

 Sure~ That's a great idea!
下午 13:56

好耶～這是個好主意！

So that, we can both enjoy the exercise and the music.

下午 13:57

這樣一來，我們就能一邊運動一邊享受著音樂了。

聊天金句大補帖

What did you have in mind? 你心裡在想什麼？

這句話可以用於任何活動或計畫，藉由詢問的方式討論或探知彼此的意見或想法。比如說兩個人要一起吃晚飯，尚未決定吃什麼，就可以用這句話問另外一個人是不是想吃什麼或者想去什麼地方吃等等。

Unit 5

瘋狂派對夜

What is the party about?
這個派對是關於什麼的？

- It's a baby shower. Gifts are not necessary but highly appreciated. 這是個新生兒送禮會。不一定要送禮物，可是若有禮物，我們會很感激的。

- It's a bachelor / bachelorette party. 這是一個告別單身趴。

- Halloween is coming. It's a costume party. Please wear costumes. 萬聖節要到了。這是個化妝舞會。請變裝打扮。

> **Word Power!**
> - baby shower
>   **phr** 新生兒送禮會
>   →嬰兒出生前，替懷孕的媽媽準備的派對
> - bachelor [ˈbætʃələ]
>   **n** 單身男子
> - bachelorette
>   [ˌbætʃələˈrɛt]
>   **n** 未婚女子
> - costume [ˈkɑstjum]
>   **n** 服裝

When will the party begin?
派對什麼時候開始？

> **Word Power!**
> - RSVP **abbr** 敬請回覆
>   →從法文 "répondez s'il vous plaît" 縮寫而來

- Seven o'clock tonight. Don't be late. 今晚七點。別遲到了哦。

- It is up to the host. But he is not here yet. 這要看主持人。但他現在還沒到場。

- After everyone comes. 等大家都到了。

> 這樣說不禮貌
> It's on July 3rd. Didn't you RSVP?
> 七月三日。你沒回覆邀請函嗎？

Where is the masquerade?
化妝舞會在哪舉行？

> **Word Power!**
> - masquerade
>   [ˌmæskəˈred]
>   **n** 化妝舞會
> - lobby [ˈlɑbɪ]
>   **n**（旅館的）大廳
> - hall [hɔl] **n** 大廳；會堂

- On the sixth floor. 在六樓舉行。

- It will be held in the lobby of the Four Seasons. 在四季酒店的大廳。

- It's held in the diamond hall. 在鑽石廳舉行。

- Follow me, please! I'll go to there, too. 跟著我吧，我也要去參加那個舞會。

> 這樣說不禮貌
> I don't think you are invited to the party.
> 我不認為你有被邀請參加這個派對。

Who will join the party with you?

誰和你一起參加聚會？

- I will go by myself. 我自己一個人去。
- I want to go to the party with my colleagues. 我想和我同事一起去。
- I asked one of my male friends to go with me, but he hasn't replied yet. 我約了一個男性友人跟我一起去，但他還沒回覆呢。
- My girlfriend of course. I won't go anywhere without her. 當然和我女友一起，沒有她的地方我不去。

Word Power!
- join [dʒɔɪn] v 參加
- male [mel] n 男性的
- reply [rɪˈplaɪ] v 回覆
- anywhere [ˈɛnɪ.hwɛr] ad 任何地方

Do you want to join the party?

你想參加這次聚會嗎？

- Yes, I am looking forward to it so much. 是的，我超級期待。
- I'm not sure if I should go. But I heard it's going to be a great party. 我還不確定該不該參加。可是我聽說這會是個很棒的派對。
- It depends on who is going to the party. 我要看看誰會參加派對再決定。

Sentence Power!
- I heard (that)... 我聽說…
- I would rather... 我寧可…

這樣說不禮貌

No, I don't like noisy places. I'd rather stay home and rest. 不，我不喜歡吵雜的地方。我寧願待在家休息。

Can I smoke at the party?

我能在聚會時抽煙嗎？

- I'm afraid you can't. 這個恐怕不行。
- Smoking is not allowed in public. 公共場合禁止吸菸。
- Smoking is prohibited at the party. 這個派對上是禁止吸菸的。
- There will be a smoking room at the party. 派對地點有吸煙室。

Word Power!
- smoke [smok] v 抽煙
- in public phr 公然地
- prohibit [prəˈhɪbɪt] v 禁止

更多…
派對好好玩
- pool party 泳池派對
- booze-party 狂飲派對
- bachelor party 告別單身（男）派對
- bachelorette party 告別單身（女）派對

2 虛擬實境口說練習
on your iMessenger

從最簡短到最豐富，讓你實際和老外練習口說和聽力

| 當朋友詢問你要不要去一個他在家舉辦的派對時 |

❶ **Thanks for the invitation!**
謝謝你的邀請！

reminder 提醒
notice 通知
reply 回覆

❷ **I will bring some booze.**
我會帶一些酒。

pizza 披薩
pasta 義大利麵
bread 麵包

❸ **How many people have you invited?**
你邀請多少人了？

did you invite （過去式）邀請…了
will you invite （未來式）將會邀請
do you plan to invite （現在式）計畫邀請

| 當你和別人討論一個你將要舉辦的派對時 |

❶ **We have a swimming pool in the backyard.**
我們後院有一個游泳池

garden 花園
garage 車庫
tree house 樹屋

❷ **There will be at least fifty people.**
至少會有五十個人。

a maximum of 最多
a minimum of 最少
a total of 總共

| 當你在派對的場合想邀請大家一起做某件事時 |

❶ Let's have a toast.
我們舉杯敬酒吧。

> get down to business 來做正事
> file a lawsuit 提告
> stand up to him 起身反抗他

❷ The dress code is leopard print.
今天的著裝標準是豹紋。

> black 黑色
> white 白色
> rainbow 彩虹

❸ It's time for dancing!
跳舞的時間到了！

> to dance 跳舞
> that we dance 跳舞

| 當你和朋友說到上一個你參加的派對時 |

❶ I ended up falling asleep on the couch.
我最後在沙發上睡著。

> kissing a stranger 親了一個陌生人
> going home with someone else
> 和另一個人回家
> not remembering a thing 不記得任何事

❷ My boyfriend came and drove me home.
我男友載我回家。

> blamed me for staying up so late 責備我熬夜到太晚
> cooked me lunch 幫我做午餐
> bought me a gift 買給我一個禮物

3 虛擬實境網路聊天
on your iMessenger

在手機或電腦上，利用打字就可以聊出千言萬語

Brat

星期三 下午 13:45

Do you know why I enjoy working in this city so much?

下午 13:45

你知道為什麼我喜歡在這個城市裡工作嗎？

Why?

下午 13:46

為什麼？

Because this is a sleepless city. There are so many things you can do no matter what time of day it is.

下午 13:47

因為它是個不夜城。不論那個時段總是有許多事情可做。
不眠的
無論

I agree with u.

下午 13:48

我同意。

For some people, life begins when the sun goes down.

下午 13:49

對有些人來説，一天的生活是從太陽下山後才開始的。

But where do people go?

下午 13:50

但他們可以去哪裡呢？

There are 24-hour bookstores where you can just sit, relax, and browse away at your favorite magazine.

下午 13:51

有二十四小時營業的書店，你可以去坐坐、放鬆一下，翻閱你最喜歡的雜誌。
瀏覽

Sounds pretty nice!

下午 13:52

聽起來超讚的！

Brat

星期三 下午 13:45

And if you are hungry, there are many restaurants that open 24 hours as well.
So long as u don't find it too much trouble to go out at night, there're nothing u can't find!

下午 13:53

要是你餓了，還有許多二十四小時營業的餐廳呢。只要你不嫌晚上出去麻煩，沒有什麼找不到的。

只要

MG, this place is great! I should sleep less and go out more.

下午 13:54

天哪，這地方真是太棒了！我應該少睡一點，多出去走走。

My God. 的簡寫

下午 13:55

I almost forgot when was the last time I slept earlier.

下午 13:56

我都快忘記我上次早睡是什麼時候的事了呢。

Shut up! I can't even wait for tonite.

下午 13:57

噢快閉嘴！我簡直要等不及今晚了呢！

tonight 的簡寫

聊天金句大補帖

It's always darkest before dawn. 否極泰來

當我們聽到身邊的人遭遇不幸、心情低落時，我們可以用這句話來安慰他，字面意思是「黎明之前總是最黑暗的」，意指黑暗過後，光明即將來臨，引申為否極泰來。

Unit 6 少不了的是祝福

Do you have a special plan for your Mother's Day?
你有為母親節準備特別的計畫嗎？

Word Power!
- celebrate [ˈsɛləˌbret]
  v 慶祝
- fancy [ˈfænsɪ]
  a 高級的
- travel around **phr** 周遊
- bouquet [buˈke]
  n 花束
- carnation [karˈneʃən]
  n 康乃馨

- Sure. We are going to celebrate it at a fancy restaurant. 當然。我們要去高級餐廳慶祝。

- My mother and I plan to travel around Europe. 我和媽媽計畫要環遊歐洲。

- I prepared a bouquet of carnations for her. 我準備了一束康乃馨給她。

Happy New Year!
新年快樂！

不能不會的小技巧
當朋友送上節日祝福時，回答時一般是把同樣的祝福送給對方，並祝對方好運。

Word Power!
- resolution [ˌrɛzəˈluʃən]
  n 願望

Sentence Power!
- Bottoms up! 乾杯！

- Happy New Year! 新年快樂！
- Best wishes! 祝福你！
- Happy New Year. Bottoms up! 新年快樂。乾杯！
- What is your New Year resolution? 你的新年願望是什麼？

Merry Christmas!
聖誕快樂！

Word Power!
- merry [ˈmɛrɪ]
  a 歡樂的
- festival [ˈfɛstəvl]
  n 節日
- country [ˈkʌntrɪ]
  n 國家

- Hi! Merry Christmas. 哈囉！聖誕快樂！

- Thank you. This is the biggest festival in our country. We must celebrate it. 謝謝，這是我們國家最大的節日，我們要好好地慶賀一番。

- Merry Christmas! Are we going to exchange gifts?
  聖誕快樂！我們要交換禮物嗎？

這樣說不禮貌
Do you have any gift for me?
你有禮物要給我嗎？

Today is Arbor Day. What are you going to do?

今天是植樹節，你有什麼打算嗎？

- Yeah. I want to plant some trees with my father. 當然，我打算和我的爸爸一起去植樹。
- I'll plant trees with my classmates on the hill. 我要和同學們一起去山丘上種樹。
- Would you like to plant some trees with me? 你願意和我一起去植樹嗎？

這樣說不禮貌
Do people actually plant trees on Arbor Day?
真的有人會在植樹節種樹嗎？

Happy Labor Day.

勞動節快樂。

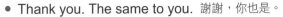

- Thank you. The same to you. 謝謝，你也是。
- Yes. Where will you go during the holiday? 是的，假期你準備去哪？
- Thanks. It's certainly sunny. We should have a picnic. 謝謝，天氣一定很好，我們該去野餐。
- Thanks a lot! I'm going back home today. How about you? 謝謝。我今天會回家。你呢？

Happy April Fool's Day.

愚人節快樂！

- Great! I have a chance to play jokes on somebody. 太好了，我有機會開某人玩笑了。
- Let's play tricks on someone. 我們一起去捉弄人吧！
- It's going to be funny today! 今天肯定很好笑！

這樣說不禮貌
Don't come here! I know you have some cunning tricks.
別靠近我！我知道你在打什麼鬼主意。

2 虛擬實境口說練習
on your iMessenger

從最簡短到最豐富，讓你實際和老外練習口說和聽力

┃當你詢問某人是否要與你共度某個節日時┃

❶ **What's your plan for Christmas?**
你聖誕節計畫做什麼？

the weekend 周末
the vacation 假期
the Chinese New Year 農曆新年

❷ **Would you like to come over and have dinner together?**
你想要過來我家一起吃晚餐嗎？

go on a trip 旅行
spend the holiday 度過假期
grab some food 找點東西吃

❸ **Why don't we visit Germany for the holiday?**
我們這個假期去德國玩好不好？

France 法國
the Philippines 菲律賓
Korea 韓國

┃當你的朋友問你下個連假有何計劃時┃

❶ **I will probably stay home.**
我可能會待在家。

visit my parents 拜訪我的父母。
take a nap 睡個午覺

❷ **I plan to visit my friends in Italy.**
我計畫去義大利拜訪朋友。

go shopping 購物
visit the Leaning Tower of Pisa
參觀比薩斜塔
visit all the famous attractions 參觀所有知名景點

| 當你告訴朋友你利用上個連假去哪裡玩時 |

❶ I took a day trip to Kenting.
我去墾丁玩了一天。

> rode a scooter 騎機車
> walked barefoot 赤腳步行

❷ It takes about five hours to drive there.
開車到那裡需要大約五小時。

> an entire day 一整天
> a whole week 一整周
> one month 一個月

❸ You should definitely visit there!
你一定要拜訪那裡！

> absolutely 絕對
> undoubtedly 毫無疑問地
> without doubt 毫無疑問地

| 當你要介紹你的國家有哪些特殊節日給朋友聽時 |

❶ We eat rice dumplings to celebrate Dragon Boat Festival.
我們吃粽子慶祝端午節。

> moon cakes 月餅
> turkey 火雞

> the Moon Festival 中秋節
> Thanksgiving 感恩節

❷ New Year's Eve is a time when all family members get together.
除夕夜是全家團聚的時候。

> Thanksgiving 感恩節
> Christmas 聖誕節

> we should be grateful 心存感激
> we celebrate the birth of Jesus 慶祝耶穌出生

3 虛擬實境網路聊天
on your iMessenger

在手機或電腦上，利用打字就可以聊出千言萬語

Sherry

星期三 下午 13:45

> Why is there almost no one on the streets today?
>
> 下午 13:45

為什麼今天街上都沒有人呢？
街道

> 下午 13:46

> Cuz everyone's at home resting.
>
> 下午 13:47

因為大家都在家裡休息了呀
because 的簡寫

> 下午 13:48

> Does that apply to people who work in restaurants as well?
>
> 下午 13:49

餐廳也都是這樣嗎？
適用於

> Sure!
> And not just restaurants, but businesses and companies as well.
>
> 下午 13:50

當然！不只是餐廳，公司行號也都是。
商業活動

> IC.
> So meanwhile this place is going to be like a ghost town, huh?
>
> 下午 13:51

我懂了，那麼，這裡很快就會成為一座空城了吧？
其間
被遺棄而無人煙之村鎮

Sherry

星期三 下午 13:45

> Actually, a lot of things are happening indoors.
> Last night, there were fireworks in the air; families were having reunion dinners.
> Gambling games were going on, elders were passing out red envelopes

下午 13:52

事實上，很多事情正默默進行著。昨晚天空放了煙火，家家戶戶都團聚吃年夜飯、玩賭博遊戲，長輩也正在發紅包呢！

`在室內`
`煙火`
`團圓飯`
`賭博`
`長輩們`
`分發`

> That sounds like so much fun~ I'm sorry if my company sent me over at a bad time for you.

下午 13:53

聽起來非常有趣～很抱歉我的公司派我過來的時機這麼不對。

`送過來`

> What RU talking about?
> All expenses in the next few days are paid for by the company.
> It's great!!!!!!

下午 13:54

你在說什麼啊？我們這幾天的花費都由公司出，感覺棒透了！

`花費`

下午 13:55

聊天金句大補帖

You are the boss. 你決定就好。

我們常常對一件事沒有意見，或者認為由他人決定即可，這句話就可以派上用場。讓別人做老闆來下決定，相當的貼切。

Chapter
8

出發社區巡禮

Viewing our community.

Unit 1 信件集散地

Unit 2 錢財通通交到這

Unit 3 沒事別進出的地方

Unit 4 店員什麼都會

Unit 5 記得守規矩

Unit 6 個人情報保衛戰

Unit 1 信件集散地

How do you want to send your mail?
你的信件想怎麼寄？

- I want to send it as an ordinary letter. 我想寄平信就好。
- As a registered letter. 用掛號寄。
- Airmail special, please. 麻煩寄航空快遞。
- As printed matter. 以印刷品寄。

Word Power!
- ordinary [ˈɔrdnˌɛrɪ] a 平常的
- letter [ˈlɛtə] n 信件
- registered [ˈrɛdʒɪstəd] a 登記過的
- airmail [ˈɛrˌmel] n 航空郵件
- print [prɪnt] v 印刷

更多…
郵寄方式
- ordinary letter 平信
- registered letter 掛號
- special delivery 限時

Where's the parcel post counter, please?
寄包裹的櫃檯在哪？

- It's at window number 2. 在 2 號窗口。
- You should go to the next window. 你應該去隔壁窗口。
- You can ask the service agent. 你可以問一下服務人員。
- The place where many people are waiting. 有很多人等的地方便是。

不能不會的小技巧
郵局的服務其實相當多元，除了一般的寄信、匯款等服務之外，許多國家的郵局也可以幫你保管信件，只要事先提出申請，在一定的期間內郵局便會幫你保管原本要投遞給你的信件。此外，變更郵件投遞地址、查詢包裹或快捷的狀況等也都是很常見的。

Word Power!
- parcel [ˈpɑrsl] n 包裹
- post [post] n 郵寄

Is there anything I can do for you?
有什麼我能幫你的嗎？

- I want to send an EMS. 我想寄國際快捷。
- I want to deliver a parcel. 我想郵寄一個包裹。
- Can you weigh my parcel? 你能幫我稱一下我的包裹嗎？
- I want to send money to my sister. 我想為我妹妹匯錢。

Word Power!
- EMS abbr 國際快捷
  = express mail special
- deliver [dɪˈlɪvə] v 運送
- weigh [we]
  v 稱…的重量

更多…
- 郵件種類
- small package 小包裹
- printed matter 印刷品
- post card 明信片
- parcel post 包裹

May I help you?
我可以幫忙嗎？

- I want to pick up my package. 我來領包裹。
- How much is an airmail letter? 寄一封航空信要多少錢？
- How much would it cost to send this to Germany by registered mail? 這封掛號信寄到德國要多少錢？
- Please give me ten 5 dollar stamps. 請給我十張五塊錢的郵票。

Should I show my ID if I send money?
如果我要匯錢我是否要出示身份證？

- Yes, you must. 是的，你必須出示。
- Yes, this is the rule. 是的，這是規定。
- No, you needn't. 不，沒有必要。
- It's better if you take it. 如果你帶的話會更好點。

Can I have this money order cashed?
我可以在這裏兌現這張匯票嗎？

- Yes, but you'll have to endorse it first. 可以，不過你得先在背面簽名。
- Yes, but you should show me your ID. 可以，但你要給我出示你的身份證。
- Sorry, we don't offer this sort of service. 對不起，這兒沒有這項服務。

這樣說不禮貌

Oh, no, you should go to the post center.
哦，不行，你應該去郵政中心。

2 虛擬實境口說練習
on your iMessenger
從最簡短到最豐富，讓你實際和老外練習口說和聽力

| 當你想寄一個包裹給國外的朋友時 |

❶ **How can I send this parcel to London?**
我可以如何把這個包裹寄到倫敦呢？

> postcard 明信片
> package 包裹（美式用法）
> packet 小包（裹）

❷ **The parcel contains foods.**
包裹裡裝的是食物。

> document 文件
> glassware 玻璃器皿
> fragile items 易碎物品

❸ **How many days will it take?**
大概花幾天時間會寄到？

> hours 小時
> weeks 週
> months 個月

| 當郵局人員告知你郵寄服務的計價方式時 |

❶ **The fare is calculated based on the weight.**
郵寄費用是以重量計算。

> the height 高度
> size 尺寸
> the length 長度

❷ **Thanks for your help.**
謝謝你的幫忙

> assistance 協助
> support 支持
> guidance 指導

當你想詢問寄東西的計價方式時

❶ How much does it cost to send it to Rome?
把這寄到羅馬要多少錢？

ship it to Taiwan 船運到台灣
transport it to Japan 運到日本
cart it to the market 運送到市場

❷ How do you calculate the price?
費用是如何計算的？

wage 薪水
expense 支出
stipend 津貼；獎學金

3.How much is the price for a package that weighs 5 kilograms?
一個重五公斤的包裹的郵寄費用是多少錢？

grams （重量單位）克
hectograms （重量單位）百克
pounds （重量單位）磅

當你要使用郵局無摺匯款或劃撥匯款時

❶ Please fill out the remittance slip first.
請先填寫匯款單。

application form 申請表
questionnaire 問卷
survey 調查

❷ I brought the bank book with me.
我有把存款簿帶在身上。

signet 印章；私章
work permit 工作許可證
academic transcript 成績單

3 虛擬實境網路聊天
on your iMessenger

在手機或電腦上，利用打字就可以聊出千言萬語

Amos

星期三 下午 13:45

Hey~ where did you go?
下午 13:45

嘿～你去哪兒了？

I was in a meeting.
下午 13:46

我剛去開會。

How was it?
下午 13:47

開得怎麼樣？

**Nothing in particular~
I mean,
What else could
happen at a meeting?**
下午 13:48

沒什麼特別的～
我是說，開會還能有
什麼新鮮事呢？
特別的

**We talked about some plans in the
near future, some ways to cut down
costs in the company.
I think there'll be another meeting
tomorrow which you'll need to go to.**
下午 13:53

我們討論了一些未來
的計畫，以及怎麼減
低公司的各項開銷成
本。另外，明天還有
一場會議，我想你也
得參加。
削減

**Is it going to be about the joint
venture between our companies?**
下午 13:54

是討論兩家公司之間
的合作計畫嗎？
聯合的
投資活動

Amos

星期三 下午 13:45

You got it!
I know meetings can get boring,
but try not to fall asleep, ok?

下午 13:55

沒錯！我知道開會總是很無聊，但儘量別睡著好嗎？

Don't worry~ I'm not a sleeper,
but I can't say the same about the
other people over at my company.

下午 13:56

別擔心～我不是個瞌睡蟲，但我們公司的其他人我就不敢說了。
愛打瞌睡的人

下午 13:57

But who can blame them?
Meetings can get stale,
especially on a Monday lol.

下午 13:58

但能怪他們嗎？開會是如此枯燥無味，特別是星期一的時候哈哈。
厭倦的

I can't deny it!

下午 13:59

我完全同意你！

聊天金句大補帖

It can't be. 這不可能。

在談話當中，倘若對方提出了一件新的消息是你認為無法置信的、或太不可思議的事情，就可以用這句來表達你的驚訝或無法相信的態度。也可以用這幾句來代替：

• I can't believe it!

• It's incredible!

Unit 2 錢財通通交到這

Good morning, may I help you?
早上好。有什麼可以為您效勞的？

Word Power!
- draw out **phr** 取出
- withdraw [wɪð`drɔ] **v** 提領
- deposit [dɪ`pazɪt] **v** 存入
- account [ə`kaunt] **n** 帳戶

- I want to draw out NT$5000. 我想領 5000 塊錢。
- I want to ask you how to withdraw money? 我想請問一下怎麼提款？
- I want to deposit some money in my account. 我想存點錢。
- I want to get a credit card. 我想辦一張信用卡。

Which account would you like to open?
你想開哪種帳戶？

Word Power!
- current **a** 通用的
- savings [`sevɪŋ] **n** 存款

更多…
- current account 活期存款帳戶
- savings account 活期儲蓄帳戶；
- checking account 支票存款帳戶。

- I'd like to open a current account. 我想開一個活期存款帳戶。
- How do I open a savings account? 我應該如何開立活期儲蓄帳戶呢？
- How do I open a checking account? 我應該如何開立支票存款帳戶呢？

What kind of service does the bank offer?
銀行提供哪幾種業務？

Word Power!
- fixed [fɪkst] **a** 不動的
- transfer [træns`fɝ] **v** 轉帳
- handle [`hændl] **v** 處理

- We have fixed deposits. 我們有定期存款。
- We can offer transfer account service. 我們也有轉帳業務。
- We have withdraw-deposit service. 我們有存提款業務。
- We can handle a credit card for you. 我們可以為你辦信用卡。

What can I do for you?
我能為你做點什麼嗎？

Word Power!
- password [`pæs͵wɝd]
  n 密碼
- fund [fʌnd] n 資金
- freeze [friz] v 結冰
  → freeze-froze-frozen
- service charge
  phr 手續費

Sentence Power!
- whether 是否（引導名詞子句）
  → whether…or not 不管是…或是（引導副詞子句）

- I forget the password of my card. 我忘了銀行卡的密碼。
- My credit card is missing. 我的銀行卡丟了。
- My funds are frozen. 我的資金被凍結了。
- I want to know whether there is any service charge. 我想知道是否需要手續費。

這樣說不禮貌
What can you do for me?
你可以做什麼？

Why isn't the bank open for business?
為什麼這間銀行沒營業？

不能不會的小技巧
在台灣，銀行的營業時間多半是周一至周五的早上9點至下午3點半；但在美國，各行的營業時間都不太一樣，有到下午4點，也有的周六也會營業。因此若出國旅遊前，也可先查詢一下當地的銀行營業時間，免得臨時要跑一趟時卻沒開哦。

- It is not the hours of operation. All the staff is off now. 現在不是上班時間。工作人員都下班了。
- The system is broken. 系統壞了。
- Because guards are escorting in transportation. 因為保全正在護送運鈔車。
- Robbers forced their way into the bank. 搶匪闖入銀行了。

Word Power!
- escort [`ɛskɔrt] v 護送
- robber [`rɑbɚ] n 搶匪
- force [fors] v 武力

What kind of investment(s) does the bank offer?
銀行有哪幾種投資？

Word Power!
- investment
  [ɪn`vɛstmənt] n 投資
- welfare [`wɛl͵fɛr]
  n 福利
- education [͵ɛdʒu`keʃən]
  n 教育
- unemployment
  [͵ʌnɪm`plɔɪmənt]
  n 失業
- futures [`fjutʃɚz]
  n 期貨

- We have a health and welfare fund. 我們有健康福利基金。
- We have education insurance. 我們有教育保險。
- We have unemployment insurance. 有失業保險。
- You can try our futures investment. 你可以試試我們的期貨投資。

2 虛擬實境口說練習
on your iMessenger
從最簡短到最豐富，讓你實際和老外練習口說和聽力

▎當你想在銀行開立新的戶頭時 ▎--------------------------------

❶ I'd like to open a new account in your bank.
我想要在你們銀行開戶。

apply for a credit card 申請信用卡
deposit some money 存一些錢
find a job 找個工作

❷ I'm opening this account for my new job.
我開這個帳戶是為了新工作。

a trip abroad 出國遊玩
my daughter's college fund 我女兒的大學基金
a business plan （商業、創業）計畫

❸ I forgot to bring my seal.
我忘記帶我的印章了。

my passport 我的護照
my driver's license 我的駕照
my ID photo 我的大頭照

▎當行員向你要求身份證明或其他文件時 ▎--------------------------------

❶ Here is my ID card.
這是我的身份證。

the agreement 協議
the contract 合約
proof 證明

❷ I left my credit card in the car.
我把信用卡留在車上了。

on the bus 在公車上
in the taxi 在計程車上
in my husband's wallet 在我老公的皮夾

| 當你要使用預借現金的服務時 | ────────────────

❶ Can I get a cash advance with my credit card?
我可以用我的信用卡預借現金嗎？

> pay the bill 付帳單
> transfer the money 轉帳
> make a transaction 交易

❷ What is the maximum limit per transaction?
每筆交易的最大額度是多少？

> minimum limit 最小額度
> service charge 手續費

❸ Do I need to provide any documentation?
我需要提供任何文件嗎？

> financial statement 財力證明
> proof of purchase 購買證明
> birth certificate 出生證明

| 當你想在銀行換外幣時 | ─────────────────────

❶ I'd like to exchange some American dollars for euros.
我想把一些美元換成歐元。

> GBP (Great Britain Pound) 英鎊
> Japanese Yen 日本
> Hong Kong dollar 港幣

> canadian dollars 加拿大幣
> renminbi yuan 人民幣
> Australia dollar 澳幣

❷ What is the exchange rate for New Taiwan dollars?
請問兌換新臺幣的匯率是多少？

> Peso 披索（菲律賓貨幣）
> Thai baht 泰幣
> Rupee 盧比（印度貨幣）

3 虛擬實境網路聊天 　在手機或電腦上，利用打字就可以聊出千言萬語
on your iMessenger

Jeffery C. Kim

星期三 下午 13:45

 Uh… Do u hav time?
I need a talk, plz.

下午 13:45

呃…你現在有時間嗎？我想説點話，拜託。

Sure. I'm happen to be free now.

下午 13:46

當然。我剛好現在有時間。
碰巧

 Hav u noticed how localized the news is?

下午 13:47

你注意到這兒的新聞報導相當本土嗎？
地區的

下午 13:48

I mean, there is hardly any in-depth coverage of international issues.
The news is on 24-7, but it's the same thing over and over.

下午 13:49

我的意思是，很難看到他們報導比較深入的國際議題。他們二十四小時全年無休地報導新聞，但似乎都是重複的新聞一再播報。
幾乎不
深入的
新聞報導

That's exactly it.
And do you know why?
Cuz that's what the people want to see!
And all that the media cares about is its ratings.

下午 13:50

的確是這樣，你知道為什麼嗎？因為觀眾想看的就是那些！而媒體唯一關心的就是收視率。
關心
收視率

Jeffery C. Kim

星期三 下午 13:45

OMG.

下午 13:51

我的天啊。

People want to see blood and gore. They want to see perversion, adulteration and occasionally, politics.

下午 13:52

大家想看聳動的消息，想看扭曲的、劣質的題材，或者是政治。

血塊
虛假
曲解
偶爾

下午 13:53

It's likewise with newspapers. I noticed it's almost always community news on the front page. It's really worrying at times…

下午 13:54

報紙也是這樣。我注意到幾乎所有的頭條新聞都是社會新聞，這種情況真令人擔憂…

同樣地
頭版

I'm on the same page as u. Hope with further education, people can expand their horizons.

下午 13:55

我跟你所見略同，而且我希望未來的教育能夠擴大民眾的眼界。

想法相同
擴展
地平線

聊天金句大補帖

I'll get it. 讓我來做吧。

當我們與他人在一起時，我們想要負責做某件事情，不需要對方操心或行動時，這句話就表示我們能夠搞定，比方說付錢、幫對方拿自助餐具等等。

Unit 3

沒事別進出的地方

What is wrong with you?
你怎麼了？

- My throat is scratchy. 我的喉嚨不舒服。
- I guess I may get the flu. 我猜我得了流感。
- I cannot see clearly and I've been feeling run down these days. 我看不清楚，而且我最近總覺得很疲倦。
- I have a toothache. It must be my wisdom teeth. 我牙痛。一定是我的智齒在作怪。

Word Power!
- scratchy [ˈskrætʃɪ] a 癢的
- flu [flu] n 流感
- run down phr 由於過度勞累而疲憊
- toothache [ˈtuθˌek] n 牙痛
- wisdom teeth n 智齒

更多…
症狀
- running nose 流鼻水
- cough 咳嗽
- sore 疼痛發炎的

What a surprise meeting you here.
在這裡見到你真有點意外。

- I came here to meet my wife. She is a nurse. 我和我太太約在這裡見面，她是護士。
- I came here to have a systemic check-up. 我到這兒來做全身檢查。
- I came to get some pills. 我來拿一些藥。
- I came here to take a blood test. 我來做抽血檢驗。

Word Power!
- systemic [sɪsˈtɛmɪk] a 全身的
- check-up [ˈtʃɛkˌʌp] n 檢查
- pill [pɪl] n 藥丸
- blood test n 驗血

Why did you come to the hospital?
你為什麼去醫院呢？

- I work in here. 我在醫院工作。
- I came to visit a patient. 我來探望一個病人。
- I've been suffering from a bad stomachache for a week. 我的胃已經痛了一個星期。
- I have a friend who is a doctor, I am visiting him in passing. 我有一個朋友是醫生，我路過這兒來看看他。

Word Power!
- patient [ˈpeʃənt] n 病人
- suffer from phr 因（疾病）而痛或不舒服
- stomachache [ˈstʌməkˌek] n 胃痛

更多…
部門
- ICU 加護病房
- CMD 胸腔內科
- REH 復健科

What do you think of the hospital?
你認為這個醫院怎麼樣？

8 Chapter

出發社區巡禮

- I think the environment is good. 我覺得環境很好。
- The nurse is kind and the doctor is responsible.
護士和藹，醫生負責任。

這樣說不禮貌

- Just so-so.
馬馬虎虎吧。

I never liked hospitals.
我從來都沒有喜歡過醫院。

不能不會的小技巧
若對方問你對於某間醫院的意見為何時，通常表示他／她有可能正在對這家醫院的醫療服務進行評估，並考慮自己或自己認識的人應不應該到那家醫院就診。因此，對於這種比較嚴肅的問題，你應該提出最真實的看法。

Word Power!
· hospital [ˋhɑspɪtl]
  n 醫院
· nurse [nɝs] n 護士
· responsible
  [rɪˋspɑnsəbl]
  a 負責任的

Do you know the doctor?
你認識這個醫生嗎。

不能不會的小技巧
碰到類似情況時，若你認為這家醫院醫生的醫術不錯，就該大力推薦；但若你認為這家醫院有需要改進的地方時，也不需要害怕得罪別人，而要大膽提出。

- No, it will be the first time I meet him. 我不認識，這是我第一次見他。
- It is my friend who recommended him to me. 是我朋友把他介紹給我的。
- Yes, he is my private doctor. 是的，他是我的私人醫生。
- I am not familiar with him. 我跟他不是太熟。

What about the patient's situation?
病人的情況怎麼樣了？

Word Power!
· serious [ˋsɪrɪəs]
  a 嚴重的
· recover [rɪˋkʌvɚ]
  v 恢復
· had better phr （勸告，建議說）最好做某事
· X-ray [ˋɛksˋre] n X 光
· further [ˋfɝðɚ]
  ad 進一步地
· observation
  [ˌɑbzɝˋveʃən] n 觀察

- It is not serious. 不嚴重。
- He should have a good rest. Several days later, he will recover. 好好休息，幾天過後就會好起來的。
- He'd better have an X-ray. 他最好照一下 X 光。
- We need further observation. 我們需要進一步觀察。

2 虛擬實境口說練習
on your iMessenger

從最簡短到最豐富，讓你實際和老外練習口說和聽力

| 當你要向醫生描述你的症狀時 |

❶ I'm feeling a little nauseous.
我感覺有點噁心。

> sore （肌肉等）痠
> itchy 癢的
> depressed 沮喪的

❷ My shoulder is aching.
我的肩膀在痛。

> ankle 腳踝
> wrist 手腕
> elbow 手肘

❸ My shoulder hurts when I lift my arms.
當我舉起手臂的時候肩膀會痛。

> feet 腳
> nose 鼻子

> go for a jog 跑步的時候
> take a deep breath 深呼吸的時候

| 當你在醫院掛號時 |

❶ I'd like to make an appointment.
我想要掛號。

> schedule an appointment 掛號
> cancel the appointment 取消掛號
> move the appointment 改期掛號

❷ I have an appointment with Dr. Smith.
我有預約史密斯醫生。

> Professor Snow 史諾教授
> Father White 懷特神父
> Sister Helena 海倫娜修女

| 當醫生建議你做某些治療時 | - - - - - - - - - - - - - -

❶ **I will prescribe some pain medication.**
我會開給你一些止痛藥。

> liquid medicine 藥水
> ointment 藥膏
> tablet 藥片

❷ **You should get an annual physical examination.**
你應該每年都做健康檢查。

> health check 健康檢查
> dental exam 牙齒檢查

❸ **I suggest you consider hospitalization for further examination.**
我建議你考慮住院接受進一步檢查。

> go home and rest 回家休息
> take three tablets a day 一天服用三片藥片

| 當醫生向你說明你可能是生什麼病時 | - - - - - - - - - -

❶ **You might have caught the flu.**
你可能得流感了。

> caught a cold 感冒了
> got allergies 過敏了

❷ **These are symptoms of pneumonia.**
這些是肺炎的症狀。

> cancer 癌症
> AIDS 愛滋病
> food poisoning 食物中毒

3 虛擬實境網路聊天
on your iMessenger
在手機或電腦上，利用打字就可以聊出千言萬語

Judy

星期三 下午 13:45

Oh, dear. You know what?
I've only been here for a few
days but I'm starting to notice
how people from different
cultures behave in different ways.

下午 13:45

親愛的，你知道嗎，
我才到這兒幾天而已，
但是已經發覺到許多
文化差異。

表現

Yeah… It's about time.

下午 13:46

恩…也該是時候了。

Just the other day,
I noticed one of the workers
in ur company going through
someone else's desk.
I went over and asked what he
was doing and he told me that
he was looking for something.
What I meant to say was he
should stop what he was doing!

下午 13:47

幾天前，我看到一個
員工在翻搜另一個人
的辦公桌。我走過去
問他在做什麼，他說
他正在找一樣東西。
我的意思其實是要他
停止他當時的舉動！

員工

仔細查找

尋找

Going through other people's
things is considered rude
almost everywhere.

下午 13:48

不論在何處，翻搜別
人的東西大概都會被
視為無禮的舉動。

粗魯的

下午 13:49

However, in some cultures it may
be accepted more than in others.

下午 13:50

但是在某些文化當中
卻可以被接受。

Judy

下午 13:51

In America, going through other people's belongings is illegal. You can be sued for invading other's privacy.

下午 13:52

在美國，亂動別人的私人物品是違法的。侵犯他人隱私可能會被告上法院。

所有物
違法的
控告
侵犯
隱私

Well, we sure to do something to enhance people's concept of privacy here.

下午 13:53

嗯，我們確實應該做點什麼來加強人們的隱私觀念。

How about announcing it during our next meeting?

下午 13:54

在會議時加強宣導的話你覺得如何？

Not bad. I'll take it into account.

下午 13:55

不錯耶。我會考慮看看的。

聊天金句大補帖

I don't feel so hot. 我覺得不太舒服。

這句指的是身體或心理等方面覺得不太舒服，不僅僅是生理上的感覺而已。通常這樣說的時候並非指什麼嚴重或需要治療的疾病，而是感覺上不太對勁之意。比方說在一間空氣不流通的地方待了一會兒，我們可能就會以這句話來表達當時的不舒適感。

Unit 4 店員什麼都會

What do you want to buy?
你想要買什麼？

- A couple of turkey burgers and some jelly beans.
  幾個火雞漢堡和雷根糖。

- I have no idea. How about some twizzlers?
  不知道耶，買一些扭扭糖如何？

- I would like to buy some potato chips and snacks.
  我想買些洋芋片和點心。

Word Power!
- turkey [ˋtɝkɪ] n 火雞肉
- jelly bean n 雷根糖
  →彩色豆狀的軟糖，
  有各式各樣的口味
- twizzler n 扭扭糖
  →條狀螺旋紋的甘草
  味糖
- chip [tʃɪp] n 洋芋片

更多
- nutella 榛果可可醬
- cheese stick 起士棒
- pretzel 蝴蝶餅

How much do they cost totally?
一共多少錢？

- 40 dollars all together. 一共是四十美元。

- Let me check it, please. It is 20 dollars.
  請讓我看看。20 美元。

- All items in our store are buy one get one free today. So the total cost is 10 dollars.
  本店的商品正在買一送一。所以總共只要 10 美元。

不能不會的小技巧
在購買物品前，一定要先問清楚價格。尤其是碰到特賣或是大減價的時候，有時候標籤上的定價不一定代表售價的價格。

Word Power!
- all together ad 總共
- buy one get one free phr 買一送一
- do the math phr 算數學

這樣說不禮貌
Can't you do the math?
你不會自己算嗎？

I would like to buy a file holder, can you give a recommendation?
我想買個檔案夾，你有推薦的嗎？

- What color do you like? We have a lot of colors to choose from. 你喜歡什麼顏色？我們這有好多種顏色供你選擇。

- What about this one? It's very fashionable today. 這款怎麼樣？最近很流行的。

- Which styles do you prefer：the round one or the long one? 你是喜歡圓的呢還是長的呢？

Word Power!
- file holder n 檔案夾
- color [ˋkʌlɚ] n 顏色
- fashionable [ˋfæʃənəbl] a 流行的
- round [raʊnd] a 圓的
- comment [ˋkɑmɛnt] n 意見

How would you pay for it?
你用什麼方式付款？

Word Power!
- wallet [ˋwɑlɪt] **n** 皮夾
- receipt [rɪˋsit] **n** 發票
- purse [pɝs]
  n（女用）錢包

Sentence Power!
- keep the change 不用
  找錢

- In cash and keep the change please. 現金，不用找錢。
- Credit card; may I? 信用卡可以嗎？
- E-wallet, and keep my receipt inside please. 電子錢包，發票幫我存在裡面。
- Sorry! I left my purse on the table. 很抱歉！我忘記帶錢包了。

Can I have a Slurpee?
有思樂冰嗎？

Word Power!
- Slurpee **n** 思樂冰
- size [saɪz] **n**
  尺寸；大小

- Sorry, we don't have it. Would you like other drinks? 抱歉我們沒有，其他飲料可以嗎？
- What a pity! They are sold out. 很遺憾，已經賣光了。
- Yes. You can choose the cup size first. 有的，你可先選要什麼大小的。
- No, but there are some sodas. 沒有，但有一些其他汽水。

What's the special for today?
今天有什麼特價東西嗎？

Word Power!
- roll cake **n** 蛋糕捲
- merchandise
  [ˋmɝtʃənˌdaɪz] **n** 商品

Sentence Power!
- …% off 打…折
  →前面填入的數字是
  指商品被扣除掉的價
  格，所以打八折會說
  20% off，打九折會寫
  成 10% off。

- The chocolate roll cake with small Latte is 39 dollars today. 巧克力蛋糕捲搭小杯拿鐵只要 39 元。
- All merchandise in the store is 50% off. 全店商品五折。
- The Pocky series. But they are sold out, sorry. Pocky 全系列。但已經售完了，抱歉。

這樣說不禮貌

There is nothing left today. Come early tomorrow.
今天的特價品已經沒了。明天請早。

2 虛擬實境口說練習
on your iMessenger

從最簡短到最豐富，讓你實際和老外練習口說和聽力

| 當你想請店員幫你操作機台時 |

❶ I have some problems using the copy machine.
我不太會操作那台影印機。

> making a decision 做決定
> reading a map 看地圖
> finding the direction 找方向

❷ Can you give me a hand with the machine?
你可以幫我操作那台機器嗎？

> project 企劃
> case 案子

❸ The copy machine is jammed.
那台影印機卡紙了。

> broken 壞了
> out of order 壞了
> running out of ink 墨水快用光了

| 當你想問店員商品的位置時 |

❶ Where are the iced drinks located?
請問冷飲區在哪？

> is ... canned food 罐頭食品區
> are ... baked goods 麵包糕餅區

❷ Can you point out where the dairy products are?
你可以指給我看乳製品區在哪裡嗎？

> frozen food is 冷凍食品區
> produce is 農產品區

┃ 當你詢問店員手上的商品是否有優惠價格時 ┃

❶ What discount do you have for bottled water?
你們瓶裝水有什麼折扣？

> tampon 衛生棉條
> tissue paper 衛生紙
> body lotion 乳液

❷ It says "Buy two get one free", right?
它說「買二送一」，對吧？

> No refund 不接受退費
> On sale 特價中

❸ Do I get 20 percent off by paying in cash?
我付現的話會打八折嗎？

> get a coupon 拿到一張禮券
> get a free gift 得到免費禮物
> accumulate any point 累積任何點數

┃ 當店員在結帳時，詢問需不需要塑膠袋或其他物品時 ┃

❶ It's 250 dollars in total.
總共是兩百五十元。

> 10 pounds 十鎊
> 20 rupees 二十盧比
> 50 pesos 五十披索

❷ Would you like to buy a plastic bag?
你想要買一個塑膠袋嗎？

> buy one more item and get a discount
> 多買一件然後可以打折
> get a free sample 拿一件免費的試用品

3 虛擬實境網路聊天　在手機或電腦上，利用打字就可以聊出千言萬語
on your iMessenger

Lucas

星期三 下午 13:45

You know, man. I'd love it if you could show me around.

下午 13:45

老兄，你知道。如果你能陪我逛逛，我會很高興的。

帶某人四處參觀

Sorry, man.
Actually, I just got a call from the office. They need me back there.

下午 13:46

事實上我剛接到公司的電話，我想他們需要我回去公司一趟。

Well, I'm okay with being alone.

下午 13:48

嗯，我一個人也可以的。

下午 13:49

Is there anything I should watch out for on my own?

下午 13:50

有沒有什麼事是我一個人逛街需要注意的呢？

注意

As you know,
The expensive shopping area is just around the corner.
Most store clerks in there speak English.

下午 13:52

你知道的，買名貴商品的地方就在這附近。裡頭大部分的店員都會說英語。

店員

Rite.
What about the traditional souvenirs?

下午 13:53

好的。那麼傳統的紀念品呢？

Lucas

星期三 下午 13:45

> You can get all of them from there.
>
> 下午 13:53

你在那裡可以買到所有你要的。

> IC.
>
> 下午 13:53

我知道了。

> After you are done shopping there, get on the bus I told you about.
> Remember, the places that sell those traditional items may not accept credit cards.
> Be sure you withdraw some cash.
> And!
> Watch out for pickpockets!!
>
> 下午 13:54

你在那兒買完東西以後，去搭我告訴過你的公車。別忘了，很多東西都是不接受信用卡付費的，所以記得去領些現金。另外千萬要小心扒手！

扒手

> Sure! Thx, bro!
> CU for now.
>
> 下午 13:55

當然！謝啦老兄！先掰啦！

See you. 的簡寫

下午 13:56

聊天金句大補帖

Did what? 你做了什麼？

• V+what

是一個很好用的句型，對於別人說的話不甚明白時都可以使用這樣的句型。除了確認對方所說的事情為何外，也能以更有效率的方式增加雙方的互動。

Unit 5
記得守規矩

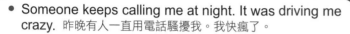

一定要會的問答句
90% 的老外都是用這些句子開始聊天。

What can I do for you?
有什麼需要幫忙的嗎？

Word Power!
- drive sb. crazy
  phr 把某人逼瘋
- windbreaker
  [ˋwɪndˏbrekɚ] **n** 風衣
- smuggle [ˋsmʌg!]
  v 走私

- Someone keeps calling me at night. It was driving me crazy. 昨晚有人一直用電話騷擾我。我快瘋了。
- I lost my wallet and passport. What should I do? 我的皮夾和護照都不見了。我該怎麼辦？
- Did you see the man in the dark windbreaker? I think he is smuggling drugs. 你有看到那個穿深色風衣的男人嗎？我覺得他在走私毒品。

What kind of wallet did you lose?
你弄丟的是怎麼樣的錢包？

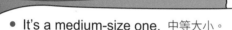

- It's a medium-size one. 中等大小。
- It's a red leather one. 是紅色皮質的。
- It's a man's purse. All of my important certificates are in it. I really need to get it back. 是一個男用錢包。我所有的重要證件都在裡面。我一定要找回來。
- It's a purse with polka dots on it. 錢包上面有點點圖案。

不能不會的小技巧
不論國內外，人多的地方都要小心扒手。特別是觀光客容易聚集的風景名勝，更容易成為他們的下手目標。因此若出國在外，重要物品跟錢財最好是貼身放置，盡可能不要露白。如此一來，才能保證出去玩時的安全及好心情哦。

Word Power!
- leather [ˋlɛðɚ] **n** 皮革
- polka dot **n** 圓點花樣

What was in the wallet?
裡面有什麼？

- My ID and driver's license. 我的駕照。
- A ticket of train, a ring of keys, a ring. 一張火車票、一串鑰匙、一枚戒指。
- More than $200 in cash. 兩百多塊現金。
- An easy card, $3000 in cash, and a picture of my girlfriend. 一張悠遊卡、三千塊現金、和我女友的照片

不能不會的小技巧
一般來說，當民眾到警察局報案時，受理報案的警員會問一些細節問題，通常這是標準程序，不需害怕或緊張，只要把知道的資訊據實告訴警員即可。當出國旅遊時，重要證件如護照及簽證等一定要隨身保管，不要讓竊賊有機可趁。

Word Power!
- license [ˋlaɪsn̩s] **n** 執照

Who is Captain Fluellen?

誰是弗艾倫上尉？

Word Power!
- captain [ˈkæptɪn]
  n 上尉
- uniform [ˈjunəˌfɔrm]
  n 制服
- pistol [ˈpɪstl] n 手槍
- on duty phr 執勤中

更多…

軍階排排站
- colonel 上校
- commander 中校
- major 少校
- lieutenant 中尉，少尉

- The man in the uniform is Captain Fluellen. 穿著制服的那位就是弗艾倫上尉。
- The man sitting by the window. 坐在靠近窗戶位置上的那個人。
- He is the one with a pistol. 配備著手槍的那位。
- He is not in the office right now. He is on duty. 他現在不在辦公室。他正在執勤中。

Thank you for helping me find my car.

謝謝你幫我找回車子。

Word Power!
- citizen [ˈsɪtəzn] n 市民

- You are welcome. It's our duty. 不用謝，這是我們應該做的。
- It's a piece of cake. 小菜一碟。
- It was the least we could do. 至少這是我們能夠做的。
- Helping citizens is our responsibility. 幫助市民是我們的責任。

Where did you lose you ID card?

你的身份證在哪裡弄丟了？

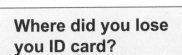

不能不會的小技巧
若在國外碰到緊急事故，例如證件、護照弄丟、碰上扒手、強盜，導致回國困難的話。可撥旅外國人緊急服務專線求助：
- +886-800-085-095（付費）
- 800-0885-0885（免付費）。

Word Power!
- classroom [ˈklæsˌrum]
  n 教室
- somewhere
  [ˈsʌmˌhwɛr] n 某處

- In the library. 在圖書館。
- I can't remember, sorry. 我想不起來，抱歉。
- Maybe in the classroom. 可能是在教室。
- Somewhere on my way to the gym. 應該是我要去體育館的路上某處。

2 虛擬實境口說練習
on your iMessenger

從最簡短到最豐富，讓你實際和老外練習口說和聽力

| 當你到警察局報案時 |

❶ **I'd like to report a robbery.**
我想要通報一起搶劫案。

a theft 竊盜案
a burglary （入室）竊盜案
an assault 襲擊；攻擊

❷ **It's in the convenience store near my house.**
就在我家附近的便利商店。

across the street 在對街
two miles away 在兩英哩外

❸ **I just witnessed a car crash.**
我剛剛目擊了一起車禍。

a murder 一樁謀殺
a suicide 一樁自殺

| 當你因為捲進紛爭被帶到警察局，並且要辯解時 |

❶ **I swear I have never met this guy before.**
我發誓我從沒見過這個人。

heard about this guy 聽過這個人
sneaked into his house 偷溜進他家
scratched his car 刮他的車

❷ **I have the right to remain silent.**
我有權保持緘默。

call my lawyer 打給我的律師
refuse treatment 拒絕治療

| 當警察請你詳細描述案件發生的細節時 |

❶ A guy ran in and took my purse.
有個人跑進來然後拿走我的皮包。

> stabbed me in the back 從後面刺我一刀
> shot me in the shoulder 往我肩膀上開一槍
> hit me in the face 朝我臉上揮拳

❷ He is about 6 feet tall and has blonde hair.
他大約六呎高且有一頭金髮。

> 5 feet and 10 inches tall, and has blue eyes.
> 五呎十吋高,且有藍眼睛。
> 6 feet tall and has red hair.
> 六呎高且有一頭紅髮。

❸ In the purse are my ID, mobile phone and credit cards.
皮包裡有我的身分證、手機跟信用卡。

> In the handbag 手提包裡
> In the pouch （小）袋裡
> In the pocket 口袋裡

| 當你想向警察道謝時 |

❶ Thank you for your effort!
謝謝你的努力!

> your contribution 你的貢獻
> your hard work 你的努力

❷ I can't thank you enough for everything you did.
對於你所做的一切,我怎麼感謝都不夠。

> protecting our community 保護我們的社區
> raising us up 撫養我們長大
> giving me the opportunity 給我這個機會

3 虛擬實境網路聊天
on your iMessenger

在手機或電腦上，利用打字就可以聊出千言萬語

Rudolf

星期三 下午 13:45

Hey~
Did you happen to bring an umbrella?
I think it's raining outside.

下午 13:45

That reminds me!
I was going to ask you something.

下午 13:46

下午 13:47

What's the deal with girls carrying umbrellas when it's not even raining?

下午 13:48

HEE HEE

下午 13:49

I think they just don't want to become dark from the sun.

下午 13:50

Americans and Europeans love a good tan.
Why has that not affected the people here?

下午 13:51

嘿～你剛好有帶雨傘嗎？我覺得外面在下雨。

這倒提醒我要問你一件事。
提醒

那些女生在晴空下也要帶著傘到底是怎麼回事？
…是怎麼回事

我覺得她們只是不想被太陽曬黑。
（皮膚等）微黑的

美國人和歐洲人都喜歡把皮膚曬成健康的小麥色。為什麼這樣的觀念沒有影響到東方人呢？
棕褐色的皮膚

Rudolf

星期三 下午 13:45

 I think it's the skin color.

下午 13:52

我覺得跟膚色有關。

下午 13:53

 Because Americans and Europeans have a lighter colored skin.
Ladies here want to be white, however, It's a psychological thing.

下午 13:54

因為美國人與歐洲人的膚色比較淺，因此我們這邊的女人就會想要變白。這是心理因素。

淺色的
心理的、精神的

IC~
That means,
If you're dark you want to be white, and when you're white you want to be dark.

下午 13:55

我懂了。這表示當你很黑你就會想要變白，而當你很白的時候，你就會想曬黑一點。

 Smart you~

下午 13:56

真聰明～

聊天金句大補帖

I'll overlook it this time. 這次就算了。

這句話是當別人不小心犯了一個錯、或不經意冒犯你的時候，很常用的一句話。不要太計較，日子也會過得比較愉快，因此就可以用這句話來原諒對方，也是很適合的。

Unit 6

個人情報保衛戰

I have heard a lot about you.
我聽說過關於你的許多事情。

Word Power!
- introduce [ˌɪntrəˈdjus]
  v 介紹
- R&D abbr 研發部門
  = research and
  development
- council [ˈkaʊnsl]
  n 學生議會
- UM abbr 密西根大學
  = University of
  Michigan

- Really? Allow me to introduce myself: Oliver King, R&D manager at Ford Company. 真的嗎？讓我自我介紹一下，我叫奧利弗・金，是福特公司的研發經理。

- Excuse me. I don't think we have met before. I'm Ann Landess. 對不起，我想我們以前沒見過。我叫安・蘭德斯。

- Good morning, I'm John Brown from the student council of UM. 早安，我是密西根大學學生會的約翰・布朗。

My name is Jack. Nice to meet you.
我叫傑克。見到你很高興。

不能不會的小技巧
"Nice to meet you." 一般是指初次見面時的打招呼，而 "How do you do?" 則是熟人之間的打招呼方式。

- Nice to meet you, too. I'm Kate. 見到你也很高興，我叫凱特。

- Allow me to introduce myself. My name is Linda Palmer. 讓我自我介紹。我是琳達・帕默。

- May I introduce myself: Richard Emerson. 容我自我介紹：我是理查・愛默森。

You look younger than your age.
你看起來比實際年齡年輕耶。

不能不會的小技巧
在歐美，除非你跟對方即將成為朋友，或是除非你想讚美對方看起來很年輕，最好不要隨便評論與年齡有關的話題。

Word Power!
- fool [ful] v 愚弄
- appearance [əˈpɪrəns]
  n 外表
- real [ˈrɪəl] a 真實的
- compliment
  [ˈkɑmpləmənt] n 讚美

- Don't be fooled by my appearance. I'm actually 40 years old. 別被我的外表騙了。其實我四十歲了。

- How old do you think I am? 要不你是認為我幾歲？

- Yes, no one can tell my real age. 是的，沒人能看出我的實際年齡。

- Is that a compliment? 這是讚美嗎？

How old is your child?
你孩子多大了？

Word Power!
- daughter [`dɔtɚ]
  n 女兒
- bear [bɛr] v 出生
  → bear-bore-born

Sentence Power!
表示年齡時，year 前的數字如果不與 year 用「-」相連，則 year 要加 s，如果數字與 year 用「-」相連，則 year 不加 s，如：
- He is an 8-year-old boy. = The boy is 8 years old.

- My daughter is five-year-old. 我女兒五歲了
- My son was born two months ago. 我兒子才剛出生兩個月。
- I have two boys. One is 12, one is 9. 我有兩個兒子。一個十二歲，一個九歲。
- I have no children 我沒孩子。

My favorite pastime is dancing. How about you?
我最喜歡的娛樂是跳舞，你呢？

Word Power!
- pastime [`pæs‚taɪm]
  n 娛樂

Sentence Power!
- How to say?
  該怎麼說？

- How to say? Maybe, I haven't found what is my favorite pastime. 怎麼說呢？也許，我還找不到什麼是我最喜歡的娛樂。
- Favorite pastime? This is a good question! I like seeing movies. 最喜歡的娛樂？這絕對是一個好問題！我喜歡看電影。

這樣說不禮貌

Sorry, I don't like any kinds of pastime.
對不起，我不喜歡任何形式的娛樂。

Do you like your job?
你喜歡你的工作嗎？

Word Power!
- interested [`ɪntərɪstɪd]
  a 感到有興趣的
- hate [het] v 厭惡
- bottom [`bɑtəm]
  n 底部

Sentence Power!
- in the beginning 在一開始時
- from the bottom of my heart 打從心底

- Yes , I like my job very much. 是的，我非常喜歡我的工作。
- In the beginning, I disliked my job. But I am interested in my job now. 剛開始我討厭我的工作。但是現在，我對我的工作很感興趣。
- No, I really hate my job from the bottom of my heart. 不，我打從心底討厭我的工作。

這樣說不禮貌

Well, my job is just something I do.
呃，工作就是份工作。

2 虛擬實境口說練習　從最簡短到最豐富，讓你實際和老外練習口說和聽力
on your iMessenger

| 當你和你的朋友討論你們的工作時 |

❶ **I work for a famous law firm.**
我在一間知名法律事務所上班。

> an international accounting firm
> 一間國際的會計事務所
> a transnational corporation
> 一間跨國企業
> a local business 一間本地企業

❷ **My duty includes negotiating between international corporations.**
我的工作內容包含為國際企業談判協商。

> contacting the potential clients 聯絡潛在客戶
> cleaning up the office 打掃辦公室
> teaching two classes 教導兩個班級（或兩門課）

❸ **I feel lucky to be able to work in such a friendly environment.**
我覺得能在這麼友善的環境工作非常幸運。

> leading company 領先的公司
> competitive surrounding 競爭的環境
> prominent corporation 著名的企業

| 當你被他人問到你的年紀時 |

❶ **I'm turning 25 this year.**
我今年將滿 25 歲。

> becoming 成為
> approaching 接近

❷ **I was born in 1985.**
我在 1985 年出生。

> given birth to 出生（被…生出來）
> deserted 遺棄
> orphaned 使… 成為孤兒

| 當你被他人問到你和女友／男友的感情狀況時 |

❶ I just broke up with my girlfriend.
我剛跟我女朋友分手。

fell in love again with 再次愛上
had a fight 吵架
popped the question to 求婚

❷ We have been seeing each other for 5 years.
我們交往五年了。

dating each other 交往；約會
divorced 離婚
living together 住在一起

❸ He proposed to me last night.
他昨晚跟我求婚。

broke up with me 跟我分手
broke off with me 跟我分手
asked me to marry him 跟我求婚

| 當你向他人介紹你的身家背景時 |

❶ I grew up in the countryside.
我在鄉下長大。

in a big city 在大城市
with two sisters 跟兩個姐姐一起
in a rural village 在一個偏遠的小村莊

❷ I have two siblings, a brother and a sister.
我有兩個手足，一個哥哥跟一個妹妹。

two pets, a dog and a cat.
兩隻寵物，一隻狗跟一隻貓
two teachers, one for math and one for English
兩個老師，一個數學跟一個英文
two best friends, a girl and a boy.
兩個好朋友，一個男生跟一個女生

3 虛擬實境網路聊天
on your iMessenger

在手機或電腦上，利用打字就可以聊出千言萬語

Rookie

星期三 下午 13:45

Someone looks upset~
下午 13:45

You want to know what happened to me last night?
下午 13:46

下午 13:47

Not really lol.
But ur going to tell me anyway, rite?
下午 13:48

I was out with this girl I met at a teashop.
The whole date was great until the moment we were saying goodbye.
下午 13:51

Let me guess, you kissed her?
下午 13:52

No, I didn't.
She dodged as fast as if she were dodging a bullet.
下午 13:54

有人看起來不太對勁喔～
沮喪的

你想知道昨晚發生了什麼事情嗎？

不太想哈哈。不過不管怎樣你都會告訴我的，是吧？

昨天我跟那個在茶館認識的女孩出去，一直到我們道再見之前，整個約會都很順利。
直到

讓我猜猜，你吻了她？

沒有，我根本沒吻到。她像閃避子彈一樣很快地閃過我的吻。
躲避
子彈

Rookie

星期三 下午 13:45

下午 13:55

And after slamming the door in my face, she wouldn't pick up my calls.

下午 13:56

然後她在我面前把門重重地摔上之後，就都不接我電話了。
把某人拒之門外
接聽

Although western culture is becoming more and more accepted, kissing on a first date is one of those things you just have to watch out for. Even if it's just a kiss goodbye. She probably thought you were trying to move in too fast.

下午 13:57

西方文化越來越能被大家所接受。第一次約會就吻對方是得小心點。即使只是一個道別吻。她可能會覺得你進展太快了。
即使是

Thanks, Casanova.

下午 13:58

謝了，大情聖。
風流人物

聊天金句大補帖

...set the record straight. 澄清某事

當我們被誤會或大家對你有所誤解時，就可以用這句話來表示你的清白，並且釐清一些觀點。講清楚，說明白，才能避免自己遭受不明的委屈。

Chapter

9

聊得更深入

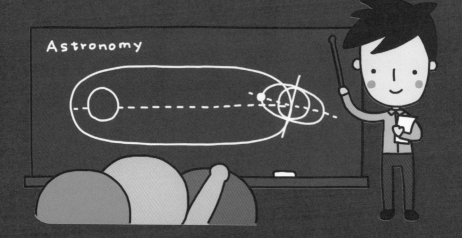

Unit 1 有話就是要直說

Unit 2 十萬個為什麼

Unit 3 請告訴我

Unit 4 信不信由你

Unit 5 真相只有一個

Unit 6 給認真的自己比個讚

Unit 1 有話就是要直說

What is your suggestion to improve the library?
你對於改進圖書館的建議是？

Word Power!
- improve [ɪm`pruv]
  v 改進
- extend [ɪk`stɛnd]
  v 延長
- enrich [ɪn`rɪtʃ]
  v 使豐富
- efficiency [ɪ`fɪʃənsɪ]
  n 效率

- Extend its opening time. 延長開放時間。
- Enrich the books in store. 增加藏書。
- It should have a large reading room. 應該有一個大的閱覽室。
- The efficiency of service must be improved. 服務效率有待於提高。

How about going to visit Professor Landon this evening?
今天晚上去看蘭登教授怎麼樣？

不能不會的小技巧
在給他人建議或詢問他人的意願時，態度一定要明確，只要口氣有禮，便能達到良好的溝通目的。另外，也可以適時詢問對方的意見和想法，不僅能幫助自己從不同角度思考，也代表你很尊重對方哦。

Word Power!
- seminar [`sɛmə͵nɑr]
  n 研討會
- under the weather
  phr 身體不舒服

- But I heard Professor Landon has gone to Paris for the seminar. 但我聽說蘭登教授去巴黎開研討會了。
- I'd love to. But I have class tonight. 是的，我也想去，但我今晚有課。
- Sorry, I can't. I'm feeling under the weather. 對不起，我不能去，我不太舒服。

Why don't we go to the exhibition?
為什麼我們不去參觀展覽？

Word Power!
- sort [sɔrt] n 種類
- Egyptian [ɪ`dʒɪpʃən]
  a 埃及的
- mummy [`mʌmɪ]
  n 木乃伊
- admission [əd`mɪʃən]
  n 入場許可
- artistic [ɑr`tɪstɪk]
  a 有藝術細胞的

- It depends on what sort of the exhibition it is. 這要看是什麼樣的展覽。
- Sure. I heard the exhibition about Egyptian Mummies is extremely popular. 當然好！我聽說這場埃及木乃伊的展覽非常受歡迎。
- Yes, how much does the admission cost? 好呀，入場費是多少？

這樣說不禮貌
Sorry, I'm not as artistic as you are.
對不起，我不像你這麼有藝術天份。

Have you thought of going to the formal party tonight?

你今晚想不想去參加正式晚會？

- I'm definitely going. It's a momentous occasion. 一定會的。這可是個重大的場合。

- Yes, I've been looking forward to it for a long time. 想呀，我已經期盼好久了。

- Not really. Everyone I know is going to it. But I'm afraid that I'm not really into socializing. 不太想。我認識的人都會參加。但我不是很喜歡社交。

這樣說不禮貌

If it's not mandatory, I'm not going.
如果不是強迫性參加的話，我就不去。

I'll give you a clear answer in ten days, is that okay?

十天後我將給你一個明確的答覆，好嗎？

- Ok, I'm counting on you. 好吧，我就靠你了。

- But you made the same promise last week. 可是上星期你也這麼保證的。

- Sorry, it's too late. The deal is off. 抱歉，太遲了。交易取消。

這樣說不禮貌

No, it's not okay. I need your answer right now.
不行。你現在要馬上給我答案。

What 's your opinion about the exploration?

你對這次探險有什麼看法？

- I'd say it is not worth the risk. You'd better not go on with it. 我覺得並不值得冒這個險，你們最好就此打住。

- Take my advice and don't go there alone. 聽我的話，不要一個人去那裏。

- The exploration will be a little bit risky, but I think it's necessary. 這次探險會有點冒險，但我覺得這是必要的。

這樣說不禮貌

To be honest, it's just a waste of your time.
老實說，這根本在浪費你自己的時間。

315

2 虛擬實境口說練習
on your iMessenger
從最簡短到最豐富，讓你實際和老外練習口說和聽力

| 當你對於政府實現的政策有意見想表達時 |

❶ In my opinion, the government should place more emphasis on social welfare policies.
在我看來，政府應該放多一點重點在社福政策。

diplomatic 外交的
educational 教育的
national security 國家安全

❷ We should protest against the new bill!
我們應該抗議那條新法案！

stand up to 起身對抗
stand for 支持
denounce 譴責

❸ The government has failed the people's expectations.
政府沒有達到人民的期望。

infuriated the people 激怒人民
implemented a new policy 實施一個新政策
launched a new scheme 發起一個新計畫

| 當你向客戶要求明確回覆你的疑問時 |

❶ Would you elaborate on your question?
你可以詳細說明你的問題嗎？

your project 你的專案
your proposal 你的提案
your answer 你的答案

❷ I don't quite understand what you meant.
我不太了解他的意思。

what he suggested 他暗示的
how he achieved it 她怎麼做到的
what he mentioned 他提到的

│ 當你被朋友問到你對於他的人生計劃有何建議時 │

❶ **Have you considered studying abroad?**
你有想過出國讀書嗎？

having a baby 生一個小孩
accepting his proposal 接受他的提議（求婚）
dating a foreigner 跟一個外國人約會

❷ **Taking a gap year may be beneficial to you.**
休一年空檔或許對你有幫助。

reading a good book 讀一本好書
exercising regularly 規律運動
going to bed early 早睡

❸ **I advise you to consult your professors.**
我建議你諮詢你的教授。

counselor 諮商師
doctor 醫師
psychiatrist 精神科醫師

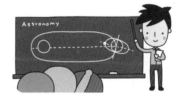

│ 當你購買一項商品卻發現不如預期，想要投訴店家時 │

❶ **I'd like to file a complaint about the clothes I ordered online.**
我想要投訴關於我在網路上訂的衣服。

the misconduct of your employee
你員工的失職（濫權）
the service you offered
你們提供的服務
the delay of the flight
班機的延誤

❷ **I'm requesting a refund due to the delay of the delivery.**
因為寄送的延遲，我要求退費。

an apology 一個道歉
an explanation 一個解釋
a discount 折扣

3 虛擬實境網路聊天
on your iMessenger

在手機或電腦上，利用打字就可以聊出千言萬語

Hamilton

星期三 下午 13:45

 So,
Where would you be if you didn't come with your boss and work at your current company?
下午 13:45

那，假如你沒跟你的老闆來這邊工作的話，你現在會在哪兒呢？
現在的

Well, I don't know where exactly~
But I'd probably be traveling somewhere in the world.
下午 13:46

這個嘛，我並不能精準的說出我會在哪裡～不過我想應該是在世界的某個角落旅行吧。

 Seriously?!
下午 13:47

你認真？！

Of course!
I used to take trips to different locations all over the world in the past.
And not for vacation, but for exploration.
下午 13:48

對啊！以前我經常到世界上各個不同的地點去探險，而不光只有去度假而已。
地點

Wow, you have such a free spirit.
下午 13:49

哇，你這麼富有冒險精神。
精神

Hey, what about you?
下午 13:50

那你呢？

Oh, I've always wanted to start my own restaurant.
下午 13:51

我一直想開一間自己的餐廳。

Is that why you love eating so much? LOL!
下午 13:52

那是你這麼愛吃的原因嗎？

Hamilton

星期三 下午 13:45

 Perhaps, I don't know.

下午 13:53

下午 13:54

 But I've always pictured myself in a traditional styled restaurant overlooking everything.
When customers come in, I would greet them like old friends, sit down at their table, and say, "drinks are on the house!"

下午 13:56

Cool, man!
If that dream ever becomes a reality, I'll be sure to come by for a glass of your free drink.

下午 13:57

或許，我不知道。

不過我總幻想我的餐廳是傳統風格、視野很好的那種。當客人進門的時候，我會像歡迎朋友一樣歡迎他們，而且輪流在不同的桌子跟客人哈拉，並大叫「今天的飲料全部算我的」！

想像
俯瞰
招呼
免費

那是你這麼愛吃的原因嗎？酷耶老兄！假如這個夢實現的話，我一定會去你那兒喝一杯免費的酒。

現實
無可否認地

聊天金句大補帖

Personally,... 就我個人而言，…
當我們對於別人所說的話或某些事物不認同，想表示一些意見時，我們就可以用這句強調，只是抒發己見，表達個人看法而已。

Unit 2 十萬個為什麼

Why do you seem to be so tired today?
你今天為什麼看起來這麼累呢？

Word Power!
- explain [ik`splen]
  v 解釋
- burn the midnight oil phr 熬夜
- loudly [`laudlɪ]
  ad 大聲地

Sentence Power!
- can't stop 無法停止
  →後接動名詞。類似用法：can't help but + Ving，有「不得不、不禁」之意

- Let me explain. I burnt the midnight oil last night. 讓我解釋一下，我昨晚沒睡。
- My neighbors were fighting loudly last night. 我的鄰居昨晚吵架吵得很大聲。
- It's because my friend couldn't stop talking to me on the phone last night. 那是因為我朋友昨晚和我講電話講個不停。

Why are you late for class?
你為什麼遲到呢？

不能不會的小技巧
每個國家對於守時的觀念不太一樣。例如祕魯就曾被世界公認為最不守時的國家，對於約定好的時間，遲到一小時到才是正常的，也因此才會有「祕魯時間」的說法。

Word Power!
- lose track of
  phr 失去…的線索

- Because I got up late. 因為我起床晚了。
- I lost track of time. 我忘記時間了。
- Sorry, the traffic is too busy today. 抱歉，今天路上太塞了。
- I had a fever this morning. So I came here after I saw the doctor. 我早上起來發現發燒。所以我先去看了醫生才過來

Why does she looks so sorrowful?
她為什看起來那麼傷心呢？

Word Power!
- sorrowful [`sarəfəl]
  a 悲傷的
- ill [ɪl] a 生病的
- quarrel [`kwɔrəl]
  n 爭吵
- criticize [`krɪtɪ͵saɪz]
  v 批評
- advising professor
  n 指導教授

- The reason is that her cat is ill. 因為她的貓生病了。
- It's because she had a quarrel with her boyfriend. 因為她和她男朋友吵架了
- Because she was criticized by her advising professor. 因為她的指導教授批評了她。
- Because her company played a joke on her. 因為她的同伴捉弄了她。

Why do you love him? ♥

你為什麼喜歡他呢？

Word Power!
- gentlemanly
  [ˈdʒɛntḷmənlɪ] **a** 紳士的
- in common **phr** 共同
- ambitious [æmˈbɪʃəs]
  a 有雄心的
- personality [ˌpɝsṇˈælətɪ]
  n 人格

Sentence Power!
- put in another way
  換句話說

- You know, he is very gentlemanly and handsome. 你知道的，他很紳士又英俊。

- We have so much in common. 我們有很多共通點。

- He is definitely going somewhere. Let me put in another way, he is very ambitious. 他一定會有所成就的。換個方式來說，他很有抱負。

- He has a great personality and an amazing smile. 他個性很好，而且他的微笑很吸引人。

Why do you give him compliments?

你為什麼稱讚他？

Word Power!
- compliment
  [ˈkɑmpləmənt]
  n 讚美的話
- make progress
  phr 取得進步
- speak highly of
  phr 讚揚
- diligent [ˈdɪlədʒənt]
  a 勤奮的

- Because he's making a great progress in his studies. 因為他在學習上有了很大的進步。

- I must speak highly of him for his good performance. 對於他的出色表現，我必須大力讚揚。

- He is a diligent student. That's why I gave him compliments. 他是個勤奮的學生。所以我才會讚美他。

Why don't you go to see the doctor?

你怎麼不去看醫生？

Word Power!
- have faith in **phr** 信任
- scare [skɛr] **v** 恐懼
- injection [ɪnˈdʒɛkʃən]
  n 注射
- illness [ˈɪlnɪs] **n** 病
- go away **phr** 消失

- Actually, I have no faith in doctors. 我不太相信醫生。

- I just need to stay home and drink lots of hot water. I'll be much better tomorrow, trust me.
  我只需要待在家休息，並喝大量的水。
  明天我就會好多了，相信我。

- I'm scared to have an injection.
  我害怕會要打針。

這樣說不禮貌

The illness will just not go away! I've done everything, but still no changes.
這個病就是不趕快好！我已經試過一切方法了，但都沒好轉。

2 虛擬實境口說練習
on your iMessenger
從最簡短到最豐富，讓你實際和老外練習口說和聽力

| 當你想知道一件事的原因時 |

❶ Would you kindly explain to me the cause of the incident?
你可以解釋給我聽那個事件的起因嗎？

the assignment of this week's class 這周的作業
the point of the lecture 講座的重點
the idea of the professor 教授的想法

❷ How did the fight start?
爭鬥是怎麼開始的？

fire 火（災）
rain 雨
quarrel 爭吵

❸ Who do you think caused the problems?
你認為是誰引起這些問題的？

triggered the fight 引發爭吵
kindled the fire 點燃這場火

| 當你問其他人你的朋友為什麼沮喪時 |

❶ He has been a little depressed. What happened?
他最近有點沮喪，發生什麼事了？

exhilarated 異常興奮的
hyper 亢奮的
bummed out 難過（失望）的

❷ What can we do to help him?
我們可以做什麼來幫助他？

catch the attention 吸引注意
get through the tough times 熬過這困難的時光
raise more money 募到更多錢

| 當你問你的朋友為何不試試其他方法解決問題時 |

❶ Why don't you try an alternative way?
你為什麼不試試一個替代的方法。

> a different method 一個不一樣的方法
> a contingency plan 一個應急計畫

❷ Think outside the box and you will figure it out.
跳出框架思考，然後你就會想出辦法的。

> Don't stress yourself out 不要給自己太大壓力
> Think from another perspective 從另一個觀點想
> Give yourself a break 讓自己休息一下

❸ How about asking Mary for help?
不如請瑪莉幫忙？

> taking a trip to the summer house
> 去夏天度假小屋旅行
> taking a couple days off 休幾天假
> seeing the doctor 看醫生

| 當你問你的老師課業上的問題時 |

❶ I'm confused. Could you help me solve the question?
我很困惑。你可以幫我解決這個問題嗎？

> perplexed 困惑
> baffled 困惑
> distracted 困惑；分心

❷ What can I do to catch up with the class?
我可以怎麼做才能跟上班上的大家？

> score well on the test 考試考高分
> succeed in exam 考試考高分
> perform well on the task 在那項工作上表現好

3 虛擬實境網路聊天
on your iMessenger

在手機或電腦上，利用打字就可以聊出千言萬語

Joyce

星期三 下午 13:45

 Hey,
Do you know there's been word that the company is out searching for new blood?

下午 13:45

嗨，妳知道有傳言說公司即將要招募新血嗎？
尋找

Is that right?
What kinds of people does the company need most?

下午 13:46

真的嗎？公司最需要什麼類型的人才呢？

Well~ Let me see.
People who have creative minds to promote their products are very welcome.

下午 13:47

嗯～我想想。那些懂得用創意概念去包裝行銷產品的人都十分歡迎。
推銷

Are you able to find people who are on a par with the company?

下午 13:48

你有辦法找到符合公司標準的人嗎？
與…同水平

Afaik, we've been quite successful.

下午 13:49

據我所知，我們一直都還算滿成功的。
As far as I know 的簡寫

And how do you manage to find these people?

下午 13:50

那你打算怎麼去找到那些人呢？

Our HR doesn't really like the idea of stealing talent from other companies. So we're going to use the old fashioned way.

下午 13:512

我們的人力資源部不太喜歡從別的公司去挖角人才的想法。所以，我們決定用老方法。

Joyce

星期三 下午 13:45	
	Like? 下午 13:53
	像是？
Placing ads in newspapers, posting listings online, and of course, by word of mouth. 下午 13:54	
	在報上登廣告、網路上貼徵人訊息，當然，還有靠口頭傳播的力量。 放置 張貼 口耳相傳
No offense. I just want to make sure it works nowadays? 下午 13:53	
	沒有冒犯的意思。我只是想知道這種方式直到今天還有用嗎？
Let's wait and see! 下午 13:54	
	我們就等著看吧！
OIC. GL to you! 下午 13:55	
	噢我懂了。那祝妳們好運啦！ Oh, I see. 的簡寫 Good luck 的簡寫
下午 13:55	

聊天金句大補帖

What do you mean? 你這麼說是什麼意思？

這句是用以質疑對方的話，希望對方為他的說法提出讓你滿意的解釋。在某些情況下說這句話可能也帶有責備意味，並希望對方給你一個能夠說服你的理由。

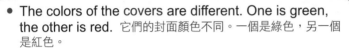

Unit 3 請告訴我

Can you tell me the differences between the two books?
你能告訴我這兩本書的不同之處嗎?

Word Power!
- difference [ˈdɪfərəns] n 差別
- cover [ˈkʌvɚ] n 封面
- be written by phr 由…所著
- author [ˈɔθɚ] n 作者
- content [ˈkɑntɛnt] n 內容

- The colors of the covers are different. One is green, the other is red. 它們的封面顏色不同。一個是綠色,另一個是紅色。

- They are written by different authors. 它們出自不同的作者。

- They have different contents. 它們的內容不同。

I heard Grace is married. Is that true?
聽說葛瑞絲結婚了,是真的嗎?

Word Power!
- true [tru] a 正確的
- perfectly [ˈpɝfɪktlɪ] ad 完全地
- nosy [ˈnozɪ] a 好管閒事的

- It's true. She got married last month. 是真的。她上星期結婚了。

- Yes, I can confirm it. I attended the wedding. 是的,我可以證實。我有參加婚禮。

這樣說不禮貌

Why are you always so nosy? 你為什麼總是這麼多管閒事?

- That is perfectly correct. 完全正確。

Can you tell me about some traditional festivals in Taiwan?
你能告訴我一些台灣的傳統節日嗎?

Word Power!
- tomb [tum] n 墳墓
- as known as phr 又被稱為
- in memory of phr 紀念
- loyal [ˈlɔɪəl] a 忠誠的
- subject [ˈsʌbdʒɪkt] n 臣民

更多…
台灣節日還有這些
- Lantern Festival 元宵節
- National Day 國慶日

- Tomb Sweeping Festival. 清明節。

- Mid Autumn Festival, as known as Moon Festival. 中秋節。

- Dragon Boat Festival. It's in memory of Chu-Yuan who was a loyal subject in ancient China. 端午節。這是為了紀念古代中國的一個忠心的臣子,屈原。

We don't have any plans for this Saturday, do we?
我們這個星期六沒什麼計畫吧？

Word Power!
- precisely [prɪ`saɪslɪ]
  ad 對，確實如此
  →用於肯定的答覆
- amnesia [æm`niʒɪə]
  n 健忘症

Sentence Power!
- as far as I know 據我所知

- Not as far as I know. 就我所知是沒有。

- Precisely. Do you have anything in mind? 沒錯。你有什麼想法嗎？

- We're going to Elsa's wedding party. Don't you remember? 我們要去參加艾莎的婚禮啊。你不記得嗎？

這樣說不禮貌
We're going to go camping this Saturday. Do you have amnesia or what?
這星期六我們要參加一個派對。你是有健忘症還是怎樣？

The earth travels around the Sun, is that true?
地球圍繞太陽轉，對嗎？

Word Power!
- earth [ɝθ] n 地球
- astronomy [əs`trɑnəmɪ]
  n 天文學
- all wet phr 【俚】完全錯了；大錯特錯

- Yes, of course. 是的，當然。

- That's true. You're so smart. 正確，你好聰明哦。

- I'm not good at astronomy. Sorry. 我天文學不好，抱歉。

這樣說不禮貌
You are all wet, actually.
其實你全搞錯了。

What do you do on weekends?
你週末都做什麼呢？

Word Power!
- buff [bʌf]
  n 【美】愛好者
- movie buff n 電影迷
- kite surfing
  n 風箏衝浪

Sentence Power!
- to name a few 列舉一小部分

- I enjoy playing football, reading, and swimming, just to name a few. 我舉例，像是踢足球、閱讀和游泳。

- I usually go to the movies with friends or family. I'm a movie buff. 我通常和朋友、家人看電影。我是個電影迷。

- Let me think. I often go kite surfing on the weekends. 我想一下。週末我通常會去玩風箏衝浪。

這樣說不禮貌
Just do nothing.
什麼也不做。

2 虛擬實境口說練習
on your iMessenger
從最簡短到最豐富，讓你實際和老外練習口說和聽力

| 當你想搞清楚一件事的來龍去脈時 |

❶ **Can you tell me what exactly happened?**
你可以告訴我究竟發生什麼嗎？

> how it happened 如何發生
> why it happened 為何發生
> where it happed 在哪裡發生

❷ **Can you tell me how you successfully got there?**
可以告訴我你怎麼成功抵達那裡的嗎？

> you managed to overcome the problem
> 你怎麼成功克服問題
> he made it to the Lincoln center
> 他怎麼成功到達林肯中心
> you found out the truth 你怎麼找到真相

❸ **Can you tell me the reason you decided to do it?**
可以告訴我你決定要做的理由是什麼嗎？

> why he needs the financial aid
> 為什麼他需要財務支援
> why you are applying for this scholarship
> 為什麼你要申請獎學金
> why you can't afford it
> 為什麼你無法負擔

| 當你想問朋友你究竟該怎麼做時 |

❶ **What should I do about it?**
關於這件事我該怎麼做？

> react to 對… 反應
> say about 對… 說
> interact with 與… 互動

❷ **Can you tell me what to do?**
可以告訴我要做什麼嗎？

> give me some instruction 給我一些指示
> give me some advice 給我一些建議
> give me some aid 給我一些協助

| 當你想問他人究竟發生什麼事時 |

① Please tell me everything about it.
請告訴我關於它的所有事情。

> the entire story 整個故事（事件）
> the reason behind it 背後的原因

② Would you tell me what went wrong?
可以告訴我什麼出錯了嗎？

> how to get there 怎麼抵達那裡
> where to find a clothing store 哪裡可以找到服飾店
> what to say 要說什麼

③ It would be kind of you if you can tell me what happened.
如果妳可以告訴我發生什麼事的話，你人就太好了。

> help me out 幫助我
> give me a hand 幫助我
> explain it to me 解釋給我聽

| 當你問你的朋友是如何面對孤獨感時 |

① I want to know how you deal with loneliness.
我想知道你是怎麼面對孤獨感的。

> depression 沮喪
> melancholia 憂鬱症
> bereavement 喪親之痛

② Please tell me some tips on tackling loneliness.
可以告訴我一些面對孤獨的訣竅嗎？

> getting a high score 拿到好分數
> winning her heart 贏得他芳心
> conquering the difficulty 克服困難

3 虛擬實境網路聊天
on your iMessenger

在手機或電腦上，利用打字就可以聊出千言萬語

Nelson

星期三 下午 13:45

Ding dong!
I'm going over to the break room to grab a cup of coffee. You want anything?

下午 13:45

叮咚！我要去茶水間喝杯咖啡，你要什麼嗎？
茶水間
拿取

I'll go with you!
If we're lucky, Katherine might be there.

下午 13:46

我跟你一起去！假如運氣好的話，凱薩琳說不定會在那兒喔。

下午 13:47

I think someone has the hots for the prettiest girl in the office.

下午 13:48

我想有人迷上辦公室裡最美的女孩囉。
迷上

HEE HEE

下午 13:49

I do not~~
I admit I find myself staring at her sometimes, but can you blame me?

下午 13:50

我才沒有咧～我承認我有時會盯著她看，但是這可以怪我嗎？
承認
緊盯
責怪

Then why don't you ask her out on a date? She's single!

下午 13:51

那你怎麼不約她出去？她單身耶！

Nelson

星期三 下午 13:45

No way!
She doesn't even know who I am!

下午 13:52

當然不要啊！她連我是誰都不知道。

不可能

下午 13:53

How about u? How's it going with u n ur girl ha? Haven't seen her around for a few days?

下午 13:54

你呢？你和你女朋友還好嗎？好幾天沒見到她了？

下午 13:55

She's mad at me because she saw Katherine talking to me the other day. If she knew what Katherine said to me, I would be dead on the spot.

下午 13:56

她在生我的氣，因為有一天她看到我和凱薩琳在講話。而且，若她知道凱薩琳跟我說什麼的話，我一定會死得很慘。

當場

聊天金句大補帖

I wonder why. 不知道為什麼。

在談話當中，當我們想表達我們對於某事物的好奇、困惑時，便能以這句話表達我們的疑慮，同時也能自然而然挑起他人的回應。

Unit 4 信不信由你

Do you believe that doomsday will come?

你相信世界末日會到來嗎？

Word Power!
- doomsday [ˈdumzˌde]
  n 世界末日
- take seriously
  phr 認真對待
- physicist [ˈfɪzɪsɪst]
  n 物理學家

- Doomsday? You can't possibly take that movie seriously. 世界末日？你不可能把電影當真吧。
- It could be true. The famous physicist Hawking said it could be in 2030. 有可能是真的。
  有名的物理學家霍金說過世界末日可能會在 2030 年時降臨。

這樣說不禮貌
Yeah, sure. Run for your life.
哦，對。那你快逃命吧。

Do you believe that she is Obama's relative?

你相信她是歐巴馬的親戚嗎？

Word Power!
- relative [ˈrɛlətɪv]
  n 親戚
- trick [trɪk] v 哄騙

Sentence Power!
- Get out of here. 別開
  玩笑了；那怎麼可能

- Get out of here. 少來了。
- Oh, don't trick me. 別騙我了。
- I'm convinced that it's true. Because they both live in Hawaii.
  我相信這是真的。因為他們都住夏威夷。

這樣說不禮貌
Uh…but it doesn't really matter to me.
呃……但這對我來講無所謂。

Do you trust John to be in charge?

你相信約翰可以負責嗎？

Word Power!
- trust [trʌst] v 信任
- in charge phr 負責
- confidence
  [ˈkɑnfədəns] n 信心
- ability [əˈbɪlətɪ] n 能力
- honesty [ˈɑnɪstɪ]
  n 誠實
- integrity [ɪnˈtɛgrətɪ]
  n 正直

- Well, he's my best friend. I have perfect trust in him. 這個嘛，他是我最好的朋友，我完全相信他。
- Yes, I have full confidence in his ability. 我非常相信他的能力。
- Yes, I can always count on him. 是的，我總是依靠他。
- I trust his honesty and integrity. 我相信他的誠實和正直。

I have already finished all of my work. Can you believe it?
我已經完成了工作，你信嗎？

- You're so efficient. I know I can trust you.
  你真有效率，我就知道可以相信你。

- I think it's so incredible. That work is very complex.
  我覺得這太神奇了，那項工作很複雜。

- Let me check it first. 先讓我檢查看看。

這樣說不禮貌
I don't buy it in the least.
我才不相信。

Do you think you are better at English than Paul is?
你覺得你的英文比保羅好嗎？

不能不會的小技巧
當你被問到類似的問題
時，記得先衡量自己和說
話人的關係再回答。因為
若是不太熟的人問你這
種問題，你比較不會知
道說出口的話會被轉述
到哪，所以在這種時候，
保持誠實但也別忘了謙
虛是最好的做法。想要使
別人信服的話，舉出實例
會比空口無憑更有效果。

- No, I dont. I think he is better. 不，我覺得他的英文比較好。
- Yes, at least, in oral English. 是的，至少在口語方面。
- No, Paul is the best in our class. 不，他在我們班是最好的。
- He is better than me. But he is not better than others. 他是比我好，但卻比不了別人。

I should have handed in my homework yesterday, but I had a headache. Could you pardon me?
昨天我就應該交作業，但我昨天頭痛，你能原諒我嗎？

- I trust you. Hand in your homework tomorrow.
  我相信你。明天再交作業。

- Oh it's absolutely fine. Do you feel better today? 哦那完全沒關係的。
  你今天有好一點嗎？

這樣說不禮貌
Do you think I would believe in your lies?
你以為我會相信你說的謊嗎？

2 虛擬實境口說練習
on your iMessenger
從最簡短到最豐富，讓你實際和老外練習口說和聽力

| 當你懷疑你的女／男朋友背著你偷吃時 |

❶ Who do you hang out with these days?
你最近都跟誰混在一起？

> spend time with 和⋯混在一起
> sleep with 和⋯睡

❷ Are you cheating on me with Laura?
你背著我跟蘿拉在一起嗎？

> secretly seeing someone 偷偷跟誰在一起
> dating Daniel 跟丹尼爾約會
> having an affair 有婚外情

❸ Who is the girl you had dinner with last night?
昨晚跟你吃晚餐的女生是誰？

> walking beside you 走在你旁邊的
> you were chatting with 跟你說話的
> you took home 你帶回家的

| 當你要說服上司相信你是真的有急事需要請假時 |

❶ I'm terribly sick and need to take a day off.
我病得很嚴重所以需要請一天假。

> infected with virus
> 被病毒感染
> debilitated by chemotherapy
> 因化療而變得很虛弱
> injured in a car accident
> 在一場車禍中受傷

❷ My dog passed away this morning, so I can't come in to the office today.
我的狗今早去世，所以我今天不能進辦公室。

> My car broke down 我的車拋錨
> I had a fever 我發燒

| 當你被人無故誣賴一件事情時 |

❶ I think you have misunderstood me.
我認為你誤會我了。

got me wrong 誤會我
misinterpreted what I said 誤解我的意思
misread the message 誤讀那則訊息

❷ I didn't intend to offend you.
我不是有意要冒犯你。

upset you 讓你不開心
wake you up 叫你起床
hurt you 傷害你

❸ You need to know that I'm innocent.
你必須知道我是清白的。

I didn't steal anything 我沒有偷任何東西
he robbed me of my wallet 他搶走我的皮夾
he committed the crime 是他犯的罪

| 當你信任你的朋友而借錢給他時 |

❶ You can return the money whenever you can.
你方便的時候再還我錢就好了。

talk to me 跟我說話
ask for help 請求幫忙

❷ Take the money and don't think too much.
就拿著錢吧然後不要想太多。

Leave the house 離開那間房子
Run away from here 逃離這裡

3 虛擬實境網路聊天　　在手機或電腦上，利用打字就可以聊出千言萬語
on your iMessenger

Felix

星期三 下午 13:45

Does it worry you that the economy is in a slump?

下午 13:45

你擔心經濟的衰退嗎？
衰落

Hmmm...

下午 13:46

It does not worry me. Do you worry?

下午 13:47

我並不擔心。你呢？

It keeps me suspended at the edge of my seat!
Especially in recent years with all the fuss over China and Taiwan.

下午 13:48

我總是憂心忡忡！特別是這幾年來中國跟台灣之間的爭論不休。
懸掛
邊緣
尤其是
爭論

Yeah, I think that contributes to some of the shifts in economy as well.

下午 13:49

是啊，我想這也導致了經濟的波動。
導致
轉換

You don't think about your job ever getting affected?

下午 13:50

你不認為你的工作會受到影響嗎？
影響

I think the company is affected.
However, I'm not worried about my job.

下午 13:51

我想公司確實受到影響了，但我並不擔憂我的工作。

Felix

星期三 下午 13:45

You sound very confident.
下午 13:52

你聽起來很有自信呢。

I just believe in this company and the people that work here. I think if problems arise, we'll think of the best way to deal with them.
下午 13:53

我只是對這家公司以及員工有信心罷了。我想要是有什麼問題，我們都會找出最好的解決辦法。
發生

I wish I could be as open-minded as you.
下午 13:54

但願我也像你這樣有開闊的想法。
開明的

下午 13:55

What you need to do is watch less of those political talk shows!
下午 13:56

你只要少看那些政治性的談話節目就好啦！
政治的

Yup, maybe you're right.
下午 13:57

對啦，也許你說得對。

聊天金句大補帖

I wouldn't bet on it. 我真懷疑。

這句話通常用於你不相信一件事時，用以表達質疑、不信任、懷疑等態度。照字面解釋就是「我不會在那上面打賭的」。就是指這件事太可疑了，讓你不會想去打賭。

Unit 5 真相只有一個

What's wrong with her?
她怎麼了？

- Judging from her face, she must be ill. 從她的臉色來判斷，她定是生病了。

- Based on my observation, I'll say she failed the final exam. 根據我的判斷，我想她期末考應該沒過。

- She doesn't seem to be quite herself today. 她今天好像不開心。

不能不會的小技巧

在待人處事上，除了應對要有禮之外，偶爾主動關心別人也是很體貼的做法。若你擔心你的直接反而會讓對方起疑或保持距離，也可以透過詢問他的好友或身邊的人來了解對方。

Word Power!
- judge from
  phr 根據…作出判斷
- based on
  phr 以…為基礎
- be oneself phr 自然地

Who is her younger brother?
誰是她弟弟？

- Judging from appearance, it must be the boy beside her. 從外表來判斷，一定是她旁邊的那個男生。

- She has no brother, that one is her classmate. 她沒弟弟，那是她同班同學。

- Sorry, I don't know the background information of her family. 對不起，我不知道她家的情況。

Word Power!
- beside [bɪˋsaɪd]
  ad 在旁邊
- background
  [ˋbæk͵graund] n 背景

What's the weather tomorrow?
明天天氣怎樣？

Word Power!
- thick [θɪk] a 厚的
- forecast [ˋfor͵kæst]
  n 預報
- approaching ad 將近

- I think it will rain. There are so many thick clouds. 我覺得會下雨，你看那麼多厚重的雲。

- The weather forecast says that it will be a fine day.
  天氣預報說會是晴天。

- Looks like it might rain tomorrow.
  看起來明天會下雨。

這樣說不禮貌

A typhoon is approaching. So what do you think the weather will be like?
颱風正在靠近中，那你覺得天氣會如何？

How does the shirt look?
這件襯衫看起來怎麼樣？

Word Power!
· pretty ['prɪtɪ] ad 相當地
· be good at phr 擅長

Sentence Power!
· In my opinion
在我看來

- It is just like your style. 這根本就是你的風格。

- In my opinion, it looks nice on you. 在我看來，你穿起來蠻適合的。

- I'm pretty sure we will find a better one in the next store.
我想我們在下一家會找到更好的。

- I am not good at picking up clothes.
我不擅長挑衣服。

這樣說不禮貌

Wow, you have really bad taste.
哇，你的品味真的很糟。

Who broke the window?
是誰打壞了玻璃？

Word Power!
· naughty ['nɔtɪ]
a 頑皮的
· clue [klu] n 線索
→ no clue with...
對…沒有想法
· remain [rɪ'men]
v 留下

- That naughty boy did. 是那個頑皮的男孩。

- I don't know, perhaps the wind. 我不知道，或許是風吧。

- It must be those three boys who are playing football over there. 我想應該是在那邊踢足球的三個男孩吧。

- I don't know, there are no clues remained. 我不知道，這裡沒有留下任何痕跡。

Who is the author of that poem? Is it written by Robert Burns?
這首詩的作者是誰啊？是不是羅伯特 · 伯恩斯？

不能不會的小技巧
羅伯特 · 伯恩斯（1759-1796）是一位著名的蘇格蘭詩人。詩作內容主要與民族自由相關，被視為浪漫主義的先驅。

Word Power!
· poem ['poɪm]
n （一首）詩
· poetry ['poɪtrɪ]
n 詩歌（總稱）

Sentence Power!
· I guess so. 我猜是吧。

- I guess so. 我想應該是。

- I bet it is not Robert Burns. 我猜絕對不是羅伯特 · 伯恩斯。

- I'm not familiar with that poem. 我對那首詩不太熟悉。

- Sorry, I don't know. I don't like poetry. 對不起，我不知道，我不喜歡詩歌。

2 虛擬實境口說練習
on your iMessenger

從最簡短到最豐富，讓你實際和老外練習口說和聽力

| 當你告訴朋友關於一部經典電影的評價時 |

❶ **The movie is highly acclaimed.**
這部電影大受好評。

> highly rated 評分很高
> highly recommended 高度推薦
> highly praised 高度讚揚

❷ **The movie is criticized for its lack of special effects.**
這部電影因為它缺少特效而被批評

> the lengthy description of the characters 冗長的人物敘述
> the tedious plot 枯燥無味的情節
> its inappropriate casting 不適當的演員陣容

❸ **Movie critics tend to think the original book is better than the movie adaptation.**
影評家大致認為原書比電影改編好。

> worse than 比… 差
> as good as 跟…一樣好

| 當你當場抓到某人在做壞事時 |

❶ **I caught you stealing the apples!**
我抓到你在偷蘋果！

> shoplifting 偷竊
> smoking 抽菸
> sneaking out 偷跑出來

❷ **Hey! Are you trying to break into the house?**
嘿！你是想要闖進那間屋子嗎？

> kidnap the boy 綁架那個小男孩
> smuggle the drugs 偷渡那些毒品
> bribe me 賄賂我

| 當你想詢問餐廳使用的食材品質時 | -------------------------------

❶ Where do the ingredients come from?
這些原料是哪裡來的？

> do the lobsters 龍蝦
> does the mutton 羊肉
> do the spices 香料

❷ Do you sell fair trade coffee?
你們有賣公平貿易的咖啡嗎？

> handmade pastry 手工（酥皮）點心
> homemade wine 自釀葡萄酒
> sugar-free drink 無糖飲料

❸ Are these certified produce?
這些是認證過的農產品嗎？

> dairy products 乳製產品
> genetically engineered foods 基因改造食品

| 當你要劇透朋友正在看的劇集結局時 | -------------------------------

❶ Do you know he ends up marrying his coworker?
你知道他最後跟他同事結婚了嗎？

> getting a divorce 離婚
> having three children 有三個小孩
> living by himself 自己一個人住

❷ Sorry, I didn't realize you haven't watched the latest episode!
對不起，我不知道你還沒看過最新那一集！

> finished the latest season 看完最新一季
> had a chance to watch it 有機會看它
> discussed it with anyone 與任何人討論

3 虛擬實境網路聊天
on your iMessenger

在手機或電腦上，利用打字就可以聊出千言萬語

Lacey Feng

星期三 下午 13:45

It just makes no sense to me!

下午 13:45

我覺得一點都沒有道理啊！
合理

下午 13:46

I'm talking about the conversation between the girls here.
It seems that the topic never runs far of dieting.

下午 13:48

我是説這裡的女生談論的話題，好像永遠都離不開減肥這檔事。
節食

Ahaha, I know what ur talking about.

下午 13:49

哈哈，我懂妳在説什麼。

Look at the girls around the office! Most of them are thin, and the others are really thin. Why are they still talking about trying to lose weight?

下午 13:51

妳看看這辦公室的女生！她們絕大部分都很瘦，而且有一些是超級瘦。她們為什麼一直不斷地想減肥呢？

Well~
It's just the society that we live in.
It keeps on promoting that thinner is better.

下午 13:52

我們的社會就是不斷地宣導越瘦越好這種觀念。
生活
不停地

Lacey Feng

星期三 下午 13:45

下午 13:53

Girls receive the image that if ur not thin, ur unattractive and unhealthy. But what's really unhealthy is this society's view on women!

下午 13:54

I just hope one day girls will realize that being thin isn't the only way to be healthy. And that we are attractive no matter what society says!

下午 13:57

I totally agree with u!

下午 13:58

「假如你不苗條，你就沒有魅力而且不健康」的觀念，不斷地傳送給這個社會的女性。不過，真正病態的是這個社會對女性的看法！

不吸引人的
不健康的

我只希望將來有一天，女性能夠了解，變瘦不是唯一擁有健康的方法。此外，不管這個社會怎麼說，我們都一樣很有魅力！

我完全同意妳！

聊天金句大補帖

Great minds think alike. 英雄所見略同。

當我們表達與對方想法相同時，可以試著用這種有趣的說法表示，這句話不僅誇了對方也誇了自己，表示兩人同為英雄，當然所見略同囉！

Unit 6 給認真的自己比個讚 1

What do you think about his performance?
他的表演怎麼樣？

- I must take my hat off to him for his performance. 我要為他的出色表演向他致敬。
- I've always admired his ability. 我一向很佩服他的能力。
- He deserved the highest praise. 他應該得到讚賞的。
- I really have to express my admiration for his talent. 我真的對他的才華表示欽佩。

Word Power!
- take one's hat off to　phr 向‥表示讚賞和欽佩
- admire [əd`maɪr]　v 敬佩
- express [ɪk`sprɛs]　v 表現
- admiration [ˌædmə`reʃən]　n 欽佩
- talent [`tælənt]　n 天資

What do you think about my new coat?
你覺得我的新外套怎麼樣？

- It's very lovely! 真漂亮！
- I do envy you, it suits you very much. 真羨慕你，真的很適合你耶。
- You look very nice in it. 你穿起來非常好看

不能不會的小技巧
對別人的新衣服或新行頭給予意見時，若對方並非跟自己很熟的人，千萬不要給予太嚴苛的批評，才不會傷害到別人的感覺喔。

Word Power!
- lovely [`lʌvlɪ]　a 秀美的
- chubby [`tʃʌbɪ]　a 豐滿的

這樣說不禮貌
You look a little chubby in this coat. 你穿這件外套看起來有點肉。

How do you feel after being encouraged?
在得到鼓勵之後你感覺怎麼樣？

- I will get some energy. 我將會有許多能量。
- It makes me feel optimistic. 它讓我感到樂觀。
- Encouragement makes me feel confident about myself. 鼓勵會讓我感到很有自信。
- I feel I can achieve anything I want. 我會覺得沒有任何事難得倒我。

Word Power!
- encourage [ɪn`kɝɪdʒ]　v 鼓勵
- energy [`ɛnədʒɪ]　n 活力
- optimistic [ˌɑptə`mɪstɪk]　a 樂觀的
- encouragement [ɪn`kɝɪdʒmənt]　n 鼓勵
- achieve [ə`tʃiv]　v 達成

I find spelling is the hardest thing for me.
我覺得拼字對我來說是全世界最難的事了。

Word Power!
- spelling [ˈspɛlɪŋ] n 拼字
- get sb. down phr 使⋯沮喪
- hang [hæŋ] n【口】訣竅

Sentence Power!
- Practice makes perfect. 熟能生巧。
- Keep your chin up. 振作起來。
- Look on the bright side. 看向光明面。
- Never say die. 不要洩氣。

- Don't let this get you down. You will get the hang of it. 不要灰心，你會找到訣竅的。
- Don't worry. Practice makes perfect. 別擔心！熟能生巧。
- Keep your chin up. Try to look on the bright side. 別氣餒！樂觀一點。
- Never say die. 不要放棄。

What do you think the poem praises?
這首詩歌頌了什麼？

Word Power!
- praise [prez] v 讚揚
- freedom [ˈfridəm] n 自由
- esteemed [əˈstimd] a 受人尊敬的
- philosopher [fəˈlɑsəfɚ] n 哲學家

- I think it praises freedom. 我認為它在歌頌自由。
- It's praising esteemed love. 它在稱頌崇高的愛情。
- A mother's love, definitely. 一定是母愛。
- It may be praising the Greek philosophers. 它應該是在稱頌希臘的哲學家們。

I'm afraid I'll fail the oral test.
我怕我的口試會不及格。

Word Power!
- oral test n 口試
- positive [ˈpɑzətɪv] a 積極的
- faith [feθ] n 信念
- give up phr 放棄

- Maybe you won't if you have more confidence. 或許你多點信心就不會不及格了。
- Be positive. Things are not that bad. 有信心一點。情況並沒有那麼糟啊。
- Cheer up. You should have more faith in yourself. 加油，你要對自己有點信心。
- Come on! Don't give up! 加油！堅持下去！

這樣說不禮貌

You wouldn't fail if you had enough practice.
若你事前多練習，就不會不及格。

2 虛擬實境口說練習
on your iMessenger

從最簡短到最豐富，讓你實際和老外練習口說和聽力

| 當你想幫準備考試的朋友加油時 |

❶ **The exam is going to be** a piece of cake **for you.**
那個考試對你來說根本很輕鬆。

> very easy 很簡單
> a snap 是件簡單的事
> a breeze 輕鬆自在

❷ **You have never** let us down, **so don't worry.**
你從沒讓我失望過，所以別擔心。

> failed the exam 考試不及格
> fell behind the class 落後班上同學
> given up 放棄

❸ **We are** always here for **you.**
我會永遠支持你。

> standing by 支持
> rooting for 支持
> supportive of 支持

| 當你想鼓勵工作面試失敗的朋友時 |

❶ **Don't worry. You can do better.**
不要擔心，你可以做得更好的。

> chill out 冷靜
> break a leg （加油）祝你好運
> knock them dead 加油

❷ **Relax!** It's not the end of the world.
放鬆！這又不是世界末日。

> You deserve better 你值得更好。
> He's not going to fire you. 他不會解雇你的。
> You will get hired! 你會被雇用的！

| 當你的朋友手舞足蹈的逗難過的你開心時 |

❶ **Thanks for your encouragement.**
謝謝你的鼓勵。

advice 建議
suggestion 建議
feedback 回饋

❷ **You are my best friend.**
你是我最好的朋友。

dearest 最親愛的
closest 最親密的
intimate 親近的

❸ **You always know how to cheer me up.**
你總是知道怎麼鼓舞我。

what to do 做什麼
what to say 做什麼
where to go 去哪裡

| 當你和家人或朋友談到今天使你心情不好的事時 |

❶ **I feel really bad about what happened today.**
對於今天發生的事我感到很難過。

sorry 遺憾
regretful 後悔
repentant 後悔

❷ **My dog passed away.**
我的狗過世了。

became ill 生病
went astray 迷路
got lost 迷路

3 虛擬實境網路聊天
on your iMessenger

在手機或電腦上，利用打字就可以聊出千言萬語

Sammy

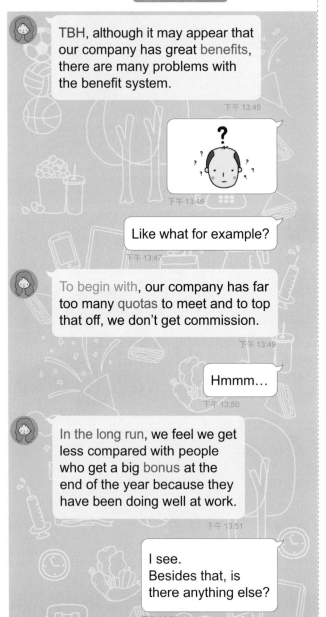

星期三 下午 13:45

TBH, although it may appear that our company has great benefits, there are many problems with the benefit system.

下午 13:45

下午 13:46

Like what for example?

下午 13:47

To begin with, our company has far too many quotas to meet and to top that off, we don't get commission.

下午 13:49

Hmmm…

下午 13:50

In the long run, we feel we get less compared with people who get a big bonus at the end of the year because they have been doing well at work.

下午 13:51

I see.
Besides that, is there anything else?

下午 13:52

老實說，雖然我們公司好像福利很不錯，但是卻存在著制度層面的問題。

To be honest 的簡寫
利益

比方說？

首先，我們公司的業績額度訂得太高，很難達到那個要求，因此我們拿不到佣金。

首先
額度

嗯……。

就長遠的角度而言，其他公司的人可以因為工作表現佳而在年終時領到額外的獎金，這點我們就比不上人家。

長期下來
額外獎金

我懂了，除了這點以外，還有其他問題嗎？

Sammy

星期三 下午 13:45

IMO, I think the biggest problem is that there is much to improve, but not enough people speaking up.

下午 13:54

Maybe when you get promoted, you can take matters into your own hands.

下午 13:55

下午 13:55

I hope so~

下午 13:56

That's exactly what I think. But I hope it isn't too late to change.

下午 13:56

Nothing is never too late! Just do it!!!

下午 13:57

就我個人的想法而言，最大的問題癥結在於需要改善的地方很多，挺身說話的人卻太少了。

In my opinion 的簡寫
大聲說出

也許等你升官了，妳可以自己推動改革。

希望如此囉～

那正是我所想的。但我希望到那時再改變還不算太晚。

太⋯以致於不能

永遠不會太晚的！
就試試看吧！

聊天金句大補帖

I've been in your shoes before. 我經歷過跟你相同的狀況。

當朋友因為挫折或困難而感到沮喪時，如果你也有相同的經驗，就可以用這句話來安慰他，讓他知道他並不孤單、不可憐，你也跟他遭遇同樣的事情。

笨蛋！
英文學不好的關鍵是「用錯方法」啦！

想要學好英文，就一定要用「老外的方法」！

> I'm so tired now. I stayed up all night preparing for today's test.

> Me, too! I'm afraid I might doze off in the next class.

Unit 2 校園風雲榜 Classmates
學校裡大家都在聊什麼？《詳見書中117頁》

> What?! There is a test today? Are you kidding me?

《全圖解用老外的方法學英文》
1書＋1MP3／349元

本書4大特點，
完全針對「老外學英文的方法」設計！

特點 ❶ 單字群組搭配彩圖記憶　　特點 ❸ 文法重點搭配醒目筆記

特點 ❷ 生活情境搭配萬用句型　　特點 ❹ 專業外師親錄英語例句MP3

國家圖書館出版品預行編目（CIP）資料

想要和你用英文聊聊天／ 陳子李 著
. -- 初版. -- 臺北市：我識，2016. 05
面； 公分

ISBN 978-986-5785-97-0（平裝附光碟片）

1. 英語　2. 會話

805.188　　　　　　105004625

書名 / 想要和你用英文聊聊天
作者 / 陳子李
審訂 / Michael Coughlin
發行人 / 蔣敬祖
專案副總經理 / 廖晏婕
副總編輯 / 劉俐伶
主編 / 謝昀蓁
執行編輯 / 黃琮軒
校對 / 李靜宜
視覺指導 / 黃馨儀
內文排版 / 健呈電腦排版股份有限公司
插圖 / 我識文創
內文圖片 / www.shutterstock.com
法律顧問 / 北辰著作權事務所蕭雄淋律師
印製 / 金濆印刷事業有限公司
初版 / 2016年05月
出版單位 / 我識出版集團－我識出版社有限公司
電話 / (02) 2345-7222
傳真 / (02) 2345-5758
地址 / 台北市忠孝東路五段372巷27弄78之1號1樓
郵政劃撥 / 19793190
戶名 / 我識出版社
網址 / www.17buy.com.tw
E-mail / iam.group@17buy.com.tw
facebook網址 / www.facebook.com/ImPublishing
定價 / 新台幣 379 元 / 港幣 126 元（附光碟）

總經銷 / 我識出版社有限公司業務部
地址 / 新北市汐止區新台五路一段114號12樓
電話 / (02) 2696-1357　傳真 / (02) 2696-1359

地區經銷 / 易可數位行銷股份有限公司
地址 / 新北市新店區寶橋路235巷6弄3號5樓

港澳總經銷 / 和平圖書有限公司
地址 / 香港柴灣嘉業街12號百樂門大廈17樓
電話 / (852) 2804-6687　傳真 / (852) 2804-6409

I'm

我識出版社
17buy.com.tw